STONE HEART

'*Stone Heart* is a polished, sparkling debut from an expert storyteller. It is a gripping, beautifully written thriller that will have you reading deep into the night...Des Ekin weaves a tangled, complex web of deception and intrigue in a modern Irish novel that captures the savagery of murder and the poignancy of a love struggling to survive against the backdrop of a brutal killing. It makes for marvellous reading and I loved it.'

Cathy Kelly, author of *Woman to Woman* and *She's The One*.

'This is a powerful piece of work and a brilliant first from Ireland's finest new novelist. Ekin has an inimitable ability to combine tension with emotion against a compelling backdrop of death and intrigue. Read it.'

Paul Williams, author of *The General* and *Gangland!*

'Des Ekin just keeps twisting the knife, a thrilling debut from a born storyteller.'

Colin Bateman

DES EKIN was born in County Down, Northern Ireland. He is a journalist and columnist with the *Sunday World*, Ireland's top-selling newspaper. He lives in Dublin with his wife and three children.

STONE HEART

DES EKIN

THE O'BRIEN PRESS
DUBLIN

First published 1999 by The O'Brien Press Ltd.,
20 Victoria Road, Dublin 6, Ireland.
Tel. +353 1 4923333; Fax. +353 1 4922777
email: books@obrien.ie
website: http://www.obrien.ie

ISBN: 0-86278-584-7

British Library Cataloguing-in-publication Data
Ekin, Des
Stone heart
1.Detective and mystery stories
I.Title
823.9'14(F)

1 2 3 4 5 6 7 8 9 10
99 00 01 02 03 04 05 06 07

Cover design: Jeremy Butcher
Cover image: Graphistock, Inc.
Book layout and design: The O'Brien Press Ltd.
Colour separations: C&A Print Services Ltd.
Printing: Cox & Wyman Ltd.

To Sally

ACKNOWLEDGEMENTS

Michael O'Brien of The O'Brien Press knew I was capable of writing a book long before I did. I hope this first novel vindicates his confidence in me.

It owes its present form to Íde ní Laoghaire and Alison Walsh, both brilliant editors whose unerring eye identified its key weaknesses and built upon its strengths. Their suggestions for its improvement were inspired. Thanks also to Mary Webb, Chenile Keogh and all the staff at O'Brien, who helped shape it and whose contributions were invaluable.

I was lucky to be surrounded at my workplace by talented people whose positive attitudes were a huge help. Eddie Rowley, Cathy Kelly, Paul Williams, Sean Boyne and Dave Mullins – all authors themselves – gave me constant morale-boosting encouragement, and it meant more to me than they'll ever know.

Thanks to the gardaí who helped me with background, and to Sean Lavelle of Achill Island, County Mayo, for his help and advice on the fishing-boat sequences. If any mistakes slipped through the net, they are my own.

I'm indebted to Colm MacGinty, editor of the *Sunday World*, for his support and for helping me rediscover my lifelong pleasure in writing.

Thanks also to Jo Keating, Colin McClelland, Alwyn James, Sarah Hamilton and to countless others who helped me along the way – you know who you are. To my mother, brother and sister for their support; and to my good friends Peter and Marian Humphries, who provided the haven of peace and tranquillity in County Kerry where the best parts of this book were written.

To Christopher, Sarah and Gráinne for putting up with a dad who often seemed bionically joined to a word-processor.

And above all, heartfelt thanks to my wife, Sally. We planned all this out together, teasing out the plots and characters during long walks in the County Wicklow hills. If the clichéd phrase 'the better half' leaps to mind, it's only because half of this book is rightfully hers and it is, of course, the better half.

D.E.

CHAPTER ONE

TARA ROSS stirred restlessly as the midsummer sun burst over the Burren hills and forced its way through her bedroom window. She made a half-hearted attempt to straighten her tangled bed sheets and to plump up a single pillow that had been flattened by the unaccustomed weight of two heads. Then, wearily, she closed her eyes and tried to get back to sleep.

Seconds later – at least, it seemed like only seconds – she was awakened by the high-pitched piping of her mobile phone.

Tara groaned. For a moment, she wondered if she'd mistaken the day and overslept. No, it was definitely Sunday. And Sunday was her only day off.

Her groping hand knocked over a glass of water as she fumbled for the phone and picked it up on the sixth or seventh ring. 'Hello,' she said without enthusiasm.

But the voice on the other end was urgent.

'Tara? Steve here. I can't hang around, but I've got something you might be interested in.'

Tara sat bolt upright, fully awake now. Steve McNamara was the local garda sergeant. He was a family friend and one of her best contacts. And he wasn't the sort to phone at eight o'clock on a Sunday morning, unless he had a very good reason.

'There's been a murder. The detectives from Ennis are on their way.'

'Are you serious?' gasped Tara. Immediately she felt like kicking herself. What a stupid bloody thing to say. 'Hang on a minute. Let me get a pen.'

She struggled out of bed and pulled back the curtains, expecting to see a frenzy of activity outside. But Claremoon Harbour looked as peaceful and calm as it always looked, Sunday or no Sunday.

It wasn't as though murder was a regular occurrence in Claremoon Harbour. In fact, nothing was a regular occurrence in Claremoon Harbour, unless you counted the steady routine of life that ebbed and flowed as predictably as the tide over the rippled sands of nearby Trá Mór. The last time the sleepy County Clare township had hit the headlines had been over forty years ago, when a fishing boat had foundered with the loss of three crewmen. People still talked about it as though it had happened yesterday.

'Where, Steve? Who?' Tara was trying to hold the phone under her chin, open the clinging pages of a new notebook, and pull the top off a ballpoint pen with her teeth, all at the same time.

'Ann Kennedy. Up at Barnabo. I found her just after seven this morning. Stabbed with a kitchen knife or something. Over and over again, dozens of times. Jesus, what a mess.'

His throat seemed to catch on the last few words.

Tara lowered the notebook as an icy numbness spread through her limbs. She sat down unsteadily on the side of the bed.

'Ann Kennedy?' she repeated, hoping he wouldn't notice the shaking in her own voice. 'But she didn't have an enemy in the world.' She took a deep breath. 'What was it, a burglary or something?'

'No, domestic killing. It was the son. We're taking him in this afternoon under Section Four.' He was whispering now. 'But for God's sake don't quote me on that. At the moment, the official line is that we're keeping an open mind.'

'But Steve...'

'Listen, kid, I've got to go. Just thought I'd give you the chance to get in there ahead of the posse. Talk to you later.'

Tara sat staring at the tiny black phone, long after the line had gone dead, as though it held the answers to the questions that raced through her mind. She just couldn't bring herself to believe Ann was dead. Ann Kennedy, the farmer's widow who had achieved national status as a women's rights campaigner. She had been a familiar face on TV discussion programmes, a recognisable voice on morning radio. She was a legend. She was her friend. And now she was dead.

Tara rubbed her eyes and forced herself to concentrate. She realised she was just erecting mental barriers, preventing another, even more disturbing, thought from entering her mind. The other vital bit of information that Steve had given her.

It was the son. We're taking him in.

Not Fergal. It couldn't be. Wasn't he...

Tara stood up and savagely punched numbers on her mobile phone. She couldn't hang around. She had work to do.

Now it was afternoon, and the little twisting road that led up from the village to the townland of Barnabo was congested with garda cars and the Dublin-registered Toyotas of the national press. After forty years, Claremoon Harbour had finally hit the headlines again.

Tara sat on a warm dry-stone wall, just outside the perimeter of the police warning tape that sealed off the house and its grounds, and waited for Fergal Kennedy to be escorted from the old farmhouse and into the waiting patrol car. Would he have a coat or a blanket over his head? she wondered. Or would he be able to look at her as he walked down the potholed laneway towards the aluminium gate where the car waited with its engine already running?

In the surrounding fields, police wearing blue boiler suits and gumboots were combing every single inch of turf and mud, raking grass, sifting weeds, sorting litter and farm debris into sealed evidence bags. There were more officers examining the barn, the outhouses and the charred framework of what had once, years ago, been a sizeable cowshed. Grim-faced forensic experts from the Garda Technical Bureau, dressed head to toe in sterile white coveralls, wandered in and out of the house where, Tara reminded herself with a shudder, the body of Ann Kennedy would stay in the kitchen until the pathologist arrived.

In the meantime, Tara had done all she could. All her phone calls had been made, and now there was nothing to do but wait.

And there could be worse places to wait. Behind her rose the hills that led towards the Burren, a bleak and eerily beautiful moonscape of snow-white limestone slabs and fissures where fully mature thorn trees grew hand-high like natural bonsais, and where lakes would appear and vanish as though by act of sorcery.

Tara strained her eyes to look out over the sea, now a sparkling blue-green with only tiny specks of white. Force four or five, she guessed expertly, and unlikely to change much today; but you could never tell with the Atlantic Ocean. And yes, there were a couple of fishing-craft about a mile out to sea. She thought she could make out the out-line of the *Róisín Dubh*, her father's fishing boat, but at this distance it was impossible to tell.

On any other day, Fergal might have been out there with him, helping to bring in the silver catch of salmon. On any other day, things might have been so different...

'And who might you be, love?'

Tara looked up. At first she thought the man in the blue suit was a detective, but he didn't have that cop air about him and, anyway, not many gardaí could afford Comme des Garçons suits. He carried a state-of-the-art laptop computer which had probably cost more than Tara's car, and a mobile phone – the latest model, with so many features that it could probably do your Christmas shopping for you. Nearby was a new-reg blue Mazda sports car, abandoned beside a police no-parking cone, its door left carelessly ajar.

Tara took an instant dislike to the man's fixed sneer and his patronising tone, but she smiled back and answered politely enough.

'Tara Ross,' she said, stretching out her hand. 'And who might you be?'

Uninvited, the man sat down close beside her on the sun-warmed dry stones – too close – and waited just a little too long before accepting her outstretched hand.

'Gerry Gellick,' he introduced himself, before handing over a business card. It identified him simply as a freelance journalist.

Tara knew she'd recognised him from somewhere – the arrogant face, the pug nose and the carrot-red, painstakingly gelled hair. The photo regularly accompanied his byline in several newspapers. He had a reputation for getting the interviews nobody else could get. He also had a reputation for getting interviews that the interviewees could not remember giving. He quoted cops, priests, housewives, politicians and prostitutes, but somehow they all sounded exactly alike.

Tara dug into her jeans pocket and produced her own card.

Gellick looked critically at her photo and then at Tara's face, comparing the two.

'You don't look like your photo,' he said at last. He tossed a lit cigarette-end into the dry bracken of the hillside.

'I wouldn't do that,' she said absently, pointing to the bracken. 'You could easily start a fire.'

'No, you're much prettier.' He edged closer, and the smell of expensive aftershave couldn't disguise the wine he'd had with lunch. She realised with irritation that he was half-smashed. He wasn't drunk, as the police witnesses would say in court cases around these parts, but he had drink taken.

In any other circumstances, she might have been pleased with the compliment. She couldn't resist glancing at the photo and then at her reflection in the window of the Mazda. She looked quickly away again, because she'd always been sensitive about her own appearance and the way it set her apart from most of the other women in her village – the ones with reddish brown hair and pale Celtic skin.

('You're more Spic than Mick,' Steve McNamara, who wasn't above a bit of racism now and again, used to tease her. 'That jet-black hair, that lovely olive skin, those big brown eyes and that classic nose. I wouldn't be surprised if you were descended from the Spaniards who were washed ashore with the Armada.')

Now, Tara realised with annoyance that Gerry Gellick was edging closer still, his twisted slit of a mouth distorted in what he no doubt took to be a disarming smile.

'What did you do to get sent to this dump on a nice Sunday afternoon?' he asked.

Tara followed his contemptuous stare down to the pretty little village.

'Well, nobody actually sent me to this dump, Gerry,' she said slowly. 'I was born and brought up in Claremoon Harbour. This dump happens to be my home.'

But the irony in her voice was wasted on him.

'Oh. Then you might be useful.' He said it as though it would be her privilege to help him. 'Do you know anything about the guy they're questioning?'

Tara shifted uncomfortably. 'A bit.'

'What's his story? Do you know whether he's got an alibi?'

'An alibi?' To her intense annoyance, she felt her face begin to redden.

Gellick gave an exaggerated sigh of frustration. 'I mean, what does he claim he was doing at the time of the murder?'

Her stomach tightened.

'Look, Gerry.' No matter how hard she tried, she couldn't meet his eyes. 'He's been locked in there all morning with two detectives from Ennis. How should I know what he's said?'

'Okay, okay.' Her answer seemed to satisfy him. She relaxed again.

Gerry Gellick lit a cigarette thoughtfully. 'You shouldn't be stuck down here in the bogs, a nice girl like you,' he said at last. 'I know a lot of the right people in Dublin journalism. I could get you a job in the big smoke if you play your cards right. You might have to start at the bottom and work your way up, though. Where are you working at the moment? A firelighter?'

'Firelighter?'

'A little paper in the sticks?' He grinned and waved his open hand as though explaining a joke to a backward child.

Tara smiled thinly. 'No, I'm not employed by the local paper. But I do work as a stringer for them from time to time.'

'Well, what *do* you do?'

'I'm a cyberhack.'

'A what?'

'I edit my own online newspaper, the *Clare Electronic News*. It's on the Internet. I've got thousands of readers all over the world.'

'Jaze, that's a good one. Where did you learn to do that?'

'I taught myself all about computers. And I learned journalism at college and later at the *Evening Mercury* in Dublin. I was features editor there for two years.'

His eyes widened. He was impressed. 'So why the heck did you return to Bally-go-backwards?'

Oh, God, she thought. Here we go again. How many times would she have to answer that question? She could have told Gerry Gellick all about her messy break-up with Chris Calder in Dublin. She could have explained how she'd decided, in a sudden rush of bravado and defiance, to start afresh by launching her own business in her home town. (After all, she kept telling herself, this was the age of the global village, wasn't it?) And how, after a few months, she'd decided that Claremoon Harbour was really the only place in the world she wanted to be.

But the last thing she felt like doing was to open her heart to this man Gellick – especially at this time.

'Because I like it here,' she replied at last. It was the truth.

Gellick shook his head. 'Come on, love, nobody in her right mind likes it here. It's a crappy little pit in the arse-end of nowhere.' He pointed disdainfully down at the tiny village as though it were self-evident. 'Listen. I can put in a word with the right people and get you back to the real centre of things. I don't know what you did to get the boot from the *Evening Mercury*, but I could fix it for you to get back in there, if you like.'

He was absolutely serious, but when he saw her angry reaction, he changed tack. His face crumpled in a grotesque caricature of a backwoods politician on the election trail. 'I can fix anything, love,' he said, mimicking a music-hall west-of-Ireland accent. 'Whether it's a drink-driving charge or a job in the civil service or just a pothole in the road, I can fix it for you, if you just be nice to me, pet...'

The mimicry was perfect. He leaned towards her, grinning evilly in character, and his hand began stroking the leg of her jeans, up and down from knee to thigh. 'Just you be nice to me...'

Tara knew the technique. It was common in Ireland – the grope disguised as a joke. If you objected to it, you were a humourless killjoy who couldn't take a bit of fun. If you submitted to it, you were still getting someone's hands all over you. A grope in quotation marks was still a grope.

'Take your hand away,' she warned icily.

'I'll even get you a council house, pet.' The mock-leer remained and the spidery fingers were edging towards her inner-thigh.

'Look! Someone's coming out of the house,' Tara said abruptly. Rising, she leaned on the largest and wobbliest rock on the dry-stone wall and sent it tumbling down to smash painfully on the toe of Gellick's brightly-buffed shoe. 'Oops, sorry,' she said, eyes still glued to the house. 'False alarm.'

She noticed with satisfaction that the sharp granite stone had cut a gash in the leather toecap of what was obviously an expensive piece of footwear. 'Now, if you'll excuse me,' she said, moving off.

But Gellick's face was a mask of black fury. 'You did that deliberately, you culchie bitch,' he shouted. 'Hey! Come back here. You don't just walk away from me like that!'

He had grabbed her arm. Even through the thick material of her jacket, the grip hurt and was obviously meant to. Gellick wasn't particularly well-built, but he was wiry and he had a streetfighter's strength.

She stood stock-still, looking him directly in the eye. 'Let me go,' she said quietly.

He hesitated for a few moments, weighing her up, then slowly released her arm.

Tara shook herself free and walked over to the blue and white boundary tape, where a heavily built man in garda uniform was helping a squad car to execute a twelve-point turn in the narrow laneway.

'Steve. I need to talk to you.'

Steve McNamara pulled off his police cap and wiped his brow. 'That's it, you're clear now. Work away,' he called out to the squad car driver, banging twice on the roof with a fist the size of a bowling ball. The driver winced and drove off.

'Are you all right, Tara?' Steve turned around to face her. 'I was watching you out of the corner of my eye and you seemed to be having a bit of trouble with that fella. If you want, I'll go over there and soften his cough for him.'

'It's okay, Steve. I can look after myself.' She glanced around at Gellick, who was examining his mutilated shoe and glaring balefully at her, resentful as a poker player who's just folded without calling his opponent's bluff. 'Listen, I really need to talk to you. About the murder.'

Steve replaced his cap. 'I can't talk now, Tara. I'm really up to my tonsils. How about if I call round to your house tonight, after I get off duty? Things should have quietened down by then.'

Tara bit her lip tensely. 'Yes. I suppose that'll be okay.'

'Tara.' His voice dropped to a whisper. 'You already know everything I know about this case.'

'It's not what *you* know, Steve,' she said. 'It's what...'

Her voice tailed off as she realised he wasn't listening. Following his eyes, she understood why. There had been a sudden explosion of activity outside the Kennedy home. Two bulky detectives were emerging from the farmhouse, a third figure sandwiched awkwardly between them.

Tara turned back to the sergeant. But he'd already gone.

'A 29-year-old man has been arrested under Section Four of the 1984 Criminal Justice Act in relation to the murder of women's rights campaigner Ann Kennedy...'

It was seven-thirty, and Tara had finished for the day. Taking longer than usual to decipher her pages of short-hand notes, she had typed up the news story and sent it down the computer line to the national paper which employed her as part-time stringer.

Then she'd turned her attention to her own Internet newspaper. The *Clare Electronic News* had been Tara's own brainchild. Working with a single computer in the cramped conditions of her own bedroom, she had created a full-scale Web publication that looked and read exactly like a local newspaper, complete with ornate Victorian masthead.

She designed a new front page, making the Kennedy murder the main story. From her library of archive photos, she selected a picture of Ann Kennedy and placed it top-centre of the page. Ann's clear blue eyes looked out at her, almost in amusement, as Tara typed up a brief tribute to the work of this extraordinary campaigner and launched it into cyberspace. Satisfied, Tara switched off the computer, popped open a can of chilled Perrier and used the cold metal to massage her aching temples.

A 29-year-old man has been arrested...

For legal reasons, the man could not be identified. But everyone in County Clare would know it was Fergal Kennedy, Ann Kennedy's elder son.

She sat back and closed her eyes. The thirty seconds that it had taken Fergal to walk down the muddy driveway, escorted by the two grim-faced detectives, were burned on to her mind's eye like a bare lightbulb burns into the retina. The scene played and replayed in her consciousness like a loop of film, until the sequence of frames was as familiar as the footage of the first moonwalk, or the ambush of that presidential limousine in Dallas.

Fergal looked much the same as he'd always looked. That was the surprising thing. For some reason she'd expected a haggard, red-eyed figure with a heavy growth of stubble. But he looked so ordinary – his solid frame dressed in his usual checked workshirt and jeans, his bewildered face partly hidden by the downward flop from his mass of unruly brown hair.

As the cameras flashed and the photographers jostled for position, Fergal had paused for a second at the gate. Then he'd spotted her face among the crowd.

And he'd winked.

She had anticipated an apprehensive look, an expression of anguish, maybe even a hint of tears. What she didn't expect was that rapid flick of the eyelid, so virtually imperceptible that she was sure no one else had even noticed.

It was a wink. Definitely a wink.

It was a wink that said: 'Don't worry. I'm innocent.'

A few seconds later, he was pushed into the garda car, and he was gone. For a while she'd watched the flashing lights disappear down the road towards Ennis and listened to the roar of the motorcycle escort. And then she'd taken a short-cut along a sheep-track through the bracken, and walked slowly home.

Her copy filed, her job done, she looked back at those shorthand notes which had taken so long to decipher. The pages were dotted with random marks, odd little circles that had smudged the ink and soaked through the paper like raindrops.

That was nothing extraordinary. Her notebooks had lots of pages that looked like that. It usually happened when she conducted interviews outside in the rain.

Only today it hadn't rained at all.

CHAPTER TWO

IT HAD rained the first day she met Fergal.

Lord, how it had rained.

It wasn't just the usual rainfall you get around the west coast of Ireland, the constant mizzle of shower and mist that folk describe euphemistically as 'a soft day'. This was a lashing downpour, flogged into a frenzy by a March storm somewhere out there in the slate-grey Atlantic Ocean. It was lashing hard enough to hurt. It made you feel that the whole world was made of cascading water. Even the hard granite of the paving stones became alive with thousands of liquid explosions as the rain battered mercilessly against the stone.

Running from her rusted, leaking old Fiat into Claremoon courthouse, Tara was soaked in seconds. Her navy woollen overcoat repelled some of the rain, but her legs were spattered with mud, and her flimsy shoes seemed to suck up the water underfoot like blotting paper.

'*Waterworld*!' she shouted as she burst through the door in a flurry of flying moisture.

'*Rain Man*,' responded Pat McEndle.

'*Splash*.'

'*Singing in the Rain*.'

'Okay, you win.'

Tara grinned back at Pat McEndle, the middle-aged court clerk, as they played their familiar game. Every month for the past two years she'd covered this same court in Claremoon Harbour, and every time they met they played the same game of wits and movie-buff skills.

It had begun as a joke about the courthouse, which was actually a courthouse in name only. Claremoon District Court was held in the local cinema, a run-down fleapit that looked grim even by the romantic glow of the silver screen at night. In the harsh light of day, it was even more shoddy and dilapidated. But it had been the only building available after the old church hall had been condemned as unsafe.

Claremoon Harbour was so far away from anywhere else that it had its own district court session. The judge would travel all the way from Ennis and spend the morning dealing with traffic cases, agricultural infringements and minor drink-related offences while grumbling publicly about the courtroom conditions in the hope that someone in authority would one day take heed. No one ever did.

So once a month the long-suffering judge would take his seat at a table just under the moth-eaten screen, while the solicitors and garda witnesses would crowd into the front rows of red velveteen tip-up seats. The only people who got any fun out of the arrangement were Tara and Pat McEndle, who would vie with each other to dream up the most likely feature film to suit the weather conditions.

Tara shook out her sodden overcoat and hung it over the back of her metal chair. She shared a table with Pat, which suited her fine because she could easily get names and addresses from the charge-sheets. 'Anyone due to be sent to Devil's Island this morning?' she asked.

He shook his head. 'Not unless they shoot the judge. We've just got the usual minor stuff – speeding, parking, thumping, peeing in the street and drinking after hours. Want a look?'

'Thanks.' She accepted the thick sheaf of charge-sheets and began flicking through it.

'There's one case you might be interested in,' mused Pat. 'Francie Mahony, up on six charges of receiving stolen goods, namely one gate.'

'A gate?'

'Yes. One of those big country-and-western jobs. You know – two giant cartwheels and a big pair of cow-horns and lots of brasswork, the sort of thing that self-made businessmen like to put up in front of their Dallas-style bungalows. Francie stole one of them somewhere around

Kilkenny last year and he's sold it six times since. Here we are.' Pat pointed to the relevant summons. 'In Carlow, Kildare, Meath, Westmeath, Galway and finally in Clare. What he'd do was, he'd offer it around the bungalows and sell it to some sucker for two hundred cash. No questions asked. Then he'd come back at three in the morning with his van and his screwdriver and steal it right back again.'

'That's a nice one. You're sure it's going ahead today?'

'No doubt about it. Francie isn't turning up, but we're holding the party without him.'

Tara took down the details and then sifted rapidly through the rest of the summonses. One name leaped out at her – Fergal Kennedy, Barnabo, due up on a charge of driving without due care and attention on the main Ennis road.

Pat pointed to the summons sheet. 'Know him?' he asked.

'Yes. Well...yes and no.'

She'd known Fergal since childhood, but there were more than three full years between them, and at that stage he had seemed almost like a member of an older generation. When she was still climbing trees and raiding orchards, he was already learning to drive and dating the sixth-year convent girls who seemed to her to be the epitome of bored, worldly-wise sophistication.

Even as a child, she had heard the rumours about Fergal. How those cuts and bruises that he seemed to carry like permanent tattoos were not, as he claimed, the result of schoolyard tussles or falls downstairs. How on a still night the neighbours could almost time their watches by the interval between the moment his morose, embittered father Martin Kennedy left Breadon's pub, and the moment the first young voice would cry with sudden pain and terror from their hillside farmhouse.

And even at that early stage, while chattering childishly behind the red brick buildings of the tiny school, Tara had encountered the most potent rumour of all – that the

Kennedy farmhouse on the hill concealed some shameful secret which even the grown-ups in the village talked about only in the most guarded whispers.

'That's him over there,' said Pat. 'The one who looks like a character out of a Monty Python sketch. He's a lumberjack, and he's okay.'

She glanced around the threadbare seats. They were rapidly filling up with defendants, witnesses, and curious spectators waiting to see the most interesting entertainment Claremoon Harbour had to offer on a wet Wednesday.

Finally her eye settled on a tall figure at the back. He was wearing a heavy red-checked lumbershirt, open necked with a white T-shirt underneath. A brown leather jacket, spattered black with raindrops, lay across his lap.

At first she didn't recognise him as the spidery, under-developed lad who'd left Claremoon Harbour when she was barely out of her teens. The years in Canada had been good to him. He was heavier-built and his skinny face had rounded out and matured, but the green eyes remained the same – bright and alert, like those of some watchful bird of prey. They seemed to flicker around the room, eager for challenge, missing nothing.

The unruly dark brown hair still looked as though it refused to submit to the control of brush or comb, but he now wore a neatly-trimmed moustache. It suited him, she thought casually, as she returned to her work and moved on to the next case on the list.

'Poor old Fergal,' mused Pat. 'Just back from Canada the two months, and he's in trouble already.'

'Why? Has he been in trouble before?'

'Fergal? No, he's a good lad. Never had much of a chance, that's all. His da, now...that was a different story. He was a regular customer of ours. In and out so often we practically had to give him a season ticket. Drunk and disorderly, the odd assault. And all down to the same old problem. John Barleycorn.' Pat raised an imaginary bottle to his lips. 'Sober, he wouldn't say boo to a goose. But once he'd had a jar, there was no living with him. I don't know how Ann Kennedy put up with it all those years.'

Tara gave a token tut-tut of concern and got back to work. She liked Pat, but she sometimes wished he wouldn't talk so much when she was trying to take notes.

The task of copying details from the charge-sheets had to be done quickly, before the judge finished his morning cup of tea, otherwise her job of reporting the often-chaotic courtroom proceedings would be very difficult indeed.

'I could never stand a man who beats up his kids,' Pat was saying. 'I mean, the odd swipe at the wife is okay – only joking, Tara – but *children*. My God. They say that as soon as he got back from the pub every night, he'd wake up his two young lads, Fergal and Manus, and make them per-form for him.'

'Perform?' That got Tara's full attention.

'Yes, perform. Recite their Catechism, do their twelve-times tables, sing a song they'd learned at school, whatever. Then, at the first slip they made, out would come the blackthorn stick from the cupboard.' Pat shook his head. 'It was almost as though, in his poor whiskey-fuddled mind, he was getting revenge for everything that had gone wrong in his own miserable life.'

Tara had almost finished. 'Well, he can't hurt them any more, can he?' she said distantly.

'That's true. He's been dead, what? Five years now. And Fergal didn't even bother coming home for his funeral.'

Tara finally reached the end of the list. She handed the batch of summonses back to Pat with relief. 'Yes, I remem-ber. There was a big scandal in the village over that,' she said. 'Everyone expected Fergal to take over the family farm after Martin died. But he just ignored the whole busi-ness and stayed put in Canada.'

Pat checked his watch. The judge was taking longer than usual over his morning cuppa.

'Well, you can't blame young Fergal,' he said. 'He hated the whole idea of becoming a farmer. As soon as he finished art college, he was out of Ireland like a shot. He had big ideas about making a name for himself as an artist in Vancouver, but from what I hear, it didn't work out and he ended up working in the forestry service or something. Then he got fed up with that, and came home again with his tail between his legs.'

Tara nodded. The story of Fergal's six-year exile and his eventual homecoming had been thoroughly discussed in a community where most emigrants never came back at all.

'I heard there was another reason,' she told Pat. 'A more personal one.'

'What was that?'

'They say there was a woman,' she said. 'And when they broke up, he was so devastated that...'

But Pat wasn't listening. He'd sprung to his feet in deference to a small, rotund figure who was walking towards his allotted place under the silver screen and trying his best to look dignified in circumstances which he knew quite well were utterly ridiculous.

'All rise,' Pat shouted.

Fergal's case, like most of the others, seemed routine and almost boring until the arresting officer gave evidence. It appeared that Fergal had been driving his imported 1966 Corvette at seventy miles per hour on an open stretch of road, ignoring the fact that there was an overall speed limit of sixty, when he rounded a corner and rear-ended a vehicle that was parked by the side of the road about fifty yards past the bend.

'What sort of vehicle?' yawned the judge.

'An ambulance, Judge.'

A titter of laughter rippled through the sodden ranks of the spectators. This was more like it.

'An ambulance?'

'Yes, Judge. A local resident had fallen off his roof and was being removed to hospital.'

'Was anyone injured in the crash?'

'Only Mr Kennedy himself, Judge. He was knocked temporarily unconscious. They just lifted him out of his car and straight into the ambulance, and took the two of them to hospital together.'

'Forty pounds,' said the judge, trying to keep his face straight.

An hour later the court ended and the disappointed spectators filed out of the cinema, once again cheated of any sex, violence or major scandals in the village.

Tara stood up and tried to brush the dried mud from her legs. At least the rest of her navy suit seemed to have dried out. Now for a bite of lunch and on to the town commissioners' meeting at two thirty...

'You from the local paper?'

She sighed inwardly, half in embarrassment and half in irritation. She'd been finding it impossible to scrape off a particularly stubborn spat of mud. And she was used to people approaching her after court cases, asking her, in effect, to censor their names from her report of the court proceedings.

In a small community like this, publicity in the local paper was more of a punishment than any penalty imposed by the court. Over the years, she had become hardened to tales of fathers with weak hearts who would drop dead at the shock of seeing their son's or daughter's name in print for double-parking.

'Yes, I'm working for the *Clare Independent* today,' she replied without looking up.

'I'm Fergal Kennedy.'

She glanced up for the first time. The green eyes were direct and serious.

'Hello, Fergal. I'm Tara Ross.'

He laughed. 'Not Tara Ross from Rathmitchel? John

Ross's little daughter? Well, I'll be damned.'

In Claremoon Harbour, you always remained somebody's daughter or somebody's son. Tara closed her notebook and forced a smile. 'Not so little any more, Mr Kennedy. Now what can I do for you?'

'You can keep this damnfool case out of your bloody paper.'

The accent was an attractive mixture of Clare and Canada, but the phraseology and the direct approach was purely transatlantic. An Irishman would have made the same request obliquely, putting on what locals called 'the poor mouth', wheedling, coaxing, and asking her if she could see her way clear to letting the hare sit.

They left the cinema together, Tara delivering her well-practised speech almost automatically.

'Look, I'm really sorry, but my job is to report all the cases. The editor of the *Clare Independent* decides whether or not they're published.'

'What a load of bull, Tara. You know as well as I do that he hasn't a clue which cases are going on. You could drop one without him even knowing.'

She laughed in spite of herself. It made a refreshing change from the tales of woe she normally had to endure.

'What's so funny?' His eyes were fixed on her, bright and wary as a falcon's. He couldn't see the joke. His muscles tensed and, just a fleeting instant, she had the ridiculous impression that he was about to hit her.

'I'm sorry, Fergal, but that's the way it is,' she said, turning serious. 'Really.'

He snorted. 'I'm having enough trouble trying to insure the goddam 'vette in this country as it is.'

She spun around and confronted him. 'So that's what it's all about – saving money on your insurance?' she challenged.

A typical Irishman would have been offended. But Fergal just nodded. 'Sure it is. Can you think of a better reason?'

By this time they were out in the street. The torrential rain had eased off, and a pale yellow sun was trying desperately to break through the mist.

'Can't do it. Sorry,' Tara shouted over her shoulder as she dashed between a tractor and a filthy delivery van to get to her ancient Fiat. Claremoon Harbour was unusually busy today. However, once the court traffic had dispersed it would return to its usual state of contented sleepiness. The most exciting thing about the afternoon would be pick-up time at the tiny national school; three hours later there would be evening Mass at the old Victorian church; then a bit of lively *craic* in Breadon's pub. That was how it was; that was how it had always been, for as long as Tara could remember.

She opened the car door quickly – there was never any reason to lock it in Claremoon Harbour – and tried to start the car. The tiny electric motor whirred gallantly but nothing happened. Wait, she reminded herself. Pause for five seconds. Try again. Wait five seconds.

Whirr, clunk, silence.

Damn it, she thought. It's finally kicked the bucket.

'Damp plugs,' said a familiar voice. 'I'll fix it for you...if you keep that case out.'

She looked around furiously. His head was halfway through her driver's window, grinning insolently.

'You go to hell,' she shouted. And for the next ten minutes she worked in the misty drizzle, head halfway into the rear engine compartment, replacing the spark-plugs with spares and trying to dry out the distributor.

Her fury grew as she watched him lounge against his shiny red Corvette, judging all her efforts with a critical smile. But finally she finished the job. Jumping triumphantly into the driver's seat, she turned the ignition key...only to find that the battery had gone flat.

'Well?' she said at last. 'Aren't you going to laugh?'

He shook his head, the grin temporarily gone.

'Nope. Not at all. You did everything right. Where did

you learn to be such a good mechanic? Here,' he offered, 'I'll start it from the Corvette's battery with these jump-leads. No charge, no conditions, no hidden agenda. Honest.'

She looked at him and saw he was serious. 'Okay. Thanks,' she said, watching carefully as he attached the leads to the battery with crocodile clips. If he put them on the wrong terminals, they'd both be in trouble. 'I learned a bit about motor maintenance with the diesel on the *Róisín Dubh*,' she explained. 'If you could keep that old engine going, you could fix anything.'

As Fergal opened the hood of his American car, Tara contrasted its sleek, shiny paintwork with the pitted surface of her own rust-bucket. 'Mind you, this old Fiat is something of a special challenge,' she admitted. 'It was a great car in its day. But it should have been allowed to die a natural death years ago.'

'Well, let's do a Frankenstein.' Fergal clipped on the jump-leads, and the Fiat's engine roared instantly to life. He turned to her and grinned. 'We have achieved a miracle, Igor!'

Tara revved up the motor and nodded her appreciation.

After disconnecting the leads, Fergal wiped his hands on a clean J-cloth and offered another one to her. He looked down towards the harbour where John Ross's fishing boat lay waiting for the tide. 'Funny you should mention the *Róisín Dubh*,' he said nostalgically. 'I used to help your da occasionally when the cod were coming in. The pay wasn't great, but I always enjoyed it. I wouldn't mind doing it again.'

'Why? Are you at a loose end?'

He looked slightly offended. 'No, not at all. I'm an artist. I'm trying to organise an exhibition of my paintings. But I could spare him a bit of time now and then if he needs help.'

'He always needs help,' said Tara. 'Give him a call. And thanks again for the jump-start.'

She was about to drive away when he signalled her to stop. 'Listen, Tara. I owe you an apology. I acted like a bit of a heel.'

She smiled. 'A bit? I'd say you were more of a giant platform job.'

'Let me make it up to you,' he said genuinely. 'I have a real news story that you might be interested in. Let me tell you about it over dinner tonight.'

Tara shook her head. 'Thanks, but no thanks. Call me cynical, but I'm used to men inviting me out to dinner to give me real news stories. The stories usually don't exist, and I end up fighting them off afterwards when they think that buying me a meal gives them a right to stick their tongue into my ear. Sorry for being direct, but you were direct with me.'

His eyes had grown wide with surprise and she steeled herself for another outburst. Instead, he roared with laughter.

'Good for you, girl. That's the spirit.'

'But,' she continued, 'I'm always interested in news stories. It's my job. If you really have one, I'll listen. Come over to Breadon's and I'll buy *you* a coffee. What was the phrase you used? No conditions, no hidden agenda.'

'Agreed.'

Almost immediately, she found herself regretting her invitation. From a professional point of view, she would almost certainly be wasting her time. She'd been in journalism long enough to know that most people's idea of a good news story had nothing in common with an editor's idea of a good news story. But – and here was the difference – he was Ann Kennedy's son. She was curious about him, intrigued by him, interested to know whether he'd anything at all in common with the women's rights campaigner she'd always respected and admired. So far, the answer seemed to be a definite no.

They entered the bar, passing through the tiny old-fashioned grocery shop at the front where the local women would still pop in for a packet of tea and stay for a half-pint of stout or a whiskey to keep away the winter chill; and on into the sanctum of marble, brass and polished wood which for years had been reserved for males only.

It turned out, to Tara's surprise, that Fergal did have a real news story. It was an environmental issue involving a plan to erect a giant electricity transformer in a field just a few yards from a primary school in the next village. The scheme had been kept quiet, but Fergal had got wind of it through a friend in the council.

'They'd never get away with it in Canada,' he pointed out as they drank their second coffee and then, all caution to the wind, ordered sandwiches as well. 'There's all sorts of scientific research indicating a possible link between these transformers and increased rates of cancer, especially among kids. Nobody knows for sure, but until we find out it's as well to keep them away from schools. I'll get you photocopies of the research if you like.'

She'd checked it out, and struck gold. She spoke to international experts about the possible dangers involved, and to other experts who claimed there was no danger at all. The following week she broke the story on her own Internet paper, the *Clare Electronic News*. It sparked off a furore and suddenly everyone wanted to know more about transformers and health risks. Tara not only made the front-page lead of the *Clare Independent*, but the main pages of all the national newspapers as well. In the course of one hectic week, she was interviewed four times on radio, and once on a peak-time TV show.

Meanwhile, Tara and Fergal continued to meet regularly to discuss progress on the transformer issue over lunch, or over a few beers. After a while it just became an excuse. When the transformer plan was finally scrapped, they didn't have an excuse to meet any more. But they kept meeting anyway.

Strange thing was, Fergal's careless-driving case never did make it into the paper.

Oh, Tara had included it, all right: six lines, name, address, date and location of offence and penalty, in the middle of a long list of similar offences, treating it exactly as she would have treated any other case.

But that week there had been a major public inquiry into a proposal to site a wind-generator farm on the County Clare coastline, and it had forced everything else off the news pages – including the entire proceedings of Claremoon Court.

Tara didn't care. She got paid anyway. 'It's an ill wind-farm that blows nobody any good,' she told Fergal.

They were sitting in a pub at Clarinbridge, about ten miles outside Galway city, lunching on oysters, wild mussels, smoked salmon and home-made brown bread. Through the window, they could see a river estuary teeming with wildfowl – chiding gulls, aloof swans, officiously busy little oyster-catchers. It was a beautifully mild Saturday afternoon, and the pub was abuzz with the laid-back, pleasurable energy of the weekend.

'Fergal,' said Tara, 'can I ask you a personal question?'

He bristled. 'What?'

'Do you always wear the same clothes? Every time we've met you've worn the same-coloured tartan shirt and blue jeans. I'm beginning to think they're sprayed on.'

He relaxed visibly. She wondered what question he thought she was going to ask.

'Not always,' he said. 'Sometimes I wear tartan trousers and a blue denim shirt. Just for a change.'

'Ask a silly question.'

'And underneath I wear tartan underpants and blue denim socks. Why do you ask?'

'Just curious.' She had to admit the outdoorsy Canadian-lumberjack look suited him.

'I hate clothes,' he explained. 'I hate shopping for clothes. I hate having to make my mind up what to wear. Be honest, now – how long did it take you to decide what to wear today?'

Tara glanced down at her own outfit – a heavy bleached-cotton jumper worn over faded black jeans. 'Five to ten minutes,' she answered honestly.

'See what I mean? That's ten wasted minutes, every morning. That's over an hour a week. What could you do in a year if you had an extra hour every week? You could do all the things you wanted to do but didn't have the time. You could master Spanish. You could read *Ulysses*. You could learn to hang-glide. So all my clothes are exactly the same. I have a dozen red workshirts and a dozen pairs of blue Levis. It's not high fashion, but it makes life goddam simple.'

'Do you wear pyjamas with tartan tops and blue pants?' Tara asked with deadpan seriousness.

'Do you want to find out?'

Tara smiled for a moment, enjoying the light-hearted sexual challenge. Their eyes met.

'Hey!' she said suddenly. 'Look what I've found in my mussel.'

Hidden in the folds of the wild seawater mussel, she had found a natural pearl. It was only tiny, about the size of a large coffee granule, but it was spherical, creamy-white, and absolutely perfect.

'I'm going to give you a present of this,' she laughed, polishing it with a napkin and setting it on the centre of her palm. 'I was born in June, so my birthstone is the pearl. This must be an omen. We're being blessed with good fortune, Fergal.'

She placed her hand on the table, palm uppermost, and glanced up at him, expecting him to lift the pearl. Instead, he gently placed the tip of his forefinger on top of it. His eyes never left hers as he began rotating the miniature pearl, under the lightest of pressure from his forefinger, around the centre of her palm.

She held his gaze, giving nothing away. But deep inside, she experienced a tiny, exquisite shiver of pleasure, because the sensation was intensely and unexpectedly erotic. The pearl circled her palm, lingering in the valleys of the life and fate lines, teasing at the crevices between her fingers. As it returned to the sensitive hollow at the centre of her palm, she felt her entire body flex in response, rising a fraction of a millimetre above her chair as though she were caught in the downward plunge of a rollercoaster. It was a familiar sensation, dangerous yet thrilling and enjoyable. She hadn't felt it for a long time.

'Well?' she challenged at last. 'Are you going to mess around forever, or are you going to go for it?'

He smiled. 'Oh, I'll go for it,' he said. Wrapping the pearl in a twist of paper, he clutched it to his bosom and assumed the voice of a bad actor in an old-fashioned melodrama. 'I'll always keep it next to my heart.'

Emphasising the point, he tucked it into the right-hand breast pocket of his lumbershirt.

'Fergal?'

He was refastening his button. 'What?'

'Your heart's on the left.'

The ancient diesel engine gave a few cantankerous knocks, then coughed and spluttered to life with all the enthusiasm of a hangover-ridden chain smoker waking up to a wet Monday morning.

'She's past her best, I'm afraid,' said John Ross, frowning at the oily black monster that juddered and shuddered just beneath the deck of his fishing boat. 'A bit like her owner,' he added with a shrug, looking up at his daughter as she stood on the harbour wall.

Tara swung her slender legs over the wall and jumped expertly on to the weather-worn deck of the *Róisín Dubh*. She flung her arms around her father and kissed his grizzled cheek.

'Dad, you've been saying that about yourself every day for the past twenty years,' she laughed. 'That old engine still has a lot of life left in it. And so have you.'

Here in the tiny harbour, with its smell of fish and salt and oil and seaweed, Tara felt most at home. She loved the sounds – the regular slop and slap of water between hull and harbour wall, the rattle and clank of the rigging on the handful of yachts, the deep throb of the diesel engines, the voices that echoed for hundreds of yards across the open sea on a calm night.

'A lot of life,' she repeated, squeezing his arm fondly.

John Ross smiled and eased himself into the skipper's seat. 'God willing,' he said. 'God willing. If He can perform the miracle of making that old engine start, perhaps He can spare me for a few more years. And talking of miracles, it would be a miracle if you put that kettle on just once without being asked.'

His deep brown eyes twinkled with humour and life. Yet, Tara thought as she ignited the gas stove, it was not so long ago that John Ross had lain suspended in that limbo between life and death, looking as though the slightest breeze would dislodge soul from body like a dried-up leaf from a tree.

She remembered how rapidly he had begun to fade after her mother had passed away. Looking back on it now, it was obvious that her father, left alone without the wife he adored, had been slowly dying of a broken heart. Tara couldn't pretend that her own return to Claremoon Harbour had been inspired by the noblest of motives, but at least her presence had helped him to recover his old zest for living.

John Ross pushed forward the throttle, concentrating on the rising note of the engine. He wasn't a big man, but he had an air of quiet self-sufficiency and determination that commanded respect. In his prime, he had resembled the young Sean Connery, and while the advancing years hadn't been nearly so kind to him as they'd been to Connery, Tara's father still cut a strikingly handsome figure for a man in his mid-sixties. His hair may have become grizzled, but it remained thick and wiry, and his weather-beaten face still showed the deep contentment and satisfaction of a life lived to the full.

When the kettle had boiled, he switched off the engine and they sat in silence, drinking their tea and enjoying the companionship of those who are so close that talk can serve only as a distraction.

'I see you and young Fergal Kennedy have been walking out together,' he said at last, eyes scanning the horizon where two large demersal trawlers were sluggishly passing the Aran Islands on their way north to Rossaveel.

'You don't miss anything, do you, Dad?'

'Fishermen's eyes can see further than most people's,' he smiled, turning back to her again. He lit one of the strong Sweet Afton cigarettes that were strictly forbidden by his doctor.

Tara, who'd never smoked, still felt a surge of pleasure as the woody scent of the tobacco mingled with the tang of the salt breeze. The combination of smells evoked a myriad of childhood memories.

John Ross took a long sip of his tea. 'That's a grand cup,' he said with genuine appreciation. 'So strong you could float a donkey shoe on top. Just be careful, love,' he said without changing his tone.

'Careful?' Tara looked at him in puzzlement. A yacht tender passed by, its little outboard engine clattering noisily.

'The Kennedy family have had a lot of problems over the years,' said John. 'It's not Ann's fault, Lord knows. The woman is almost a saint. But that husband of hers was an animal. No one could have blamed her for what she did.'

'Did? What did she do?'

John stubbed out his half-finished cigarette on the edge of a steel bucket, sending an avalanche of sparks down the metal surface. 'It doesn't matter, love. What's done is done. That isn't what I wanted to tell you about. All I'm saying is that Fergal and his brother, young Manus, had a rough childhood. It probably left them scarred for life.'

'Fergal hated his father,' said Tara. 'But he never talks about Manus at all.'

She looked out to sea. The sun had become an enormous disc of fiery copper, suspended inches above the liquid horizon. In a few moments it would sink, almost hissing, into the ocean.

Up on the harbour wall, two little girls were fishing, their outlines silhouetted against a backdrop of pure orange.

'It doesn't surprise me that he never talks about him,' said her father. 'Manus left home seven or eight years ago, in circumstances that were strange, to say the least.'

Tara wrinkled her brow as she tried to remember the stocky youth with the acne-scarred face and the dense mass of curly brown hair. He had reminded her of pictures of the younger Beethoven.

'Yes, I remember now,' she said. 'He got a job on a salmon farm in Scotland, or something.'

'That was the story,' he said with sudden gravity. 'The truth is different. Only a few of us know that truth, and we've kept it quiet for Ann's sake. I think you should know, too. But I know I can rely on your discretion, Tupps.'

Tupps. Short for Tuppence, his childhood nickname for her. Tara felt a glow at the private term of endearment. 'You know you can, Dad.'

John rubbed his hands. It was growing colder with the dusk. He put on an oiled-wool fisherman's jumper and a battered denim cap.

'Lord knows I don't stand in judgement on anyone,' he said at last. 'But Ann's husband was the most brutish man I've ever known. He beat her and he beat his children. He enjoyed it. We all tried to stop him – Dr Maguire, the parish priest, even Sergeant Flynn down at the garda station – but he didn't care about any of us. Once it became so bad that I called out the social workers all the way from Ennis, but the children swore they'd fallen off their bikes or something and Ann, God bless her, was too terrified to testify against her husband.'

'Then she was part of the problem, I suppose,' said Tara.

'That's something she's had to live with ever since. And over the past five years, she's worked harder than anyone to try to stop other women falling into the same trap. But don't you sit in judgement on Ann, either,' warned her father. 'Things were different in those days. It was practically impossible to get the authorities to interfere in family matters, unless something drastic was done.'

'I'm not judging Ann, Dad. She's the one who's helped to change the old system.'

John Ross nodded. 'Anyway, Martin was allowed to get on with raising his family as he saw fit,' he said. 'Until one night, one terrible night in January seven years ago, it seemed that Manus just couldn't take any more.'

Tara shivered, only partially because of the cold breeze.

'I suppose he would have been in his late teens at the time,' John continued. 'But he must have decided that was the last beating he'd take from Martin Kennedy. After it was over, he waited until his father had gone to sleep, and he went out to the cowshed where the cattle were peacefully bedded down for the night. He poured paraffin all over the hay, jammed all the doors closed, threw in a match and watched it go up.'

Tara stared open-mouthed. 'But I remember that fire. Something like two dozen cattle died. You told me it was an accident.'

'Yes, I did, love. But it was no accident. I'll never forget it so long as I live, Tara – the cries of the beasts and the burning flesh.'

'What happened to Manus?'

'He lay low in the woods for a while, living rough. A couple of days later a woman out in Sixmilebridge came home to find a strange, bedraggled man in her kitchen, wolfing down lumps of bread like some wild animal. The police caught him soon after that. He gave his name as Manus Kennedy.'

'I never heard any of this before,' Tara protested. 'Did it make the papers?'

'It didn't even make it to trial. The judge ordered a psychiatrist to have a look at him, and the psychiatrist diagnosed that he was...oh, I can't remember the phrase he used. But the end result was, he was put in some sort of a nursing home out in the midlands. Martin and Ann signed the papers authorising his treatment, and everyone agreed the fire had been accidental. It was all kept very quiet around here.'

He stood and began organising the boat in readiness for the fishing trip at first light.

'Hang on a moment,' Tara protested, her journalistic scepticism aroused. 'How do we know that the fire wasn't really an accident? How do we know Manus had anything to do with it?'

'Because Fergal caught him in the act. He tried to stop him. They actually fought each other outside the cowshed, with the flames leppin' up around them. It was all Fergal could do to stop Manus setting fire to the farmhouse as well. I know, because Fergal told his mother and Ann told me.'

'And what happened to Manus? Is he still in the hospital?'

Her father stacked up the fish boxes and put the gutting-knives back into their sheaths. 'He was discharged in January. He was supposed to live in a sheltered dwelling for a while, but he disappeared and hasn't been seen since. Some people said he emigrated to America and that he's working on the building sites in Boston. Others say they've spotted him living rough around these parts. Nobody knows for sure. Well, maybe Ann knows, but she's never said.'

Tara was intrigued by these revelations. It was a story more fitting to a Steinbeck novel or a Greek tragedy than to a sleepy little fishing port in County Clare.

'I know why you're telling me all this, Dad,' she said after a moment. 'You're warning me that anger and violence could run in the Kennedy family's blood. But those two brothers are totally different, even in their appearance. They're chalk and cheese.'

John Ross stared at her for a long while. Then he busied himself by positioning a barrel of seawater to one side of the deck. As the tide went out, it would act as ballast, encouraging the boat to settle against the harbour wall.

'Maybe,' he said finally. 'Maybe not. Just watch yourself, that's all. And remember, not a word of this to anyone. Not even to Steve McNamara. He knows nothing about it – he was transferred to Claremoon Harbour years after the fire.'

'Sure.' Tara nodded. 'Oh, incidentally, there's one way you might get to know Fergal a little better. He says he'd be keen to give you a hand with the boat. Says he got a taste for sea angling in Vancouver, and he might get a chance to put a line over the side.'

John Ross sighed. 'I could certainly do with some help now that young Colm has taken the big jumbo to San Francisco. And you're right, it might give me a chance to get to know Fergal again after all these years. Tell him to come along on the first of June. But I can't guarantee he'll have any free time for sea-angling.'

Tara knew exactly what he meant. The first of June was a special day on her father's calendar. It was the start of the salmon season, two months of hectic make-or-break for those inshore fishermen lucky enough to have a licence.

'That time of year again?' she said. 'Now it's *my* turn to warn *you* to be careful.'

She looked pointedly to the stern of the boat, where his tangle-nets lay ready for 'shooting', or letting out into the sea. It could be a dangerous business, because once the nets gained momentum under the weight of their huge anchor-stone, they were virtually unstoppable. One young lad's arm had been literally wrenched from its socket after his wristwatch became entangled in the flying meshes of a tangle-net.

'Don't worry, Tupps. I know you're concerned about my health.' He held up his left hand to display a missing forefinger. 'But I can't afford to lose another one of these. Sure how would I be able to smoke?'

Tara shook her head in mock-despair. She constantly worried about her father's safety at sea. John Ross was an experienced skipper, but he was out in all weathers, from early February until late October, and danger was always present. Fish was one of the few remaining supermarket foods that *Homo sapiens* still went out to hunt.

'I give up,' she smiled. 'Let's go home.'

John Ross locked up the cabin and checked the boat's mooring ropes. Together, they walked the few hundred yards to her father's house.

'Good night, Dad,' said Tara as she headed up the hill towards her own cottage.

He squeezed her hand. 'Take care, love.'

It was now almost dark. Around the port and high up on the hillside, dozens of lights flickered on and Claremoon Harbour settled gently into night.

CHAPTER THREE

'I'VE FINISHED with sex, thank God,' said Melanie O'Driscoll. 'I've moved on to child abuse.'

'And after that?' asked Tara.

'Oh, then I'll be doing masturbation – not too much of that – and then there's birth control. Oh, and somewhere along the line, I have to get in some sexually transmitted diseases.'

It was just a small coffee shop and there was no such thing as a private conversation. At the next table, an elderly man cleared his throat disapprovingly, folded up his copy of *The Irish Catholic*, and left.

'Better keep your voice down a bit, Mel,' warned Tara with a grin. She sipped her coffee and shook her head in admiration. 'It must take a lot of self-discipline to write a book. How many chapters are there altogether?'

'Well, I'm trying to cover every subject from abortion to zits, with every topic from sex to unplanned pregnancy in between, and make it all understandable to teenagers. I suppose a dozen chapters in all. It's the title that's the problem. The publishers are suggesting *The SUSS Survival Guide* but I'm not keen on that. Still, I'd better get the damn thing written first.'

'Hang in, there. I'm sure it will be a huge success.'

Melanie nodded her thanks. 'And what have you been up to for the past two months, while I've been slaving away over a hot word processor?'

'Oh...nothing so productive. Desperately trying to get sponsorship and advertising for the *Clare Electronic News*. Covering the town commissioners' meetings and the courts. Going out with Fergal Kennedy.'

Melanie looked at Tara in astonishment. 'Fergal Kennedy? Get away out of that, with you. You're not serious.'

'Why shouldn't I be serious?'

'Oh, come on, Tara. Tell me you won the Lotto. Tell me you've been shortlisted for the first Irish moon mission. But don't tell me you're going out with Fergal Kennedy.'

'Yes, I am. Why shouldn't I? Mel, this is very offensive. Stop it. I'm going to take offence. I mean it.'

Melanie ham-acted a heart attack and collapsed over the formica table of the coffee bar. In spite of her irritation, Tara couldn't help smiling. Infuriating as she was, Mel was her best friend and, besides, she was so compulsively entertaining that it was impossible to stay angry with her for long.

'Heart. Heart. Pink tablets. Resuscitation. Oh...too late.'

'Oh, open your eyes and sit up, Melanie. For God's sake. Everybody's staring.'

The mop of Titian-red hair on the table remained still, then gradually rose. The eyelids slowly opened to reveal green, mischievous eyes.

'It's all been a dream,' Mel intoned. 'A terrible nightmare. I dreamed you said you were Fergal Kennedy's girlfriend. I'm glad it was just a figment of my fevered imagination. I'll never touch the magic mushrooms again, doc.'

Tara ignored her and studied the street outside the café. Bright sunshine battling through showers. Flashes of colour against the grey, as shoppers dashed across the street in multicoloured windcheaters and golfing umbrellas.

Melanie touched her arm. 'Sorry, Tara. You took me by surprise, that's all. You've always said you'd do anything to help Ann Kennedy, but I'd no idea that included dating her appalling son. How long has this been going on?'

Tara tugged irritably at the plastic top on the UHT milk container and poured the contents into her coffee. She hated UHT milk. 'A few weeks. But don't worry. It's nothing serious.'

'Not serious. Oh no-oh.' Melanie stirred her coffee and hummed the first few bars of 10CC's "I'm Not In Love".

'I thought I could confide in you,' said Tara. 'Obviously I was mistaken.'

There was a sudden chill. Mel defused it by the simple device of sticking out her tongue at her friend. She'd learned over the years that it was the best way to deal with Tara's moodiness.

Tara glared at her and then burst into laughter. 'Mel, stop fooling around, would you? I'm in a dilemma and I need a bit of advice. I'm very fond of Fergal' – she frowned – 'I think I'm getting really involved with him, actually. And he seems even more serious about me.'

Melanie shook her head mockingly. 'I thought you said you weren't going to have any more long-term relationships after the great Chris Calder catastrophe. What was your firm resolution? Ah yes. Three dates and they're out.'

'Yes, I did say that, didn't I.'

'So now you're in exactly the same position as you were with Chris. It's just that you've swapped a good-looking, intelligent, rich barrister for an unemployed artist with a personality disorder. Just remind me again why that's an improvement in your situation.'

'What do you mean, personality disorder?' Tara demanded.

Melanie said nothing.

'You know what I need?' Tara said thoughtfully. 'I need to get myself a friend. Ever heard of that term? You know, one of those people who takes *my* side in these matters. Any idea where I could find one at short notice?'

Melanie transformed herself from jester to counsellor in two seconds flat. For counsellor was exactly what she was in everyday life. At the age of only twenty-nine, she was the most sought-after psychotherapist in Galway city. Perhaps, Tara thought for the thousandth time, her off-duty levity was really a reaction to a life spent listening to other people's problems.

'Okay,' she said. 'Get on the couch. But remember, I'm like Lucy in *Peanuts* – I charge five cents per session.'

Tara smiled, recalling the *Peanuts* cartoons in which Lucy Van Pelt offers counselling to the eternally-bewildered Charlie Brown under a sign that says 'Psychiatric help, 5c.'

'I can't quite make up my mind how I feel towards Fergal,' she confessed. 'He has a touch of the outlaw about him, and that's what I love about the man. He's impulsive and unpredictable and he doesn't give a stuff what anybody thinks. And he makes me laugh. You know, I'd almost forgotten that dating could be fun, not just a matter of solemn duty – meeting the right people and being seen in the right places.'

'In other words, Fergal's an antimatter version of Chris Calder. He's everything that Chris isn't.'

'I suppose so. I'd be less than honest if I didn't admit that.' Tara rolled an empty sugar sachet into a tight cylinder and stared at it. 'But you're making it sound negative. It's not. It's more like...oh, like a release after a long term in confinement. Or that wonderful feeling you have when you get healthy again after a bad dose of 'flu. But is that enough, Mel?'

'Enough for what?'

'Enough to build a long-term relationship on.'

Melanie sighed. 'I can't see inside your head, Tara, although I suppose it's my job to. All I know is that most of us create our relationships slowly, building on a gradually growing love and respect. And in the best relationships, these feelings evolve and grow and change in pace with the growth and change of the individuals. You want my advice? Enjoy the fun part. But take your time. Don't be rushed into anything.'

'I suppose so.' The bill arrived and Tara reached for her purse.

'No – this one is on me.' Mel paid the waitress. 'But for God's sake, put it in perspective, Tara. You've been going out together for how long? A few weeks? It's hardly time for either of you to be thinking of long-term commitments at this stage. Don't let him pressurise you if you don't feel like it. Let it grow.'

Tara nodded. 'You're right, of course, Mel. As always.'

'Of course I am. Slow down, enjoy. Now...my five cents, please.'

Tara tossed her five pence. 'Just one more thing. Why did you react so negatively when I mentioned Fergal?'

'Because he's a geek,' replied Mel candidly. 'Sorry, but that's a highly technical term that we Freudian psycho-therapists use.'

'What do you mean?' Tara was serious now.

Mel shrugged. 'Okay, he was a bully. He made life a misery for me and my sister on our way to school. I was delighted when he left the village.' She grimaced. 'I'm sorry, Tara, I just didn't like him. That's all. I suppose that blows my chances of becoming bridesmaid?'

'It's true that he can be a bit high-handed,' said Tara, thinking of their row outside the courthouse. 'But, come on, Mel. Schooldays were a long time ago.'

Mel nodded. 'Sure they were. Listen, I've got to go. Just one tip. If you ever decide to start buying rings and going through books of carpet patterns, make sure you know all about him. I mean everything.'

More than any woman Tara had ever met, Ann Kennedy possessed that indefinable quality summed up by the word 'presence'. Even in the most crowded, noisy room, the atmosphere would change subtly when Ann entered. You could have your back turned to the door and still sense the charisma, the electricity. You would know that she was there.

But tonight the public persona had been left aside and Ann was the perfect hostess, warm and welcoming, as Tara and Fergal joined her for dinner.

'More tiramisu, Tara?' she asked.

Her voice was warm, with a hint of her native County Antrim in the accent. She was a tall woman, but, unlike many tall women, she didn't stoop to disguise her height. She carried herself proudly. Her greying gold hair, tied back in a bun, betrayed her Viking ancestors. So did her Scandinavian features – the wide, generous mouth, the finely structured features and the friendly but penetrating blue eyes.

'No, honestly, thanks, Ann. It was delicious, but I really couldn't manage.'

Ann smiled. 'I'm glad you liked it. Fergal?'

'Not for me, thanks.'

The dining-room – a modern extension to the old farm-house at Barnabo – faced directly west, catching the full glory of the setting sun over the Atlantic. Tara could just make out the silhouette of the *Róisín Dubh* near Chicken Point.

Ann Kennedy followed her gaze. 'How does your father find the fishing these days?' she asked.

'He's kept busy,' Tara admitted. 'It's the salmon season and he'll be working flat-out from now until the end of July. After that, it's back to the lobster pots. Not nearly so hectic.'

'And how is he, in himself?'

'Much better, thank you. He had us all worried at one stage, but he's much improved.'

'I'm glad. He's a good man.' Ann's eyes wandered to a framed photo above the mantelpiece. It showed a couple on their wedding day. Ann, her young face shining with happiness, the full mouth smiling and sensual, and Martin, formal and solemn as befitted the occasion. His dark hair was brylcreemed into place and his deep-set brown eyes stared challengingly at the camera from beneath heavy eyebrows that met over the nose. It was a picture of youth and hope.

'You knew my late husband, didn't you, Tara?' she asked.

'I often met him,' said Tara, 'but I don't think we ever had a conversation. Apart from the usual exchanges about the weather, of course.'

'We'd just celebrated our silver wedding anniversary when he died,' said Ann, still staring at the photo.

'Twenty-five years. That's a long time.'

Ann searched Tara's face for signs of a deeper meaning behind the remark, but found none. 'Yes,' she said simply.

The meal had been a gourmet's delight – roast Clare lamb with wild garlic and rosemary straight from Ann's herb garden – but all the small talk had been exhausted and this latest exchange had created an awkwardness that no one had intended.

'And now I must make some coffee,' said Ann brightly, snapping out of whatever mood had captured her. She stood up and stacked the plates, carefully avoiding any splashes on her classic beige suit.

As the kitchen door swung closed behind her, Tara rose and walked over to the wall opposite the window. Another framed picture had intrigued her throughout the meal, but it had been half-hidden by the bright reflection of the setting sun on the glass.

Looking at it from a better angle, she could see it clearly. It was an original oil painting – a view of Claremoon Harbour from high on the hill. The composition was rushed, almost as though it had been dashed off in a hurry. The scale was all wrong. But the bright, savage colours sang out as joyfully as a gospel chorus. It was magnificent.

'Like it?'

Fergal was standing behind her, offering her a replenished glass of red wine.

'It's absolutely wonderful,' said Tara, with genuine feeling. 'I've never seen anything quite like it before.'

'The colours,' said Fergal.

'That's it, of course,' said Tara, studying them more closely. 'They're not true to life, but somehow they sum up how you feel when you stand up on the hill on a bright, windy day looking down over the harbour. It's got a sort of...' She searched for the word... '*pagan* quality about it.'

'It's been compared to the work of Matisse or Derain,' said Fergal. He laughed. 'I only wish it was even a fraction of the value.'

Tara peered at the scribbled signature in the corner. 'Michael de Blaca,' she read. '*The* Michael de Blaca?'

'The very same,' said Fergal, pouring himself another glass of the Hermitage which Ann had laid on for dinner. 'Recognise the viewpoint?'

Tara studied the painting again, checking angles and perspectives. 'It must have been painted from around here,' she said at last.

Fergal nodded and gestured to the picture-window that offered a panoramic view of the bay. 'Not just around here. Exactly here. Just there, a few feet from where you're standing. That was about three decades ago.'

Tara knew very little about art, and even less about Michael de Blaca. She knew he was a moderately famous Irish artist who had lived for a few years in Claremoon Harbour before moving permanently to the Continent. He had donated a sculpture of a Celtic cross to the village about fifteen years ago. It still stood in the main street.

As the only famous person ever to have had any connection with Claremoon Harbour, his name was dropped constantly in the tourist season. There was even a De Blaca Gallery, which had absolutely nothing to do with the artist and through which an unctuous art dealer named Godfrey Villiers hawked very bad local watercolours to gullible Americans. Villiers wasn't his real name – *nobody* was called Godfrey Villiers – and there were dark rumours that his shop was nothing more than a money-laundering outlet for some heavy criminal elements in Limerick city.

'Did your parents know de Blaca well?' Tara asked.

'Very well,' said Fergal. 'He was a guest of theirs from time to time. He loved the view from this house, and they allowed him to paint here.'

There was a sudden, inexplicable tension in the air. Tara turned around to see Ann standing in the open doorway carrying a cafetière and a stack of cups.

'Fergal,' she said casually, but there was a strain in her voice she couldn't disguise, 'give me a hand with the coffee.'

'Here, let me.' Tara relieved her of the cafetière. 'Fergal's just been showing me the seascape by Michael de Blaca. It's beautiful. You must be very proud of it.'

Ann poured the coffees. 'I'm not keen on it myself,' she shrugged. 'I had it wrapped up and stored away in the loft. Fergal brought it down only this afternoon.'

She looked at her son. The last few words of the sentence were unspoken, but clearly understood: *against my wishes*.

'Come on, Mom.' Fergal was smiling, but his voice was almost a shout. 'It's a crime to have such a great painting rotting away up in the loft, hidden from view. Don't you agree, Tara?'

Don't drag me into this, Tara wanted to say. Whatever this family dispute was about, it was about more than a painting.

She smiled. 'I think it's a matter of individual taste. And speaking of taste – could I have one of those delicious-looking oatmeal biscuits?'

Ann looked at her with amused gratitude and passed the plate.

Fergal stalked over to the window and stared out towards the Burren hills. 'Somebody's forgotten to close the gate on the far field,' he said irritably. 'I'd better go do it, or we'll have the cows all over the lawn again.'

'I'll come with you.' Tara stood up. 'I'd enjoy the walk.'

'No.' It was an order. 'You stay here. Relax.'

The kitchen door slammed. They watched his figure disappear across the fields, bent slightly forward, almost as though his body was at war with itself, his head racing his feet to get there first. His bullish posture was exaggerated in the long shadow cast by the setting sun.

'Do you always let him order you around like that?' asked Ann, half in amusement, half seriously.

Tara laughed. 'I'm a guest in your house, Ann. Things would be different if we were on neutral territory.'

Ann poured more coffee and smiled back at her. 'I'm glad to hear it,' she said. 'Fergal would boss the whole world about if he thought he could get away with it.'

'Don't worry.' Tara added milk to her coffee and passed the jug across. 'He sometimes tries it on. But I can give back as good as I get. I value my independence, Ann, and I don't let anybody walk over me.'

'Yes, so I've heard.'

Tara glanced sharply at her. What did she mean?

But Ann seemed preoccupied. 'I'm glad you're strong in that way, Tara, because...well, Fergal can be a bit over-whelming at times. I suppose he gets that from his father.'

Trying not to make it too obvious, Tara peered over Ann's shoulder at the groom's face in the wedding photo. She failed to discern any facial similarity between father and son.

'There's no harm in him,' Ann continued, 'but you just need to take a firm stand with him now and again. And it's difficult to do that, I know, because he's been through a bit of a rough time.'

'Yes, I realise that.' Tara became serious. 'His father's death. And then the break-up with his girlfriend in Canada.'

She looked out across the fields. Fergal's figure had become dwarfed against the ancient limestone hills. The dramatic white outcrops of rock had been tinted salmon-pink by the sunset. Sheep huddled underneath the twisted, dwarfish thorn trees. From this perspective, Fergal looked for the first time frail and vulnerable, like some lonely reaper in a Van Gogh landscape.

'I never met Mathilde,' Ann was saying. 'I offered to fly out once or twice, but Fergal always put me off. He said it wasn't the right time. Then they broke up, and of course he came back here. He was pretty devastated, Tara. It's no secret that you've caught him on the rebound.'

'I know that, Ann. And I know what you're trying to tell me.'

Ann Kennedy smiled. 'My, my. You are perceptive, aren't you?'

'It's okay. I've no intention of letting anyone rush me into anything. We're just going to take it nice and easy. Enjoy the fun part. See what happens.'

'Good.' Ann glanced out the window. Fergal had closed the gates and was trudging purposefully back across the fields.

She smiled, then glanced at her watch. 'Good Lord, is that the time? I have to dash out to address a meeting of the Irish Countrywomen's Association, and I'm already late. I hope you don't mind, Tara.'

'Not at all. Thank you for a wonderful meal.'

'My pleasure,' said Ann, struggling into a light raincoat and searching for her car keys. 'I'm sure it won't be our last.'

Tara and Fergal listened in silence as Ann's Honda Civic growled throatily down the lane towards the village. 'Silencer,' sighed Fergal. 'I keep right on fixing it, it keeps right on breaking. It's all those damn potholes. There's...'

'Don't tell me. There's more tar in a pack of Silk Cut than there is on the roads around here,' Tara supplied, using his favourite line but getting in first.

He threw the remains of a bread roll at her. She returned it deftly, like a tennis serve.

'They wouldn't stand for it in Canada.' He frowned at her, almost as though it were her fault.

'Hey, hang on a minute,' she said in mock annoyance. 'If Canada was so great, how come *it's* over there and *you're* over here?'

'What do you mean?'

'If you liked it so much, why didn't you stay there?'

His grin faded. She had inadvertently touched a sore point. He thought carefully for a moment before replying.

'I wanted to make it as an artist,' he said. 'That was the only thing that was really important to me. Vancouver has a thriving art culture – in many ways, it reminds you of what Paris must have been like in the last century. But even though I painted my goddam heart out and produced some of my best work ever, it just didn't happen for me. I staged two full-scale exhibitions. They were well reviewed, but they didn't put any money in my pocket. The whole exercise left me broke.'

Tara sipped her glass of wine. 'Was that the only reason?' she asked.

'You want honesty?'

Tara smiled assent.

'I lost Mathilde.'

The voice was matter-of-fact and devoid of any trace of self-pity.

'Your girlfriend in Canada?'

'Yes. She was very special to me. And, well, once it became clear that I wasn't special to her, there seemed no real point in hanging around Vancouver any more. It was all very civilised, very mature. We kissed goodbye and told each other we would always remember the good times.'

'But it took you a while to get over her.'

He shrugged. 'It took a while, but I got there.'

'Can I see some of your paintings?' Tara asked suddenly.

Fergal nodded. 'Of course. I'd love you to. But not tonight. There's something else I want to show you.'

They rose from the dinner-table and moved into the sitting-room. It was exactly as Tara had imagined it – glass-fronted cabinets bulging with Irish crystal, mock-Jacobean leather suite, a reproduction antique globe in the corner. A bay window overlooking a well-hoovered lawn and a disciplined parade of columnar juniper trees.

'Here,' said Fergal without warning. 'Catch.'

Tara spun around and stretched out her hand, too late to catch a heavy roundish object about the size of a tennis-ball. It fell with a muffled thud on the carpet, inches from her foot. It was a tiny, roughly-fashioned stone sculpture.

'For God's sake, Fergal,' she exploded. 'I hope that isn't anything breakable. And even if it isn't, my toes are.'

'Don't worry,' he laughed. 'It's used to rough treatment. And I'm sorry about narrowly missing your toes.'

'Apology accepted.'

'I'll get them next time.'

He picked up the artefact and handed it to her. Tara took it over to the window and inspected it in the fast-fading light.

'Tell me honestly what you think,' he prompted.

'It's absolutely horrible,' she said. 'It's obscene, puer-ile and disgusting.'

'But *apart* from that, you like it?' he laughed.

The object in her hands was a crude sculpture of an obese naked woman, with giant, pendulous breasts, in a pose that would have made a gynaecologist blush. The head was completely bald and crowned with monkey ears. The face, though recognisably human, was hideously ugly and the features were twisted into a grotesque expression. Under its base were etched the letters '*Sng1 – mdB*'.

'It's like something you'd see sketched in a school toilet,' she retorted, handing it back to him. 'Where on earth did you get it? And more to the point, why are you showing it to me?'

'You don't know what it is?' he persisted.

'Of course I know what it is.' She looked sharply at him. 'Fergal, if this is some childish attempt to embarrass me...'

'Hey. Hey, hey! Calm down. You know me better than that. It's relevant. Just sit down and listen.'

She sat down.

'Did you ever hear of the sheela-na-gig?' he asked.

'It's an ancient form of stone decoration.' She frowned, trying to remember. 'You find them in very old churches and ruins of monasteries. One of them was hacked off a wall and stolen a couple of years ago. I remember reading it in the papers.'

'Very good.' He looked impressed.

'But that's all I know. Except that they've recently been a source of great embarrassment to the Church because they're so sexually explicit. What are they, some sort of pagan fertility symbol?'

Fergal shook his head. 'No, the exact opposite. They may have their roots in the pagan era, but in mediaeval times the sheela-na-gig was used as a sort of protective talisman to warn pilgrims of the dangers of one of the seven deadly sins. Guess which one.'

'Let me think. It wouldn't be lust, by any remote chance?'

Fergal went to the bookshelf and extracted a slim volume. 'Nobody's quite sure of the origin of the name,' he said, consulting the book. 'It could be derived from the Irish phrase *Sighle na gCíoch*, "the old hag of the breasts", or from *Sile ina giob*, which roughly translates as "Shiela on her hunkers". The word Shiela was early Irish slang for a woman. Either of those two derivations makes sense, for these sculptures were aimed to dampen the desires of men – mainly pilgrims travelling to faraway shrines – by depicting women in the most hideous possible way.'

'The original sex objects,' mused Tara as she took the book from his outstretched hand. She flicked through dozens of photographic plates showing statues and engravings of naked women with gaunt skeletal heads, monkey faces or features twisted like gargoyles. The focus was always on the exposed and gaping genitals. 'They're as ugly as sin.'

Fergal liked the phrase. 'That's it. That's *precisely* it. The mediaeval Christians were terrified of falling victim to the sin of lust. If they did, they believed they would go to a special circle of hell where the punishment would suit the crime. Let's not go into details, but you can imagine. So a monk would use the sheela-na-gig as a constant reminder that, although the woman he lusted after might seem beautiful, the sin of desiring her was repulsive.'

Tara closed the book. 'All very interesting to a student of sexual psychology,' she said lightly. 'But to be honest with you, Fergal, it's not something I particularly want to discuss on a beautiful evening like this. I know, let's drive to Ennis – there's a new singer I'd like to check out, and she's performing at Brannagan's tonight.'

'Wait.' He seemed agitated at her attempt to close the subject along with the book. He gestured at the small sculpture on the carpet. 'I haven't told you about this particular sheela-na-gig.'

'What about it?' A thought suddenly occurred to Tara. 'This isn't the one that was stolen from the abbey a few years back?'

He laughed. 'I may be a rogue, but I'm not a thief.' He lifted up the sculpture. 'No, I was just giving you the background. This is a typical sheela-na-gig, but it's not ancient. It's a modern interpretation of the same theme, sculpted by a talented artist less than thirty years ago. By the same talented artist whose picture you were admiring in the dining-room.'

'Michael de Blaca?'

'Yes. It's part of a series of twelve sheela-na-gigs he made. He didn't exhibit them or sell them, because he felt Irish society wasn't ready for that, and he was probably right. But he gave them as gifts, to people who were very special to him.'

Realisation began to dawn on Tara. 'And he gave one to Ann,' she said slowly.

'Close. He gave it to Ann, to hold in trust for me. It was a gift to celebrate my birth just over twenty-nine years ago.'

Tara put down her empty wine glass. She had an idea

where all this was headed. But she was terrified of leaping to the wrong conclusion.

'Okay,' she said at last, seeking refuge in forced humour. 'Some people give babygros to celebrate a birth. Some people give changing-bags. Some people even lay down a case of fine vintage port. But Michael de Blaca thought it would be a good idea to give a dirty sculpture of a naked woman. It's different, I'll grant you that. But I can't see the trend catching on.'

He watched her with studied amusement. He was in no hurry.

'That sculpture,' he persisted, 'was a gift to me. From my father.'

So he had come out with it. But still, her professional instincts warned her to tread carefully, to check everything twice.

'Let me get this straight,' she said. 'Are you telling me that Michael de Blaca is really your father?'

'Yes.'

'How do you know?'

'Oh, come on, Tara. The whole of Claremoon Harbour knows Martin Kennedy was not my father. You must be the only one who hasn't heard the rumours. And I know why – your father would never have allowed gossip to be repeated in his house.'

Tara felt suddenly out of her depth, like a person who had been invited to a coffee morning and had found herself in the middle of an intensive group-therapy session instead. 'Can I have another glass of wine, please?' she asked weakly.

He ignored her. 'Now do you understand why I have such a passion to paint? Why painting means everything in the world to me?'

She nodded. But she didn't want to be side-tracked down that road – at least, not just yet. 'Did your father – Martin, I mean – know about this?' she asked.

'He knew.'

'And when did *you* find out about it?'

'Oh, it started very early. I heard schoolyard taunts and innuendo I didn't understand, about my mother having an affair with an artist, and sometimes the drunks outside Sluther's would shout the same sort of thing across the road at me as I walked home from school. I asked mom about it, but she just told me they were stupid, spiteful people and that I should ignore it.'

Tara laid her hand on his arm. She knew how cruel people could be in a small village.

'Don't worry, I'm fine,' he assured her. 'Those were the earliest indications. After that I began listening more closely. To things Martin said when he was drunk. To things that the grown-ups in the village said when they thought I wasn't listening, or that I was too young to understand them. But I was absorbing it all, taking it all in. And eventually I was able to piece together the whole story – how de Blaca had had an affair with my mom, and how he'd run out on her when she became pregnant. I learned it all. And you know how it made me feel?'

'I can imagine.' Tara's voice was sympathetic. 'You were devastated.'

'No!' His face was lit up with pleasure. 'It made me feel...whole. Fulfilled. At last I knew who I was. I wasn't the son of a pathetic drunk – I was the son of a brilliant artist. I didn't belong here on the farm. But I belonged.'

'Was it official? I mean, on your birth certificate?'

He shook his head impatiently. 'This is holy Ireland we're talking about here, Tara. I was registered as Martin Kennedy's son even though everyone knew it was a lie. The truth is that my veins don't contain a single drop of blood from that sad white-trash lowlife creep, and if it weren't for my mother, I'd shout the fact from the cliff tops.'

His eyes flashed with fury. Tara spoke soothingly. 'Fergal...Fergal.' She held his hand between hers. 'I understand how you must feel. But you obviously realise it would destroy your mother if you were to turn a rumour into a fact, in a small community like this. Does she talk about it at all?'

'No. I've tried to talk to her, but she would never open up to me.' Fergal's hand was stiff, still tense with the coiled-up anger that had been trapped inside him since his teens. 'She just kept repeating that some things about the past were better left alone.'

He removed his hand brusquely and refilled their glasses. 'When I pressed her, all she would say is that her conscience was clear before God. She was certain God would understand, and she hoped her family would. I couldn't get another word out of her.'

There was a long silence. 'How long did their affair last?' asked Tara.

'Who knows? By its very nature it had to be kept hidden. We're talking about three decades ago, Tara,' Fergal pleaded, his anger turning to a fierce urge to explain and justify.

'How did he get within a mile of your mother? They seemed to inhabit totally different universes.'

Fergal passed the sheela-na-gig between his hands, almost as if in a private ritual, as he told her how he believed it had all happened. He could never know for sure, he explained, but, again, he had pieced together the story from local gossip, and information dropped by both his parents in times of anger.

De Blaca had begun by painting the fishermen at work down by the harbour, but had rapidly tired of the subject and moved further up the hill to get a wider view of the bay. The best viewpoint of all had been from the roadside just outside the Kennedy household, and that's where he had planted his easel. Like some modern-day Turner, he painted outdoors in all weathers, trying to capture the constantly changing moods of the volatile Atlantic Ocean.

It had been Martin who had encouraged the artist, regarding him as a potential drinking buddy whose bohemian nature would allow him to join him in early-afternoon drinking sessions. But that illusion was soon dispelled. De Blaca was fond of his Jameson, but painting was his all-consuming passion and he allowed nothing to get in its way.

Once or twice Martin had gone to watch him paint on the cliff top, offering him a hip-flask to keep the cold at bay. De Blaca had accepted politely but had returned to his task. After that he had responded with curt monosyllables to the farmer's attempts at conversation.

Martin wrongly interpreted de Blaca's self-absorption as bad temper caused by discomfort and cold. He took a few more slugs of the whiskey and arrived at what he thought was the perfect solution.

'Why don't you come in to the house, and paint?' he offered after they had finished the hip-flask between them. 'Better than freezing your arse off out here in the middle of a heap of sheep droppings.'

De Blaca had turned his penetrating stare on him. 'The word around town is that you should never invite me into your house,' he said. 'You never know what I might steal.'

Fergal slowly set down the sheela-na-gig. 'It was a fair warning, man to man,' he told Tara. 'But Martin still insisted on bringing him back home and giving him the freedom of his house.'

'But why...?'

Fergal shrugged and said nothing.

Tara lifted the statue and looked at it with distaste. 'And de Blaca was as good as his word,' she said. 'He did steal something from him.'

'The only thing de Blaca stole from him,' said Fergal, 'was something that was never his in the first place.'

CHAPTER FOUR

TARA'S OLD school echoed to the clatter of size-twelve boots and the cackle of communication radios. It was the day after the murder. The children were on summer holidays, and the empty building had assumed a new role as a garda incident centre. A note on the blackboard read: 'See you all in September.'

Two detectives were in the headmaster's study, explaining the case to a superintendent from Dublin who was due to address a press conference at eleven-thirty.

After a hot shower and a good breakfast, Tara felt her spirits rise as she walked through the familiar corridors. Whoever had committed this murder, it was not Fergal. That would very soon become obvious, if it hadn't been made so already. His release was probably imminent.

But at the same time, she couldn't take any chances. She searched the building for Steve McNamara, the local sergeant, and finally found him drinking a mug of tea in the junior infants' classroom. She was relieved to find that he was alone.

It was no secret in the small village that Steve had a soft spot for Tara. Although he was in his late thirties, he had never married. For her part, Tara had grown very fond of this gentle Kerry giant who had played football for his county, and whose generosity and kindness were legendary. They were good friends, but Tara had to send out regular tactful signals to the sergeant that their relationship was no more than that. He seemed to accept the hints good-naturedly, and their friendship continued to grow.

Tara stole quietly in and closed the door behind her. 'Steve, I really need to talk to you,' she whispered. 'It's important. It's about...'

'Oh, feck it, Tara.' A guilty expression flickered over

Steve's rough-hewn face and he clapped his huge hand to his brow. 'I was supposed to call around to your house last night, wasn't I? We were due to get extra men in at nine, but they didn't turn up,' he explained. 'I was on overtime 'til midnight.'

'It doesn't matter, Steve. This is as good a time as any.'

The door burst open, striking Tara painfully between the shoulder blades. 'Oh, Jesus, sorry,' said a woman garda with a Donegal accent. 'Steve, the Super wants you in his office right away. He needs to check something before the press conference.'

'Oh, shine a light.' Steve sprang to his feet and drained his mug. 'It'll have to wait, Tara. Hey! Don't look so dejected.' He clapped her on the shoulder. 'I'll talk to you immediately after the press conference. I'll fill you in on everything. And that's a promise.'

The press conference was being held in the assembly hall, a large room decorated with road safety posters and surrounded by cardboard boxes of gym gear. There were about twenty journalists perched on wooden folding chairs. Most of them were from Dublin, one was from the *Examiner* in Cork, and two or three were from local print and radio outlets. TV crews from RTÉ and TV3 were setting up their equipment directly in front of a low platform containing three empty chairs, a table and a large backdrop cloth bearing the crest of the Garda Siochána.

Tara took a seat near the front, nodding hello to a few of her colleagues. She glanced at her watch, checked the time, and wrote it at the top of a fresh page in her notebook.

She closed her eyes and tried to fight off the feeling that she was some sort of impostor. It was her job to be present at this press conference – at least three papers were depending on her for their coverage. And yet, she felt she had no right to be impartially reporting on a tragedy in which she was so closely involved. If only she'd had a chance to talk to Steve...

'Good morning. Do you mind if I protrude and take this seat?'

Tara glanced up, puzzled. Oh, she realised suddenly. He meant 'intrude'.

'No, not at all,' she said, shifting the handbag she'd thoughtlessly abandoned beside her on the only empty seat in the row.

'Thank you.' The tall stranger sat down. Behind the slight hint of CK aftershave, he carried with him a fresh smell of wind and open air, like sheets that have just been brought in from an outdoor clothesline on a gusty day. 'Have I missed anything?'

Tara stole another glance at him as she shuffled her chair to give him more room. He was obviously a journalist of some sort, but he stood out from the rest of the press corps as distinctively as Tara herself stood out among the pale-skinned redheads in her native village.

For a start, his clothes were different. Most male reporters she knew dressed either in chain-store suits or smart-casual gear with Polo logos ostentatiously stamped all over them. This man wore a black leather jacket over a well-worn olive green shirt and black cotton trousers. His sturdy leather boots obviously had a lot of miles up on them. He looked as though he'd hiked across Ireland to get here.

And then there was that odd accent – what was it? Scandinavian? German? Or just that strange, almost Chinese, intonation that Donegal people developed when they'd been living in London for years?

'No, nothing's happened yet.' She pointed up at the empty platform. 'It was due to start at eleven-thirty, but there seems to be some delay.'

He smiled. 'It's par for the court in Ireland. Nothing ever starts on time.'

Par for the course, she wanted to tell him. It's par for the course.

Instead, she was distracted by his dark, intense eyes.

They were not old eyes – he was probably in his mid-thirties – but they seemed experienced, almost war weary. Yet they were warm with friendly humour as he smiled back at her.

'I'm trying to place your accent,' she confessed after a moment's silence. 'It's not Swedish, it's more...Eastern European or something.'

'Well, it's what you would describe as Eastern Europe, but it is really closer to central Europe. I come from Estonia. It is one of the Baltic States...'

'North-east of Poland, north of Latvia, just across the gulf from Finland. I know. I've been there.'

His eyes opened in surprise. 'You have?'

She nodded. 'A few years ago. Just after the collapse of communism.'

'And what the Dickens took you there?'

What the Dickens. He spoke like a character from one of those old black-and-white movies they showed on Sunday afternoons. She decided to leave him guessing.

'Oh...a spying mission, of a sort,' she said mysteriously. She didn't divulge the more prosaic truth that she'd been sent by her editor to spy out the pubs and restaurants as an advance guide for Irish soccer fans on their way to World Cup games in the Baltic. 'And what brings an Estonian to Ireland?'

He smiled. 'That would take a very long time to explain. I fled Estonia in the mid-eighties because I didn't like being ordered about by the Russians. After a while I settled in West Germany and got a job with *Magnus*, the news magazine.'

Tara glanced up at the platform. Still nothing happening.

'Are you based here in Ireland?' she asked politely, although she didn't really care. She had the impression that the Estonian was using their meeting as an opportunity to polish up his atrocious English. Admittedly he was very good-looking, and under any other circumstances she would have been tempted to play along, but today she just didn't feel in the mood. She was too worried about Fergal.

'Well, I've recently been appointed as their correspondent in Ireland, so, yes, I have a home in Dublin now,' the man was saying. 'But for the last few years, I have not been based in any one place.' He gave a self-deprecating smile. 'My editors were good enough to let me travel the world playing cowboys and Indians at their expense. I was given the job of reporting on wars and conflicts all over the world.'

Tara nodded guardedly. 'I've always admired the great war correspondents,' she said. 'People like Robert Fisk and Maggie O'Kane. I've just finished a book by that German journalist Andres Talimann about his experiences on the war fronts. He's covered everything from the Chechen uprising and the Rwandan massacres to the Drumcree riots last summer.' She shook her head sadly. 'His writing is so damn good, you want to just give up and go back to journalism college.'

His face remained impassive. 'Not German. Estonian,' he corrected her. He stuck out his hand. 'It was terribly rude of me not to introduce myself. I am Andres Talimann.'

'You wrote that book?' Tara was so astounded she forgot to give her own name. 'You wrote *Unholy War*?'

Andres nodded. 'Well, I wrote the original version in German. The version available here is a translation, but I am told it is a very good translation. I am determined to improve my English – that is one of the reasons I came here.'

'Wow. I really am delighted to meet you,' she said genuinely. 'That article you wrote about Nelson Mandela in Robben Island Prison is one of the classics of modern journalism. I've read it and reread it so many times...oh, I'm sorry.'

The hand was still outstretched and Tara suddenly realised that she hadn't shaken it yet. 'My name is Tara

Ross. But I'm afraid my own life isn't nearly so exciting,' she admitted. 'I'm a cyberhack. I edit an online newspaper, the *Clare Electronic News*, but, to tell you the truth, at this stage most of my income comes from working as a free-lance stringer.'

Seats shuffled and notebooks rustled. The press conference was about to begin.

'I know who you are and what you do, Tara,' whispered Andres, staring up at the platform where a uniformed garda superintendent was taking a seat. 'I also know that you have more than a professional interest in the fate of Mr Fergal Kennedy. But we must be silent. The gentleman is about to speak.'

CHAPTER FIVE

THE UNIFORMED officer sat motionless until the room had become completely silent.

'Thank you for coming here this morning, ladies and gentlemen,' he said at last. 'My task to pass on to you whatever information we have on the tragic killing of Mrs Ann Catherine Kennedy at or near her home at Barnabo, Claremoon Harbour, late on Saturday night or in the early hours of Sunday morning.'

He paused. A technician, bent double, scuttled forward underneath the cameras to adjust a microphone.

'We intend to be as open as we can with you, and hope that in return you will treat this matter responsibly, assisting us with appeals to the public for information and, so far as is possible, respecting the privacy of the people of this village who have been visited by tragedy. Before proceeding, I would like to extend the sympathy of the Garda Siochána to Mrs Kennedy's family, relatives and friends at this terrible time.'

He paused. At the back of the hall, there was a very audible whisper: 'Oh, get on with it.'

The heads of the other journalists turned disapprovingly towards the source of the interruption. But, sitting alone in the back row, Gerry Gellick was busy taking notes and didn't appear to have noticed them.

'So, let us proceed,' he said, shuffling his notes. 'The facts are these. Mrs Kennedy, a widow of fifty-two and mother of two sons aged twenty-nine and twenty-seven, lived at her family farm at Barnabo with her elder son Fergal. On the eve of the murder, she was last seen leaving a social function at around midnight.

'So far as we can ascertain, she proceeded directly back to her house. The following morning at around seven-twenty am, as a result of a phone call, a garda sergeant visited the scene and discovered her body on the floor of her kitchen. She had been stabbed more than twenty times with a kitchen knife or similar instrument. At any rate, a long and very sharp blade. At this stage we are endeavouring to establish precisely the time of death.'

'Who called the gardaí to the house?' asked a reporter in the front row.

'The local garda sergeant, Sgt Stephen McNamara, received a phone call just after seven am. The phone call was from Mrs Kennedy's son Fergal, who informed us that he had just discovered the body.'

'And do you believe him?'

The superintendent ignored the question. 'Mr Kennedy informed us that he had come home at around six forty-five am and, on walking into his kitchen, had discovered his mother's body on the floor.'

'Were there any other witnesses?' asked a woman with a Cork accent.

'None that we know of. That's where we hope you can help.'

'Any sign of a break-in?'

'No, but so far as we can establish Mrs Kennedy was in the habit of leaving her doors unlocked.'

A skinny blond woman who looked about sixteen years old shouted: 'Was she raped?'

The superintendent looked pained. 'No. There was no sign of any sexual assault.'

'But was she fully clothed?' persisted the blonde.

'She was in night-gown and dressing-gown. It was very early in the morning.'

'Anything stolen?' asked a red-haired man with a Belfast accent.

'No. Robbery does not appear to have been the motive. Now –' The Superintendent looked at his watch – 'now, if there are no further questions, I think we'll...'

'How long can you hold Fergal Kennedy without charging him?' another pressman called out.

The superintendent shot him a warning glance. 'The official position is that a man aged twenty-nine was arrested at six pm yesterday under Section Four of the 1984 Criminal Justice Act, which, as you know, enables us to detain an individual if it is considered necessary for the proper investigation of any serious crime. Last night, under the powers granted by that same Act, a senior garda officer directed an extension of his detention and it was agreed that questioning be suspended between midnight and eight am for the purposes of sleep.'

'How optimistic are you that charges will be preferred against this man?'

'No comment.'

'Off the record, super...did he do it?'

'No comment.'

'Have you any comment on anything?' It was the same voice that had given the highly-audible whisper.

The superintendent ignored him. 'We are appealing to the public for any information that may lead to the apprehension of the killer or killers. Anyone who saw anything in the vicinity of the Kennedy house at any time between nine pm on Saturday and around seven-twenty am on Sunday should contact detectives at Ennis, or his nearest garda station.'

He gathered his notes together with an air of finality.

'Hang on, Super,' called out a national newspaper reporter. 'You haven't told us anything about the junkie theory.'

'I have no knowledge of any drug link in this killing. But we are anxious to trace a man who was seen on the road between the village and Barnabo late on Saturday night. At this stage, we simply wish to eliminate him from our inquiries. He was heavily built, wearing rough working clothes and a woollen cap.'

'Age?'

'Mid-twenties up to around thirty. Witnesses said it was hard to tell.'

'So more than one person saw him?'

'Three altogether, we believe. None of them got close enough to describe his face.'

'Are you checking Ann Kennedy's will? Was there any dispute over who would inherit the farm?'

'We are of course exploring every avenue that could lead to a resolution of this case. Every avenue.'

'What about insurance? Could young Kennedy have done it for the insurance money?'

'No comment.' The superintendent scooped up all his notes. The TV tape would have to be tightly edited for legal reasons, he thought. Better have a word with the programme producer just in case he didn't realise.

'That's all, gentlemen and ladies,' he said. 'And in view of the tenor of some of your questions, I would remind you that gardaí are keeping a very open mind on this case.'

He walked off the platform. 'We are, in me arse,' he muttered under his breath.

There was a sudden release of tension and a deafening hubbub of talk. The television crews cornered the superintendent for individual interviews, and the daily newspaper reporters began talking urgently into cellphones.

Tara closed her notebook with a snap and turned to Andres Talimann. 'And just what the hell did you mean by that?' she demanded.

'What?' he asked innocently.

'You know damn well what. "More than a professional interest." That.'

Andres sighed. 'You can rest easily, Tara. The secret of your close friendship with Mr Fergal Kennedy is safe with me. I do not intend to publish it. But I do not know for how long it will remain secret, in the circumstances. You should be aware of that.'

Tara stared at him. How had he learned so quickly of a relationship she'd tried so hard to safeguard? She maintained what she hoped was a poker-face.

'Thank you for your advice,' she said icily, 'but one day your English teacher should teach you a phrase about noses and other people's business. Excuse me.'

She rose to her feet, but the Estonian remained seated, blocking her way.

'I have only come from arriving in this village,' he said quietly, 'but already I have talked to many people. And I am concerned that you could be in some danger.'

'Oh, really?' She stopped dead. Her heart was pounding again, her stomach was doing somersaults, and her mouth had turned so dry she could hardly speak. 'From whom, exactly?'

He ignored the question. His voice dropped to a low whisper. 'Before I can tell you that, I need to know how closely involved you are with Fergal Kennedy. Are you...' He frowned as though fighting tactfully to translate some foreign phrase...'are you intimate with him?'

Tara gasped with disbelief. 'I'm going to pretend I didn't even hear that question,' she said. 'Excuse me, please.'

He rose and backed out of the row to let her past.

'I ask only because I feel you are in danger,' he repeated.

'Right. Well, I'm a big grown-up person now, Mr Talimann, and I can look after myself, thank you. And anyway, I don't see how my being in danger gives you any right to ask intrusive questions.'

'Okay, I withdraw the question. I'm sorry.' He was speaking urgently, trying to get his point across before she left. 'Let me put another question to you. Just one.'

Tara kept her silence. He took this as assent.

'Where were you on Saturday night? Prior to the murder?'

It seemed like an age before her vocal cords unglued themselves enough to voice the shock and outrage she felt.

'That is none of your damned business, Mr Talimann,' she hissed, pushing past him. 'Now excuse me. I have some copy to file. Goodbye. I doubt if we'll be talking again.'

'I will see you later,' he said.

She wasn't sure whether it was his clumsy version of a goodbye or a statement of intent.

'It's a small town, Mr Talimann,' she said over her shoulder. 'I suppose it's unavoidable.'

Walking through the hall past the other journalists, Tara felt uncharacteristically flustered, as though every eye on the room was on her. She took several deep breaths and forced herself to slow down.

In the doorway, a Dublin reporter was talking into a mobile phone, one hand protecting his free ear against the babble of noise. 'Yeah, it's him all right. No doubt. Guilty as hell. Why? You tell me. Land row or something. Disputed will. Whatever. Yes, the cops mentioned the junkie theory, but if you ask me, it was probably just some tramp. Okay, if you want, I'll do a bit of digging on that end too. Meantime, I'll have the press conference, an interview with the parish priest, some local colour. I'll be filing in twenty minutes.'

Tara pushed past him into the corridor, where brightly-coloured posters advised children to cross the road carefully and brush their teeth after every meal. At the other end, Sergeant Steve McNamara stood waiting for her.

'Get what you wanted, Tara?'

'What?' She stared at him. 'Oh, the press conference.' She glanced around quickly. 'Listen, Steve, we really need to talk.'

Steve checked his watch. 'I'm due a break in fifteen minutes. Meet me for a sandwich in the café.'

'Steve.' Her eyes pleaded with him. 'It's really, really important.'

'I'll be there, Tara.'

'Aw, lads, come on! Will yiz give us a break!'

Steve McNamara, six foot six tall and built like a granite pillar, was trying to negotiate two cups of coffee and a toasted ham sandwich through a café that was crowded with persistent press.

'Sorry. No comment. Contact the press office. Theory? The only theory I have at the minute is that my toasted sandwich will be cold if I don't get to eat it.'

He finally made it to the corner table where Tara was sitting. They had some measure of privacy, because the table in front of them was occupied by a family of Danish tourists who were totally bemused by all the activity in the village they'd chosen as a haven of Celtic tranquillity.

'Jesus,' said Steve, 'give me a good riot any day of the week. I'd sooner face a mob of English soccer fans at Lansdowne Road than cope with this lot.'

His giant face, angular as a Druid statue, shook from side to side in a comic gesture of disbelief as he passed Tara a cup of coffee and swung his bulky frame into the seat beside her. The joints of the wooden chair groaned under the strain.

'I know what you mean. Thanks for the coffee.'

'You're welcome. Who was that Russian fella you were talking to at the press conference?' he demanded suddenly. 'I'm just curious. He was trying to pump me for information earlier.'

Tara's hand quivered with annoyance as she raised her cup. 'His name's Andres Talimann. And he's not Russian. He's Estonian.'

Steve snorted. 'I don't care if he's from Outer Mongolia. Just be careful of him. I wouldn't trust him as far as I could throw him.'

Tara stared at him. Did she detect a note of jealousy in the sergeant's tone?

He caught her quizzical look. 'These foreigners are all the same,' he explained seriously. 'They're up to their necks in drug dealing and refugee smuggling.' He opened his toasted sandwich and smothered it in salt. 'And they drink like fishes.'

'Don't be ridiculous, Steve,' she said. 'You can't lump people together like that. Andres Talimann is a respected war correspondent. But if it's any consolation to you, if I ever see him in this life again, it will be too soon.'

She noticed Steve relax a little. So she'd been right.

'Well, if you ever do see him again,' Steve said through a mouthful of ham sandwich, 'ask him what he was doing yesterday afternoon while the rest of you press boyos were up at Barnabo.'

'What was he doing?'

'I'll tell you what he was doing. He was sitting in the back of the De Blaca Art Gallery with Godfrey Villiers, the two of them chatting like ould mates and working their way through a full bottle of vodka together. That's what he was doing. And I'd like to know why.' He thrust a giant finger in her direction. 'You know as well as I do, Tara, that Godfrey is thick as thieves with the Viney family from Limerick. You know, the drug dealers. Their dirty money goes in one door of Godfrey's shop and it comes out the other door on a hanger, wrapped in clear polythene and smelling of dry-cleaning. And when a stranger breezes in from Eastern Europe and gets all palsy-walsy with that crowd, I reckon our lads in the National Drugs Unit should sit up and take note. What do you think?'

Tara glanced around her. At any other time, she would have been very interested in Steve's theories of a money laundering operation in Claremoon Harbour, but right now she had other things on her mind.

'Listen, Steve,' she said urgently. 'I've been trying since yesterday to get a word with you alone.'

Steve held up his hand. 'I know, I know. You've a job to do. And you want to know about the murder investigation. Well, we have to wait for the post-mortem, but the cause of death seems straightforward enough. Place of death – no doubt about that. She was killed where her body was found. Time of death is what we need. Plus a murder weapon. None of the kitchen knives in the house is missing, and none of the ones that are there fits the profile.'

'What profile?'

'Again we have to wait for the results of forensic tests,' said Steve, forcing his words through another mouthful of ham, 'but it looks as though the knife will be easily identifiable as the murder weapon – a long blade, very sharp. Not the sort of shaggin' thing you use to butter your sandwiches.'

He opened the second half of his toasted sandwich and daubed it liberally with tomato relish. Tara winced.

'Sorry, love. You knew her a lot better than I did,' said Steve, looking up. 'But from the little I knew of her, she was a lovely woman. I just hope this hoor confesses so that we can put him away for a long time.'

Her heart sank. So Fergal hadn't been eliminated from the police inquiries after all. He'd obviously failed to tell them everything. It was all up to her, now.

'You seem convinced he did it.' Her voice was shaky.

'I'd wager my overtime on it.' Steve didn't notice her distress. He was absorbed in his sandwich.

'But what about a motive? Sons don't just kill their mothers for no reason.'

'That's a tough one, right enough. Don't pay any attention to the rubbish those fellas are talking in there – about wills and insurance and suchlike. We've checked the will with her solicitor. It's completely straightforward –

everything split between the two boys. But there's a fair amount of debt, so even if the farm was sold, the bottom line is nothing to get excited about.'

'And her life assurance?' asked Tara, hearing her own voice coming from a long way away. She didn't know why she was asking these questions. It was as though the journalist in her was still functioning on autopilot, while inside, all she wanted to do was scream out what was really on her mind.

'Under-insured by a mile. There had been no attempt to change the policy.'

'But all this tends to indicate he *didn't* do it,' she said, without much hope that he'd agree.

The big policeman shrugged silently.

Tara felt close to despair. She obviously wasn't getting through to Steve. Only a few miles away Fergal was sitting in a cold interrogation cell. He desperately needed her help.

'Steve ...'

'You obviously didn't know him very well,' he said. 'From all accounts, he's a fiery sort of fella, easily riled. Maybe he came back with a few jars on board and had an argument over something stupid. It happens all the time. Oops...here comes trouble.'

Tara looked up. Two figures were negotiating their way across the crowded café like skiers on a slalom, bending their bodies to keep horizontal the brown plastic trays containing bowls of soup and plates of sandwiches.

One was a local detective inspector. Tara had never met him, but knew him from some of the court cases he'd testified in. She struggled to remember his name. Rourke? O'Rourke. That was it. Phil O'Rourke.

He was a tall man of around fifty, solidly built but with a porter-belly that strained the belt of his plain brown suit.

His hair, still thick and plentiful, was steel grey. He had the ruddy face of a man who likes his whiskey.

But Tara knew better than to underestimate this officer. His reputation as a hard man was well established. A couple of decades ago, social problems that the entire justice system would have failed to solve had been settled within minutes during a personal 'interview' down a back alley between this detective and a troublemaker who chose never to make trouble again. It was an old-fashioned approach to policing that had constantly got him into hot water. His defiant response was that his patch had always stayed remarkably free of the sort of urban blight that had elsewhere forced decent people out of their homes and transformed housing estates into wastelands. He was no longer allowed to conduct back-alley interviews, and the criminal activity on his patch was increasing at roughly the same rate as his blood pressure; colleagues hoped that neither factor would kill him before he reached retirement.

His companion was a short, dumpy woman in a rain mac. She was in her late forties and her hair, dyed chestnut brown, stuck out in permed curls from beneath a red beret. Her eyes stared myopically from behind bottle-thick lenses.

'Mind if we sit here, Steve?' asked O'Rourke. He stared intensely at Tara as only detectives feel they have a right to do, checking her out, matching her to some internal computer database of faces.

'Come ahead, come ahead,' invited Steve genially, moving around to create room. 'Always pleased to give a seat to an expectant parent.' He patted the detective's rotund stomach. 'When's it due?'

'Same time as your transfer to the Aran Islands,' growled the cop. He had a deep, chain-smoker's voice. A voice like a rusty shovel scraping up damp slack in a coalyard.

'Come on. If that stomach was on a woman, she would be pregnant,' persisted Steve.

'It was,' said O'Rourke, 'and she is.'

'At the risk of interrupting all this male bonding,' said a cultured voice from directly behind him, 'may I take a seat before my soup congeals even further than it has already?'

'Sorry, Rita,' said O'Rourke, setting down his tray and squeezing himself into a seat. He stuck out a hand towards Tara. 'Phil O'Rourke. Inspector. Are you a Member, or are you unfortunate enough to have this gobshite as your friend?'

He was asking if Tara was a police officer, or a 'Member of the Garda Siochána' as the ponderous official term went. Tara smiled as she shook his hand. 'Friend, and fortunate to be one,' she said. 'Tara Ross.'

'Tara's with the *Clare Independent*,' explained Steve. 'But don't worry. She's okay.'

'Well, I'm glad she's okay,' growled O'Rourke, "cause nobody else is. I've got a pain in my arse with this murder and I'm supposed to be on my rest-day. Tara, forgive me. I'm pleased and honoured to make your acquaintance.'

The woman called Rita was taking off her mac and hanging it over the back of her seat. She sat down to Tara's left. Tara was now trapped in the corner.

O'Rourke did the introductions. 'Tara, Steve, I'd like you to meet Dr Rita Barnes, from the State Pathologist's office. She's fresh from doing the post-mortem at the hospital, although perhaps fresh isn't the right adjective to use in the circumstances.'

'How do you do,' said Rita with a thin smile. 'No, fresh is fine. I've had a lot less fresh in my time.' She attacked her oxtail soup.

'She's established the time of death from stomach contents,' mumbled O'Rourke, his voice muffled by a mouthful of bacon, lettuce and tomato.

Rita nodded. 'We can tell a lot from the process of digestion, which naturally stops at the time of death,' she explained to Tara. 'According to witnesses, this victim had supper very late the previous night – roast beef, I understand. The contents were well digested, more or less to the consistency of...well, actually, this oxtail soup would be a good example.'

She took a loud slurp of the soup and smiled proudly.

Tara nodded, determined not to express on her face the nausea she felt inside. Trapped between table and wall, she also felt a terrifying sense of claustrophobia and it contributed to her mounting panic.

'So what does this tell you?' Steve was asking.

'Well...' Dr Barnes waved her spoon around in a vague gesture, 'it's confirmation more than anything else. Combined with other factors such as body temperature, and the absence of rigor mortis at the time her body was discovered, it enables us to establish fairly accurately the point in time at which Mrs Kennedy met her, er, unfortunate demise.'

'Later rather than sooner?' guessed Steve.

'Yes,' confirmed Dr Barnes. 'Certainly not before five am. Probably later. And definitely no later than seven.'

She put a large dollop of mayonnaise on her toasted cheese sandwich and spread it carefully. Tara studied the wallpaper, trying to fight back another overpowering wave of nausea.

'So,' said O'Rourke, 'that puts paid to the idea that she surprised a burglar when she came home the previous night.'

Rita Barnes nodded vigorously. 'My evidence to the inquest will be, death between five and seven. I understand you, Sergeant McNamara, were on the scene by seven-twenty.'

'And don't forget that Fergal Kennedy discovered her at six forty-five, as soon as he got home,' Tara suddenly burst out.

She felt three pairs of eyes staring at her.

'So he says,' growled O'Rourke, after a while. 'All we can establish for sure is that he phoned Steve just after seven, so he didn't do the job after that. The times fit, all right. I'd say he topped her at around six. That gives him an hour or so to calm down, get rid of the weapon and prepare his story before phoning.'

'Talking of the weapon?' prompted Steve, looking at the pathologist.

Rita Barnes finished her sandwich and patted her precise mouth with a paper napkin. 'Blade, around fifteen centimetres long by around four, five at its widest point. Curved at the business end. Extremely sharp, as keen as a surgeon's scalpel or a butcher's knife. Handle made of wood.'

'What sort of knife was it? Any theories?' asked O'Rourke.

'Doesn't seem like a regular kitchen knife. I would suggest a butcher's blade, except there was no butcher's skill involved in the actual killing. It was a frenzied attack, anywhere and everywhere he could reach. She tried to defend herself with her hands and arms – they were pretty badly slashed as well. The man was a maniac; don't quote me on that. And you' – she turned to Tara – 'you don't quote me at all.'

Steve McNamara tried to get back to the subject of the weapon, which was his main concern. 'So I'll tell my men to look for a six-inch bladed knife with a wooden handle,' he restated.

The pathologist called for a waitress. 'Coffee? Anybody else? Four coffees, please. Yes, sergeant,' she confirmed. 'That's the basic description. There may be another, rather unusual characteristic – I'm not sure. And there's something odd about the angle of cut. I want to wait until I get a second opinion from forensic.'

'Search the house and gardens again, Steve,' instructed O'Rourke. 'And the farm outhouses, and all that vegetation down the cliff. We'll get the sub-aqua lads out tomorrow. Kennedy may even have fecked it out into the Atlantic.'

To Tara's surprise, the next voice she heard was her own.

'What about checking along the roads leading out of Claremoon Harbour?' the voice said. It sounded thin and desperate. 'I mean, it could have been dumped in a ditch by some killer as he was escaping from the village. Couldn't it?'

Steve was about to speak, but Phil O'Rourke stopped him. 'It's not her fault, Steve. All these reporters, all these media types, they've been raised on American cop shows and horror movies. They think the typical murderer is a "psycho"' – he raised saffron-stained fingers to illustrate quote-marks – 'someone in a balaclava mask, stalking a stranger. We should be throwing up roadblocks on the county line and putting out APBs to prevent another serial killing.'

'That's not what I said,' protested Tara, taking a drink of tepid coffee just to give her arid throat something to swallow. It tasted terrible. The café's usual brand had been replaced by instant mild-grade powder, probably because of the volume of demand.

'No, but it's the way you're conditioned to think,' said the detective. 'It rarely happens that way in Ireland. Here, we keep it in the family. Or at least within our circle of friends. Most killers know their victims; many are related to them; a significant number are married to them. And the vast majority aren't thugs or crazies. They're ordinary decent people, living ordinary decent lives, until one day they work themselves up into a state of fury over something. It often happens after a few drinks have distorted their better judgement.'

Dr Barnes raised a cigarette as though calling for silence. 'Getting back to the subject,' she said, 'what does Fergal Kennedy have to say about his movements on the night in question?'

'Yes,' said Steve. 'What was he doing, out until six forty-five am in the first place? Enjoying the pulsating nightlife of Claremoon Harbour?'

'He's a farmer, isn't he?' objected Dr Barnes. 'If you're a farmer, six forty-five am isn't early. It's late. He probably came back for breakfast after he'd finished milking the bullocks or something.'

'Cows,' corrected Steve.

'Sorry,' said the doctor. 'Not my field.'

'Anyway, that's not the case,' said Steve. 'Ever since the father's death, the working operation of the farm has been contracted out. Fergal Kennedy had nothing to do with it.'

Everyone's eyes turned back to the detective.

'So what was he doing before he discovered the body at six forty-five?' Dr Barnes repeated.

Phil O'Rourke looked at Tara for a long time. Unable to meet his eyes, she stared down at her coffee cup and fiddled with her spoon.

'Going walkabout,' the detective said at last. 'He didn't feel sleepy, so he went walking.'

'All night?' asked Steve incredulously. 'He went strolling around the village all night?'

'I must say that's a hopeful sign from your viewpoint,' snorted Dr Barnes. 'No jury's going to believe that.'

'Well,' said the detective, his eyes still fixed on Tara, 'we do have a statement from a fisherman who was putting out lobster pots and thinks he saw Fergal Kennedy walking down by the shore, near the harbour, sometime between six and seven. But not a single witness has come forward to vouch for his whereabouts before that. Not a single witness.'

'Tara,' said Steve, suddenly. 'Tara, are you all right?'

Tara didn't hear him. All she heard was the pounding of blood as it rushed through her head. She had the detached feeling of playing a bit-part in a movie with the volume turned down and the other players' voices sounding far, far away. When she spoke, even her own voice sounded echoing and unreal, as though it was coming back at her on a faulty long-distance phone line.

'He wasn't walking all night,' she said slowly.

'Tara, do you want a drink of water or something?' asked Steve. 'You're looking pale as a ghost. Rita, can you...?'

But the detective had thrown a large arm in front of the pathologist, preventing her from moving.

'No,' he warned. 'You said he wasn't walking all night, Tara. Do you have any information about this case? Something you should be telling us?'

Tara took a deep breath. She knew that what she was about to say would shatter the comfortable, well-ordered routine of her life. There would be a sea-change, and after this, things in Claremoon Harbour could never again be the same.

'Fergal wasn't walking all through the night,' she said at last.

'How do you know that, Tara?' asked O'Rourke. His voice has become quiet and intense.

'Because he spent the night with me.'

CHAPTER SIX

THE SUDDEN silence that followed echoed around the tiny café like a quarry-blast. People at the furthest tables felt the shockwaves and abruptly stopped talking, although they had heard nothing of the conversation. Even the Danish tourists looked up in startled surprise.

Steve McNamara laughed self-consciously. 'You have to get used to Tara's unorthodox sense of humour,' he said, his voice running out of conviction halfway through the sentence.

Dr Barnes stood up suddenly, throwing back the last remnants of her coffee. 'Well, I see you gentlemen and lady will have a lot to discuss,' she said briskly, 'and I have a lot to be a-doing. See you anon.'

She directed a quick smile of encouragement at Tara. Then her cup clattered back into its saucer and she was gone. 'No comment, no comment,' she sang cheerfully in a confident contralto as she made her way through the gauntlet of coffee-sipping press.

Steve toyed with his spoon. 'Would you like me to leave, too, Inspector?'

Tara noticed the subtle shift of atmosphere. The casual style of address had gone. This was formal.

'No, it's okay.'

The electrically-charged silence endured as O'Rourke continued to stare at Tara, quietly assessing her. At length he put a comforting hand on her arm.

'I know this is hard for you, love,' he said kindly. 'It would have been a lot easier to keep quiet.'

'It wasn't that,' she said miserably. 'Up until yesterday afternoon I assumed Fergal *had* told you the truth about his whereabouts that night. I was just waiting for someone to ask me to corroborate. When nobody did, I realised what had happened – that he'd spun you some stupid yarn to cover up for me and keep me out of the whole business.'

She glanced at O'Rourke, but his face betrayed nothing.

'So I made up my mind to tell Steve McNamara the full story,' Tara continued. 'It's just that I would have felt more comfortable talking to him. I tried to tell him yesterday, I tried to tell him this morning. And I was just about to make a full statement when you and Dr Barnes came in.'

She looked to Steve for confirmation, but the garda sergeant was staring fixedly at his oversized boots.

Tara felt irritated. 'Look, I don't give a damn about what people think.' Her voice sounded hard as flint. 'Just get it over with, and let's get Fergal out of there.'

O'Rourke nodded understandingly. 'You know I'll have to ask you to come over to my office and make a formal statement,' he said. He glanced at his watch. 'And I give you my word Fergal will be released almost immediately.'

'Of course I'll make a statement,' she said. 'I've nothing to hide.'

'Right. Let's go.'

The café had reverted to its normal hum of cross-talk. With forced levity, Steve exchanged a few jokes with the reporters as they settled their bills and left.

A short walk down the street – a street that had somehow changed character completely in the last half-hour – and she was back at her old primary school.

O'Rourke had taken over one of the classrooms as his personal office. On the wall, a hand-painted poster said: IT IS SUNNY. IT IS WINDY. IT IS RAINY. WHAT IS IT TODAY?

What is it today? thought Tara as she sat waiting for O'Rourke to begin. It is the worst day of my entire life.

The woman police officer from Donegal sat by Tara's side as the detective officially cautioned her and began to take her statement.

'Okay,' he said formally. 'You say you spent the night with Fergal Kennedy.'

She thought she detected censure in his voice.

'Yes. I'm sorry if you disapprove.'

'What makes you think I disapprove?'

'Do you?'

'That's not my area of concern,' said O'Rourke, waving a hand dismissively as he produced a packet of Camel Filter. 'Cigarette? Mind if I do? No, what I'm mostly interested in is times, Tara. Exact times.'

Tara thought carefully. 'We met at around half nine the night before. We'd arranged to have dinner together. He picked me up from home in his car.'

'What car?'

'An American Corvette. It's an imported model.'

'Why nine-thirty? Bit late for dinner around these parts, isn't it?'

It was. Most restaurants and hotels stopped serving meals at around nine. But Fergal had been helping her father on the *Róisín Dubh*. They hadn't finished until around eight-thirty, and after that Fergal had to shower and change.

'He was working late,' she explained.

'Okay. So where did you go?'

'We drove to Ennis for a drink and then a meal.'

'Long way to go for a meal.'

Tara shrugged. 'We didn't socialise much around Claremoon Harbour. People here see you together once or twice and they start asking if you've chosen the menu for the wedding reception. I'm a private sort of person, Inspector, and I'd hate being the subject of gossip and pub-talk.'

O'Rourke nodded sympathetically. If that was the case, then the statement she was giving was about to unleash her worst nightmare. From this moment on, she would be the central subject of gossip and pub-talk in the entire county.

'I know what you mean,' he said. 'Which restaurant did you go to?'

She told him the name of the tiny late-night Italian bistro they frequented from time to time.

'Good choice,' he said. 'They do a great osso bucca.'

'I had seafood carbonara with penne. He had spaghetti pesto. And we shared two bottles of Chianti Classico. I'm sorry...you probably don't need all this.' She was feeling confused and her tongue seemed to be operating on autopilot.

The young woman garda was looking at her with horrified fascination.

'That won't be necessary, Tara,' said O'Rourke. 'What time did you leave?'

'Late. Around one-thirty. They were hoovering around our feet for the last half-hour.'

'Who drove home?'

'He did. I know he shouldn't have, after drinking a bottle of wine. But I suppose a drink-driving charge is the last thing he should be worried about right now.'

O'Rourke didn't react. 'We have no evidence of any motoring offence,' he said. 'And then?'

'Straight back to my house.' She gave the address of the small two-storey cottage on the outskirts of the village. 'I invited Fergal in for a cup of coffee.'

'Time?'

'Two-thirty or so.'

He made a note. 'So you had coffee.'

She nodded. 'Coffee and brandy.'

'Coffee and cognac,' he repeated, scrupulously noting down everything she said.

'No. It was Armagnac.'

There was a long silence.

'And?'

'And what?'

'And what time did he leave?' O'Rourke asked patiently.

'Six. Roughly.'

'Exactly? I really need to know, Tara.'

'About ten to six. I remember opening the door and being surprised to see the sunshine flood in. So I looked at my watch. I'd no idea how late it was. I mean, how early.'

O'Rourke clicked his pen. 'Cup of tea?'

'No, I went straight to sleep after that.'

'I mean, would you like a cup of tea. Now.'

'Oh. I'm sorry. Yes, please. White, no sugar.'

Behind her, someone left the room. The detective surveyed his notes carefully. 'So we're talking nearly four hours in your house.'

'Three and a half. Roughly.'

'Right. Three hours, and another twenty minutes or so. That's quite a long period.'

He paused, apparently unwilling to ask the question.

'You want to know how we passed the time,' said Tara.

'Yes. I'm sorry. But I have to ask these things. Did you have sex with him?'

Oh, no. Please God, don't let this be happening. His rusted-metal voice made it sound so sordid, like some brief encounter down a back alley. She could imagine herself in a courtroom, giving evidence. The judge leaning forward. Answer the question, Miss Ross. Did you have sex-ual in-ter-course? Did you have car-nal knowledge? Did you achieve intimacy outside a state of wedlock?

It wasn't like that. Really it wasn't.

'Yes,' she said.

That night, as she looked at him she'd felt something stir within her. She knew she wanted him. Maybe it was just the effect of the wine and the candlelight and months of celibacy, but it didn't make the longing any less powerful.

By the time she'd come back from the kitchen with the pot of espresso, Fergal had already found the Armagnac and had poured two generous measures.

'I hope you didn't mind,' he said. 'I just wanted to round off a perfect evening.'

He'd dimmed the lights and lit two candles on the mantelpiece.

She accepted the glass. 'What a nice idea. Why not?'

He raised his glass. 'Here's to us.' Before she could respond, his face became tense with concentration. 'Hold it,' he ordered her. 'Don't move a muscle.'

'What? What's the matter? A spider or something?'

'No, nothing like that. Just don't move.'

He jumped up and grabbed a pencil and an A4 pad. 'You look so...so goddam *beautiful* sitting there,' he explained. 'At that angle. Your hair's shining and your face is glowing in the candlelight. And those eyes! This is an artistic emergency. You're lucky there happens to be a painter in the house. I'm going to sketch you.'

His hand moved briskly over the paper, sketching the outline and filling in the details. She smiled warmly, and only partly because she was posing. She was genuinely flattered by the compliments.

'Okay,' he announced after a couple of minutes of frantic sketching. 'Finished.'

'Let's see.' She stood up to examine the drawing, but, annoyingly, he closed the notepad at the last minute. 'Oh, come on, Fergal. Let me have a look.'

'No. It's for the artist's eyes only.'

She wasn't sure whether he was serious or only teasing. He looked serious.

'Oh, don't be such a pain. Let me see it.' She made a grab for the pad, but he passed it deftly from one hand to another, so that she had to lean across him to follow it.

'I'm warning you. Don't mess around with me,' he said, only half-jokingly, and she didn't know whether he was talking about the sketch or their relationship.

'Ooh, like I'm really afraid,' she said defiantly. She made a frantic lunge for the notepad but instead she slipped and fell across him. And then suddenly they were rolling on the carpeted floor and she was returning his frantic, hungry kisses, and his hands were inside her dress and her own hands were inside the back of his shirt, involuntarily digging her fingernails into his shoulders.

It was raw, it was rough-and-tumble, at times it was more like all-in wrestling than sex. The static sparks flew like fireworks as they tore each other's clothes off and practically devoured each other, exorcising all the frustrations that had built up between them for the past three months.

After so many months of slow build-up, this was glorious. It was anarchy. It was lovemaking with a capital F. It was frantic, lustful, panting, floorboard-rattling, cupboard-door-banging sex, so noisy that Tara was afraid they'd wake the neighbours. And the neighbours lived three-quarters of a mile away on the other side of a granite hill.

'Whooo,' she said when it was over.

'Wowee,' he agreed.

'Why did we wait so long?'

He rolled over and kissed her on the lips. 'You tell me.'

After a while, they sat upright to find themselves placed at the epicentre of what looked like a minor natural disaster. They cleared up the debris, the overturned footstools and the spilled drinks. Then they poured themselves two more Armagnacs, and moved upstairs to investigate this puzzling question further in her bedroom.

After he'd left to go home, she lay back on her bed and smiled. Every single cell, every pore, in her whole body seemed to be smiling in its own biological fashion. That was how good it had been, and that was how good she had felt, but how could she explain all this to a coldly efficient policeman? A policeman whose lips were moving right now, and asking her some sort of question...

'Pardon me?' she said.

'I asked, how long had you been going out together?' O'Rourke repeated.

'Just under three months. It began around March.'

'How often would you go out with him?'

Tara thought for a minute. 'I suppose about twice a week. Weekends and sometimes midweek. It was all very informal. We'd just go out for meals, or trad music sessions, or sometimes we'd go to Limerick or Galway to hear a rock band. The usual thing. We just enjoyed each other's company, that's all.'

O'Rourke exhaled a long plume of smoke, carefully aiming it away from her face. 'That evening. The night of the murder. How would you describe Fergal's demeanour? During the meal and...well, afterwards.'

'During the meal he was very relaxed, very mellow. In fact, he was very good company. He talked about Canada, about Clare, about his mother...' Tara stopped suddenly.

'What about his mother?'

'He told me he loved her very much. He knew how badly his father – how badly Martin Kennedy had treated her and he wanted to make it up to her by ensuring that she had everything she ever wanted.' She smiled sadly. 'It was ironic. Within a few hours he went home and found her dead.'

O'Rourke met her eyes and held them. 'That all sounds very...'

'Convenient? Perfectly scripted? I realise that's how it sounds. But that's the way it was.' She looked out the window at the playground where the blue-overalled gardaí on search duty were sitting having a break. 'He just chatted about this, that, everything.'

'And you?'

'Me too.' The tea arrived, big brown mugs from the school staffroom. 'Thanks. Yes, I was talking nineteen to the dozen, too.'

'What were you talking about?'

'I don't know. Silly things, really. About my plans and hopes for the future.'

'Which were?'

Tara smiled. 'Still are. To spend my whole life in Claremoon Harbour. I have this dream. It's a stupid dream.' She pointed out through the window to the hillside.

O'Rourke's eyes followed her pointing finger to the shell of an abandoned building. It was constructed of solid local stone, and the masonry around the doors and windows was painstakingly carved in the Art Nouveau style. But all the windows were broken and part of the roof had caved in.

'It was once a Victorian spa-house,' she explained. 'Its garden contains a natural spring which is supposed to have health-giving properties. In the last century, people came from all over Ireland and Britain to take the waters.'

O'Rourke raised his eyebrows in a puzzled gesture.

'That's what we were talking about,' she clarified. 'I've always had this dream of buying that old shell, restoring it to its former beauty and perhaps even reopening it. But I could never raise as much cash as the Dutch and Belgians are prepared to pay for property around here.' She caught herself on. Her tongue was on overdrive again. 'It was just silly talk. Four o'clock in the morning talk.'

O'Rourke nodded. He went on to ask about her relationship with Ann and about her visits to the Kennedy home. Then he sat in silence while he prepared her final statement. It was stripped to the bare details of dates and times.

She read it and signed it.

'You know, you had an advantage over us,' said the detective when she'd finished. 'You had confidential information about the time of death. It would have been very easy for you to have added half an hour or so and put Fergal completely in the clear.'

Tara, who had relaxed, sat upright. 'What do you mean? I thought he *was* completely in the clear. You can't possibly think that he left me at ten to six, drove home, killed his mother without a motive, went for a walk along the shore and then phoned the police by seven!'

O'Rourke didn't look up. 'It's technically possible.'

Tara sighed with exasperation. 'But not likely. No jury

would think it likely. You know that.'

O'Rourke remained silent.

'You know he has a brother,' Tara said at last. 'Manus has a history of mental instability. He is the one you should be interested in.'

'We're always interested in all possibilities, Tara.'

'So why don't you take *him* in for questioning?'

'We can't find him. He was discharged from hospital six months ago. He spent a bit of time in sheltered accommodation near the hospital and then vanished. Nobody knows where he is. It's quite possible he doesn't even know his mother is dead.'

Tara finished her tea. The sugar lay at the bottom of the mug in a gelatinous heap. 'One question. When are you going to release Fergal?'

'Well, that depends on whether that's a question from Tara Ross, journalist, or from Tara Ross, private citizen. In the first case, no comment. In the second case, he was freed...' He looked at his watch... 'exactly half an hour ago. And we have no plans to re-arrest him. Not after your evidence.'

Tara checked her own watch. It was precisely two-thirty. 'I don't understand,' she said. 'I've only just completed my statement. Yet you say he was released at two o'clock, before we'd even started.'

O'Rourke fished out a spoonful of damp sugar from the bottom of his own mug and put it in his mouth. 'Read up on your newspaper-law, Tara. You're supposed to know these things. Section Four permits us to hold someone for six hours, give him an uninterrupted night's sleep between midnight and eight, and then detain him for another six hours maximum. His six hours have just elapsed.'

Tara looked at him directly. 'Tell me the truth. You do believe he's innocent, don't you?'

'Who's asking the question?'

She smiled. 'Tara Ross, private citizen.'

He thought for a moment. 'I think that there are cases

in which women make up alibis to protect their men,' he said at last.

Tara felt a chill in the pit of her stomach.

'But this isn't one of them.'

'Thanks. That's a relief.' Tara rose to leave. 'Anyway, I'd better find Fergal and tell him that he can stop this nonsense of pretending we didn't spend the night together.'

O'Rourke shook his head. 'No need,' he said, apparently engrossed in sorting through his pile of papers. 'He's already told me he slept with you that night. In fact, it was the very first thing he told me.'

Bastard.

It was all Tara could do to stop herself hissing the word out loud at the detective as she spun on her heel and stalked towards the door, realising that she'd fallen victim to one of the oldest tricks in the book.

'Tara?'

She paused.

'It's not going to be easy. Finding your dream in Claremoon Harbour. Not after this. You know that.'

Tara ignored him and slammed the door behind her. She had walked through the corridors, out through the playground and into the village street before it suddenly dawned on her that O'Rourke had not answered her last question at all.

CHAPTER SEVEN

TARA WAS walking down a long alleyway, colder and darker than the streets of hell. She was shivering, wet and cold. She knew someone was following her, but she dared not turn around. She walked faster and the mysterious follower quickened his step as well. She ran and the pursuer broke into a run, too.

She tried to scream for help but her lungs would only produce a muffled moan. There was a doorway. She tried to hammer on it for help, but her limbs were moving as slowly as a swimmer's through water.

Suddenly she was inside, in a room where the stifling warm air was as thick as treacle. It was suffocating her, slowly, breath by breath. An old-fashioned black phone was ringing persistently. It rang and rang and rang. She had to answer it and get help. But every movement she made took an eternity, every step towards the table left her drained and exhausted.

Her screams of frustration, howled with all the strength in her lungs, emerged as weak, stifled groans from behind a gag of cotton wool. The phone kept ringing. And ringing. And...

'Hello.'

'I thought you'd never answer.'

'Fergal! Where are you? How are you?' Tara switched on her bedside lamp. The alarm clock showed six thirty-two am.

'Sorry to phone you so early, but I need your help to get home. That is, if they don't put me in jail first.'

She sat upright. Two seconds later the full force of a mighty hangover struck her and she wished she were back in her nightmare. Doom, doom, doom went the steel hammers inside her head. It was as though a contractor's wrecking ball was demolishing an empty gasometer inside her skull.

She remembered the previous night. After Ann's removal ceremony Fergal had left Claremoon to escape the media and had spent the night with friends in Ennis. Meanwhile Tara had brought Melanie back to her cottage. Before retiring, they'd been unable to resist a small night-cap. But with Melanie in charge of the bottle, it had inevitably become a large night-cap. Never again, she groaned silently. Never, ever again.

Tara massaged her aching head. 'Where are you phoning from?'

'A phone box in Ennis.'

Doom, doom, doom went the wrecking ball.

'I'm seeing a lawyer this afternoon, after the funeral. A real one this time, not the redneck hick who's supposedly been looking after my interests so far. I can tell you, I'll be suing. And just in case they've got your phone tapped...I'm not settling for less than a hundred grand, guys.'

Tara, head pounding, resisted the impulse to say: Well, if you're going to be so bloody rich you can call yourself a taxi.

'Anyway,' he said, as though reading her thoughts, 'I came away without any money for a taxi and I haven't time to wait for the first bus. Besides, I need to talk to you. I must see you, Tara. Can you pick me up?'

'Go for a coffee in Maguire's,' she instructed. Coffee. The very thought made her feel slightly better. 'It's a café that opens early for farmers and market workers. Read a paper. I'll be there by a quarter to eight.'

She put down the phone and sank back exhausted on to the bed. She could have risen straight away and made it by seven, but she needed that extra forty-five minutes. God, how she needed it.

The little Fiat rocked and rolled along the potholed road

from Ennis back to Claremoon Harbour. Every metal-on-metal clunk of the shock-absorbers was another hammer-blow in Tara's hangover-ridden head. But hangover or no hangover, she was overjoyed to be alone with Fergal again for the first time since his release. Although they'd met briefly at the removal, the watching eyes had forced them to remain distant and formal. This morning, when they'd met in Ennis, she had run up to him and flung her arms around him passionately.

'Not now,' he'd said, disentangling himself. 'Not on the street.'

They had almost reached Claremoon Harbour when Tara steered the Fiat into a lay-by overlooking the town. She switched the engine off and threw herself into his arms. This time she met no resistance.

'I think you should get out of the area for a while,' she said after a while.

He looked astonished. 'Why? How can you say that? I haven't done anything wrong. And anyway, I want to stay with you, Tara.'

Tara said: 'You saw the looks you were getting last night, Fergal. Everyone's going to shake your hand today at the funeral and wish you the best. But after that, you'll see the other side of this town.'

Fergal shook his head incredulously. 'Tara. Look at me. I haven't done anything. I'm innocent,' he repeated.

'I know that. You know that. But you know what it's like. You grew up in this village. Best neighbours in the world if you're in trouble – if your cow falls into a ditch or your boat gets wrecked. But if they sniff out a different kind of weakness, over something they disapprove of, they'll form a queue to destroy you. They scent blood, and in a small community, that can cause a sort of collective hysteria. You know the way gulls gang up on an injured bird?'

She frowned and stared at two black-backed gulls who, coincidentally, were soaring overhead with fluid grace. She sensed his irritation. 'This isn't what you want to hear at a time like this,' she said.

Fergal fell silent. 'I *was* going to say that you shouldn't be giving me all these problems just before my mother's funeral,' he said after a while. 'But now I realise that only a true friend would.' He tugged at his moustache, a sign that he was deep in thought. 'I'm going to stay,' he announced finally. 'To hell with 'em all.'

They sat for a while, looking over the cluster of rooftops – black, terracotta, navy, flaxen with thatch. The houses, like many in the west of Ireland, were painted in colours that seemed to have been dreamed up by a confectioner on acid. Bright pink, pale blue, lavender, impossible shades of purple and orange. Anywhere else in the world it would have been brash and tasteless. But here, in the sea-bright Atlantic air, it created a Mardi Gras atmosphere of cheerful and almost childlike innocence.

'Such a beautiful place,' said Tara, as though seeing her home village for the first time. 'The most peaceful place in the world in the summer. Yet in the winter you get gales that lash in from the ocean with enough fury to uproot concrete. Most people here would give you their last penny if you thought you needed it, but some of them would turn their own daughter out in the rain if she got pregnant out of wedlock. Two facets of one personality. It's like this country as a whole, I suppose.'

They sat for a while in silence.

'I think you're crazy to stick around,' said Tara, 'but you can rely on me. Whatever it means. Whatever it takes.'

Fergal smiled and squeezed her hand. 'I know that already, you half-wit. Thanks. Anyway, after what I went through on Sunday morning, everything else will seem...what?...petty. Not petty. Irrelevant.'

Tara looked at him directly. 'Would it help to talk about it? Or not?'

He nodded emphatically. 'It would help. It definitely

would help. I'd love to talk about it. I'd love to shout about it and get it out of my system. But that's the trouble, Tara. I can't find any words to describe how...' he struggled for an adjective and failed to get one... 'how bad it was.'

Tara smiled encouragement. 'I know. There aren't any in the dictionary. At times like this, they all seem inadequate.' She was thinking of her own mother. She forced herself to stop, to concentrate on the needs of this man who had not only experienced that same grief, but also the unspeakable horror of finding his mother murdered.

'After I left your house, I drove straight home,' Fergal said woodenly, as though repeating a story he'd told a thousand times. 'It was broad daylight. I was afraid of waking her, so I parked the 'vette out on the road and took a short walk up into the Burren, to clear my head and think things through. I climbed to the top of the hill just behind my house and just stood there for a while, looking out to sea. It was so calm at that hour of the morning, so...eternal. I thought about what we'd talked about, and about our future – my future, I mean, and yours, and how they might relate.'

Tara stared at him. 'Hang on a minute. You walked up into the Burren?'

He seemed annoyed that she'd interrupted his soul-searching. 'Yes, I just told you. I climbed the top of the hill behind my house. It only takes fifteen minutes if you're in good shape. Then, after a while, I came back down and walked around the house to the back door. I had a key for the front door, but I knew I could just walk in through the kitchen door and make less noise. It's always kept on the latch, you know, no matter how many times I warned her how dangerous it is.'

Tara nodded. Her own father did exactly the same thing. Old country habits died hard, even though city-based gangs of violent criminals regularly blitzed remote rural areas in search of easy pickings.

'I mean, I thought I'd got the point through to her when

we had a break-in a week or so beforehand,' he said. 'Well, it wasn't really a break-in. Whoever it was just walked in through the unlocked door. But it should have served as a warning to her. To both of us.'

'A break-in?' Tara sounded puzzled. 'You never told me.'

'Well, we weren't sure. Nothing was taken. Not a single thing. The guy must have just wandered around, poked about a bit, and walked out again. We had banknotes and cheques stuffed in the teapot, and some jewellery in the drawer, but none of it was touched.'

'So how did you know...?'

'Some things were just shifted around a little. Mom thought I'd done it and I thought she'd done it. We didn't even realise it had happened until a few days later.'

'But Fergal.' Tara gripped his arm. 'This could be important. Have you told the police?'

He nodded. 'Yes, but I could see they didn't believe me. No evidence of any break-in. Same thing on Sunday, of course. That was the reason it hit me so hard.' His eyes closed. He was back at the murder scene again. 'I mean, if there had been a smashed window or a busted lock I might have been prepared, you know what I mean? Instead I just opened the door and found her lying there.'

His hand, still on hers, tightened at the memory.

'She lay twisted on the floor, her body covered with knife slashes, her arms cut where she tried to defend herself. Blood everywhere. Absolutely...everywhere.'

He swallowed. 'What amazed me was how calm I was. I knew there was no point summoning medical help – she was beyond that sort of aid. You know the calm part of us that takes over in a crisis? That's what took control. I just stepped over her body and phoned the police. Then I phoned the priest. I was Mr Cool, Mr Capable. It was only afterwards, hours afterwards, that I cracked up.'

Tara opened her window slightly. She could practically smell the odour of death. 'I know exactly what you mean,' she said. 'The feelings kick in later. First gear, second gear, third gear, then into overdrive.'

Fergal nodded silent agreement. Then he turned his head away and looked out of the passenger window for a while. When he turned back, she could see his eyes swollen with tears which he refused to release.

'It's okay,' she whispered. 'It's all right. I understand.'

But Tara could find no words to comfort him, any more than Fergal could find words to express his feelings. She silently held his hand for a few minutes. Then she started the car and drove back home, taking a back-route to avoid the centre of the village.

Home for Tara was a nineteenth-century fisherman's cottage that had been extended and modernised by its previous owners, a German couple who'd moved back to Berlin at the same time as she had returned to Claremoon. She'd been lucky to get it, because its unrivalled views of the harbour and the Burren hills had placed it in great demand.

'I'll make us some breakfast,' she said practically, as she searched for her door-key.

'Sounds good,' he replied.

But as soon as they were inside the house, they both knew that breakfast could wait. The door had hardly closed behind them when they were in each other's arms, their lips locked together, oblivious to everything else.

'Tara.' His voice was husky, urgent. 'I've missed you. God, how I've missed you.'

'Yes.' She felt her own body respond to his, an overwhelming ache of desire. 'I've missed you, too.'

Afterwards, they breakfasted in bed on buttered toast and chilled cranberry juice. He told her how beautiful she was, and how the past few days had made him realise how much she meant to him; she nuzzled his ears and neck and told him of her own feelings, of the hesitations and uncertainties that she was sure had now vanished for good.

'You are such a wonderful lady,' he said. 'So goddam gorgeous. So goddam special.'

She kissed him softly on the lips. 'You know, you're pretty special, yourself.'

'Tara.' Suddenly his voice sounded strained and awkward. 'Something I wanted to talk to you about. It's about that dream home of yours. You know, the old spa house...'

Something made her lay her forefinger gently across his lips. 'Not now, Fergal. Not now.'

They made love a second time, slowly and lingeringly, savouring the sheer luxury of having stolen a couple of hours for themselves on a day when they would otherwise never be out of the public eye.

'I suppose,' he said unconvincingly as he sat on the edge of the bed, dressing himself, 'I suppose today was not exactly the right time to do this.'

He pointed to the rumpled bedclothes, as though she could have missed his point.

She knelt on the bed, put her arms around him, and kissed his neck. 'When it comes to giving love,' she said, 'I don't think there's ever a wrong time.'

The noise began slowly and softly, like a rumble of distant thunder. It gathered strength and confidence as it rolled and yawed through the crowd in an ocean-swell of sound.

It had its own irregular rhythm, an unexpected rhythm, almost like a work by some obscure modern Russian composer.

Yet it was a strangely primitive noise, carrying emotions that would have been familiar to the prehistoric folk who had built their own giant stone edifices of pagan worship on the hills overlooking the graveyard.

It was the most basic noise that human beings could create – a mumble of voices, low and steady and constant, building a solid bulwark of resistance against the forces of chaos that appeared to fill the universe.

'...lead us not into temptation, and deliver us from evil.'

The prayer drew to a close and the cemetery fell silent again.

Standing with her father among the scores of mourners, Tara watched as Fergal stood, head bowed, alongside the priest at the graveside. Beside him on one side were Ann's only surviving relatives, an uncle from County Antrim and a cousin from Dublin. On the other side stood two tall, dour men who turned out to be Martin Kennedy's brothers.

The weather had been kind. A break in the rain left the churchyard suffused with clear, wet sunlight, the sort of shimmering, unnatural light you get only in the west of Ireland. It was like being on the inside of a child's soap bubble.

As the religious service ended, there was a stirring of bodies in the assembly as they prepared for an equally ancient ritual – the chats by the roadside, the exchange of platitudes, the few drinks, even the prospect of the sale of a car or a cow or the renting of a few acres of land.

All crowds have a life of their own, and a wordless communication that travels through them like ripples in a pond. Those in the front rows paused first, and tensed; and within seconds the same tension spread back through the crowd, right to its outer fringe, and all without a single word having been spoken. The message was clear. Wait. Don't leave yet. Something is happening.

Heads craned. A small, elderly, monkish man emerged from somewhere in the crowd and whispered something to the priest. Fergal and the other relatives looked up in puzzlement – clearly, they had not expected this.

The priest consulted with Fergal, who stared at the white-haired newcomer with astonishment and then nodded his head.

'Brothers and sisters,' the priest had called out, 'we

have a gentleman here, an old friend of our dear sister Ann, who would dearly love to say a few words in her memory. Silence, if you would.'

And the obedient crowd fell silent, so silent that you could actually hear the faint voices of the men in fishing-boats far out in the bay. They waited in anticipation.

It was a full half-minute before the monkish man opened his mouth to speak. He didn't shout, but his clear voice effortlessly carried across the graveyard and beyond, into the trees and rocks that bordered it on two of its three sides.

'Sweet love of youth, forgive if I forget thee,
While the world's tide is bearing me along;
Other desires and other hopes beset me,
Hopes which obscure, but cannot do thee wrong.

'No later light has lightened up my heaven,
No second morn has ever shone for me.
All my life's bliss from thy dear life was given,
All my life's bliss is in the grave with thee.'

He bowed his head as the silence of expectation was replaced by the silence of bewildered anticlimax.

He thanked them politely, then shook hands with the priest and – briefly, formally – with Fergal and the other relatives. Then the monkish man turned back into the crowd and was gone.

On the other side of the cemetery, the local schoolmaster, Tommy Ardill, was heard to proclaim loudly that he recognised the poem as an obscure work by Emily Brontë, and that he considered it in damn poor taste to recite it in the circumstances.

But that wasn't what the villagers wanted to know.

'Who in God's name was that?' The same question ebbed and flowed around the bemused crowd. And just as swiftly the answer came back. The same name was on everyone's lips in broken synch, like a verbal Mexican wave.

'Who?' asked the man beside Tara when he heard the name.

His neighbour yawned and loosened his tie. 'Nobody,' he said at last. 'Just some artist fella she used to know.'

CHAPTER EIGHT

'WHERE DID he go?' asked Tara.

'De Blaca? I've no idea,' said Fergal. 'He just seemed to disappear. I turned around for just one second, and when I turned back again he'd gone.'

Nobody, it turned out later, had seen Michael de Blaca leave Claremoon Harbour. Nobody saw him drive off, nobody saw him hire a taxi, nobody saw him queue for a bus. And he certainly didn't hitchhike, as it was quite common for elderly people to do around these parts. He just seemed to vanish, not just from the graveyard but from the entire district.

'I imagine he felt a bit embarrassed,' suggested Tara. The artist's eccentric behaviour at the funeral seemed to have thrown Fergal into an even more downcast mood, and it wasn't helped by the gloomy emptiness of the function room where they sat, gamely trying to work their way through platefuls of ham sandwiches.

As though reading her mind, a waiter moved forward with a giant teapot. 'Would you like some tea, ma'am?'

Tara nodded. The waiter dispensed three meagre teacups from a pot designed to cater for two dozen. He handed the cups to Fergal, Tara and Melanie and retreated in obvious embarrassment to his serving position behind a huge table laden with untouched plates of sandwiches and salads.

'You might as well clear all this away,' Fergal told him. 'Looks like nobody else is going to turn up.'

'If you're sure, sir.'

'Yeah, yeah, I'm sure. Tell Eamonn Breadon not to worry, I'll pay for it all anyway. Just...just give the stuff to an orphanage, or something.'

Tara took his hand, silently comforting him. What

could she say to console someone who'd been cold-shouldered by an entire community? In keeping with tradition, Fergal had laid on refreshments for the dozens of mourners at his mother's funeral. There had been no conspiracy, no concerted plan to boycott the function. It was just that every single person in Claremoon Harbour had decided to find something else to do.

'Well,' said Fergal, standing up suddenly. 'I suppose there's no point sticking around here, is there?'

'Hang on a minute.' Melanie frowned and raised her hand for silence. 'What's that noise?'

The smooth hum grew steadily louder and then abruptly stopped. Peering through the stained-glass windows, they saw Andres Talimann dismount from a BMW R1100 motorbike and remove his helmet. His face seemed anxious and distraught as he hurried towards the function room.

'Who the hell is that?' demanded Fergal. 'And why's he coming here?'

Before she had a chance to reply, the Estonian burst through the door. His troubled eyes scanned the room and lit up with relief when he spotted Tara.

'Excuse me.' Fergal stalked forward belligerently to meet him. 'This is a private function.'

'I know that, Mr Kennedy. I apologise for the intrusion. My name is Andres Talimann. I'm a journalist and...'

'Well, if you're a journalist, you can get the hell out of here. That's what you can do.'

Fergal stomped past him and threw open the door to assist his exit.

Tara hurried forward. 'It's okay, Fergal. I know this man.'

Slowly closing the door, Fergal retreated with bad grace to the table. He kept his eyes on Andres, watching him suspiciously.

'What's the matter, Andres?' Tara could see that something was troubling him. 'Is anything wrong?'

Andres removed his gloves, fished into his leather jacket and removed a folded copy of a newspaper.

'Yes,' he said. 'Something is wrong. Something is very wrong indeed.'

Tara stared at the opened newspaper. The message that confronted her was starkly simple – just three words combined with a colour photograph – but it was enough to make her stomach churn with nausea.

'I wanted you to see it before anybody else does,' said Andres. 'This is the early edition. I collected it outside the print works in Dublin and drove up here as quickly as I could. The delivery van will not arrive for at least another hour. At least that will give you some time to prepare.'

Tara didn't even hear him. Her attention was focused on the front page of the *Evening Report!,* a London-based tabloid which had recently opened an office in Dublin and was pulling out all the stops in a desperate bid to win Irish readers. The byline on the article was that of Gerry Gellick.

The entire page was dominated by a giant, grainy colour photograph of herself and Fergal outside the coffee shop where they'd met in Ennis early that morning. They were embracing. Tara was smiling. Fergal was grinning as though he'd just won the Lottery.

In stark contradiction of the image, the headline in ninety-six point gothic type said: THE GRIEVING LOVERS.

The words were obviously intended to be taken ironically. Behind the disingenuous surface message, the innuendo was clear: Fergal and Tara were celebrating Ann Kennedy's death.

Tight-lipped with silent fury, Tara read the text.

Exclusive by Gerry Gellick:

Lovers Fergal Kennedy and Tara Ross were united

in grief this morning...only a few hours before the burial of Mr Kennedy's mother, murder victim Ann Kennedy.

The twosome kissed and canoodled unashamedly in the centre of Ennis, County Clare, shortly after Ms Ross had admitted to gardaí: 'We slept together on the night of the killing.'

Ms Ross's crucial evidence about their sizzling all-night love tryst has finally solved the mystery of Mr Kennedy's whereabouts at the time of the murder that has stunned the nation.

As a result of her unexpected statement to detectives, Mr Kennedy was finally freed to leave Ennis Garda Station after twenty hours of questioning.

Police are now no nearer to solving the brutal knife-slaying of the 52-year-old women's rights activist in Claremoon Harbour on Sunday morning.

'We're right back to square one,' one frustrated garda told me.

Meanwhile, the pair of lovers embraced, then walked together to a waiting car which they drove to an isolated spot overlooking the beautiful County Clare coastline.

After spending forty-five minutes together in the car, they drove back to the murder town of Claremoon Harbour with only a short time to spare before the funeral.

Then Mr Kennedy stood solemnly by the graveside as Ann Kennedy's corpse was lowered into the ground. Ms Ross is believed to have been absent due to another more pressing engagement.

Twenty-four hours earlier, as Fergal Kennedy was still being questioned by detectives, gorgeous Tara (27) proudly declared her love for him.

In an exclusive interview, she told me: 'I was delighted to be able to give Fergal an alibi, even though I know no one in the village believes me. I'd do anything to keep my lover out of jail.'

The beautiful 27-year-old brunette added: 'Ann is dead, and nothing can bring her back again. All we can do is rebuild the shattered pieces of our lives. I love Fergal passionately. We want to marry and make beautiful babies together.'

Tara tossed the paper away with a loud groan of despair. 'Give me a break,' she said to the ceiling. 'If he's going to make up quotes for me, he could at least make up original ones. These are the oldest clichés in The Bad Journalist's Dictionary Of Hackneyed Phrases.'

'Calm down, Tara,' said Melanie. 'There's no point getting yourself upset.'

'I'm not going to calm down. This isn't journalism. This is writing by numbers.'

'Bloody reporters. They're all the same,' said Fergal, who was glaring over her shoulder at the article.

Tara and Andres both looked up sharply.

'Present company excepted,' Fergal said. 'Of course.'

'You can't generalise like that,' said Tara. 'The other evening papers, the *Evening Herald* in Dublin and the *Evening Echo* in Cork, have been reporting the story fairly. The same goes for my old paper, the *Evening Mercury*. Ninety-nine percent of journalists are honest professionals who'd never dream of inventing a quote or fabricating a story. You get bad apples like Gellick in every profession.'

Fergal frowned as he read down through the report. 'Did you really say all those things to him?'

Tara gasped. 'Of course I didn't, Fergal. He's making it all up.' She shook her head incredulously as she re-read the article. 'He's depicting me as a cretin as well as a heartless bitch,' she moaned. 'I'm not sure which I object to most.'

They lapsed into an uncomfortable silence.

Andres put his hand on her shoulder. 'We have succeeded in buying some time,' he reminded her quietly, 'but not too much time. Within forty-five minutes, this will be in the local shops.' He looked at her keenly. 'What do you propose to do?'

Tara sighed. 'I really don't know.'

It was true. For a start, she had found herself temporarily unemployed. She had naturally declared her involvement in the Kennedy murder case to the editors of all the newspapers she contributed to. Some of them had been delighted with the prospect of having a writer with the inside-track on the big story of the week. But Tara had refused to write another word on the topic, explaining truthfully that she was following legal advice. Instead, she'd decided to grant herself some long-overdue holiday leave.

Since then her mobile phone had been hopping out of her pocket with requests for TV and radio interviews and news-analysis articles. If she'd really been the heartless schemer portrayed in the *Evening Report!* story, she thought ruefully, she could have made herself a fortune. Instead, she'd switched her phone over to an answering service.

'What'll I do? Go home, I suppose,' she said vaguely.

To her intense annoyance, Talimann began shaking his shaggy head. 'I do not think so,' he said, his strange Estonian accent making his words seem more dictatorial than they were meant to be.

'What?' she demanded, hackles instantly raised.

Fergal leaped to her defence. 'Why the hell shouldn't she go home?' he asked Andres angrily. He glared round at the two women as though seeking support. 'Listen, whatever your name is...'

Andres stood up to face him. 'My name is Talimann. Andres Talimann. And I would remind you, Mr Kennedy, that I am trying to help.'

'Help? By trying to stop Tara from going home? To her own house?' Fergal's face was only inches from Andres's. 'This is Ireland, friend. You're not in Russia any more.'

'I am not Russian,' said Andres with dangerous calmness. 'I am an Estonian.'

'Stop it!' Tara raised her hands. The two men slowly backed away from each other.

She walked over to Fergal.

'I think we owe Andres a great debt of gratitude for travelling all the way from Dublin to warn us about Gellick's article in person,' she told him firmly. 'He tried to warn me yesterday, but I didn't believe him.' She glanced apologetically at Andres. 'I also know why he's warning me not to go home. Within the next hour, there'll be a steady stream of reporters calling at my front door. Maybe even camera crews. The place will be under siege.'

Andres nodded confirmation. 'The first ones are already there.'

Fergal took a deep breath and let it out slowly. 'Sorry,' he said curtly, shaking the Estonian's hand. 'I misunderstood you, Mr Talimann. We'll talk this over. But not here.' He glanced around the function room. 'It's too depressing. Come up to my house and we'll discuss it over a beer.'

Melanie looked up from behind the newspaper and smiled for the first time. 'Beer?' she repeated. 'Did somebody say the magic word?'

Tara was prepared for an emotional jolt when she returned to the kitchen of Ann's farmhouse for the first time since their last dinner together. But what shocked her most was its sheer, normal, humdrum ordinariness. There were no overturned chairs, no smashed crockery, no shattered shards of glass.

Once the forensic experts had completed their arcane trade, the cleaners had moved in and left the place immaculate. It looked exactly as it had looked on the evening of her visit – a visit that seemed to have taken place several lifetimes ago.

Tara half-expected Ann to emerge from behind an open door, carrying a steaming casserole and smiling a welcome.

Instead, Fergal was handing out longneck bottles of chilled Labatts. 'Canadian lager okay for you, Mr Talimann?' he called out from behind the fridge door.

But Andres wasn't listening. He was standing stock-still, like a pointer dog spotting a pheasant.

'Wow,' he said at last. It was a long, low syllable of pure worship.

Tara followed the direction of his gaze. He had spotted the Michael de Blaca seascape that had transfixed Tara herself during her first visit.

'De Blaca,' he breathed, recognising the painting from twelve feet away and at an impossibly sharp angle. 'It is...magnificent.'

Fergal looked impressed despite his efforts not to be. 'You're familiar with his work?' he asked.

'De Blaca? He's among my top three favourite Irish painters,' said Andres, almost bounding towards the picture. 'Along with Louis le Brocquy and Colin Middleton, naturally.' He paused, preoccupied with a close-up examination. 'Look at that brushwork. It's like he's piling it on with a trowel. He did it exactly the way he wanted to do it. And yet it works. You can practically smell the salt and seaweed.'

'That's because the window's open,' muttered Fergal grumpily. 'It was painted from this room.'

He pointed through the window at a scene that had remained virtually unchanged for three decades.

'I don't believe it,' breathed Andres. 'He lived here?'

'Well...yes and no,' Fergal admitted. 'It's a long story.'

'Show him the sculpture, Fergal,' suggested Tara.

Andres whirled around. 'Sculpture? You have a

sculpture as well?'

Fergal looked uneasy. He glanced at Tara, as though seeking advice. She shrugged.

Abruptly, he seemed to make up his mind. Tara watched the two men disappear into the living-room and shortly afterwards saw Fergal hand Andres the stone sheela-na-gig. After an interval, she joined them.

'And that's how it happened,' Fergal was saying.

Tara caught his eye. This time it was his turn to shrug, in a sort of 'what have I got to lose?' gesture.

'That is absolutely...incredible,' said Andres, turning the stone piece over and over in his hands. 'And you're sure about this? Absolutely certain?'

Fergal looked at him for a moment without saying a word. His face grew darker than the dense clouds that were gathering over the slate-grey Atlantic. 'I hope you're not doubting my word, friend,' he said softly.

Andres held up both palms defensively. 'Hey, hey. Please do not take umbrage. It was just a...what do you say? A figure of speech. No offence meant and none, I hope, taken.'

'Forget it.'

There was a silence as Fergal continued to stare out the window and Andres continued to examine the sheela-na-gig in the light. They were all relieved when the door-bell rang.

Melanie answered. 'Fergal,' she called from the hall. 'It's Godfrey Villiers. From the art gallery.'

'What the blazes does he want?' muttered Fergal with irritation. He unwillingly extracted himself from an armchair and headed for the hall.

Andres turned to Tara. 'He seems rather prone to take offence, your friend,' he whispered.

'For God's sake, Andres, he's been living through a nightmare,' Tara exploded. She was secretly seething over Fergal's churlish attitude, but she knew she had no right to complain at a time like this. 'How would you feel?'

Andres said nothing. He looked puzzled, turning the small statue over and over, apparently lost in deep thought.

Tara was irritated by his silence. 'So do you mind telling me what that was all about?'

The tall Estonian sipped his lager slowly. 'I don't know. That is the short answer. There is just something odd.' He looked up suddenly and his eyes were frank with genuine perplexity. 'I honestly don't know what I mean, Tara. It seems I shall have to return to...kindergarten. You have kindergarden in English?'

He pulled such a ridiculously sad face that Tara couldn't help laughing out loud. The noise echoed unnaturally in the empty sitting room.

Andres smiled and rose to his feet. 'And now, I must return to Dublin. No, it's all right, I shall leave by the back door. Please give my goodbyes to Fergal.'

Tara shook his hand. 'Goodbye, Andres. And many thanks for your kindness. After all this, I'm sure you'll be glad to see the last of Claremoon Harbour.'

She leaned forward and gave him a quick kiss on the cheek. She had to admit that she was beginning to warm to this eccentric Estonian, but at the same time, she was glad he was getting out of her life for good. His presence just complicated things, in all sorts of ways that she didn't want to start thinking about. And God knows, her life was complicated enough already.

'Farewell, Tara.' Andres turned towards the door. 'But I have a feeling that we shall meet again in more tragic circumstances.'

Tara smiled at his lack of command of the idiom. 'You mean, less tragic circumstances.'

Andres shrugged.

'Perhaps,' he said.

Tara and Melanie fidgeted awkwardly in the sitting room

as they waited for Fergal to end his conversation with the art dealer Godfrey Villiers. They wanted to leave, too, but not without saying goodbye, and the exchange between the two men seemed too earnest to interrupt.

'Well, Tara?' Melanie asked eventually. 'Have you decided what you're going to do?'

Tara shook her head. 'I don't know. Maybe hide out in a B&B for a while. I can't go home, that's for sure.'

'Well, if you've no plans,' Melanie suggested, 'why not come and stay at my house in Galway? Just as long as you don't throw your dirty underwear all over the floor.' She grinned. 'You see, I wouldn't be able to tell it apart from mine.'

Before Tara could reply, the conversation outside grew louder.

'But my dear boy!' They heard Villiers' theatrical tones boom through the closed door, and then fade again.

'I don't care. Everything's changed now.'

Fergal.

Then Villiers' voice increased in volume as he moved deeper into the hall from the front door.

'But you simply must reconsider. I have to tell you, Fergal, the canvasses that you have painted are brilliant...absolutely outstanding, a classic example of the genre. To keep these hidden from the world is a crime. We must form a dynamic partnership, a synergy which will enrich the world as well as, I hope, be of material benefit to us both.'

There was a pause. His footsteps could be heard in the dining-room where the de Blaca seascape hung on the wall.

'I shall naturally give you top price for your works in an overall package deal which must, of course, include all the artistic works in your late mother's home.'

Melanie grinned at Tara, who gestured for silence.

'You've got a bloody nerve coming here on the day of my mother's funeral,' said Fergal.

Villiers began to protest, but a few seconds later the front door slammed.

'But time, my dear boy! Time is of the very essence!' pleaded the art dealer from outside the house.

'You're quite wrong, my friend,' murmured Fergal, returning to the sitting room with a face like thunder. 'I've got all the time in the world.'

CHAPTER NINE

LATER THAT night, Andres Talimann sat in his eyrie high on the sea-cliffs overlooking Dublin Bay. His hands flew over his computer keyboard, assessing facts, sorting information. The lights on his modem flickered frantically as they signalled contact with computers spread out over five continents. Laid out before him, in all its daunting complexity, was the vast storehouse of information known as the World Wide Web.

Andres completed his research for a magazine article on the Loyalist paramilitary organisations. He was about to close down the computer when, almost without his brain realising it, his hands typed in three words. Seconds later his screen changed its appearance, like the surface of a witch's cauldron, to reveal the answers he sought.

Only two documents in the entire Web contained the linked words he was looking for. One was the gossipy personal website of a Newfoundland student. The other was from the on-line edition of a daily newspaper in Toronto.

Andres ignored the student's website and opened up the newspaper article. It wasn't the current edition, he quickly realised, but an archive clipping dating back several months.

It contained a lengthy collection of news briefs that had appeared in the national news section of the Canadian paper that day. He had to scroll through it for several minutes before he found the section that was relevant to his inquiry.

Andres read and re-read it. Then he rubbed his eyes, walked around a bit, opened a can of Coke, and read it again.

There could be no doubt. No doubt at all.

Or could there?

Andres took a decision. He lifted the phone on his desk, dialled Tara's mobile phone number, and waited.

'Hello?' said Tara Ross, her voice almost drowned out by the clinking of glasses and the cacophony of shouted conversation.

'Hello?' she said again.

Andres Talimann was about to speak when he was suddenly overwhelmed by the same doubts he'd dismissed a few seconds ago. There *were* doubts, he thought. There were serious doubts. And he would have to resolve these uncertainties before he committed himself.

He checked his watch. Just after eleven pm in Dublin. Late afternoon, Toronto time. He still had time to burn up the phone lines to Canada. To plead for information from overworked cops, court officials, other reporters, anyone who would listen.

'Hello?' Tara Ross was still calling down the phone line. 'Hello? Is anyone there?'

Andres Talimann said nothing. Slowly, guiltily, he replaced the receiver.

'Another crank call?' shouted Melanie as Tara stared in bemusement at the cellphone in her hand. 'Why don't you switch your mobile off?'

'I forgot,' Tara yelled back, struggling to make her voice heard above the din of a jukebox that was belting out an early Elvis classic.

'Don't worry about it,' said Melanie. 'It was probably a wrong number. Chill out and have another beer.'

In the clamorous, almost rowdy atmosphere of The Docks, one of Galway's most celebrated pubs, Tara could relax for the first time. After the traumatic events of the past forty-eight hours, it was sheer bliss to find sanctuary with Melanie in the cosmopolitan capital of the West, far away from Claremoon Harbour and its poisonously oppressive atmosphere.

'No, I don't think it was a wrong number,' Tara said thoughtfully as the Elvis song ended and the jukebox went silent.

'Well, what was it? Abuse or heavy breathing? If it was heavy breathing, pass him over to me next time. I'll heavy-breathe right back at him.'

'Neither. Just silence. There was someone there, but he just hung up.' Tara frowned. 'I've a feeling it was Andres Talimann.'

'What are you, telepathic all of a sudden? He said nothing, but you still think it was Andres?'

'Because of the Bach,' Tara said.

'Bach?' Melanie obviously thought her friend had taken leave of her senses.

Tara finished her glass of lager and tried to explain. 'Andres Talimann always works with Bach playing in the background, no matter where he is in the world,' she said. 'It's a quirky habit of his. He mentions that in his book.' She chewed her lip thoughtfully. 'And there was Bach music playing in the background in that phone call.'

'Suddenly you're an expert on Bach?' Melanie smiled.

Tara shook her head. 'It was the whatsit, the cigar-ad tune. Everybody knows that.'

'The Air on a G-String?'

'That's the one.' Tara's brow furrowed. 'What did he want? Andres may be a bit eccentric from time to time, but he doesn't seem the type to make nuisance phone calls. Maybe he was trying to tell me something.'

'Maybe he dialled your number by mistake and then hung up when he realised,' said Melanie, more practically. 'Or maybe this is all just wishful thinking on your part. Aural hallucinations. We shrinks learn all about it at college. Recognised treatment is another round of beer.'

'Don't start all that,' said Tara. Taking Melanie's hint, she summoned the barman and ordered two more lagers. She set the mobile phone on the table and peered at its dial to make sure it was functioning. 'Do you think he'll call back?'

'He never phones, he never writes...' Melanie teased. 'That's the fourth time you've checked your phone. You're like a sixteen-year-old hoping her boyfriend will call back after a first date.'

'Oh, shut up.' Tara paid the barman. 'I haven't changed my mind about Andres Talimann. He's still a bit of a pain in the neck.'

'No, he's not,' Melanie argued. 'I had a bit of a chat with him earlier. He doesn't mean to sound arrogant or intrusive. It just comes across that way because of his accent. Underneath it all, he's okay.'

Tara pushed the cellphone across to her. 'Then the two of you can have another chat if he phones back.'

Melanie shook her head. 'I did a bit of research on him,' she said suddenly.

'On who?'

'Andres. I rang up my publishers in London. They're the same people who publish *Unholy War.*'

'And?'

'Well, it seems he's had something of a tragic personal life, although he's never written about it. I talked to Carla, who does his publicity. She says he married a Mexican schoolteacher during his travels abroad and took her back to Estonia with him. But she died suddenly, five years ago. Some sort of accident or something. Carla says he never talks about it, but it seems to have been some tragedy that could have been prevented if he'd been there. But he wasn't, and he feels he let her down. And he's been blaming himself for her death ever since.'

Melanie raised her voice to a holler as the latest summer holiday hit blasted out of the jukebox. 'Carla got the wrong end of the stick, as usual,' she shouted. 'She thought that, just because he happened to be a good-looking man, I had designs on him.'

'Perish the thought.'

Melanie ignored her. 'But what intrigued me was the advice she gave me. She said: "Don't waste your time, honey. Sure, he's plenty photogenic and all that, but as far as steady relationships are concerned, the guy just can't be trusted to commit. As soon as he gets close to anyone, he jets off to the other side of the world and leaves her in the lurch. He's left a trail of broken hearts from here to the Urals." That's what she told me.'

Tara said nothing.

'But then Carla always was prone to exaggeration,' shouted Melanie. 'I'm just passing it on for what it's worth.'

CHAPTER TEN

TARA STEERED her rickety Fiat down the hill towards Claremoon Harbour. The very experience suggested a vortex, a return to a gravitational base. The worst of the nightmare was over, she thought. Things might never be the same, but at least her life would return to some semblance of normality.

It had been a restless, unsatisfactory, disjointed week: too many days pacing the claustrophobic, maze-like streets of Galway like some neurotic polar bear trapped in a cage; too many late nights at pub sessions with Melanie, building up a sixty-a-day passive-smoking habit, carefully constructing hangovers that lasted all morning and caused time to blur and smudge beyond recognition.

In the main street, she double-parked her tiny car on the outside of another motor, a twenty-five-year-old Mercedes that had a haybale serving as its rear seat. She slammed the rusty door and paused for a second to let the road-tension leave her body as she breathed in the sweet air of sea and hillside. It was a heady combination of salt and half-rotted seaweed and grass and dung and gorse-blossom. It was home.

She knew this feeling of peace and contentment couldn't last, but what surprised her was that it was shattered almost instantly.

'Hey, you. You can't leave that thing there.'

Tara turned quickly. 'Oh, hello Steve,' she said. She wasn't sure whether the aggressive tone was a joke but felt she'd better play it safe. 'It's great to see you again. I'm just nipping across for a pint of milk. I'll be right back.'

Normally, it wouldn't have been a problem. Double and triple parking was almost part of the highway code in rural villages. It created a sort of acceptable level of chaos from which tractors and lorries disentangled themselves with continental bravado.

But today was different.

Sergeant Steve McNamara responded with all the warmth and flexibility of an Albanian border guard. 'Your vehicle is causing a serious obstruction. Please move it.'

'Steve!'

'Very well.' He reached into his pocket and removed a black notebook.

'Oh, for God's sake!' Tara jumped back into the Fiat and revved up its engine more than was necessary.

He leaned on the window. The vast bulk of his head cast a shadow over the front seat. 'You've also got a defective silencer.'

She searched his features for any human emotion. There was none. This had once been the face of a close friend, but now she was dealing with Robocop.

'So has everyone in bloody County Clare. It's the pot-holes in the roads. Nobody fixes them. Remember?'

But Steve was determined to do it by the book. He handed her a slip of official paper. 'Please have it fixed and report to your nearest garda station as soon as it's done.'

Tara didn't care about the ticket, but she did want to repair a damaged relationship.

'Steve. Listen to me.' She was almost pleading. 'I realise that things have gone badly wrong between us and I'm sorry that you feel the way you do. Let's meet up for a drink tonight and sort it out, friend to friend.'

'Move on, please. You're still causing an obstruction.'

His head suddenly vanished from the window, and the summer sun seared her eyes like a laser beam. She winced. It was almost as though he had struck her physically.

Angered by the cold rejection from Steve, Tara was more than ready for the abuse from the drunks at Sluther's pub. Unfortunately, they were not ready for her.

As she walked past the grubby bar, with its nauseous

smell of Jeyes Fluid and recycled slops, she saw two of the pub's regulars hanging around its doorway.

'Here she comes,' sniggered Zip-Down Seanie, loudly enough for her to hear. 'The town bicycle.'

'And not just the town, either,' wheezed his mate Davy. Davy had lost one lung and still smoked forty a day. 'I hear she makes sixty quid a night around the Limerick docks.'

'Jaysus,' said Seanie. His weasel face twisted in mock concentration. 'At a fiver a time, that's some goin', even for her.'

He flicked a lighted cigarette end into the street. It hit the hem of Tara's cream lambswool skirt and bounced off in a shower of sparks.

She knew what was about to happen. As she drew alongside the doorway, Seanie stepped out in front of her. It was early in the day, but already his breath smelled of stout and the cheap wine he'd consumed before opening-time.

'Hey, love. What about giving the local fellas some of what you give to the Yanks? Eh?'

Davy was alarmed by this development. 'Come on, Seanie. Slagging's one thing, but for God's sake don't be hassling her.' His remaining lung thumped hollowly with the effort of producing the rush of words.

'She's lovin' it, aren't you, me oul' flower? Eh? Eh? What?'

'Come on in out of that, Seanie. I'll buy you a pint.'

'Excuse me, please. I want to pass.'

'Okay. Okay.' Seanie pretended to search in the pockets of his filthy jacket. 'How much is it? A tenner? Twenty? How come murderers get it for free? Eh? What's that? Eh?'

His unshaven face was close up against hers, his bad teeth at eye level. They looked like broken headstones in an untended cemetery and smelled like an uncleaned rabbit-hutch.

'Seanie. Seanie. Give it a miss.' Davy was looking around frantically.

Tara side-stepped, but Seanie was surprisingly agile.

She knew he was about to assault her, and she was prepared. When his bony, blackened hand swooped towards her breast like some predatory vulture, she reacted swiftly.

She hardly moved, but her knee raised itself just a fraction. Her leather boot connected side-on with his left leg, and immediately skidded painfully down along his shinbone. Her heel, perfectly aimed, landed hard on his ankle-joint with every single ounce of her body-weight behind it.

Seanie hadn't expected it. He staggered backwards in agony, not sure which wound was hurting the most – the bruise just beneath his knee, the savagely skinned bone of his shin, or the damage to the soft tissue and tendons of his foot.

Tara glanced quickly at Davy to see how he would react. If he had attacked, she would have been ready for him, too. But Davy had disappeared. He was one of this world's born pot-stirrers, a man who delighted in provoking others into action and then vanishing into the shadows at the first sign of trouble.

Tara calmly circumnavigated Seanie, who was in no position to pose any threat to her, and walked on towards her waiting car.

She felt good again. Really good. And then she felt bad about how good she felt. And after that, she didn't really care.

'Very impressive, Tara.'

The voice came from behind her. A different sort of voice. Cooler, calmer, with no hint of aggression. No sarcasm or irony. Just a normal voice. It sounded wonderful. She could have hugged him just for his neutral tone.

Whoever he was.

'Thanks.' She didn't turn around, but kept walking. Take no chances.

'Basic Self Defence, one of the classic moves. Book or evening class?'

The way he said 'class' gave him away. It was more of a Limerick city pronunciation, with a wide and elongated vowel. She recognised the deep, gritty, furnace-shovel voice and felt her muscles relaxing slightly. But she didn't answer his question.

If she had, the answer would have been 'neither'. She remembered the long night-town shifts in her Dublin newspaper office where, during quiet times when they were both bored, a friendly security man named Ciarán would patiently teach her a series of simple moves that were guaranteed to disable a much heavier opponent in case of sudden attack. He would watch and criticise as she practised them over and over again. One day, he told her, this move could get you out of serious trouble, or that move could save your life. Don't think about how much it will hurt him. Just do it, quickly, without delay. Surprise is everything.

Ciarán himself was a burly six foot three martial arts champion. Ironically, his only recorded defeat would come at the hands of a five-foot-nothing junkie wielding a syringe filled with his own HIV-infected blood. It's the only thing you can't fight, he'd told her philosophically as he'd sat in a clinic awaiting the results of the Aids tests he'd have to keep taking for years.

Now, as she reached her car, Tara wrenched open the faulty door and simultaneously wrenched herself back into the present.

'I've already been done for double-parking and for breach of noise abatement by-laws,' she said. 'What are *you* going to bust me for, Inspector?'

The detective, Phil O'Rourke, smiled thinly. 'You'll have to excuse Steve McNamara,' he replied. 'He's been taking a lot of slagging from his colleagues. The usual juvenile stuff, but it gets to you after a while. And you did make a bit of an eejit out of him, Tara.'

'Whether I did or I didn't, and I don't think I did, it's none of your bloody business.' Steady on, she told herself. You're becoming incoherent.

'Don't worry about the traffic ticket. I'll sort that out.' He held out his hand.

Tara looked him squarely in the face for the first time. Then she handed him the ticket. 'Okay. Thanks.'

Over his shoulder she could see Seanie. He had stopped rubbing his ankle and was standing upright, glaring at her with an expression of pure hatred.

Phil O'Rourke noticed but didn't even glance around. She realised he'd been monitoring the whole scene through the reflection in her rear window.

'And especially don't worry about Zip-Down Seanie. I'll be having a word with him tonight. We'll have a drink together and I'll remind him about certain little episodes he'd rather forget. He won't bother you again. Unless, of course, you want to press charges?'

Tara shook her head.

'I think that's a wise decision. After all, it's not as though he hasn't received some degree of punishment. He'll think twice before pulling that sort of stunt again.'

As he talked, Davy edged warily out of Sluther's and handed Seanie a small spirit-bottle. Seanie swiped him aside peevishly, keeping his eye fixed on Tara, then appeared to change his mind. He took a swig from the bottle, and then both men walked back towards the pub. Tara noticed with satisfaction that he was limping painfully.

'Yes,' she said. 'I suppose he will.'

O'Rourke lit a cigarette. 'It's not generally known, but Seanie has a special interest in this particular case,' he said, still staring at the reflection in the window. 'At one stage, his unsavoury personal habits included molesting his twelve-year-old daughter. The authorities either couldn't or wouldn't act. Nobody did anything about the problem until Ann Kennedy intervened and persuaded his wife to move out with her family to one of her Safe Houses. Then they had him barred from the family home. At a single stroke, Seanie's power over them was broken. He's one of the few people in the world to have harboured a grudge against Ann.'

Tara glanced back towards Sluther's pub. Seanie had gone inside, but she could still make out his bitter, twisted features staring at her through the grubby window.

'Is he a suspect in the murder investigation?' she asked, unable to keep the note of hope out of her voice.

'No.' His voice was sympathetic but firm. 'Seanie has many vices, most of them highly unpleasant, but they do not include murder.'

'So how can I help you, Inspector?' Tara's tone became formal.

'Call me O'Rourke. Everyone else does.'

She didn't respond but continued asking the same question with her eyes.

'Let me buy you a coffee.'

She thought about it for a moment and then shrugged her shoulders. 'Sure.'

They walked in silence to a roadhouse just outside the village. They passed through the crowded lounge bar and made their way into a deserted disco room marked 'Closed'. Its huge dancefloor looked sad and empty in the meagre amount of daylight that was managing to filter through the dusty windows.

O'Rourke steered her to a table well out of anyone's earshot. Then he walked back out to the bar and returned with a pot of black coffee, a cream jug, a fork, some sugar and two large beakers.

From his overcoat pocket he removed a double-measure bottle of whiskey, of the type served on aeroplanes. 'Want to make it an Irish?' he asked.

She nodded wearily. 'Why the hell not? I'm the town slattern after all.'

The adrenalin buzz from her encounter with Seanie was fading fast and was being replaced by an enervating mental fatigue.

He poured the whiskey, added some sugar and coffee, and whipped up a creamy head with polished expertise. 'Four years as a part-time barman in the States,' he explained. 'You never lose the technique.'

Tara was amused. 'I think the idea is that *you* buy *their* whiskey, and they mix it for you,' she said.

O'Rourke made a contemptuous noise with his lips. 'They're used to me here,' he said. 'They don't mind. I get the miniatures from a friend at Shannon Airport. I do him favours, he does me favours.'

'I thought policemen never drank on duty,' she said. She was curious rather than judgmental.

'I'm not on duty.'

Tara stared at him and tried to imagine what sort of home life or social life he must have.

'*Sláinte*.' He raised his cup. Tara responded, and they sat for a moment in silence, appreciating the smooth comforting mixture.

'Tara,' he said at last, 'I want you to listen to me. Have you ever heard of ASPD?'

'Anything to do with the NYPD or the LAPD?'

He smiled. 'No, nothing to do with police departments. It's a relatively new concept in psychiatry – Antisocial Personality Disorder.'

'And what on earth is that?'

'You already know about psychopaths,' he explained. 'Remorseless, cold-blooded, aggressive criminals. You could call people with ASPD "socialised psychopaths". They're not necessarily criminals, but they exhibit all the classic symptoms of psychopathy – they're cold, manipulative, deceitful, impulsive, superficially charming, blameful of others, unable to sustain relationships and totally lacking in guilt.'

He took another slug of his Irish coffee and leaned forward. 'We all know someone with ASPD,' he said. 'The kind of person we might describe as "a cold fish" or "a real sonofabitch". You know the sort of man who endlessly uses people, who talks *at* you rather than *to* you, who has about as much emotional depth as a cardboard cut-out? Chances are he's got ASPD.'

She shrugged, unconvinced.

'Okay,' he said. 'Let me try a little test on you.'

'Go ahead.'

'Which two of these words would you link together: "warm", "loving" and "cold"?'

Tara didn't hesitate. 'Warm and loving.'

'There you are. Most of us would say the same. But people with ASPD tend to link "warm" and "cold". They're totally incapable of understanding how an emotion like love could be "warm". They've grown up to believe that the world is a bleak and hostile place where, in order to survive, you either have to trample on everybody else, or else use superficial charm to manipulate them. Of course, they don't make many friends that way – but it only reaffirms their view that they are outsiders in a world where it's every man for himself.'

'Every *man*?'

'Yes. Men are five times more likely than women to have ASPD. No one knows why. But when they grow up and realise that they're not quite like other people, they do one of two things. They can become hardened criminals and spend the rest of their lives in and out of prison.'

'Or?'

'Or they can camouflage their disorder. They learn to fake sincerity and act out the emotions that they see in other people. Their relationships are equally spurious and short-lived. They seek out jobs where their talents are in demand – think of Gordon Gecko in the movie *Wall Street*, for example. Anywhere that greed is good and ruthlessness is an asset, you'll find no shortage of high-flyers with ASPD.'

Tara fell silent. 'You obviously think Fergal Kennedy has ASPD,' she said at last. 'Or you wouldn't be telling me all this.'

He paused, long enough for her to realise that his true answer was yes. 'I don't know,' he said finally. 'I'm not qualified to say. All I know is that people with ASPD are unreliable, unpredictable, and prone to sudden bouts of aggression and even violence.'

'But Fergal's not a bit like that.'

O'Rourke was silent, then he leaned forward and looked directly into her eyes. 'There's no cure for this disorder, Tara. And women who get into relationships with ASPD men always end up regretting it. The only problem is that they don't find out until it's too late.'

She met his gaze without flinching. 'Thanks for the warning, O'Rourke. But I've no immediate plans to get into a long-term relationship with Fergal Kennedy. If I do, you'll be the first to know.'

He finally looked away. 'There's been a lot of wild speculation about Ann's murder,' he said. 'You've heard theories about robbery and sex attack. We've dismissed both. Ann was not sexually assaulted in any way. And anyway, sex murderers tend to strangle their victims. As for robbery, the idea that she was mugged by some Dublin drug addict is a non-starter. Of the three sightings of this alleged junkie, we can't get one that's totally reliable. No cash was stolen. No saleable goods taken either. Video, TV, even jewellery, all intact.'

'That's easily explained. He's surprised in the act. He knifes her and runs.'

'Without taking anything?'

'He's in a panic.'

'So why did he spend at least three minutes stabbing her?'

'Did he?'

'Yes. Even as she lay on the ground. Long after she'd stopped struggling. Probably long after she was dead. At that particular moment, the killer hated Ann Kennedy very much indeed.'

She shook her head. 'Well, that clinches it, then. Fergal loved his mother. He was absolutely devoted to her. I'm certain of that.'

'Blind rage can overcome all sorts of positive emotions. Read up on your criminology: rage is the reason for most domestic murders. Rage, often fuelled by alcohol. Cheers.'

O'Rourke raised his cup and drank. She didn't.

'And remember,' he said, 'that people with ASPD are accomplished actors. He led you to *believe* that he loved his mother very much. That's all you can say with certainty.'

She waited for him to go on.

'Listen, Tara,' he said, 'I brought you here for three reasons. One, to ask you if you know anything else at all about that night. Any little thing, however insignificant, about his demeanour. Anything he said or did.'

Tara thought long and hard. 'No. I've told you everything,' she said truthfully.

He checked his notebook. 'You said he was wearing jeans and a checked shirt.'

She nodded.

'We've checked the house. His entire wardrobe seems to consist of jeans and checked shirts.'

Tara frowned. 'So?'

She saw him make a conscious effort to slow down his mental processes to match hers. 'So it's important. After an attack like that, we would expect him to have had blood all over his clothes. But he hadn't.'

Tara gasped incredulously. 'Excuse me if I sound dense, but isn't that a sign of his innocence?'

'Could be. Could also be that he disposed of his blood-soaked clothes and changed into other ones that were almost identical. Can you describe the ones he was wearing when he left your house?'

She gave every detail she could remember.

'Okay,' he said, writing them down. 'Point two is the murder weapon. You've already heard the description – a very sharp knife with a wide, curved blade and a wooden handle. But it will be easily identifiable. The forensic guys have established from microscopic examination that it must have been broken near the tip. So we're looking for a knife with a distinctive notch or cut at the end. Incidentally, Tara, we're keeping that bit quiet to discourage cranks and false confessions. Now, we've searched the entire area and we can't locate the knife – any more than we can locate any bloody clothes. Anything you can think of that would match that description, in your house or his? Think hard. It's important.'

'I have been thinking, for over a week. No, there's nothing I know of.'

O'Rourke produced another miniature bottle and poured it into his empty cup, this time neat. 'Why bother with the coffee?' he asked. He fished for another bottle. She touched his arm lightly and shook her head.

'Why did Fergal phone New York from your house that night?' he asked suddenly.

'What?'

'You heard me, Tara. Why did he make a phone call to a Manhattan number at around five am? Just two hours before his mother was found dead?'

She shook her head in bewilderment. 'I haven't the remotest idea what you're talking about.'

'You've no knowledge of that call? Yet you were with him all the time?'

'Yes...well...' She searched her memory. 'Well, I did go to the bathroom a couple of times.'

'For how long?'

'I don't know. Maybe ten minutes or so.'

'Around five am?'

'I don't know, O'Rourke. I honestly don't know. I might

have. What's all this about?'

'I'm not sure yet. But I'll tell you as soon as I do know.' He swirled his whiskey restlessly. 'Do you know a man called Andres Talimann?'

His relaxed mannerism had disappeared. The questions were coming thick and fast.

'Yes. He's a journalist and writer. He works for...'

'I know all that. Any idea why he should have spent Sunday afternoon drinking vodka with Godfrey Villiers?'

'You mean after Ann's body was discovered?'

O'Rourke nodded.

Tara shook her head. 'I've no idea. He was probably just trying to pump him for info. He's a reporter, after all.'

O'Rourke said nothing. He was obviously unconvinced.

'Why shouldn't he talk to Villiers?' Tara demanded. 'I know his gallery is a bit shady, but...'

'It laundered over a hundred grand for the Viney family in Limerick last year,' O'Rourke stated flatly. 'Admittedly that's only a small fraction of the money they earned from distributing cannabis around the south-west, but it's still an important outlet.'

'But Villiers himself isn't into dealing drugs.'

'No. But he's a lush and a gambler. From what I hear, he's been skimming a bit off the drugs money to fund his high-rolling poker sessions. Always a dangerous thing to do. The last guy who crossed the Vineys was trussed like a chicken and buried up to his neck in mud in the Shannon estuary. He had to wait six hours for the tide to come in and drown him.'

Tara shuddered. 'But what has all this got to do with Andres Talimann?'

O'Rourke reached into his inside pocket and produced a folded photograph. It showed Andres about to enter a pub with a fresh-faced young man who was dressed in a golf-club blazer and slacks.

'That's one of the Vineys' main distributors,' he said.

'He shifts most of the gear in the Cork area. No heroin. Hash from Asia, some home-grown grass.'

Tara studied the picture. 'When was this taken?'

'A couple of days ago. While you were in Galway. It was part of a general surveillance by the National Drugs Unit.'

She handed the photo back to him. 'And what do you make of all this, O'Rourke?'

He shrugged. 'I don't know. Talimann was just spotted once. There's no evidence that he's broken any law. But if we see him again, he'll go on to our files for further investigation.'

Tara drained her cup. 'Well, I've told you everything I know,' she said. 'I'm not holding anything back. You see, O'Rourke, I genuinely believe in Fergal's innocence. And I'm convinced you're after the wrong man.'

'The right man being...?'

'I don't know. I'm not in the habit of making assumptions.' She waited for the barb to sink in, then continued. 'But surely you should at least investigate Fergal's brother Manus? From what I've heard of his past, he fits your description of a classic psychopath.'

He turned to her. 'We are, Tara, we are. We're still searching for Manus. As I've told you, he was discharged from Inismaul Mental Hospital around six months ago. We've heard he could be in Boston, but we've had no luck with US immigration; if he's in the States he's there illegally, so he'll be hard to track down. Our inquiries are ongoing, even as we speak.

'But what do you suggest we do if we find him? Arrest him because he's had psychiatric treatment? We haven't even the slightest shred of evidence that Manus was even in this country at the time of Ann's death, never mind in County Clare, never mind near the scene of the murder. If we tried to extradite him from America on that basis, the judge would still be laughing come Thanksgiving.'

'But if you *could* find him?'

'Well, yes, I'd be keen to put some questions to him.

Very keen.'

'You wouldn't dismiss it out of hand? It could help clear Fergal?'

He seemed taken aback. 'It would depend on what he had to say, Tara. If there were any suspicions at all, well, yes, it would shift the focus of our inquiry.'

She nodded. 'That's all I wanted to hear.'

He looked at her. 'You're not planning on doing anything stupid, are you, Tara?'

'It all depends what you mean by stupid. Standing by and doing nothing while an innocent man suffers is hardly intelligent. Point three.'

'What?'

'You said you had three points to raise. We've had two.'

'Okay.' He seemed off-balance, no longer so completely in control. 'Point three is more personal.'

She stiffened.

'Point three is a warning, Tara. A woman who stands by a murderer has her own life ruined alongside his, when he finally comes clean and admits the offence. It's particularly wasteful if she does it out of a misplaced sense of loyalty rather than...love, or passion.'

He seemed ill at ease with the words.

'Nothing you've told me indicates that you are deeply in love with this man. Don't throw your life away because of him. Socialised psychopaths don't love and they don't feel friendship. They just pretend to.'

'Fergal isn't like that. He doesn't have...whatever it is, ASPD. And he is not a murderer. I'm convinced of that.'

'But *if* he is.'

'He's not.'

'But *if*.' He came in hard, like an unexpectedly aggressive return on a tennis serve. '*If*, Tara. Just consider the possibility. In that case, you could be in grave danger. You could even be his next victim. A man who can kill in that manner could easily kill again. All I'm asking you to do is to be careful.'

'You saw how I handled Seanie today. I'm a big girl now. I can look after myself.'

'So was Ann Kennedy. Kind, sweet, but tough as nails after everything she'd been through. Besides,' he finished his whiskey and grabbed his coat, 'boots aren't much defence against a frenzied knife attack.'

He scribbled two numbers on a beermat. 'This is a direct line. This is my mobile number. If anything worries you, or if anything occurs to you that you didn't think of before, give me a call immediately. Promise?'

She nodded. But she felt O'Rourke was getting off too lightly. 'And what will you lot be doing in the meantime?' she asked. 'Besides following Fergal around twenty-four hours a day and booking me for dropping litter?'

He winced. Perhaps he'd been getting the same criticism from his superiors.

'There are things going on behind the scenes. Things I can't tell you about. We've a lot of forensic still to go through, and we still have to find the murder weapon. But as far as I'm concerned, Tara, the killer has been found.'

He stood up. The flush on his face could have been from the whiskey or obsessive determination. 'You can tell him from me that I'll be on his case for as long as it takes.'

They left the bleak disco and re-entered the lounge. O'Rourke strode over to the bar and slapped some money down on the counter. The young barman looked at it and his face brightened. 'Thanks, Mr O'Rourke,' he said with a wide grin.

O'Rourke gave him a don't-mention-it wave and re-joined Tara at the door. 'For however long it takes,' he continued with deadly seriousness. 'Weeks, years. Decades.'

Tara was speechless.

'It may seem crude,' he said, 'but it's the only way to crack cases like this. And when he finally does break, and when he finally comes grovelling into court pleading for mercy, where will you be, Tara? Down on your knees with him? Or standing on your feet without him? It's entirely up to you. But act quickly before it's too late.'

He stared at her challengingly.

She stared back at him, trying to project an aura of certainty and confidence while, inside, her mind was a deafening babble of contradictory voices.

Tell this pushy cop to get lost, one voice was telling her. Tell him you'll stick by Fergal, through thick and thin. Tell him you're prepared to go through hell with him. Because you know in your heart that he's innocent.

But what if O'Rourke is right? another voice kept asking. What if Fergal really does suffer from this frightening disorder, this ASPD? Wouldn't it explain a lot of things that had been bothering her, all those concerns that had kept her tossing and turning in uneasy sleep each night for the past week? Fergal's bullish determination – was it fortitude, or just selfishness? The impulsiveness, the rebelliousness, the scornful independence she'd found so attractive – were they really qualities to be admired, or just manifestations of a mind untrammelled by conscience or guilt?

'Unreliable. Unpredictable. Prone to sudden bouts of aggression and even violence...'

Her mind flicked through the events of the past few weeks. His reaction outside the courthouse when she'd laughed at him and he'd seemed almost on the verge of striking her. His hectoring, almost bullying behaviour towards his own mother. Ann's concern for Tara, and those words of caution that were almost, but not quite, a warning...

Stop it! For God's sake stop, she screamed inwardly. *If I keep on like this, I'm going to go crazy.*

The squabbling voices fell silent.

O'Rourke continued to stare at her, his bloodshot eyes demanding a response.

It was at that instant that she decided it was time to

stop herself being swept along helplessly on this chaotic flash-flood of events. It was time to regain some sort of control over her life.

'I intend to act soon, inspector,' she said, choosing to address him formally. 'I'm going to do your job for you.'

'And just what the hell do you mean by that?' He was more intrigued than offended.

'I'm going to find Manus Kennedy.'

Before he could reply, she was gone.

'Dad, I have to head off for a few days to do a bit of research,' Tara explained.

'Okay, love.' John Ross looked up from his newspaper. 'Where are you off to, this time?'

'I don't know. I realise that sounds stupid, but it's true.' She kissed him on the forehead. 'I'll probably be out of touch for a while. But I'll phone you as soon as I get back.'

A flicker of concern passed across her father's face. He was used to Tara's business trips, but he seemed to know there was something different about this one.

'Tara,' he said simply, 'just take care of yourself.'

She smiled reassuringly and patted his shoulder. 'You, too.'

'Then I'm coming with you,' said Fergal.

'No, you're not.'

'The hell I'm not. Just try to stop me.'

They faced each other off. Tara was first to look away.

'What on earth are you painting?' she asked at last.

He stepped back from the giant canvas that covered one entire wall of the farm outhouse. Red paint dripped from the overloaded decorating brush. It covered his hands and spattered his clothes.

'I don't know,' he admitted, surveying the half-completed work with a critical eye. 'I'm just trying to work all this angst out of my gut and on to the canvas. What do you think?'

'I don't know about angst.' Tara studied at the writhing shapes of red, black and green. 'It looks more like a bout of indigestion to me.'

'Thanks for the insight.' He attacked the canvas again. 'Good job Picasso didn't have you around when he painted *Guernica*. "Forget all those twisted faces and horses' heads, honey. Just take a dose of Bisodol and you'll be fine".'

Tara laughed. 'Sorry. I shouldn't be criticising it before it's finished.' She shivered in the chill sea wind that swept through the open door. 'Anyway, it's getting dark. You should take a break soon. Come inside and I'll make us some coffee.'

'Artists don't take coffee breaks. We're not civil servants.'

'Fergal,' she said, 'why did you make a phone call to New York from my house?'

Fergal turned around slowly. 'Say what?'

'You phoned Manhattan. At around five am that Sunday morning. The day your mother died.'

He gave a relaxed grin. 'My God, you've caught me out. Technology? Isn't it great?' He reached into his pocket and pulled out a crumpled fiver. 'Sorry. I meant to pay you later on Sunday but, well, I had other things on my mind.'

'It's not the money.'

He pushed the brush into the paint and resumed his task. 'I know five am sounds an unreasonable time to call anyone,' he called over his shoulder, 'but remember, it was only midnight in New York. I had to make a quick business call, so I took the opportunity while you were in the bathroom. I didn't tell you at the time because...well, it's not exactly the most romantic thing to do during a night of passion, is it?'

She felt her face begin to redden. Trust O'Rourke to make a big issue of such a little thing.

He turned around to face her again. 'Are you serious about searching for Manus?'

She nodded, grateful for the change of subject. 'Yes. Why not? The police are doing nothing to find him. And if there's the slightest chance of proving your innocence, we'd be crazy not to take it.'

'Well, then, I'll have to come with you.' He loaded the brush again and described a giant spiral on the canvas. 'You'll need all the help you can get.'

Tara shook her head. 'You haven't been listening, Fergal. Having you with me wouldn't be a help. In fact, it would be a disadvantage.'

He bristled. 'You saying I'm useless?'

'I'm saying it wouldn't make sense. Think about it. Everywhere you go you're being followed by the police. If I'm going to find Manus I'll have to go into a lot of shady areas and talk to a lot of dubious people. That's fine – I've done that sort of thing before. But imagine how far we'd get with a squad car in tow.'

'Then we'll lose the squad car.' He stuffed the brush aggressively into the red paint.

'And that would play into their hands. Make you look even more guilty. For once in your life, Fergal, just stop for a minute and think things through.' She grabbed his paintbrushing hand and held it firmly before it could return to the canvas. 'Just think. What if we actually find Manus? Is he more likely to talk to me, or you?'

He glared at her until she released his wrist. Damn, she thought. Now her own hand was plastered in paint as well.

'It doesn't matter who he talks to,' he said, applying the brush to the canvas with a loud slap. 'If I find that he's guilty of murdering my mother, I'll kill him.'

'You don't mean that.'

He didn't reply.

'I can understand why you should feel that way,' she said softly. 'And that's one more reason why you shouldn't go.'

Fergal grunted and turned his back to her.

Tara found a sink in the corner of the outhouse and washed the red paint from her hands, trying to avoid associations with Shakespearean tragedies.

'I'm going, Fergal,' she said as she dried herself on a paint-spattered towel. 'And I'm going alone.'

He didn't turn around. Silently, she left the outhouse and walked through the darkened farmyard towards her waiting car.

Fergal didn't even notice that she'd gone. He carried on painting.

'Don't be stupid, Tara,' he said at last, when he'd become uncomfortable with the silence. 'You'll never find Manus by yourself. Where would you even begin to look?'

CHAPTER ELEVEN

MARBLE STATUES of gloomy-eyed saints stood guard over the bleak entrance of Inismaul Psychiatric Hospital. Inside, the hallway was dominated by an enormous Victorian painting of the Crucifixion – the type that depicts the torture and mutilation in gruesome detail. Above the door of the cafeteria, framed by sickly green plaster, another faded canvas portrayed the Martyrdom of St Stephen.

Tara stared around her in disbelief. If you weren't depressed and suicidal *before* you came here, she thought, you certainly would be as soon as you walked through the door.

'Can I help you?'

'Oh, pardon me.' Tara turned around to face the blue-rinsed receptionist. 'I have an appointment. With Dr Ian Westwood.'

The receptionist nodded. 'Be with you in a moment. Hello, Inismaul Hospital. Hold on, please. Hello, Inismaul Hospital. Hold on, please. Hello, Inismaul Hospital. Which ward is he in? Hold on and I'll check.'

It took a full five minutes before the constant flow of phone calls eased long enough for the receptionist to contact Dr Westwood. 'He's in Group,' she explained at last. 'He'll be with you in ten minutes. Would you like to wait in the restaurant?'

She motioned across the hall to the door marked 'Cafeteria'.

Tara thanked her and walked into a large open-plan room with a self-service counter at one end and a piano at the other. Patients in dressing-gowns and cardigans sat at melamine tables with their visitors. Other patients sat alone, mumbling quietly to themselves. At the far end of the room, an elderly woman with an acute curvature of the spine sat hunched at the piano stool. Her physical affliction placed her head below the level of the keyboard, but her hands reached up and played nonetheless. They danced across the keys with surprising agility. Tara recognised the second movement, the Romance, from Mozart's Twentieth Piano Concerto. From this combination of twisted bones and afflicted mind, warped wood and over-stretched metal, was emerging a clear beauty that transcended them all.

She ordered a coffee and sat down at a table near the door, hoping that she would be able to spot Dr Westwood when he arrived.

'Excuse me.'

She paused in the act of stirring her coffee. A tall young man dressed in a dark-brown bathrobe was hovering over her, shifting uneasily in his tartan slippers. He was about twenty-three, she estimated, with tousled black hair and eyes that were sleepy with sedative. They were focused somewhere behind her head.

'Hello.'

'I'm William.'

'Good morning, William.'

He looked around. 'Would you mind doing me a great service?' he asked in a soft voice. The accent was south-side Dublin. Tara guessed he was a university student.

She was about to say yes, but checked herself. 'It depends. What is it?'

'Would you post a letter for me?'

Her body, already tensed, relaxed a little. 'Of course I will. I'll do it just as soon as I leave the hospital.'

William edged back and forward restlessly. 'It's just...it's just that I'm not really supposed to be in here. I have to get word out to my friends.'

Tara smiled understandingly. 'Of course.'

He looked around again. 'Here,' he said, handing her an envelope from his pocket. She saw an address but no stamp.

'That's fine. I'll see to it.'

He kept hovering. His brow was knitted with concentration. A thought was trying to swim through the miasma of chemicals to the surface of his mind.

'It has no stamp.'

'That's okay. I'll put one on.'

He nodded. 'I'm not supposed to be here, you know. I just studied too hard.'

'I understand.'

Without another word, he shuffled away, slippers brushing along the ground as though he were afraid he might lose contact with the surface of the earth. How long had he spent in this limbo, she wondered? Would he remember any of it later? Or would it all seem like a hazy dream?

She stuffed the envelope into her jacket pocket.

'Poor William,' said a voice at the next table. She glanced over. An older man, late-thirties, spectacles, cardigan, cord trousers. He had sandy hair and sharp fox-like features. He spoke in a north Louth accent, fast and clipped, the words from the side of the mouth.

'Pardon?'

'Poor William. He thinks he doesn't belong in here. He's not the only one. Most of us think we don't belong in here.'

He flashed a set of white angular teeth. 'But William, he's been diagnosed schizophrenic. He's going to be here for a while. At least until the voices stop. At least until he stops throwing fits. It took four male nurses to hold him down last time.'

He snickered. Tara noticed that the words came out far too fast, like an audio tape on fast-forward. She remembered reading something about the manic stage of manic depression.

'He wants to get back to his studies. Big deal. I want to get back to my wife and kids. It's what I want more than anything. Things to get back to normal.'

He lit a low-tar cigarette with fast, lizard-like movements of his hands. He didn't offer her one, she noticed; presumably the custom was that you smoked your own.

'Funny how you never think of things as being normal, good.' The voice was increasing in speed, words spattering out like a machine-gun. 'You only think of things as normal, bad. Like "boring, boring, boring", like "nothing's happening, I'm bored". But it's only in here you realise that normal, good is pretty-damn good. Normal, good, like you're not sick and you have a job and you have a wife and kids and there's nothing wrong.'

He stared at her, as though waiting for a reply.

'Mmm,' she said.

'And then one day it all goes wrong, it all gets screwed up, and there's no warning, it just happens, and you don't have a job any more and you're in here and you'd give anything, anything, just to be back in your nice boring house with your wife and your kids. Your lovely, lovely kids.'

He fished in his trousers pocket and brought out a dog-eared colour photo. It showed two carrot-haired little girls, not particularly attractive, grinning at the camera from the doorway of a Wendy house.

'They're gorgeous.' Tara handed back the photo. She took a sip of her coffee and looked around for Dr Westwood, spending longer than necessary scanning the room. She didn't know why, but she wanted this conversation to stop.

'You visiting?'

He wouldn't give up.

'Yes.'

'Who?'

'Well...I'm looking for Manus Kennedy.'

He grunted nasally. 'You won't find him here. He's gone. Long time gone. Woah...round Christmas, maybe.'

'Did you know him?'

'Shared a room with him. On and off. Strange guy, if you don't mind me saying so. Didn't talk to me much.'

I'm not surprised, Tara thought.

'My name's Larry.' His hand shot out rapidly like an anteater's tongue.

'Tara.'

'You family?' he asked.

'No. A family friend.'

'Girlfriend?'

'No.'

'Cop?'

'No, not a cop.'

'The cops have been round asking about him, you know. His brother's been done for the Claremoon Harbour murder.'

'Yes. I'm a friend of his brother's.'

'Hold on a minute.' The darting green-brown eyes lit on her like restless wasps. 'Yes, I remember. You're the girl that was on the front page of the *Evening Report*!'

'We didn't want it that way. Excuse me.'

She got up to leave.

'If you're looking for Manus, I know where you'll find him.'

Tara stopped in her tracks.

'Least, I know who can tell you where to find him.'

Tara walked back slowly to his table. But at that moment, with the sort of precise ill-timing that happens only in matters of vital importance, a hand tapped on her shoulder.

'Ms Ross?'

She turned, almost in irritation, to find a tall, bearded man staring at her impatiently. He was wearing a battered grey suit. He looked hassled and overworked.

'I'm Dr Westwood. What can I do for you?'

She explained as concisely as she could.

'Mr Kennedy was discharged from here nearly six months ago. I've already explained all this to the police. This is really too much. Really.' His voice hovered just on the right side of high-pitched hysteria. 'I am trying to do

my job here, Ms Ross. I have patients waiting for me.
Patients who need help. They won't employ more staff.
They won't even replace the staff who leave. Those of us
who are left have to cope with it all.'

His eyes, red with lack of sleep, glared at her accusingly as though it was all her fault.

'I am genuinely sorry about your staffing problems,'
Tara said, meaning it, 'but it is vitally important that I
locate Mr Kennedy. Vitally important. If you have a forwarding address or even a phone number...'

'Good God!' He slapped his forehead in frustration.
'How many times do I have to explain? We don't know
where Manus is. We arranged a flat for him, a sheltered
accommodation, here in Inismaul, where we could monitor him for six months. That was the plan. That was our
intention. But there was no court order, no requirement
for him to stay there. We fulfilled our obligations.'

'That's not an issue,' Tara reassured him. 'All I want to
know is, when did he leave and where did he go?'

'He left the flat around Easter. He said he planned to
find work in the United States of America. He left no forwarding address. That is all I know, Ms Ross. Now, if I may
please get back to my patients...?'

Without waiting for her to reply, he turned on his heel
and walked off with giant, hurried strides.

And good-day to you, too, Tara thought. She felt sorry
for him. She wondered how much longer it would be
before the stress, the sleepless nights and the impossible
burden of responsibility forced him to the edge of nervous
breakdown. He must know the signs, the warnings. Yet he
would be driven on by a sense of duty. And then there
would be yet another good doctor less, another doctor who
wouldn't be replaced.

She sat down again, feeling angry that her two-hour
journey to this remote midlands hospital had been wasted.

She took a swallow of tepid coffee, feeling the eyes of
the red-haired man flickering across the side of her face

like rapid-flashing disco lights.

'I can tell you,' he said again, as though there had been no interruption. 'I can tell you who can tell you where Manus is.'

She turned to face him. 'Okay, who?'

He smiled and his arms leaped into fast bargaining gestures, like a market trader on speed. 'You do me a favour, I'll do you a favour. You scratch my back, I'll scratch yours.'

Oh no, thought Tara. Here we go. 'I don't know,' she said, shaking her head.

'I don't want much.'

She said nothing.

'I don't have any money. Nothing,' he said.

She waited.

'I don't want much. Just buy the kids a surprise present, that's all. A doll or something each. Barbie, Sindy, whatever, leave it up to you, you know best.'

She recalled the two little girls in the photo. They would be in that age-group.

'She doesn't bring them to visit me any more, you see? Just a couple of dolls, that's all. Wrap them up in nice paper, keep them separate, one present each, and just send them to my home address and mark it "Love from daddy".'

She looked at his face. His fast-talking street-trader's expression had been replaced by one of near-desperation. How long had it been since he'd had a visit from his wife and children, she wondered? What had happened to make them abandon him so completely?

She tumbled the ethical dilemma over and over in her mind. For the life of her, she couldn't see what harm it could do. She was only doing what he himself would do if he had the money.

'Okay,' she said at last. 'I'll do it.'

'Good, good. Great.' He was back on turbo-drive again. He scribbled on a piece of paper and handed it to her.

'Here's my address.'

A house in one of the giant Dublin suburbs. She'd been in the estate many times. It was a soulless place, nothing to alleviate the acres and acres of bleak grey concrete.

'Now,' he said, 'you have to come with me. Don't say anything. I'll do all the talking. Okay? I'll talk, you just stick with me. Okay? Right?'

'Where are we going?'

'St Sebastian's Ward. It's the secure unit.'

He led her out through an unmarked side door and up a labyrinthine staircase which was marked at several stages 'Strictly No Admittance To Public'.

The crumbling green plaster was in even worse condition than in the rest of the building and the naked stairboards, which hadn't seen varnish or stain for decades, were badly affected by woodworm. They passed several doorways through which Tara could hear the sounds of sobbing, unnaturally animated laughter, and the muted music of a TV set.

'This gets you right past security,' said Larry, darting up the stairs like some nervous rodent. 'You can get up this way, but you can't get down. Better security on the way out.'

Somewhere around the third floor, he left the stairwell and led her down a long corridor. At the end stood a modern glass-and-metal fire door. Larry paused for a while, peering through the glass to ensure that no one was on the other side, then pressed down the metal bar to open the door.

'Public area again,' he explained. 'You're a visitor. By this stage you've already gone through reception and security.'

He closed the fire door carefully behind him. It wouldn't open again without a key. The key was in a glass case with an alarm fitted to it.

Larry led her up to a desk beside another door marked ST SEBASTIAN. A large male nurse was trying to cope with three things simultaneously: an inquiry from a visitor, a constantly ringing telephone, and a complex-looking log which appeared to monitor the dispensing of medicine.

'She's a visitor. Visitor for Paul,' said Larry, making rapid gestures at Tara.

'Yes, okay. Just knock on the door when you want to come out.'

The door leading to the secure unit was made of reinforced glass. A simple catch opened it from the outside. There was no similar catch inside. The lock closed behind them with a solid clunk of steel on steel.

They walked into a large communal-activity room with well-worn brown leather seating ranged around the edges. In the middle were other leather chairs and a three-seater sofa. High on the wall, a battered television set was showing a daytime chat show.

In the room there must have been around twenty people, Tara estimated, with others lounging or sleeping in bedrooms nearby. Many of the patients in the TV room weren't using the seats at all. They were sprawled on the floor, seated or lying, with vacant expressions on their faces.

Some of them were arguing vehemently, but their voices were directed at no one in particular. An overweight woman in her forties was explaining, at the top of her voice, intimate details about her sex life. In another corner, a pretty teenage girl, blonde and painfully thin, wept uncontrollably.

'Whoops, look out, look out,' warned Larry.

A woman was bearing down on them. She was wearing a grey tracksuit and she was walking fast towards Tara with a thunderous expression on her face. Tara tensed for a second until she realised that the woman was not looking at her, but through her. She moved out of the way and the woman walked past, speed-walking around and around the perimeter of the room.

'This way,' said Larry. He led her into one of the

bedrooms. It contained four neat beds, each with its own steel locker. Through a steel-mesh grille on the window she could see the grey perimeter wall of the hospital and, above it, the flat brown and green boglands that stretched for miles around.

'Paul,' prattled Larry, full of nervous energy, 'this is Tara. She's looking for Manus Kennedy. You remember Manus, you were his mate, the two of you talked a lot, didn't you? I said that if anyone knew where Manus was, you would. Am I right?'

'Shut up, Larry.'

The figure lying on the bed was tall, aged about twenty-five, with close-cropped hair dyed cherry red in a neo-punk style. Thin, fair eyebrows overlined his staring pale eyes. He looked ill at ease in his brown bathrobe and striped flannelette pyjamas. Tara guessed that his normal garb would be a shiny shell-tracksuit and Nike trainers.

But the clothes weren't important. If Tara had been the manageress of a pub or a nightclub, she would have turned him away from her door, not because of his clothes but because of his eyes. This man was trouble. 'You don't look at their clothes or their size – you look at their eyes,' her friend Ciarán, the security guard, had advised her once. 'The secret is not to invite trouble in. Then you won't have to put it out.'

Tara walked over to the bed. 'Hi. I'm Tara. I hope you can help me.'

'Depends. If you're a banner, you can piss off.'

He was using the old-fashioned term for a woman police officer, a Bean Garda. The title had long since been dropped for reasons of gender equality, but it lived on in the streets of Dublin.

'No, I'm not police. I'm a family friend.'

'Right.'

He pronounced it 'roi'. Inner-city Dublin.

Paul stared at her suspiciously. 'Orange?'

'No thanks.'

He yawned and helped himself to a mandarin from a bowl on top of his locker. 'Manus was a mate of mine, okay. So what?'

He stuffed the peeled mandarin, whole, into his mouth. Tara noted the use of the past tense.

'When he got out of this place, I got out at the same time, roi'? We shared the sheltered flat here in town, roi'?' The words were mumbled through a churning mass of orange pulp.

'And then Manus left to go to America.'

Paul shook his head. 'No. That's what he told everyone he was doing, roi'? He wanted to get them all off his back. Manus couldn't afford to go to bleedin' Borrisokane, never mind Boston.'

Tara felt her pulse quicken. 'So, where did he go?'

'We both left this kip together. We squatted in a gaff in Bernietown.'

Bernietown. Shorthand for Bernadette Towers, a low-rise flats complex in the south inner city of Dublin. It was an area of high unemployment and social deprivation of near-Third World standards; its name had become a byword for violent crime and drug dealing.

'And where did he go from there?'

Paul was peeling another mandarin. 'Nowhere. The bastard's still there. And he can rot in that kip for the rest of his life, far as I care.'

'So you're not exactly mates, any more?' Tara had to tread carefully.

Paul spat out a stream of invective confirming her conclusion.

'If you're planning to bust him, go ahead and tell him I sent you,' he said. 'Whatever you do to that little shit, it wouldn't be nothin' compared to what I'd do to him. If I could get my hands on him.'

'Why should I want to bust him?'

Paul shrugged. He yawned again. Either the conversation was making him very bored indeed, or his medication was kicking in.

'Were you dealing drugs there?'

'Nothing to say.'

The stock response of the career criminal to any police question.

'Where was Manus living in Bernietown?' she persisted. 'Which address?'

'Nothing to say.'

He turned on his side, away from her, and put on the headphones of his walkman. The interview was obviously over.

'And if you're gonna nail him, remember to tell him I sent you,' he shouted after her as she left. 'That's Paul Lawless. L-a-w-l-e-s-s. Roi'?'

'Thanks. Goodbye.'

'Recognise the name? Tara? Do you recognise him?' Larry was still on a manic high as they walked back down the corridor.

Tara was only half-listening to him as she tried to assess this dramatic new information. 'I don't think so,' she said vaguely, her thoughts elsewhere.

'You know. You know. The guy who was on the front page of all the papers last month.'

Tara stopped in mid-stride. It was as though someone had socked her, hard, in the solar plexus. She recognised him now, all right. The grainy black-and-white newspaper photos of a young man, anorak raised over his head, being led from a courthouse after having been charged with a gruesome series of attacks on elderly women living alone in rural areas.

'That was Paul Lawless?' She felt sick at the thought that she'd been alone in a room with a man capable of inflicting such horrors upon other human beings.

Larry was pleased at her reaction. 'Yes. Yes. That was him. That was him, all right. The same man. Nice fella, Paul. But you wouldn't want to take him home to meet your granny. What do you think, Tara? What do you think?'

She tried to filter out his non-stop monologue and concentrate. What had the detective said?

We haven't the slightest shred of evidence that Manus was even in the country...

Now all that had changed. The evidence she needed hung tantalisingly within her reach.

The male nurse at the entrance to the door of St Sebastian's secure unit hardly glanced up as they knocked on the glass door.

He reached under his desk. A buzzer sounded, an electronic lock clicked open, and they were back in the main body of the hospital.

Down the public stairway, they walked unchallenged past a reception desk where all visitors to the secure unit were vetted on the way up. Larry was nudging her and smiling smugly.

'Now,' he said as they reached the bottom floor, 'I've got to go. People to see, things to do.' His eyes shone with an unnaturally bright gleam. 'You won't forget your side of the bargain?'

He looked at her eagerly, like a puppy.

'I won't forget,' Tara promised.

'Two dolls. Barbie, Sindy. With love from daddy. Separately wrapped.'

'Got it.'

'Appreciate.' He smiled again, touched her arm in farewell, and walked off with a jerky, over-fast gait. He looked like a dancer caught in a nightclub strobe-light.

Tara stood still for a minute, taking deep breaths and trying to disentangle him from her nerves.

It had started raining, hard. It was thundering on the roof and a gully outside was choking with water.

She'd have to drive to the nearest shopping centre and get the dolls, before she forgot. A Barbie and a Sindy, he'd said. She glanced at the sheet of paper on which he'd written his address and the names of the little girls. Cathy and Julie. He didn't say which doll was for which. She supposed it didn't matter.

She began walking down the corridor towards the main exit, trying to understand why something was making her feel uneasy.

What harm could there be in sending dolls to two little children?

Why send them? Perhaps she should deliver them personally.

She tried to make her mind function amid the thunder of the rain on the roof.

If only there were someone she could ask, someone who could give her advice. It certainly wouldn't be Dr Westwood.

Come on, Tara. You're overreacting. Let's get out of here, buy the dolls, and get it over with.

No, hold on a minute. Think...

At that moment she passed the hospital chapel. The door was open. Inside a tall figure in black was rearranging chairs in preparation for evening Mass.

Before she knew it, she was standing behind him. 'Father...?'

'Yes. What is it?' His eyes were tired but friendly.

She introduced herself. 'I just wanted to ask your advice.'

'Of course. Sit down.'

'It's silly. I probably shouldn't be taking up your time.'

'Sit down.'

She said nothing about her visit to Paul Lawless in the secure unit, but she told him of her promise to send the two dolls to Larry's daughters. 'I just wanted to get a second opinion, Father. It's not against the rules, is it? There couldn't be any harm in doing it, could there? It would keep him happy. Keep them happy. Wouldn't it?'

She realised, with irritation, that she had uncon-sciously adopted Larry's turbocharged speech patterns.

'Which patient, did you say?'

She described him.

He sat down heavily. 'Ms Ross...may I call you Tara? Okay. Let me tell you about Larry. He was a bright kid. He started work at fifteen, sweeping floors in a big foreign-owned factory. By last year he was a foreman. He was earning a good wage and a fortune in overtime. He worked all the hours that God sent to buy his family a decent life-style.'

He gazed over at the flickering electric candles by the altar, as though searching for the answer to some deep and fundamental question.

'Then they took a decision in Chicago or Düsseldorf, God knows where, that the factory had to close. It was one of their most profitable factories, but it had to close because the men in the suits, the men who balanced the books at headquarters, said it had to close.

'Suddenly Larry found himself sitting at home all day, staring at the walls of his kitchen and wondering what had gone wrong. He was only thirty-eight, but he was already too old to get another job and he was up to his neck in debt.'

Tara had to fight a sudden and irrational urge to stand up and run away. She didn't want to hear the end of this story.

'So one afternoon, when his wife was out at the shops, Larry wrote a suicide note,' the priest continued calmly. 'Then he hugged his two little daughters and told them a bedtime story. He brought out a bottle of sleeping tablets and said they were special sweeties and they all had to share them because the world was too bad to live in any more.

'The doctors pumped out his stomach. He survived. The two little girls died.'

He gave a weary shrug. 'Larry is aware that they're dead, but his mind can't cope with it. That's one of the reasons why he's here. He has blocked the whole episode out of his consciousness. As far as he's concerned, the two girls are still waiting for their father to get better and come home.'

Tara felt nauseous. She said nothing.

'His wife is still living at that address. If you had sent those parcels, she would have opened them.'

He rose and patted her shoulder kindly.

'The way you're feeling now,' he said, 'you couldn't be in a better place.'

He walked off quietly, leaving her sitting alone in the false flicker of synthetic candlelight.

Twenty minutes later, Tara walked out past the reception desk towards the main door.

The weather was still filthy, she noticed. And she had a long drive ahead of her...

'Excuse me.'

She stopped. A tall figure was standing in her path, blocking her way.

'I'm William,' he said. 'I wonder if you could do me a great service and post this letter.'

She nodded, took the letter, and hurried past him.

'I'm afraid it has no stamp.'

'That's okay. I'll buy one.'

She didn't stop hurrying until she reached her car. Then she brought out the letter she'd taken from him earlier.

They were exactly the same. The envelopes were unsealed. They were obviously empty. And they were both addressed to William himself, care of Inismaul Mental Hospital.

Tara cranked the engine. Thank goodness, it started despite the rain. Then she sat for a long while, settling her nerves, thinking about her limited options.

Back to Claremoon Harbour, to admit defeat in her search for Manus Kennedy? Or onwards to Dublin, to hunt for a violent psycho in the grim concrete jungle of Bernadette Towers?

There really wasn't a choice.

She turned her wheels towards the capital.

CHAPTER TWELVE

DRESSED IN an old black leather jacket and faded blue jeans, Tara stood on the Dublin quays and looked down the River Liffey towards the sea. It was another cold summer morning, with the fine rain drifting almost horizontally along the river from the flatlands to the west.

Her bones ached. She had spent an uncomfortable night sleeping on a lumpy sofabed in the living-room of Jean Murphy's riverside flat. Jean was a former colleague who had reduced herself to near-poverty by buying a prime waterfront apartment at a price which, only a few years beforehand, would have purchased a five-bedroom mansion in the stockbroker belt. She was delighted to have got it so cheaply. Had she waited another six months, she assured Tara, its price would have been fifty per cent higher. Now she had a thirty-year mortgage, an overdraft, no social life and a smile of complacency that was hard to take.

Tara had been grateful for Jean's offer of accommodation – it saved her a fortune in hotel charges – but it had come at a price. Several of her former colleagues had joined them for a bottle of wine and a pizza. They'd all sympathised with her current predicament, but the conversation had rapidly and tactfully switched to the Dublin property boom. They had all made tens of thousands of pounds in paper profits, and they pointed out, none too subtly, that Tara would have done the same had she stayed in the capital instead of getting out at exactly the wrong time and decamping to the sticks.

And, naturally, there had been the pointed references to her former boyfriend, Chris Calder: his recent move to a £750,000 Georgian home in Ranelagh, his legal triumphs, his elevation by a magazine to the status of

Ireland's Most Eligible Bachelor.

Tara sighed and checked her watch. Nine-thirty am Good. She was exactly on time for her appointment at the Four Courts.

She was about to cross the quays to the stately eighteenth-century building when she heard a peep from a motor horn. Not a blast. Just a tiny, polite beep.

She turned around, saw his face, and experienced that sudden lurch that comes when you're transported back to an earlier incarnation, to a time when a face you've almost forgotten was the most important thing in your world. He was sitting there in his blue Daimler, waving at her, his face lit up by that famous Chris Calder smile. It was as though nothing had changed in two years, as though they'd just met as usual for lunch in La Stampa or the Ayumi-Ya and an afternoon of shopping in Grafton Street.

He beckoned her over and opened the passenger door. The inside of the Daimler smelled of old leather, fine tailoring and just the slightest hint of his Armani aftershave. Chris Calder had the sort of face that always looked freshly-shaven.

'Tara.' He smiled again as he leaned over and kissed her on the cheek. 'How have you been?'

'Fine, Chris. I was just on my way to the Law Library to see you.'

He nodded. The motion disturbed his perfectly-coiffed hair, and he automatically raised a hand to pat it back into place. She noticed that the hands were as soft and white as a surgeon's and his fingernails, as always, were precisely manicured.

'Yes, the clerk told me he'd made an appointment for you. I was just on my way in, too.' He grinned broadly, as though their chance meeting was the highlight of his morning. 'But, hey, let's just sit and chew the fat a moment first. What have you been up to?'

'Oh, lots.' She tried to sound upbeat. 'I run my own Internet newspaper in County Clare, and it's a big success and it's all...very exciting.'

She realised he wasn't really paying attention. He was looking into her eyes and smiling nostalgically. 'How long's it been, Tara?'

She looked uncomfortable. 'Since when?'

'Since we last saw each other, of course. What do you think I meant?'

'Oh, I don't know. Two years, maybe.'

Two years, two months, and fifteen days, to be exact.

'My, my, my. Is it really that long? Still, at least we can look back and laugh about it all now.'

'Yes.' Tara didn't laugh.

She stared out of the rain-streaked car window, trying not to think of the torturous days and nights that followed their break-up. The endless zombie-like days and the tear-stained nights, dragging on like a blunt execution before she finally took the decision to leave Dublin behind and return to Claremoon Harbour.

Breaking up with Chris Calder had been the hardest decision she'd ever made. And yet she'd never regretted it. True, Calder was all the things her friends said he was – rich, intelligent, good looking, the rising star of the King's Inns. But he was a closet dictator, a control freak who insisted on telling her what to do, what to say, what to wear, which of her friends should be discouraged because they were bad for her image (Melanie among them, apparently) and which social acquaintances should be cravenly cultivated. The problem reached crisis point when he made a surprise marriage proposal, ostentatiously and in public. In the course of a few seconds, she looked at the prospect of living her entire life that way, and decided she couldn't do it. Everyone had thought she was crazy when she turned him down.

'Anyway.' Chris glanced pointedly at his classic 1960s Rolex. 'You told my clerk you had a question for me and it wouldn't take much time. I'd planned to discuss it with you over coffee, but I'm running behind schedule. Perhaps we could just talk about it here and now.'

'Fine by me.' Tara forced herself to collect her thoughts and concentrate on her present task. 'I've heard that you'll be appearing for CAB in a case against the Viney family in Limerick. The drug dealers.'

Calder nodded. CAB – insiders pronounced it as in the word taxicab – was shorthand for the Criminal Assets Bureau, an organisation formed specifically to separate crooks from their ill-gotten gains. It had successfully seized the assets of several dubious characters who had made millions with no visible means of support other than the dole.

'Yes, that's true, but the case won't come up until September,' he said, sounding slightly relieved that the topic wasn't anything to do with their former relationship. 'Why do you ask?'

'I need information.'

He frowned. 'Is this for publication, Tara? Because it's highly confidential.'

'No. Purely background. I wouldn't ask if it wasn't important.'

'Well, in that case...' He whipped out a pocket organiser and a minuscule cellphone. 'Infrared connection,' he explained as he dialled a number. 'Links me up with the computer network in the office.'

A few keystrokes later, a lengthy document began scrolling across the tiny screen.

'These are the affidavits we'll be presenting to the High Court when we move to seize the Viney family assets,' Calder said. 'There are one hundred and seventy pages of them.'

'Can I have a copy?'

'Nice try, Tara. No.' He grinned to show it wasn't personal. 'What do you need? I mean, specifically? Give me a clue and I'll do a Find.'

Tara peered across at the diminutive screen. 'I want to find out if the name Manus Kennedy crops up anywhere in the Vineys' business dealings.'

He typed in the surname. 'No, I'm afraid not. No Kennedys at all.'

Tara looked out the passenger window, trying to hide her disappointment. 'Would you expect his name to appear there?' she asked at last. 'I mean, if he was mixed up with them in any way?'

'No doubt about it. This investigation is so thorough, it almost lists the people who gave the Vineys their Communion money.' He glanced at her. 'Is that it, Tara? Because...'

'One more quick search, Chris.'

He checked his Rolex again. 'Okay, shoot. What is it?'

'Villiers. Godfrey Villiers.'

He keyed in the name. 'All right. This time you're in luck.' He scrolled down through the text and whistled softly. 'Which is more than I can say for Mr Villiers. CAB are applying to have his gallery closed down. They say it exists purely for the purpose of laundering drug cash.' Calder squinted as he tried to decipher the next paragraph. 'Part of their evidence against him is that he's been seen associating with known drug dealers, to wit Christy Geaney and Paul Lawless, last known address Block C, Bernadette Towers. It's Game Over for Godfrey Villiers, I'm afraid. Serves him right for having a name like that.'

Tara sat bolt upright. 'What was that name again?'

'Christy Geaney.'

'No, the other one.'

'Paul Lawless. Mind you' – he typed a quick memo – 'that address is outdated. I think the lovable Mr Lawless is under assessment in a psychiatric hospital at the moment.'

'I know. I've just been talking to him.' Tara felt her heartbeat quicken as she took out her notebook. 'Give me that address.'

He jotted it down on a page from his Filofax, ripped it out and handed it to her. 'Remember that's in Block C, the very worst part of Bernietown. Don't even think of going there unless you've got an army escort. Preferably in a Sherman tank.' He rapidly cut the phone connection before Tara could ask for another favour. 'Is that it?' he asked.

'That's it, Chris. Thanks. I owe you one.'

'Yes. One thousand guineas. My usual fee.' He kept a straight face, then laughed as her face fell. 'Only joking.'

'That's a relief.'

'It's just one thousand euros.'

She returned his smile and felt an old familiar stirring. Somewhere deep inside, she couldn't help wondering what would have happened if she'd swallowed her pride, had a personality lobotomy and become a Stepford Wife. Maybe it wouldn't have been so bad after all. Maybe he would have changed. Maybe he would have become less dictatorial, less demanding...

'Well, I'd better go.' He hoisted his briefcase on to his knee. 'Just one thing, Tara.'

'What's that, Chris?' Tara was used to Chris's just-one-things. It was his way of introducing the most important topic on his mind.

'I have a confession to make. I didn't just happen to meet you outside the building. I was waiting for you.'

'But why?'

'Because I didn't want you to be seen inside my office. Tongues would start wagging. Especially after that *Evening Report!* article.' His voice became lower and more intense, inviting her sympathy and understanding. 'You see, I'm about to get a major role in the new Tribunal on the Family, and I just can't risk any damage to my reputation. I'll always be here for you, Tara, if you need help, but for old times' sake, please don't tell anyone you know me. Let our past stay in the past.'

Tara nodded silently.

'That doesn't mean we can't see each other from time to time,' said Chris in a different tone. 'It just means we'd have to be discreet. You could come to my London apartment, for instance, or I could visit you when I'm in County Clare.'

'You mean, you'd like the occasional fling? As long as you're not seen with me in public?'

'That's it.' He was glad she understood.

'I don't think so. Goodbye, Chris.'

She opened the car door and got out. He remained seated, obviously intending to wait until she'd got well clear of the area before daring to emerge.

'Oh, and Tara!' he called softly though his open window as she walked away.

She paused without turning around. 'Yes?'

'Do something about that hairstyle. It doesn't suit you at all.'

CHAPTER THIRTEEN

AT EXACTLY ten-thirty am, Tara drove her Fiat across Capel Street Bridge towards the south city. Timing was an important consideration if you planned to visit Bernadette Towers. Midmorning was best: the young kids would be out and about, but older troublemakers would still be asleep after a late night of beer and *MTV* and there was less chance of getting hassled, robbed or mugged.

But of course, this was just a general rule. It didn't take into account the hungry and desperate junkies, who didn't live by everyone else's time. They obeyed only their inner clock of dark cravings and compulsions. Hours didn't matter to them. And nobody, old or young, male or female, able-bodied or infirm, had safe passage when their irresistible demons demanded to be fed.

Out past the Guinness brewery and Heuston Station. Past the red-brick inner-city suburbs. Two mangy horses chomped at the heavily-littered grass as she swung into the road that led to Bernietown.

A few hundred yards of glass-strewn concrete and she was there. It was just as she remembered it from previous visits. Three grey concrete squares, Blocks A to C, each containing three storeys of flats looking down on a windy central quadrangle that was grandly known as a 'piazza'. It looked more like a prison yard.

To her left were a grimy general store, a fruit-and-veg shop, and a launderette. Back and forth between shop and flats trailed an ant-like procession of women with buggies. Many of them were mere teenagers – pale young girls with old, world-weary faces. All too often, the swelling under their cheap anoraks revealed a second or even a third child on the way. Some of them would be grandmothers by their early thirties.

Tara deliberately bypassed Block C and drove into the central square of Block B. As she got out of her car, she heard the sound of excited screaming above and to her left. She swung around. High up on the third storey, a group of young teenage kids were hanging out of a window. Suspended beneath them, clutching on to their outstretched arms and swinging wildly from side to side, was a red-haired boy who couldn't have been more than twelve years old. Ten or fifteen feet beneath him was a flat concrete roof. He was the one who was screaming, half in excitement and half in terror. The game seemed to be one of endurance. At last his hands lost their strength and he tumbled in freefall. His mates cheered. He landed awkwardly, with a solid crump of flesh on unyielding stone. It must have hurt like hell. He didn't show it. He scrambled to his feet and gave them a sexual gesture of defiance and contempt.

'Howaya.'

A voice from behind her.

Tara was startled. She hadn't noticed the half-dozen youngsters who'd emerged from the concrete caverns and surrounded her car. They were touching it curiously.

She nodded a curt greeting. 'Do you know where Barney Gould lives?'

She knew perfectly well where Barney Gould lived. He was a community leader and a former contact, and she'd been to his flat often enough. But she wanted them to know she was a friend of Barney. It meant a safe-pass for herself and her car.

The oldest boy, dirty fair hair tightly shaved, face covered with disfiguring acne, smirked suggestively. 'What's it worth?'

'Why don't we ask Barney that? I'm a good friend of his.'

'Top storey. Red door.'

One of the younger kids began picking a bit of rusted metal off the wing of the Fiat. Another, possibly his older brother, cuffed him over the back of the head.

The mere mention of Barney's name had already saved her a considerable amount of hassle. Barney was a former Olympic coach whose boxing club played a major role in preventing young kids of Bernietown from falling victim to the drug dealers. Some of the kids worshipped him, others hated him. But everyone treated him with respect.

'Up here? Thanks.'

The oldest boy leered. She could imagine the grins and the gestures directed at her back as she walked towards the stairwell. She didn't care. At least they wouldn't touch her. Or her car.

The concrete stairwell smelled exactly as public-authority stairwells smell all over the world, from Bernie-town to Birmingham, from Belfast to the Bronx. Crude graffiti on the walls, empty beer cans on the stairs, puddles in the corners. Side-stepping the obstacles carefully, she made her way to the top and rang the bell on the red door.

She waited for a few moments and then knocked as well, feeling a mounting sense of panic as the seconds ticked away in silence. No answer.

Barney wasn't at home.

She was on her own.

She looked over the concrete balcony towards Block C. It was hundreds of yards away, on the other side of a litter-strewn wasteland, but she could read the graffiti from here. The last time she'd been to that block, she'd been in the company of a burly cop and a six-foot camera-man, and it had still scared the hell out of her.

Walking from Block B to Block C was like moving into a lower circle of hell. While Block B had its share of prob-lems, the majority of people who lived there were decent folk – couples, families, single parents, all trying to make the best of what they had. Some of them loved living in Bernietown and wouldn't move away if you paid them to. Block C, on the other hand, was where nobody in his right mind wanted to live. It was where the authorities put their problem tenants – deserted mothers with uncontrollable teenage sons, young single men with violent tendencies, junkies and dealers, discharged mental patients. It wasn't meant to be that way. But like water finding its own level, that's how it had ended up.

Picking her way through the discarded mattresses and burned-out cars to Block C, she passed gangs of screaming kids, groups of wary-eyed women and – in the first shadowy corridor – a sullen coven of strung-out junkies. To her immense relief, she found the flat she was looking for on ground level. There would be no need to use the stairwell. She hated to think what unpleasant surprises it would hold at each turn of the steps.

The flat had been deserted for some time. The entrance was sealed with a metal door, and someone had sprayed the words 'Junky scum out' on the rough plywood that boarded up the windows.

A small hole had been punched through the ply. Peering through, she could make out the outline of what had once been a living room. A couple of torn mattresses on the floor. An opened bottle of what had once been milk. The remains of a loaf. A few newspapers. On one mattress, a well-used syringe and a leather belt. Some scraps of burned kitchen-foil. In the far corner, something stirred. It was a large, ugly rat.

'It's empty. There's nobody livin' there any more.'

She looked around to see an emaciated teenager in a Metallica T-shirt and skin-tight, heavily kneebagged jeans. She recognised him as one member of the group of desperate junkies who'd been hanging around the end of the concrete corridor. He was eyeing her up and down, wondering whether she was worth the trouble of mugging.

'Yes, I know that.' She glanced up and down the corridor, pretending to look for someone. 'See Barney Gould around? I'm due to meet him at eleven.'

The teenager looked away in obvious disappointment.

If she was a friend of Barney's, she wasn't a target any more.

'Know who lived there?' She gestured to the deserted flat.

'Squatters. Four or five fellas. They've moved out. Dunno where to.'

'Were they dealing?'

'Coupla them were. Others were just usin', right? Somathem weren't doin' anything, just hangin' out. Just goofin' around. Anyway, they're all gone now.' He looked at her in a new light. 'You lookin' to score somethin'?'

She didn't answer. 'Who're you waiting on?' she asked. 'Deals on Wheels?'

Deals on Wheels was the local nickname of Dave Feskin, a disabled drug peddler who'd operated a thriving business from his wheelchair. He was just one of a long line of dealers who'd used unorthodox means of transport around Bernietown. Another had ridden horseback on a mangy pony. And a third had done his deals on an eighteen-speed mountain bike – the ultimate drug peddler.

'Deals on Wheels?' The teenager laughed derisively. 'No, he's long gone.'

'Manus Kennedy?' Tara took a shot in the dark.

Four other junkies sidled up and formed a menacing circle around her.

The teenager in the Metallica T-shirt looked puzzled. 'Manus Kennedy? Dunno him.'

Tara described Manus as accurately as she could. 'He would have had a west of Ireland accent. County Clare. A bit like mine.'

To her amazement, all five teenagers burst out laughing.

'You mean Mano,' said the first junkie. 'Mano the man.'

'You know him?'

'Everyone knew Mano. He came here a coupla months ago. There was himself, a fella called Paul – he was one sick bastard – and a coupla others. One of them got the flat from the Corpo after the last crowd were driven out. There was a lot of drug dealin', but I don't think Mano was involved. He was a strange sorta fella. He just kept to himself, didn't talk much.' He kicked an empty beer can. 'Anyway, after a while Paul got done for robbin'. Then the vigos forced the rest of them out.'

Tara took a deep breath. 'Do you know where he's gone?'

'Who?'

She'd lost his attention. His junkie eyes were wandering all over the flats complex, looking for some sort of chemical salvation.

Only one member of the group, a skinny youth in an old denim jacket, kept his eyes fixed on her.

Tara tried to hide her frustration. 'Mano. The fella from Clare.'

'Already told ya. Dunno.'

He began scratching himself restlessly. 'I'm goin' over to Block A,' he said to his mates. 'See if there's anythin' doin' over there.' He turned to the skinny teenager in the denim jacket, who was still staring at Tara. 'Forget it,' he said, reading his thoughts. 'She's a friend of Barney's.'

He turned his back on them and walked off. After a moment of uncertainty, the others followed.

Tara heaved a deep sigh of relief and made her escape to Block B. She found her car undamaged, although two of the young lads were contentedly using it as a climbing frame.

Shifting them unceremoniously from the roof, she drove out past the shopping centre and towards the main road. But just around the corner, she saw a figure standing in the road trying to flag her down.

Her first instinct was to step on the accelerator. But then she recognised him as one of the group of drug users – the skinny one who'd kept staring at her.

Tara made sure both her doors were locked and pulled

up at the kerb. She wound down her driver's side window, but only by an inch.

'Well?' She kept her voice very neutral. She kept the car in gear and her foot on the clutch.

'The new address. What's it worth to ya?'

He looked jumpy, agitated, close to desperation. He kept looking at a nearby bus stop and then looking down the road for a bus. She could see clearly into his mind, as easily as you could see a mannequin through a shop window. Get a few quid, get the bus into town, he was thinking. Score some gear.

'Twenty quid. But be careful – if you sell me a fairy tale, you'll have Barney to deal with.'

'It's the truth. Honest.'

Tara took a twenty-pound note from her jeans pocket and unfolded it. 'Go.'

'Some of them moved to Ballymahon, but I don't know if Mano went with them. One of the high-rise flats. It was used for dealin' gear. It still is.'

'Which flat?'

He shook his head. She shrugged and put the note back into her jeans. Then she revved up her engine. In her rear-view mirror, she noticed a bus a few hundred yards away.

He saw it too, and quickly made up his mind. 'Christy Geaney's flat. Fifth floor, Joy McCracken Tower.'

He grabbed the outstretched note and ran off. He was afraid of retribution from the dealers. But his blood was crying out for chemicals and anyway, within half an hour or so, he would be past caring.

'I see seven towers, but I only see one way out.' The line from the U2 song 'Running To Stand Still' kept orbiting around Tara's head as her car clattered its way towards Ballymahon Flats.

Heroin. That had been the only way out for the tragic

character in the anti-drug song. And the seven towers immortalised in the lyrics were the seven soaring tower-block flats that loomed on the fuggy northside horizon.

Ballymahon had been Dublin's only experiment with the high-rise flats concept. It had never been repeated, for reasons which were obvious to everyone, but especially obvious to the people who were forced to live there. For years the Corporation had been trying to keep the experiment alive, against all doctors' advice. Now, at last, the plug was to be pulled on the life-support machine. Bally-mahon Flats were to be demolished, and few people were sorry.

Tara parked outside the shops, a spot where her car would be marginally less vulnerable to vandals. She bought a newspaper, then braved the lashing rain to walk across the patchy green towards Joy McCracken Flats.

OUT OF ORDER said the sign beside the dilapidated lift. Surprise, surprise. Tara had never actually seen it working. People had lived there for years and never seen it working. Perhaps it never had.

Now, there was nothing for it but to do what everybody in Joy McCracken Tower had been doing for a long time – put one foot in front of the other and climb all those stairs.

First flight of steps. Second flight. Third. Tara was reasonably fit, but already she was struggling and getting short of breath. Ahead of her, a young woman was trying to negotiate the steep stairs with a baby-carriage and several precarious-looking plastic bags bulging with shopping.

'Excuse me.'

'Go on ahead, love. I'm not goin' anywhere fast.'

'Want a hand?'

'Oh, that would be great.'

Tara took one end of the buggy and, together, they flew up the next two flights.

'You're a pet. Thanks, love.'

'No problem.'

'Know where you're goin' okay, love? You're not from

round here, are you? You sound west of Ireland.'

'Yes. I'm from Clare.'

'My uncle's from Lisdoonvarna.'

'I'm from Claremoon Harbour. Not too far away.' Tara took a crumpled piece of paper from her pocket. 'I'm looking for Christy Geaney's flat.'

'Jaysus, Mary and Joseph. You sure you want to go there?' The woman stared at her as though she were mad.

'Yes. I'm looking for a Manus Kennedy. Mano for short. Do you know him?'

'Listen, love, I don't know any of those hoors in that flat and I don't want to. And if you listen to my advice, you'll stay clear of it too. They're bad news. You goin' there by yourself?'

'I have to.'

The woman's face turned hard. 'I see. That's the way it is, is it?' She gave terse directions to the flat. 'It's none of my business if you want to wreck your life, love, but be careful. If the police don't get you, the vigos will.'

'It's not like that. Goodbye.'

'G'luck.'

G'luck. The curt, one-syllable Dublinism that sounded like a Klingon oath and served a dual purpose as a blessing or a malediction. It could mean goodbye. It could be used ironically to dismiss someone who had done you wrong. It could mean 'get out of my life for ever'. It could mean simply good luck.

And she would need it.

Half of the door numbers had been vandalised. It was only by painful mathematical deduction that she identified the flat she sought.

It was located right at the end of a dark corridor (the lights had all been smashed, probably years ago) and every square inch of its outside walls was covered in hate graffiti. 'Death dealers must go'. 'Junkie filth.' 'No Aids scum here' and 'Pushers out, ri'.

As in Bernietown, the front door had been reinforced

with sheet metal, probably because it had been smashed in so many times. Tara took a deep breath and knocked. Loudly, decisively. Deep down inside, she was hoping that there would be no reply.

But within seconds, she heard the sound of two metal bolts clunking back. The door opened, but only by six inches. She saw that it was restrained by a heavy-link security chain. Within the narrow band of vision, she saw the face of a girl in her late teens. Her face was pale and gaunt, the piercing eyes sunken into their sockets like those of a cadaver. Her greasy hair, dyed jet black, clung to the outline of her skull. Her expression was one of permanent, deep-set anguish. She reminded Tara of Edvard Munch's painting *The Scream*.

But as soon as she saw Tara, she relaxed. The face became cynical and businesslike. 'Howaya. What d'ya want?'

Taken aback by her directness, Tara resorted to the polite formality of the West. 'Sorry to disturb you. I'm looking for...'

'Oh, for Jaysus sake cut the crap. How much? Quick. We haven't got all bleedin' day.'

At that moment Tara caught sight of her own reflection in the polished surface of the metal door. Her hair, soaked by the rain, clung greasily to her head. Lank strands fell over a face that looked deathly pale in the poor light.

I look like her. She thinks I'm a junkie. Here to buy drugs.

Tara decided to change tack. 'I'm looking for Mano,' she said.

'Join the bleedin' queue.'

From inside the flat, a male voice. 'Who's the Madra talking to?'

The girl glanced apprehensively over her shoulder.

'He's not here?' Tara asked her.

'Who?'

'Mano.'

'No. You a friend of his?'

Tara was about to explain when another face appeared in the narrow door-crack. A man, late twenties, features hard and angular as a broken pint glass in a Saturday night brawl. Short-cropped black hair, heavy eyebrows locked together above piercing pale blue eyes. A row of half a dozen tiny gold earrings around the outer ear. Four tiny purple letters, HATE, tattooed on the neck.

'Who you talking to?' This to the girl.

'I thought it was yer wan from the third floor.' The girl stared hard at Tara and realised her mistake. 'I thought she was just here to score a turn-on.'

'Shut it, Madra, you stupid bitch.' He glared at Tara. 'What do you want, anyway?'

'She says she's a friend of Mano's,' said the girl miserably, trying hard to make amends.

'Oh, she is, is she?' The cold eyes came alive with something akin to hatred. The chain rattled. The door flew open, and before she knew what was happening, a sweatshirt-clad arm grabbed her and hauled her forcibly inside.

'Stop. You're hurting me.'

No reply. The door slammed behind her. Clunk. One bolt. Thunk. The second bolt. Rattle and clink. The chain.

The flat was a shambles. A boarded window, a bare lightbulb, a red carpet stained black with unmentionable liquids. A few broken items of junk-store furniture. Through an open door, Tara could see into the kitchen. She caught a brief glance of golden-brown powder, scales, and a pile of plastic sachets. Then someone slammed the kitchen door from inside.

'Don't look anywhere. Hear me? Look at me. Look at me.'

The man with the dealer's eyes knew what she'd seen. He grabbed her by the lapels of her leather jacket and threw her bodily against a plaster wall pockmarked by darts.

'I'm looking. I'm looking. Calm down.'

She met his eyes head-on. This was no pathetic junkie, she realised. This was a career criminal with no bad habits except a tendency to extreme violence.

'A friend of Mano's? Wha'? A mate of Mano's? Is that what you are?'

'I'm not...'

He shoved her against the wall again. 'Just shut your bleedin' face. If you're a friend of that bastard, you can start by telling me where he is.'

'I don't know where he is. That's why I came here. I was looking for Mano.'

His thick eyebrows lowered and he gestured towards the girl. 'You told the Madra you were a friend of his.'

Madra is Irish for dog. The girl raised no objection. She was obviously used to being described that way.

'I didn't say that.' Tara glanced over at the girl, seeking confirmation. The man looked around too. The girl froze.

'You did. She told me she was a friend of Mano's,' she whimpered.

It wasn't true, but the girl wasn't lying. She was just telling it the way she remembered it.

The man didn't care one way or the other. 'Tell him that if I don't get that three thousand quid back, he's bleedin' dead.'

'I'll tell him. If I see him.'

'Slowly. He's going to bleedin' die slowly. Give him that message from Christy. Got it?'

Tara nodded. 'I'll tell him if I find him. I have to go now. I've got friends waiting downstairs.'

He stared at her long and hard, then suddenly released her and whipped a small metal object from his pocket. Tara flinched. Then she recognised it as a lightweight mobile phone, a top-range model worth hundreds of pounds.

Short, nicotine-stained fingers dialled the number of another cellphone. 'Willie? Christy. Girl with black hair, leather jacket, Levis. Came up here five minutes ago. Did she come alone?'

He listened for a moment. 'Double check. Have a good look around. Sure? Okay.'

He stabbed the phone into silence with his index finger. 'Lying bitch,' he said.

'I'm not lying. I came up here with a woman with a pram. She warned me not to come here. She's worried about me. She's waiting for me to come out again.'

The eyes considered the lie and instantly dismissed it. 'If you're not a friend of Mano's, who are you?'

She could sense his emotions shift gear from anger to suspicion. She fought to control her own emotions, forcing her mind to sort through her options. Think. Think quickly. The danger level rose around her like acrid fumes from a chemical fire. Unless she acted soon, it would be out of control and it would be too late to do anything.

But he was the one who acted first.

'Carl. Come here.'

The kitchen door opened slowly and disgorged a shy-looking boy with long, lank brown hair parted in the middle. He wore glasses and a Star Trek T-shirt.

'W-what is it? W-w-who's she?' His pallid face twisted with the effort of forcing words out.

'Ever seen her before?'

Carl walked over hesitantly. He took up a position to the side of Tara, so that he could see her face but she couldn't see him.

'N-no. I d-d-don't think so. W-w-wait.'

He swung around and stared at her face-to-face. 'I'm n-not sure. Y-yes, yes, she is. She's a re-re-reporter. She was...she was... in court the day Philo went down.' He finished the sentence in a rush of triumph.

'A reporter?' Christy was suddenly very interested indeed.

'Y-y-yes. W-w-works for the *Evening M-m-m*...'

'The *Mercury*.'

The room suddenly turned chill, and Tara realised she

had a serious problem. Philo she remembered as Philip Romero, one of the most ruthless of the northside drug barons, jailed for fourteen years for operating a heroin-dealing network. Romero had specialised in getting young children addicted; there had been one boy of nine, another of eleven. What had also been remarkable about his operation was the unnecessary violence he used, routinely, sadistically, to assert his authority on the street.

If these men were in the rump of his gang, then she was in deep trouble.

'She wrote a b-b-big piece about Philo. It w-w-wasn't very nice.'

Christy appeared not to hear.

He turned his back on Tara, took a few steps away, turned around and stared at her again. This time his eyes lingered unpleasantly on her body as he looked her up and down.

'What do you think of Carl?' he asked her at last.

There was something ominous in the tone. Tara didn't answer.

'Bit of a nerd, isn't he?'

'I really have to go.'

'All the women think he's a bit of a nerd because he talks funny. He stutters so much that by the time he gets to say hello, they're saying goodbye.'

Carl was about to protest, but then he realised the direction the conversation was taking. He waited with silent anticipation.

'I'm sure you don't think that. So why don't you be the first woman who's nice to Carl.'

Tara was surprised to hear a sudden sob. It was the girl they called the Madra. She was standing directly behind Christy and she was crying with sheer terror.

'No, Christy. Please. No. Just let her go. She hasn't done nothin'.'

Christy's cold stare didn't leave Tara for a moment. But his arm lashed backwards in a semicircular motion.

She screamed as the knuckles connected with the side of her face.

The girl fell to her knees, making tearing, whimpering noises, like an injured animal.

'Like I was saying. It would be nice and friendly if you were to show Carl a good time. It wouldn't be the first time for you, bitch. Not by a long shot. But it would be the first time for him.'

Tara had been expecting this. But what she didn't expect was the chill that descended on her and turned the blood in her veins to icy sludge.

'You m-m-mean it, Christy?' Carl looked eager, like a stray dog on the doorstep.

'Yeah, why not?' He kept his eyes on Tara. 'You see, we're both up in court soon. We're about to go down for a long time. But if this deal comes off, we'll be so far away that nobody's even gonna remember our names. Either way, what have we got to lose?'

'Y-y-yeah. W-w-why n-n-not.' Carl's stutter became staccato with nervousness, and that made him angry. 'The b-b-bitch deserves it, after what she s-s-said about Philo.'

Tara knew it was no good screaming for help. In flats like this, the screams of battered wives and girlfriends were just so much background noise, like car alarms in underground car parks.

Carl was undoing his belt.

Christy was moving towards her.

Tara forced herself to remain calm. She recalled Ciarán, the security man, and the advice he kept drumming into her head: you have to move fast, or you don't get a chance to move at all. And you have to be as violent as they're going to be.

Nobody notices a rolled-up newspaper. It's almost ludicrous, something carried by city gents. Yet if you roll it up exceptionally tightly, as Tara had been doing over the past few minutes, it can be a deadly weapon. You don't use it like a club. You use it like a short stabbing sword, left hand gripping it in the middle and aiming, the palm of the other hand tucked under the end, powering it upwards.

Christy hadn't expected any attack as he moved in to pinion her arms.

He certainly didn't expect the newspaper that Tara had been twisting nervously, as an agitated person might twist a handkerchief, to come shooting up vertically towards his face.

The end of the newspaper, solid as mahogany, made contact with the fleshy area between his upper lip and nose. It caused Christy considerable pain. He was used to pain, but he wasn't used to surprise. Unprepared, his head shot backwards like a crash-test dummy's.

'Oh God, no. Oh Jesus. Jesus!' The girl.

Tara looked around at Carl. But Carl was no threat at all. He was petrified, like a small frightened animal in a car headlight.

Dash for the door, she told herself. Don't waste time. Go! Now!

She covered the few feet in a split second. Thunk. The first bolt. Clunk. The second bolt. Click. Turn the catch. Open. Freedom.

Skreek. Metal running through metal.

The chain. Oh, God. I forgot about the door-chain.

Don't panic. Lift the chain out of its holder. That's it. Now...

Two hands grabbing her. Vicious fingernails digging into her upper arm. A powerful haul backwards. Tara lying on her back, winded, vulnerable. Her wrist on fire with pain – she must have twisted it as she fell. Christy standing over her, broken nose oozing blood down his chin, lips parted in a neanderthal snarl of victory.

'We *were* gonna make it fun, lady. Now we're gonna make it hurt.'

Behind Christy, the girl in the corner, still emitting pathetic animal noises of fear, edging nervously towards the door. Fumbling with the chain. The door opening, slamming.

'Christy! The Madra's gone!'

Carl, panicking, voice breaking into a schoolgirl squeal.

'Let her go. The Madra's not going to go anywhere. Bitch has got no place to go.'

Christy, blood on his mouth, leaning over her, eyes alive with excitement. 'We're going to have a party,' he whispered.

The face lowering, close to hers. Drops of blood falling on her cheek. Tara too winded to fight, too breathless even to scream.

His left forearm resting heavily on her throat, blocking off her windpipe until she found it difficult to breathe. His right hand snaking downwards, unbuttoning her jeans. His eyes, bright and hard as steel points on a drill, remaining locked on hers, waiting for her terror to blaze and flare.

'Open up! Police! Open up!'

The door beating, battering, vibrating.

'Gardaí. We have a warrant. Open the door. Now!'

Christy on his feet in an instant. 'Jesus. The gear. Ditch the gear!'

Carl, Christy, diving towards the kitchen. Colliding in the narrow doorway. Dashing out with polythene bags of golden-brown powder. Across the floor to the bathroom. A brief second, then the sound of a flushing toilet. The roar increasing, then subsiding.

Tara, somehow finding strength, rising, moving. Half walking, half crawling, to the door. Shaking fingers fumbling with the handle, turning it.

Behind her, Christy, not bothering to pursue, just standing guard outside the bathroom where Carl is getting rid of the remaining heroin.

The front door flying open. A tall figure, silhouetted against the light, hurtling past her towards Christy, propelling him backwards against the closed bathroom door. Christy's head contacting the wood with a hollow thud.

Then both of them are on the floor, the newcomer on top, grappling, straining, cursing.

Then, behind the intruder's head, Tara spots Christy's hand holding a weapon. One of the ugliest weapons on the street...a razor blade melted into the plastic head of a toothbrush. A weapon designed and forged in prison: light, easily concealed, absolutely lethal. The blade inching towards a vein in the intruder's neck.

Tara, moving faster than she could ever have believed possible, diving across the room, grabbing the arm that holds the razor blade, sinking her teeth into the soft flesh of the wrist.

A yell of rage and pain. The weapon falling harmlessly aside. The intruder's elbow jerking backwards and upwards, then driving forwards in a disabling blow to Christy's stomach. The two figures disentangling. Christy doubled over on the floor, gasping for air, out of the fight.

Tara half crying, half laughing, in hysterical relief. 'Oh, my God. Are you all right? Thank you.'

The tall, dark-haired intruder slowly rose to his feet.

'On the contrary, Tara,' said Andres Talimann, eyeing the ugly blade that had nearly claimed his life. 'It is I who must thank you.'

CHAPTER FOURTEEN

THERE WAS only one noise from the bathroom – the repeated hollow clunk of someone trying to flush an empty cistern. Carl was still trying to get rid of the gear.

Lying on the filthy carpet, Christy was clutching his stomach in agony. His breath came in hoarse gasps. But his pale eyes still glared at them with undiluted hatred. They would haunt Tara's dreams for a long time.

This was no time to hang around. Tara and Andres half ran, half fell down the flights of gloomy concrete stairs, finally reaching the main door and bursting breathlessly into the bleak daylight of Ballymahon. Rain had never felt so good.

'This way.' Andres guided her around a corner to a half-hidden alley where his R1100 leaned on its side-stand. A teenage boy was sitting on it, idly twisting the throttle control. Andres tossed him a handful of pound coins. 'Thank you,' he said. 'Now get off.'

'No problem. It's safe. Nobody came near it.'

Andres nodded a curt acknowledgement and got on. The starter motor gave a brief, shrill whine and the engine roared into life.

Tara didn't wait for instructions. She hopped on to the pillion, feet barely finding the footpegs as Andres dropped the clutch and roared off. Powerful G-forces pushed her backwards. Her hands found the safety grip just in time.

As they powered out of the side-alley and into the main road, a bulky figure appeared in front of them. Tara had never seen him before. He was at least six foot three tall, and half as wide. He was holding a mobile phone to his ear and talking excitedly. His face was angry and anxious at the same time. His arm waved at Andres. He was ordering him to stop.

Tara took only a second to make the connection. This was obviously Christy's heavy. The man he had posted as lookout. 'Keep going!' she yelled in Andres's ear.

'Don't worry. Hold on tight.' He gunned the motor forward, straight at the burly figure in the middle of the road. At the last minute he leaned the bike over at a sharp angle. It changed direction, duping Christy's lookout and missing him by inches. Andres applied the power-assisted ABS brakes to avoid a row of bollards, and then the precision-built German engine howled as the power surged. Tara couldn't believe the acceleration – one instant she was here, the next instant she was somewhere else entirely. She glanced behind. Christy's minder had become a minuscule figure on a grey horizon. Even the tower-blocks were growing smaller by the second.

The BMW crossed a traffic light on the amber and roared off westwards. Tara recognised the approach to the M50 ring-road, then they were on the motorway doing one hundred and ten miles an hour and the rain was stinging her face like needles. She glanced around. There was no traffic within following distance apart from a tanker and a grain lorry.

After a few minutes, Andres slowed the machine and took the first exit. Then he turned off the main road and into a housing estate, where he slowly negotiated the bike through a series of streets. He reached a set of pedestrian bollards which separated one section of the huge estate from another. There was just enough room to take a pram through; with infinite caution he steered the giant BMW at walking speed through the gap. Tara realised what he was doing: anyone following them in a car would have to stop at that point and double back all the way through the estate.

Andres paused just down the road and watched the gap carefully for a while. Nothing came.

Satisfied, he killed the engine, dismounted and wiped

the rain-soaked hair from his eyes. He looked anxious. 'Are you all right, Tara? Do we need to take you to hospital?'

She got off the machine. She was soaked to the skin and shivering with cold and shock. The natural painkilling endorphins which her body had unleashed in its fight-or-flight response during her escape were starting to wear off, and her wrist hurt like hell. But otherwise she was unharmed.

She shook her head. 'No, I'm fine. I've twisted my wrist a bit, that's all. How about you?'

'I am...what's the phrase? In the pink. Top-hole.'

Tara couldn't stop herself laughing at his unusual choice of English, which at times sounded like the language of some ageing colonel from Tunbridge Wells. The laughter went on too long and began to sound shrill. She forced herself to stop. This was a hysterical reaction. She had to pull herself together.

'Where on earth did you come from?' she asked. 'You were the last person I expected to see.'

He responded with a curt shake of the head. 'Later. We shall have to get you into some dry clothes. You're in shock.'

She bristled. 'I told you, I'm fine. Before we go anywhere, I want to know how you managed to find me. You told them you were Gardaí. Are you some sort of undercover cop?'

He shook his head. 'No, I'm not. I knew you were in that flat, I knew you were in trouble, and I couldn't think of anything else to say that would make them open the door. Come on, you're shivering. Let's go.'

Tara didn't move. Her earlier paranoia about Andres was starting to reassert itself. If he could lie so convincingly about being a policeman, maybe he could lie about other things, too.

'How did you know I was in that particular flat?' she demanded. 'You still haven't told me how you came to be in Ballymahon in the first place. Were you stalking me or something?'

He sighed. 'I was doing exactly what you were doing, Tara. I was trying to find Manus Kennedy.'

'But how did you find the address of the flat?' Tara couldn't believe he had stumbled by luck upon the same lengthy, twisted trail that she'd uncovered. 'You must have been following me.'

For the first time, he seemed genuinely annoyed at her accusation. 'Please don't flatter yourself, Miss Ross,' he said. 'I am a busy man and I have better things to do with my time than to follow amateurs who take several days to complete a simple investigative assignment.'

'Amateurs?' She was outraged by the sheer arrogance of the man.

'You set out to find Manus,' he explained. 'As did I. But while your rambling method took – what? – two days to locate the flat in Ballymahon, my own method took only a few hours.'

'All right, Mr Smart Ass,' she challenged. 'You tell me how you did it.'

'Everyone needs money to live,' he elucidated with infuriating patience. 'When you set out to find anyone, you should begin by following the trail of money. Manus had left the sheltered housing at Inismaul Hospital, but his social welfare cheques were still being sent to him there. Someone was apparently forwarding them to him in Dublin. I was able to ascertain through various contacts that he had cashed the last few payments in the post office at Bernadette Towers. Having narrowed the field, it was then a simple matter of asking around. They say a good journalist is a person who doesn't know anything, but knows someone who does. I knew someone who knew. He knew that the unsavoury residents of the flat in Bernie-town had decamped to the squat in the Joy McCracken block in Ballymahon.'

'I'm impressed.'

'You shouldn't be. It was a straightforward process, nothing the police themselves could not have achieved had they wanted to.'

Okay, you're good, thought Tara. Very good. But she still wasn't satisfied. She pressed him further.

'Why are you going to all that trouble to trace Manus Kennedy?' she demanded. 'I mean, your German readers can't be that interested in an Irish murder case.'

'No, but they are interested in anything to do with Michael de Blaca.'

'Michael de Blaca?'

'The artist.' He glanced pointedly towards the grey sky. 'Do I have to explain everything while we're standing outside in the rain, Tara? Can't we talk later?'

'It won't take long. Just summarise.'

'As you will.' He knelt beside the BMW and began to reposition a section of casing that had clipped against the concrete bollards in their dash to escape Ballymahon Flats.

'I'd really no pressing reason to travel all the way to Claremoon Harbour that Sunday,' he explained as he worked. 'Although I was interested in the news angle about the murder of a famous women's rights activist, I could have handled the story from Dublin. But I have always admired the work of Michael de Blaca. It seemed a good excuse to see the town where he'd lived and worked, and to visit the gallery of his paintings there.'

'But it's not a gallery of his paintings. They just hijacked the name.'

Andres nodded. 'As I discovered, to my extreme disappointment. I found a shop packed with cheap rubbish and run by a ridiculous con-artist. Can you pass me a screwdriver from that toolbox, please?'

'Standard or crosshead? What made you distrust Villiers so much?'

'Crosshead. Thank you. When I tried to ask him questions about Michael de Blaca, he simply clammed down.'

'Clammed up.'

'I am sorry. Clammed up. He was so secretive about this artist, the very man he was ostensibly there to promote, that it made me suspicious. It was almost as though he regarded me as a rival bidder for something very valuable. I was intrigued. I noticed that he was drinking, so I brought in a bottle of very special Polish vodka and offered to share it with him.'

'I know. You spent all afternoon sharing it with him.'

He glanced up and grinned. 'Your spies are everywhere. Well, I have long mastered the art of appearing to drink heavily while actually taking only a little. I kept refilling his glass. He became more and more inebriated. More and more talkative. He told me about the late Mrs Kennedy and her secret affair with de Blaca. He told me about your relationship with Fergal. It seems he went looking for Fergal on the night before the murder, and found his car parked outside your house.'

She grimaced. 'Sneaky little toad. Still, it doesn't matter any more. Thanks to Gerry Gellick, the whole world knows the story now.'

He gave her a sympathetic smile. 'I tried to warn you. But before Villiers finally passed out, he told me a little more than he intended. By the time I left his shop, I knew that Manus Kennedy was suffering from a long-term psychological disorder and that he had been living rough around Claremoon Harbour for several weeks. I knew that he was being hunted by a family of Limerick criminals, the Vineys. I knew it had something to do with drugs. And I knew that it also had something to do with Michael de Blaca.'

Tara frowned. 'What a mixture. But remember, you can't trust Villiers. He could have been trailing red herrings to put you off the scent.'

'Trailing red herrings. I must remember that phrase.' Andres finished his repair work and replaced the screwdriver in the BMW's toolbox. 'Yes, that thought had occurred to me. And that's why I made some enquiries with sources in the Limerick underworld.'

'Let me guess. With a man in his thirties, fair hair, golf blazer and slacks?' She remembered the photo O'Rourke had shown her during their Irish coffee session in the roadhouse.

His eyebrows rose. 'It is my turn to be impressed, Tara.'

'Not bad for an amateur. You're aware that he's the main cannabis supplier in the Cork region?'

'Yes, I know that.' His face crumpled in mock apology. 'Alas, in our business, one cannot always deal with gentlemen. In the course of my career I have had to talk to torturers and mass murderers, so I would be foolish to draw the line at cannabis suppliers.'

She smiled, conceding the point. 'What did you find out from him?'

'Some very interesting information. That Godfrey Villiers is under extreme pressure to find money, fast. I don't know why...'

'It's because he's been laundering money for the Vineys and skimming some off the top for himself. They want it back.'

'I see.' He looked at Tara with a new respect. 'And according to my source, the art dealer has told the Viney family that he can get the money for them if he can find Manus Kennedy. I have no idea why. That is all I know.' He spread his arms wide. 'And that is why I want to find Manus. I am first and foremost a journalist, Tara, and this story has everything – murder, drugs, a political heroine and a major international artist.'

Tara nodded slowly. 'So you set out to find Manus because he seems to hold the key to this whole mystery. And I set out to find Manus in order to clear Fergal's name.' She frowned. 'But the fact that we arrived at the Ballymahon flat at the same time on the same day? A strange coincidence, don't you think?'

He seemed impatient with her objections. 'No, that was not a coincidence, Tara.'

'Then what?'

'I'll tell you exactly what happened if you let me. This afternoon I had arranged to meet my friend, the one who knows things, in the bar at Ballymahon Flats. He was giving me some details about the squat – the number of occupants, the purpose for which it was being used, the disappointing fact that Manus is not living there.

'My friend is not a councillor or a community leader, but he is recognised in the flats as a man who gets things done. What is the phrase, a Mister Fix Things?'

Tara shook her head. 'Mr Fixit. Go on.'

'As we sat talking, a woman came up to him in a state of some distress. It seems that she lives just above the flat we have just visited in Joy McCracken Tower. She was worried because she had seen a nice, respectable young woman from the west of Ireland go into this notorious flat. She had not seen her come out again. She thought she had heard a girl's voice crying and a male voice raised in anger. She was especially anxious, she said, because the young woman was not the usual type who might visit such a place. This kind lady is the one who really deserves your thanks. Who was she?'

'I don't know,' Tara confessed. 'I just helped her up the stairs with her baby-buggy, that's all. She did warn me not to go to the flat.'

Andres nodded. 'That is exactly what she told us. She said she saw no point in contacting the police because there was nothing concrete to report...merely her instinctive fears for your safety. She thought my friend, the local community fixer, might be able to help in some way.'

'And you realised that the woman in trouble was me?'

'Instantly. I didn't even wait to ask for a description. I grabbed my bike and got there as fast as I could. You know the rest of the story.'

'I do, and I'll be forever in your debt.' Tara already felt

ashamed over her paranoid accusations. She had obviously misjudged this man.

She hesitated before asking the next question. 'On your way up to the flat, did you happen to see a young girl, dark hair, pale face, very thin...?'

Andres didn't wait for her to finish the description. 'Yes, I know whom you mean. She was very frightened, very troubled. Who was she?'

Tara told him all she knew about the junkie girl. 'They called her "Madra" – Irish for "dog",' she explained. 'They treated her like an animal and she seemed too terrified to do anything about it. I had hoped that she was the one who had called for help for me.'

Andres shook his head slowly. 'I am afraid that there was no help forthcoming there, Tara. I asked her for directions to the flat. She told me there was no point going to that address, that there was no one there, that it was totally deserted. She lied.'

'I see.' Tara felt a sort of emptiness inside, that sock-in-the-gut feeling that is one step beyond disappointment or disillusionment, and closer to betrayal. She had been in terrible danger. The junkie girl had abandoned her, deprived her of the basic aid that one human being is entitled to ask of another. It was tempting to blame heroin addiction. But deep down in her soul, Tara realised that this was not what had prevented this girl from saving another woman from the torture and violation she knew was about to take place. What had prevented her was fear, and that was so much more disturbing because fear was universal. It dehumanised everybody, not just drug addicts.

Andres laid a comforting hand on her arm. 'Don't waste your concern on this young woman, Tara. I looked in her eyes. She is dead.'

'Yes.' Tara knew that he meant the word in both senses. The young woman they called "Dog" was already dead in spirit and, barring some sort of miracle, would soon be physically dead as well. 'Yes, you're right. But I can't help feeling sorry for her.'

'Which was more than she did for you,' said Andres, harshly. 'Forget about her.'

CHAPTER FIFTEEN

TARA'S BODY gave a bone-wrenching shudder, as though to remind her that she was still standing in the cold rain, soaked to the skin. She began shivering and the shivering didn't stop.

'We need to take you home now,' pressed Andres. 'I insist.'

This time she didn't argue. 'But first I must get my car. It's back at the flats.'

'That would be most unwise. There are some very angry people who have just lost thousands of pounds in drug money. There is no point in tempting fate by letting them know which car is yours.'

'But it's my only means of transport. If I leave it there, it'll be wrecked by morning.'

He raised a hand as though to fend off her concerns. 'Trust me. I'll take care of it.'

He produced a key and removed two motorcycle helmets that had been locked to the back of the machine. 'Here. Put one on. We'll take you back to base and get you into a hot bath. Where are you staying?'

Tara's face fell. She hadn't planned to stay another night in Dublin, and her colleague with the riverside apartment had left town for a few days. 'I don't know yet. I'll find a hotel.'

He understood right away. 'Okay. We'll sort that out later. First, dry clothes.'

Helmets on, they got back on board the bike and drove off at a more sedate pace. They rejoined the M50 and followed the main roads around the west and south of the city until they reached the sea.

The landscape changed from industrial-estate and giant housing complexes into an almost Mediterranean environment of twisting, hilly roads bordered by palms and monkey-puzzle trees. This was the Dalkey-Killiney area, nicknamed Bel-Éire because it was home to millionaire rock stars and movie directors.

The rain had stopped. Clouds reluctantly nudged each other aside to reveal the sun, and the sea changed from grey to an uncertain blue. The air was fresh and tangy with the scent of wet eucalyptus trees. Suddenly, it felt good to be alive.

Andres steered the bike into the car park of an apartment block overlooking the bay. He turned the ignition key, and the growl of the big Bavarian motor was replaced by the gentle sibilance of surf.

'This is my home,' he said, unbuckling his helmet. 'At least, one small part of it is. I think it would be a good idea if you had a hot bath here while I get those wet clothes washed and dried. Then we can sort out the matter of your accommodation. What do you think?'

He waited formally for her approval.

'I can think of nothing I'd enjoy more,' said Tara gratefully.

'Splendid!' Again, his English sounded like something from the days of the Indian Raj. He led the way through a security door and into a lift which took them smoothly to the top floor.

The apartment wasn't enormous, but the sea view from its window was magnificent. She could see all the way from the Howth Peninsula in north Dublin to Bray Head and the Sugar Loaf Mountain in the extreme south. No wonder it had been compared to the Bay of Naples.

Andres walked right past. He didn't even notice the view.

'Here we are,' he said, fetching a couple of giant white bathtowels. 'The bathroom is just down the corridor. Please excuse any mess. I was not expecting company.' He smiled for the first time since their escape. 'I have never been...what do we say?...housetrained.'

He handed her a white towelling dressing-gown. 'Also, if you could leave your wet clothes outside the door, I shall ensure that they are seen to.'

Tara put the dressing-gown to her face. It felt soft and luxurious. On the lapel was a logo which she recognised as the crest of the top international hotel in St Petersburg.

Andres gestured to a door at the end of a colour-washed corridor hung with two tiny original oils. 'Now, please. There is plenty of hot water, and feel free to use anything you find in bottles.'

'Including brandy?' She felt she needed one.

'I meant the bath oils and shampoos and stuff.' He smiled comfortingly, as though he were familiar with the strange reactions of those who had suffered a recent traumatic experience. 'Later, we shall share a drink if you wish, but for now it is best that you get warm and dry. Alcohol is not what you need at this moment.'

'Where I come from, farmers often use *poteen* as a cure for traumatised animals,' she protested as he pushed past her and turned on the hot tap. 'They give it to cows who've fallen into rivers in the middle of winter.'

He shook his head. 'Try this instead,' he said. He was holding out two small white tablets.

'What are they?'

'Arnica. A homeopathic remedy for shock. Don't worry – the dose is so tiny it's insignificant. It's perfectly harmless but remarkably effective.'

Tara glanced at the label on the bottle and took the tablets. They melted almost as soon as they touched her tongue.

She nodded thanks and disappeared into the bathroom. It was simply furnished in white tiles and mahogany – an Edwardian gentleman's bathroom. The free-standing bath was larger than average. She filled it high and hot. The bottles he'd referred to were tiny and filled with various medicinal oils. Some smelled pleasant, others smelled like ancient compost. She chose two she liked and added a few drops to the bath.

As she wallowed unhurriedly in the hot water, she felt her worries evaporating with the steam of the bath. Time slowed down. Outside, she could hear the comforting background sounds of domesticity – the purr of a washing machine, the clink of glasses and dishes, muffled piano music which she guessed was Bach but was unable to identify. At one stage she heard Andres's voice on the phone giving instructions on something or other; at another stage she heard Bach being replaced by a radio news programme. She recognised the time-signal and realised with a start that she had been in the bath for ninety minutes. Had she been asleep for part of the time or just daydreaming? She didn't know and she didn't really care.

The dressing-gown fitted as comfortably as a warm woollen glove in winter. As she emerged from the room, towelling her hair, she saw Andres seated at a small desk in front of the seascape window, typing staccato rhythms on a laptop computer.

He didn't notice her. For a long time she just stood still and watched him at work. It was a curiously restful feeling. This is what a good marriage must feel like, she thought. This is how it must feel to have someone who'll always be there to lend you strength and support whenever you need it.

She could get used to it – this warmth, this cosiness, this temporary surrender to pampering and cosseting, this willing acceptance of care and support in the knowledge that on other days, it would be the other way around, and that she would be the carer and supporter when he needed it.

He? Who did she mean, *he*?

He didn't turn around from his work. 'How was your bath?' he asked, still typing furiously at the keyboard.

She started with surprise at the sudden sound of his voice. 'It was wonderfully relaxing, thank you. I feel much better.'

His chair spun around. 'You're still rubbing your wrist,' he pointed out.

'Yes. I don't know what I've done to it. It hurts like mad.'

'Let's have a look,' Andres suggested. 'I'm not a doctor, but I have had some first-aid training and I've had to treat a lot of people for injuries in situations where no doctors were available.'

She shrugged. 'Why not? But do me a favour, don't amputate without an anaesthetic. I'm no good at biting bullets.'

He gestured for her to sit down. 'It's okay,' he said after probing gently at her hand and forearm. 'It's not broken, just a little sprained.'

He fetched a bandage and a bottle of clear liquid. 'This should help,' he promised. 'It's witch hazel. It may not be as efficacious as *poteen*, but it has also been used for centuries for this purpose. I am adding another medicinal oil to help relieve the pain.'

He prepared a compress and began to apply it to her wrist. The process was strangely relaxing; the pain didn't disappear, but it faded into the background as her tensions eased.

All the time he was reassuring her that her immediate problems had been taken care of. 'Your clothes have been washed, and are in the process of being dried and ironed by a wonderful lady who looks after my domestic needs. They should be ready in half an hour. After that, if you wish, I shall help you find a hotel. On the other hand, you are more than welcome to stay here. I have a comfortable guest bedroom and I give you my word that I shall behave as befits a gentleman.'

She checked his face to see if he was joking, but his old-world courtesy seemed genuine and unaffected.

Tara was both amused and pleased by his concern. She had often shared flats with other single people – males, females and some who were undecided – and there'd been several occasions when she'd dossed platonically on the sofas of male colleagues or friends when she couldn't get a taxi home.

But on the other hand, she hardly knew this man who had saved her life and who was now treating her with such special hospitality.

She hesitated only a few seconds before making up her mind.

'Then that is settled,' said Andres happily. 'We can have dinner and relax.'

'But what about my car? It's still at Ballymahon Flats.'

'I told you – trust me. If you were to look outside the window, which you cannot because I have yet to finish my healing work on your wrist, you would see that it is in the car park right now. My friend who knows things gained access to your car – please don't ask – and drove it across town. He assures me that it has not been linked with the curious events at Ballymahon this morning.'

'Good. That's a load off my mind.'

'He tells me there is great excitement in the area. There are several prominent gentlemen who are very upset over the loss of a sizeable quantity of heroin. The local people, on the other hand, are delighted that the dealers have suffered this setback.'

He completed the compress and secured her wrist in a white bandage, tied tightly enough to support the sprain. 'How's that?'

Her wrist glowed warmly where once there had only been a searing pain. 'It feels much better,' she said.

'Good.' He sat up. 'Now it's time to ask what the next move is to be in this general quest. It appears that, working separately, each of us has...crashed into a brick wall? Is that the phrase?'

'Usually it's "hit a brick wall", but yes, you're absolutely right. All I managed to learn in Ballymahon was that Manus, Mano, or whatever he calls himself, has disappeared and that his mate Christy blames him for the disappearance of three thousand pounds. Nobody seems to have a clue where he is. So where do we go from here? What do we do next? Any ideas?'

Andres nodded. 'I agree with your choice of pronoun. Since we have banished the mistrust between us, it makes much more sense if we pool our resources to a common end.'

Tara was more guarded. 'I wasn't actually thinking in terms of a strategic alliance. Still, I suppose you're right. But only until we get to the bottom of this business. After that...' She left the sentence unfinished but her meaning was clear.

'Agreed,' he formally shook her good hand. 'Now, as to your string of questions, I admit I do not know the answers.' He smiled. 'Yet. Let me think about it. But not on an empty stomach.'

Tara was quick to cut in. 'Let's eat out, or organise a Chinese takeaway or something. Dinner's on me. I don't want to cause you any more trouble.'

His eyes widened in mock-offence. 'I would not dream of accepting such an offer. We Estonians have a long tradition of entertaining our guests at our homes. I may not be a master-chef, but I know how to cater for myself.'

He stood. 'And I have learned some valuable lessons during my time in the Far East, one of which is that the tastiest meals are the simplest and most easily prepared, often by the roadside with nothing but a naked flame, a wok and a bamboo steamer. In short, trouble is not an emotion that is permitted past my door – and especially the door of my cookhouse.'

With this, his tanned face split into an infectious grin, and she knew he meant it.

'What I propose to make will take less than twenty minutes and very little effort, yet it is wholesome and nutritious and, I trust you will agree, quite delicious.'

He flung open the door of the kitchen and began displaying ingredients with the air of a Victorian conjurer premièring a special trick. 'You must imagine that the scene is a forest track in Cambodia or Vietnam,' he said, tongue firmly in cheek. 'There may even be mortars exploding in the distance. *Whee! Pow!* Like that. Four small fillets of chicken. Bought fresh this afternoon. Simple? Yes? We have had them marinading in Chinese rice wine, soya sauce and some finely chopped ginger and garlic for the past half-hour. Oh, and a little zest of lemon.'

'In other words, here's some you prepared earlier.' She entered into the role of the audience heckler.

'Okay, okay. Now we take everything, the entire plate of chicken and marinade, and we place them in this bamboo steamer. We put them over a wok filled with simmering water for a short while – around twenty minutes – and we let the steam cook them. Simple as that. No oil, no fat, just basic H_2O and heat.'

'Chicken in a sauna bath.'

'Precisely. Now we take some top-grade Basmati rice – never compromise with the quality of the rice, it is too important – and, having washed it, put it in this rice steamer with a little salt. It goes into a microwave for ten minutes.'

'I didn't know they had microwaves by the roadside in the Cambodian forest.'

'I am cheating just a little. In such circumstances, the rice would have been cooked in the wok. Do not make irrelevant objections. Listen and learn.'

Amused by his mock-condescension, she watched as he threw together the other ingredients and left them to cook.

They ate seated at a simple wooden table. He served up a starter of asparagus tips in melted lemon butter ('again, simplicity is best') and put on a CD. She recognised the same calm, methodical piano music that she'd heard earlier while enjoying her bath.

'Andres, this asparagus is very good indeed. What's

the music?'

'Bach's Forty-eight.' He seemed to think she'd know what he was talking about.

'Is he? Well, happy birthday, Bach. Now, tell me what the music is.' She smiled, still giddy enough to make bad jokes.

He stared at her, uncomprehending. 'It's Bach's Forty-eight. His collection of forty-eight preludes and fugues entitled "The Well Tempered Clavier",' he elaborated patiently.

'As opposed to a bad-tempered clavier? You have to be careful of those claviers when they get angry. You never know what they might do, especially after they've been drinking. What is a clavier, anyway?'

Andres kept his patience. 'It is a keyboard instrument – the precursor of the piano,' he explained. 'And well-tempered simply means well-tuned.' He glanced up and caught her expression. 'You're mocking me, aren't you?'

'Just a bit. The food is so perfect you deserve to be taken down a peg or two.'

He shook his head in a parody of despair and brought out the main course. The steamed chicken fillets were served on a bed of wilted pak-chao, which he explained was a green-leafed vegetable popular in Asia.

'Will you join me in some wine?'

'That would be nice. Thank you.'

He brought out a chilled litre bottle of white wine, and proceeded to pry off a crimped top like a beer bottle's. She was puzzled, because it seemed so out of place. In her experience, wine that came in litre bottles with prise-off metal caps was usually the cheapest of plonk, either sickly sweet or acidic enough to strip the paint off a farm tractor, and Andres didn't seem the sort of person who would compromise with something as important as wine.

But this was pleasantly crisp and dry. It smelled of mountain pasture and it tasted of elderflowers.

'It's very unusual,' she said. 'Very different. It's

delicious. It's so light and fine, it's more like spring water than wine.'

'I'm glad you like it. It's one of my favourites. And I can assure you it's much more potent than spring water.'

'Are you going to tell me what it is?'

'Wine from Switzerland. Fendant, from the Valais region along the Rhone River Valley.'

'Never heard of it.' She took another sip. Yes, Swiss. The mental image fitted the taste exactly.

'No, it is rare to find it outside Switzerland. The Swiss say their wine is so good that they drink it all themselves. Very little of it is exported, which is a great loss to the rest of us.'

'And which explains why Heidi looks so happy all the time. Cheers.'

They raised their glasses and ate.

'So,' he said, between mouthfuls of pak-chao and chicken, 'you must tell me more about yourself.'

'No!' She surprised herself with the forcefulness of her reply. 'You know quite enough about me already, Andres. Far too much. I think it's time I learned something about you instead.'

He seemed amused. 'Very well, Tara. But I must warn you, you ask at your peril. When the clock sounds one in the a.m., and I am still describing my childhood, you must shut me up and walk away.'

To emphasise his point, he took a section of bread roll and thrust it plug-like into his mouth.

But contrary to his warning, he wasn't long-winded and he certainly wasn't a bore. Like the food he served, his reminiscences benefited from being pared to the essentials. And they were well seasoned with self-deprecating humour.

He had been born in the Estonian capital of Tallinn at the height of the Cold War. His father, a highly-respected university professor, had married a doctor and they had settled in a comfortable house on the Baltic coast.

Settled was the wrong word – Professor Talimann had been given a rare freedom to travel in order to exchange ideas with other academics around the world, and the young Andres found himself exposed to cultural influences that most of his friends would never have encountered. He spent part of his childhood in Dresden, part in Prague, and short periods in Berne and Paris.

'When I reached university age, I was expected to put all that behind me and prepare for a long and productive life as a Soviet citizen,' he said. 'But I found that impossible. After witnessing Western democracy in action, I could easily see through the Soviet propaganda that portrayed it as an evil system. I resolved to get away from Estonia as soon as possible, and return only when my country was free of Russian domination.'

He found he had a natural gift for languages. In addition to the Estonian and German he learned from his parents, and the Russian he was forced to study at school, he could speak fluent French and Spanish.

'But never English,' he said with a rueful smile. 'My father blamed the British for surrendering Estonia to Stalin after the War, so I was never formally taught the language.

'But like most young people, I rebelled against my father. I secretly learned English grammar from textbooks. Then I bought a set of language-instruction records at a second-hand market and listened to them covertly in my room until I had learned something of the vernacular. I still have the records.'

He rose and bounded across to a cupboard. When he returned, he was clutching a battered old box. On the lid was a graphic artist's painting of a man in his twenties wearing a trilby hat and smoking a pipe. The title words, in 1930s art-deco type, read: LEARN SUPER ENGLISH IN JUST FOUR WEEKS. Underneath, a subheading exulted: 'Impress all the chaps at the club with your command of colloquial expressions.'

Tara burst out laughing and couldn't stop. 'Now I understand,' she managed to say at last.

'What understand? Understand what?'

'The way you speak. Your idiom. Your slang. It's frozen in a nineteen-thirties' time warp.'

'You mean...it's not modish?'

'No, it's not *modish*. But never mind. I'll give you a few lessons. We'll soon get you up to speed.' She accepted another top-up of wine. 'Now please go on. You learned all these languages, and then what?'

When he left university, Andres explained, he was immediately snapped up by the Soviet tourism agency Intourist as a translator-guide for visiting foreign VIPs. His job was to meet them at the airport, take them to their hotel, show them the triumphs of communist society during the day and, if they wished, take them around the bars and State-run whorehouses at night.

This was no problem to the young Andres, who had an easygoing approach to life, but he soon found out that there was another side to the job.

Every night, at midnight or three am or six-thirty am or whatever time the foreign dignitary staggered off to bed, he was required to fill out a full report on the VIP's activities – and particularly any sexual indiscretions or weaknesses that might make him liable to blackmail or political extortion. The report was forwarded to the murkier corridors of the State security apparatus, where it would be painstakingly studied by men with pale faces and blood as cold as the white tiles in the chilly interrogation rooms beneath their feet. They would read his report, stamp it, duplicate it and recommend whether the matter should be acted upon immediately, or simply filed away to add to their bulky dossiers.

Andres loathed that aspect of his job, and would deliberately turn a blind eye to some of the wilder activities of his guests.

But one night when he returned an almost blank report

on the activities of a French nuclear physicist who had spent most of the night indulging in role-playing games with a fifteen-stone Ukrainian prostitute, his luck ran out. The Ukrainian lady had also reported back to State security and her truthful story did not tally with Andres's work of fiction. The lady of the night was rewarded, the happily-married French scientist was compromised and forced to reveal some confidential information about his trips to certain testing-grounds in the Pacific, and Andres Talimann found himself cleaning out toilets and attending re-education sessions.

'I got off lightly,' he shrugged philosophically. 'If I hadn't been the son of a highly-placed professor, I could well have ended up rotting in a prison camp or receiving a lobotomy in one of their special psychiatric hospitals.'

However, his linguistic talents were too valuable to waste. There was a shortage of graduates who could fluently translate Estonian into Spanish. So when an elderly Estonian composer, who spoke no language other than his native tongue, was invited to travel to Mexico City to address a prestigious international cultural seminar, Andres was pulled out of toilet duty and back into a higher plane of public service.

There were three of them in the delegation – the composer, Andres his translator, and a smiling seven-foot giant from Leningrad who was there to care for both of them and ensure that they returned home safely.

The three-day event went like a dream. The famous composer was greeted as a hero. He spoke for an hour to a rapt audience, and Andres even managed to translate his obscure Estonian jokes so well that the audience actually laughed. The Important Men Back Home were delighted and phoned to say so.

As soon as he had taken the call at his hotel in Mexico City, the burly minder from Leningrad became much more relaxed. He was so relaxed he permitted himself a small Tequila in celebration, then another, then another, and finally he just ordered the waiter to leave the bottle on the table with the salt and lemon segments. Sitting in the lobby of their hotel, all three of them toasted the Revolution, and the Communist Party, and *perestroika*, and the future. At around five am, the composer slowly slid under the table. Half an hour later, the minder stood up to go to the toilet and collapsed into a potted plant. Andres surveyed both comatose bodies, calmly got up, and walked out of the hotel into the streets of Mexico City towards freedom.

The Bach CD ended, and he replaced it with Billie Holiday – impromptu, slap-happy jam sessions from the late 1930s, the era before heroin and heartbreak had destroyed her magnificent voice.

'I spent a year travelling,' Andres said. 'Taking work where I could get it, going hungry when I couldn't. For some time, I lived with the Tarhumara Indians of northern Mexico – you may have read that chapter in my book – and then I took the Pan American highway south.'

Eventually Andres managed to obtain a German passport and flew to Frankfurt, where he landed a job in a library. His multilingual talents earned him extra income as translator and researcher for the globetrotting journalists on *Magnus* magazine, which was based nearby, and when he was made redundant from the library he began submitting his own articles to the editor.

'We arrived in Germany expecting to stay there for only a few months, and we ended up living there for five years,' he said, replenishing her wineglass. 'But the magazine job involved a lot of travelling. For instance, we spent a long time in Cape Town, South Africa. It is a beautiful city. We loved it.'

Tara sipped her Swiss wine and quietly noted the subtle change of pronoun. *I* travelled to Mexico; *we* arrived in Germany.

'There were a lot of changes to report,' Andres continued. 'I talked to Desmond Tutu and FW De Klerk, and my interview with Mandela just after his release from prison in Robben Island proved the turning point in my career. It earned me my first international award, and Mandela sent me a personal letter of congratulation.'

Tara nodded. She had read the interview and, like many people, had been moved by it. 'But there were a lot of changes happening in the Baltic at that time as well,' she reminded him.

'I know. I watched the news on television and I could hardly contain my excitement. The mighty Soviet empire was being destroyed – not by intercontinental ballistic missiles, but by human voices. And it was all happening in my own little corner of the world. Thousands of people were gathering in the centre of Tallinn to sing traditional Estonian songs that the Soviets had banned for decades. It went down in history as The Singing Revolution.'

Realising that the Soviets were finally relinquishing their bloodstained grip on the Baltic States, Andres returned home to Tallinn, determined to share in these epic events.

'One magic day in 1991, peaceful protesters formed a human chain all the way from Vilnius in Lithuania to Talinn in Estonia,' he said, his voice reflecting the excitement he had experienced that day. 'A six-hundred-kilometre-long line of human beings holding hands. Can you picture it? The world watched and it was struck dumb with awe.'

'It must have been a very emotional experience for you.'

'It was. For two years at least. I felt as though I were in exactly the right place at the right time, that I had a role to play in this new drive towards freedom and democracy. And then, five years ago, I left my homeland, never to return.'

He stood abruptly and began clearing their plates. She

rose to help him, but he laid a restraining hand on her shoulder.

'But why...?'

He turned his back on her and disappeared into the kitchen.

Tara recalled Melanie's words in Galway.

'His wife died suddenly, five years ago. Some sort of accident or something...a tragedy that could have been prevented if he'd been there. He's been blaming himself for her death ever since...'

She waited until he returned, carrying a large pottery bowl filled with fresh fruit. 'Do you want to talk about it? I mean, would it help?'

He set down the fruit bowl. 'I would much prefer not to, Tara.' His tone was light, unoffended. 'Do you mind?'

He never talks about his wife.

She shook her head. 'Of course not. I understand.'

'Good. Let us change the subject,' he said lightly. 'We have talked about Andres Talimann for far too long.'

'Okay, then. Music. Is it true that you can't work unless you have Bach playing in the background?'

'Perfectly true, I'm afraid. It's the only thing that gives me the peace of mind I need to write. And needless to say, this was the source of some amusement to my colleagues.' He smiled and passed her the bowl of fresh fruit. There were oranges and apples and several unidentified fruits of various shapes. Tara reached for a knobbly fruit about the size of a ping-pong ball.

'No, no!' he seemed genuinely anxious. 'Not that one.'

'Why not? What's wrong? Is it wax, or something?'

'It's a lychee.'

'So?'

'In some parts of India, where the litchi tree has been cultivated for many centuries, there's a tradition that its fruit should be shared only between lovers. Otherwise it will bring bad fortune.'

She stared at him. Was this some sort of joke?

'I'm serious. Put it back.'

'What are you talking about?'

'They say it is a very erotic fruit. You peel off the outer layer and you expose a fleshy membrane which they say resembles...intimate human parts. That is why it should be shared only by those who are in love. It is just a silly superstition, that's all.'

She laughed. 'You're making this up, Andres.'

'I am not.' He pretended to take offence. 'The Ancient Chinese also regarded the fresh lychee as a very seductive fruit. Dating right back to 200 BC, when the Emperor Kao Tsu insisted on having them served in his royal bedchamber.'

'The Emperor who?'

'And early Cantonese literature refers to it as "nature's titillating treat". If you don't believe me, check in the National Museum's library of oriental manuscripts.'

'No problem. I go in there every day.' They were both laughing now. Tara replaced the lychee and chose an orange instead. She was going to take a banana, but God knows what those Kamasutra experts in India would have said about that.

Andres disappeared into the kitchen again and re-emerged with two espresso cups and a small cafetière.

They sat and sipped their coffee in silence as darkness fell over the Irish sea. Accustomed to west coast sunsets, Tara found it hard to adapt to an evening seascape where the sun didn't settle on the ocean horizon, like a parent kissing her child goodnight.

She was just starting to mellow nicely when Andres deliberately shattered the tranquil atmosphere.

'What do you see in Fergal Kennedy?' he asked suddenly.

She gasped in astonishment. 'Excuse me?'

'You heard me, Tara. What do you see in him? He doesn't seem like your type. Tell me if I am talking off my turn.'

'Listen, Andres.' She sat bolt upright, trembling with outrage. 'You may have helped me out today, but it does *not* give you the right to make intrusive remarks about my personal life. It does *not* give you the right to interfere in my relationships. It does *not* give you the right...'

She let him have it, with both barrels. But at the same time, she surprised herself by trying to analyse that peculiar tone she'd heard in his voice when he'd asked the question. She'd detected the same tone in the voices of other men. It usually meant they were jealous. And somehow, that thought didn't displease her as much as she thought it might.

Eventually she paused, out of breath. But her verbal onslaught hadn't deterred him in the least.

'Fergal Kennedy?' he repeated, as though she hadn't spoken at all. 'You know you deserve better than that, Tara.'

'Of course I do,' she said with heavy sarcasm. 'But Tom Cruise went and married someone else.'

'What do you know about him? I mean, what do you really know about him?'

'Tom Cruise?'

He smiled but his eyes continued to ask the same question.

'I know everything about him.' She was furious with herself for even bothering to reply, but she couldn't help it. 'We come from the same small village, for Pete's sake.'

'Yes, I am aware of that. But his missing years in Canada?'

'They're not missing years. He's told me all about them.'

'Are you sure?'

Tara avoided his eyes. She was loath to admit it, but he had a point. Fergal had talked at great length about some periods of his life in Canada, but she'd noticed that he'd adopted an almost furtive secrecy about other times.

And as for Andres's first question: what did she see in

Fergal? It may have been breathtakingly impertinent, but, if she were to be starkly honest with herself, there had often been times when she'd quietly asked herself precisely the same thing.

Right at this moment, for instance.

Exhausted by their verbal skirmish, she sat for a few moments watching the new moon shimmer through the rustling leaves of a eucalyptus tree.

'The only thing I'm sure of,' she confessed after a long silence, 'is that I'm not sure of anything any more.'

He smiled. 'Then there is at least one thing we have in common.'

Tara looked at the profile of his face silhouetted against the fast-fading light, and felt a surge of some sort of emotion she couldn't easily identify.

She didn't know why she reached across the table and rested her fingers lightly on the back of his hand. Perhaps it was meant to be a swift gesture of apology for the ferocity of her outburst. Or a simple expression of gratitude, something any woman would do for a man who had come to her rescue in time of trouble. But for some reason her hand remained there, her skin lightly touching his, maintaining contact. He didn't move, but she could feel his response as surely as though he had turned his hand around and enfolded hers.

He raised his head slowly and looked directly into her eyes. This time she didn't look away.

Andres withdrew his hand from hers and placed it gently on her cheek. She turned her head slightly towards it, responding.

'I'm sorry,' he whispered, taking his hand away. 'I promised I would behave like a gentleman.'

She looked away. Among the mishmash of emotions she was experiencing, there was one that closely resembled disappointment.

'And you have,' she smiled.

He chose to make light of the episode. 'And yet here

we are, drinking coffee, and I cannot offer you a brandy or a liqueur to go with it. And you specifically asked me for brandy earlier. That is hardly the behaviour of a good host.'

Tara finished her coffee. 'It's okay. I don't usually drink brandy, anyway,' she said ruefully. 'It makes me behave out of character. I'm not myself.'

'We should all behave unlike ourselves from time to time.'

'I suppose we should.'

He leaned forward, his face hovered over hers, and for an instant she was sure he was about to kiss her. Perhaps he was. Perhaps he changed his mind at the last minute. But instead, he simply rose to his feet, and she felt angry with herself for wondering how she would have reacted.

'But now it is time for sleep,' he said. He stared up into the night sky, where a jet was flashing its landing lights as it began the slow descent towards Dublin Airport. 'Tomorrow, I have to take an early flight to Paris.'

'Paris?'

'Paris, France.'

'I know where Paris is. It's just...I thought we had planned to work together on this business.' Her voice sounded brittle and tetchy and she hated herself for it.

'This *is* "this business", albeit indirectly,' he said. 'And as for working together, you are welcome to accompany me if you so choose. In the meantime, your room is just through there. I think I have provided everything and I hope you will be comfortable. Sleep well, Tara. Goodnight.'

'Why Paris?' Tara was exasperated. 'What has Paris got to do with anything?'

But he had already gone, and she found herself alone at the window with the new moon, the whispering eucalyptus tree, the plaintive sigh of Billie Holiday, and the untouched lychees.

CHAPTER SIXTEEN

IT WASN'T just a plane trip to another city. It was a journey through a looking-glass to another dimension, a place where no one had heard of the murder in Claremoon Harbour, where there were no grim memories of a good woman's death to blight every waking hour, and where people laughed and loved and slept peacefully at night undisturbed by dreams that slashed your sleep asunder like a knife scything through thin satin.

At least, that's how it seemed to Tara as she stood near the beautiful Place du Tertre, high above the winding cobbled streets of Montmartre, and looked over the peaceful skyline of the City of Light. A realist would probably have argued the point with her – here, there were just as many good dreams and just as many nightmares as there were at home, no more, no less – but today she would not have listened.

She still didn't know why she'd agreed to come to Paris, but once she'd taken the decision at five am, over a cup of strong black coffee brought to her room by her wide-awake and fully-dressed host, there was no going back. And no, there were no regrets.

The early morning flight from Dublin airport was packed with weary commercial reps, returning French tourists and the occasional canoodling couple looking forward to a romantic break. Tara and Andres ended up in different parts of the plane, Tara jammed in a centre-seat between two very fat businessmen and Andres enjoying the comparative luxury of an aisle seat three rows ahead, where he spent the entire flight chatting animatedly to a blonde woman with a shock of frizzy curls and the most ludicrously enormous earrings that Tara had ever seen. She looked like the sort of person who would lead the

Conga dance at a Spanish holiday disco.

The flight would have been perfect, she told herself, but for the blonde's irritatingly shrill laugh as she responded to Andres's lively chat. The fact that she could hear the sound of their voices, but not the substance of their conversation, added to Tara's irrational annoyance. From time to time, the woman would tilt her head towards Andres and fiddle with her ridiculous earrings as she burst into another teeth-gratingly shrill giggle.

Tara tried to concentrate on reading an article in the in-flight magazine, but her eyes kept wandering off the page. Of course, it was none of her concern whom Andres chose to talk to, but she thought he had better taste than to waste his time chatting up an obvious bimbo with an Essex-girl hairstyle and, to judge from that strident laugh, all the IQ of a mynah bird.

'Did you enjoy the flight?' she asked him as they disembarked.

'Yes, very much. I met a very interesting lady,' he said vaguely, looking around the airport for direction signs.

'Did you? I didn't notice. I'm afraid I dozed off for most of the journey.'

'That was wise,' he said. 'I had planned to do the same thing myself. But it's not every day that one meets a professor of Middle Eastern studies, and the opportunity was too good to miss.' He waved across the room at the blonde, who peered over her bifocals and waved her leather briefcase in response.

With no luggage to reclaim, they sailed rapidly through immigration control and right past the crowded baggage hall.

'Where do we go now?' she asked. It had suddenly occurred to her that she'd absolutely no idea where they were headed.

'We travel into the city,' replied Andres. 'We could hire a car or take a taxi, but at this time of day, Paris is little more than a slow-moving car park. We would spend the next ninety minutes breathing exhaust fumes and listening to drivers swearing at each other. Trains are faster, and, anyway, where we are going it is impossible to drive.'

He steered her towards a waiting shuttle marked 'Roissybus' which whisked them out of the airport towards the adjacent suburban rail station. They caught a train to the giant Gare du Nord in the centre of Paris. From there they switched to the underground and, changing only once at Barbes-Rochechouart, rode the shaking, rattling, exhilarating Métro to Place Pigalle.

The famous Pigalle red-light district looked tawdry in the fresh morning sunlight, like an ageing prostitute who has slept all night in her makeup. A workman in blue overalls was repairing a broken neon sign that said: SEX, SEX, SEX and trading complaints with an old woman who was sweeping up the detritus of the previous night, the residue of passion and frustration, from the pavement below.

They turned their back on yawning, scratching Pigalle and wandered just across the road to a smart, clean minibus labelled: 'Montmartrobus'.

Andres checked a timetable and consulted his watch. 'Good,' he said, 'It will leave in just a few moments. We're early. If we had chosen to travel by road, by whatever means of transport, we would still be out somewhere around the Boulevard Périphérique, fighting our way through the commuter traffic. A nightmare.'

Tara hadn't a clue about traffic flow in the French capital, but she nodded agreement all the same. She looked around her and smiled happily. She felt strangely at home in Paris; she always had. The fact that this journey had been so impulsively entered into, so unexpected, added to her feeling of lightness and freedom. She felt as freshly liberated, as unencumbered, as a backpacker who has just shaken off a heavy rucksack for the first time in days. Psychologically, she was as weightless as a moonwalker.

Even her mode of dress was, by sheer happy accident, just right for the time and the place. The black leather jacket, teamed with freshly-laundered light-blue Levis and the new white scoopneck T-shirt she'd bought at the airport that morning, made her fit perfectly among the rich Parisiennes for whom the leather-and-Levis look was *sympa*, cool, street-chic.

'This is the only way to travel around Montmartre,' announced Andres as he led her on to the minibus that the city of Paris provided for the convenience of the residents of the Mount of Martyrs.

She soon found out why as the little bus disappeared into the maze of ancient cobbled streets that corkscrewed up the steep hill, ducking and diving past lorries, cyclists and street traders, skilfully negotiating fiercely-angled bends at impossible gradients while as the same time swerving to avoid suicidal moped riders. When they got off near the Place du Tertre, she was disappointed that the rollercoaster ride had ended so soon.

Taking their time, they strolled through the Place du Tertre, brushing off the persistent street artists who kept badgering them for instant-portrait commissions.

'They should be banned,' growled Andres after getting rid of the latest hopeful painter with a volley of uncomplimentary French. 'Every centimetre of this square is history. It used to be the very heart of the village of Montmartre, where the villagers used to gather to hear important announcements and watch public hangings. It has not changed all that much. Left alone, one could recreate it all in one's imagination. But one is not left alone. These pests destroy the magic.'

Not quite, thought Tara as she watched the quick-draw artists perform miracles of draughtsmanship, and winked back at the white-painted mime artists who stood stockstill on the steps of ancient buildings pretending to be sculptures.

Andres didn't even notice them. He glanced at his

watch. 'We're still too early,' he said with relief.

'Too early for what, Andres? For God's sake, stop being so mysterious.'

'All in good time. How about coffee?'

She nodded enthusiastically. 'You've just said the magic word.'

They chose a pavement table outside a café in the heart of the ancient square and ordered two large *cafés* from a waiter who had obviously taken a master's degree in arrogance.

'Locals call this hill La Butte. It used to be the bohemian centre of Paris,' explained Andres, his arm encompassing the entire district in a sweeping gesture. 'Van Gogh, Gauguin, Toulouse-Lautrec, all the great post-Impressionists, they all painted here. This is where Picasso, Braque and Gris invented modern art. And now it has come down to this – con artists who dupe the public with their ill-executed daubings.'

'Funny, but I seem to recall that the critics used exactly the same language about the Impressionists when they first arrived on the scene,' Tara teased as she sipped her coffee.

'They had talent. These do not,' he said, taking her seriously. 'For instance, if you look at a painting by...'

He stopped in mid-sentence. A huge woman, her body almost as round and fat as a globe, had stopped in front of their table. Her skin was black – not just brown, but shiny black, like wet coal – and her eyes had a strange gleam as she offered Andres a single cellophane-wrapped rose from the bunch in her wicker basket.

'Une rose pour votre femme, m'sieur?' she asked, gesturing towards Tara.

'Non. Non, merci.'

Tara was amused at Andres's embarrassment. The woman had presumed they were man and wife.

The flower-seller refused to go away. Instead, she tried a new sales technique. This time she offered the rose to Tara and gestured towards Andres with a dazzling smile.

'Madame? Une rose pour votre mari?'

Tara smiled back. *'Monsieur n'est pas mon mari,'* she said. Andres was not her husband.

The black woman gave a clucking sound and shook her head. Her reply was too rapid for Tara to understand.

'What was that?' she asked Andres.

'Nothing. Just the usual...what's the phrase? The usual cowshit they give to tourists.'

'Bullshit. We say bullshit.' Tara wasn't satisfied. 'Tell me what she's saying.'

Andres sighed. 'She's talking nonsense. She says we are plainly meant for each other. She probably says exactly the same thing to every couple she sees.' He laughed off his embarrassment. 'She's offering to read our future in the Tarot cards for fifty francs.'

He shook his head violently and gestured at her to leave.

But the roly-poly black woman had already produced a pack of Tarot cards from beneath her floral marquee of a dress. She rapidly dealt out several cards, suddenly stopped, and laughed out loud.

Another stream of rapid-fire, colloquial French, this time directed at Tara. She couldn't make out a word of it.

'What's she saying?'

'Nothing. Absolutely nothing.' Andres was becoming extremely irritated. He produced a fifty franc note, thrust it at the woman, and ordered her to leave. She smiled, picked up the cards and began to walk away.

'What did she say, Andres?' Tara was intrigued.

'I told you. Nothing. She is a crazy woman. She is half mad. She has gone. Forget her.'

The huge black woman winked at Tara, gave a high-pitched and curiously girlish laugh, and disappeared into the crowd.

'Well, here we are,' said Andres. 'The Church of the Sacre Coeur.'

She was familiar with it, of course – she knew how this landmark church had been commissioned in the nineteenth century as an act of penitence for the bloodshed of the communard uprising, how its special white stone whitened rather than dulled with age, how its over-elaborate Gothic architecture made sensitive critics wince. But this was still the second most famous church in Paris, presiding over the wide city skyline like some sentimental Victorian guardian angel.

As she scanned the horizon for buildings she recognised, Andres checked his watch again. 'Perfect,' he said with satisfaction. 'Now all we have to do is wait.'

'Wait for what?'

He ignored her and sat down on the steps. A brightly painted funicular railway car clattered up the steep hill and tipped out a cargo of excited schoolchildren.

Tara sat down beside him, closing her eyes and raising her face to the warm rays of the summer sun. She could sense that he was looking at her, studying her features.

'The last time I was in Paris was with Manuela,' he said.

She didn't move or open her eyes.

'Your wife?'

'Yes. She loved Paris. She said it was her favourite city in the world.'

'Mine, too.'

The schoolchildren formed a laughing, chattering crocodile and walked up the steps towards the church, their teacher desperately shushing them as they approached the main entrance.

'Manuela,' said Tara. 'What a beautiful name. Was she Spanish?'

'Mexican. I met her in the Baja California peninsula.

She was a teacher. She taught a class just like that one. The same age.'

Tara kept her eyes closed and her face upraised to the sun. She didn't want to press him.

He never talks about his wife.

'We married within a few months. It was love at first seeing.'

'At first sight.'

'It was love at first sight. We travelled around the world together – to Cape Town, Frankfurt, Madrid.' He paused. 'Paris.'

The voice was neutral. No nostalgia, no pain, no emotion at all. It was almost as though he were describing a distant relative.

'And to Estonia?'

There was a long, long silence.

'Yes,' he said at last. 'When The Singing Revolution succeeded, and I wanted to go home, she agreed unquestioningly to come with me.'

But all was not well in his country, he told Tara. 'Before independence we were being terrorised and extorted by old men in grey suits. Now we were being terrorised and extorted by young men in tracksuits and designer running shoes. They hung around outside the nightclubs and hard-currency bars, talking into mobile phones, arranging drug shipments and smuggled consignments of stolen Mercedes. They called them the new mafia.'

He called over a vendor and bought two cans of Perrier. Then, slowly sipping the ice-cold springwater, he told her the whole story.

The couple had settled comfortably into their new life in Tallinn when Andres began writing a series of investigative articles about the new mafia – the extent of its activities, the scale of its corruption, the number of politicians it had in its pocket. As he probed deeper and deeper, the death threats had started coming.

'It did not deter me,' Andres was saying in a distant

voice. 'To me, the truth was above all else. The sacred truth must be told at all costs. I was too blind to see that they would not strike directly at me, but through Manuela.'

Tara took his hand and said nothing. She knew from his halting, rusted cadences that this was the first time he had told the story in a long, long time.

'When it came, it came without any further warning,' he said. 'Manuela was driving her car, an old East German Trabant, to the office where I worked. When she reached the car park a long-haired young man in a red tracksuit walked up to her, calmly pulled out a .38 handgun, and fired three times into her head, just here,' he tapped his temple. 'She died instantly, of course.'

Tara was silent for a moment. 'Andres, I can't think of any words. I'm so, so sorry.'

He shrugged. 'Five years ago, Tara. There is nothing to be gained from living in the past.'

'So you had to leave your country a second time?'

'Yes, I'm afraid I ran away, like some panic-stricken animal. I know I should have stayed and carried on my campaign, but by that time there were others who were following the same trail that I had started.'

He took a long drink of Perrier. 'I was offered a job as international war correspondent by the editors at *Magnus* magazine,' he explained. 'So off I went, following the trail of holocausts from Asia to Latin America, from the Chechen hills to the streets of Sarajevo, from Armagh to Iraq. I always needed to get closer to the action than anyone else. Some of my fellow journalists said that I was foolhardy, others that I was courageous. They were both wrong. The truth was that I really wanted a bullet to end my life, just as it had done Manuela's.'

'But you survived.'

'God protects fools.' He drained the can. 'With time, the pain began to ease. Perhaps one day it will disappear completely.'

He turned to face her for the first time. 'You're a good listener, Tara,' he said. 'It has been years since I have had a chance to talk about this to anyone.'

'I'll listen any time,' she said simply.

He hesitated. It was almost as though the effort of delivering his next words was causing him actual physical pain. 'The worst thing I have to live with,' he said at last, 'is that it was all my fault. If I had been there, it would never have happened.'

Tara squeezed his hand. 'You're being too hard on yourself.'

He shook his head. 'I had arranged to meet her in Raejoko Plats half an hour beforehand. I didn't turn up. If I had, Manuela might still be alive today.'

'But I'm sure there was some good reason why you were delayed.'

He nodded, his dark eyes filled with pain. 'There was a good reason. I was involved with another woman.'

Then, with a suddenness that startled her, he crumpled his empty can and rose sharply to his feet.

'We'd better hurry,' he said. 'Or we shall be late for church.'

Tara and Andres took a pew near the centre of the basilica. As they waited for the service to begin, a group of white-clad novice nuns entered the church in single file and sat near the altar. Down in the body of the church, the families of these young girls glowed with quiet pride.

A choir of older sisters sang; their clear, pure voices swelled and swooped and resounded through the old building.

Then an old priest began the service. He spoke into a microphone that sent his words bouncing and echoing incoherently around the church. Words shattered, sentences broke up and repeated themselves. Tara, whose French was basic but functional, couldn't understand a word and soon gave up trying.

Soon it was time for Holy Communion. The consecrated Hosts were handed to the eucharistic ministers, the lay helpers who took their places at the head of each aisle and dispensed the wafers to the patient lines of communicants. The priest himself gave communion to the nuns and the novices.

Andres and Tara remained seated. After a few moments of indecision, Andres nudged Tara and nodded his head discreetly at one of the eucharistic ministers – the one furthest away from them, at the far side of the church.

'There he is,' he whispered with satisfaction. 'Do you recognise him?'

His face was half hidden by a forest of heads and half a dozen obscuring pillars, but Tara could just about make out his features.

Oh yes. There was no doubt about it at all.

That was the man, all right.

In the very last place you'd expect to find him.

'S'il vous plaît, monsieur?' said Andres.

'Ouay?' The accent was rough, guttural, working-class Paris. He stood on the steps outside the church, a pale and ascetic figure dressed entirely in black and carrying something wrapped in dark cloth.

'This is Ms Tara Ross, a close friend of Mr Fergal Kennedy.' Andres was speaking in English now. His voice was soft, but his eyes never left the other man's.

'I know who Ms Ross is.' His pale eyes turned towards her.

'We would like to talk to you,' insisted Andres. 'About the late Mrs Ann Kennedy.'

'Ann Kennedy.' He said it slowly, as though the words were something holy, like the four words he had said over and over again to communicants in the church.

'Yes. Ann Kennedy. The woman you once loved.'

The old man glanced around as though looking for a means of escape, then shrugged his shoulders and spread out his hands in a Gallic gesture of submission.

'It is as you say,' admitted the artist Michael de Blaca. 'But not as you might think. You had better come with me.'

They followed de Blaca to his ground-floor studio in one of the most expensive quarters of Montmartre. No artist would starve in a garret here any more, thought Tara. At the very worst one would be forced to cut back on the pressed duck and truffles, or cancel the champagne, because the bank was about to foreclose on one's astronomical mortgage.

The artist led them into a side street that was almost hidden behind the huge security fence of an embassy building. 'No one gets in or out here without being captured on video,' said de Blaca. 'Just warning you.'

He didn't smile.

The tiny cul-de-sac held only half a dozen buildings. It was a natural suntrap and the warm, motionless summer air was heavy with the smell of laurel, lavender and climbing roses.

'Here we are,' announced de Blaca, leading them through a stone archway and punching a security code in a keypad beside a hefty door flanked by individual bells and nameplates. Tara noticed a doctor, a dentist and an advertising agency executive. Finally, de Blaca fished out a complex-looking key and used it to open the main door and another door in the vestibule.

'Welcome to Bohemia,' he said.

Tara knew exactly what to expect. Primed by dozens of movies and books, she knew precisely what an artist's studio in Montmartre ought to look like. There would be bare, paint-splashed wooden floorboards, rough-hewn tables and chairs, and newly-painted canvasses stacked against each other in an untidy heap. A half-finished bottle of *marc* on the table, and perhaps a pouting model half-asleep on the unmade bed.

That was how it was in the Hollywood script; unfortunately, reality turned out to be different. De Blaca's studio was as austere as a priest's study. The living room was tiled in black and white, and heavily furnished with Edwardian armchairs and a chest of drawers in age-old, unforgiving mahogany. A small Arabic rug was the only concession to comfort. In the corner was a bookcase holding an encyclopaedia; on the walls a line drawing of a street scene. There was no TV, no video, no telephone. Every surface was clean, and every polishable one was gleaming with a deep, well-tended shine.

They passed through an equally sparse dining-room and Tara caught a glimpse of a bare, functional galley-kitchen. Finally de Blaca opened a pair of wide French windows and gestured at them to follow him into a small garden dominated by a shady, scented cedar.

'Something to drink?' he offered, sitting them at a beechwood garden table beneath the tree. 'Mineral water? Fresh orange? I'm afraid there is no wine or beer. I have been teetotal for some considerable time, and you must understand that I was not expecting guests.'

He went back into the house and re-emerged with a chilled bottle of Badoit mineral water, a *pain*, and several varieties of cheese on a wooden board.

'Help yourselves,' he instructed. 'There's brie, camembert, some blue from Provence and a goat's cheese from Normandy which I think you'll find interesting.'

'You have a beautiful studio,' said Tara, making small talk as she spread some brie.

He looked at her and frowned, as though she had said something controversial that required him to think long and hard before replying.

'Beautiful?' he said at last.

'I mean, it's a fine apartment in a very scenic location. You must be very happy here.'

Again the frown and the long pause. He had removed his heavy black jacket. He wore a black polo-necked sweater which contrasted with his pale face and white hair and emphasised his priest-like appearance. He was an ascetic, a monk, a creature of the dark catacombs, out of place in the shimmering sunshine.

'Happy?' he said.

Tara felt a spasm of irritation. She was familiar with this bizarre conversational game. It was easy to play. You questioned simple statements, analysed words, demanded definitions. It had nothing to do with clarity of meaning. It had everything to do with demeaning your opponent and demonstrating your own superior intelligence. She busied herself with choosing another portion of cheese and didn't respond.

'I like the beauty of austerity,' de Blaca said after a while. 'Happy? That's not an adjective I've used in relation to myself for a long, long time.'

Tara glanced up at him and quickly looked away. He hadn't said it in a tone that invited consolation, human sympathy or even further inquiry. It was a simple statement of fact.

She tried the friendly small talk approach one more time. 'I didn't notice any paintings,' she said. 'Are you working on any at the moment?'

'Paintings?' said de Blaca, knitting his brow.

Oh God, thought Tara. Here we go again.

'It's not surprising that you didn't notice any paintings,' de Blaca said, 'since I haven't painted any for the past twenty-seven years.'

'You have to forgive Tara,' Andres butted in quickly. 'She has not studied your work as closely as I have, Mr de Blaca. I have long been an admirer of your talent, hidden as it has been.'

'Hidden?'

Your turn, thought Tara. Serves you right for being so patronising.

'I mean,' said Andres, 'that while your work has been appreciated by some of the best critics, it has not earned you the sort of financial success enjoyed by your less talented contemporaries. The sort of success you deserve.'

De Blaca looked cynically amused.

'Van Gogh sold only one work in his lifetime,' he said. 'The difference between Van Gogh and me is that he didn't care. I do. I would love my sculptures to be purchased by rich people. I don't mind if they are philistines in the Chase Manhattan Bank or the Kawasaki Futures Corporation. Critics be damned. Cheques is what I want.'

'You prefer sculpting to painting these days?' Tara was just curious.

But it was Andres who answered. 'Tara, Mr de Blaca is famous in artistic circles as the man who changed his medium from painting to sculpture in the course of twenty-four hours. It was one of the most sudden and dramatic shifts of direction in the history of modern art. You said' – he turned back to de Blaca – 'that something happened on that day that was to change the course of your life forever, and that it prompted an entire change of medium. But until this day, you have never revealed what it was.'

'No. I never have.'

There was an awkward silence. Disappointment registered clearly on Andres's face. De Blaca was obviously in no mood to divulge any secrets.

Tara also felt a flicker of impatience. What had happened that day? What momentous event had been powerful enough to change the course of this man's entire career?

'So I began sculpting that day, and I have never stopped,' de Blaca continued at last. 'My passion for stone has never diminished. Only a few hours ago I began planning my latest project. It is a series of fantastical sculptures based loosely upon mediaeval gargoyles found in

Dublin. They are said to depict the seven ages of Man. I apologise' – he looked directly at Tara – 'the seven ages of Person.'

He continued to stare at her with blank, spiritless eyes. Tara began to dislike him intensely.

'Where do you work?' Andres asked, looking around him. 'Obviously you're not sculpting here.'

De Blaca finally released Tara from his stare.

'This is my city home,' he said. 'My workshop is in Brittany, out in the far west Atlantic coast. I work there for two months at a time, then I come here for a month's rest, and so on in a regular rhythm throughout the year.' He thought for a moment. 'Would you like to see it?'

For a moment, Tara thought he was offering to take them there, and mentally formulated a polite refusal. But he vanished into the house again, and returned with a leather-bound photo album.

De Blaca sat down more heavily this time, and panted as he recovered from the effort of his short journey. Tara realised that he was not a healthy man.

The first photograph showed a panoramic view of a Breton skyline, with an ancient stone barn in the centre. The barn itself had been renovated and was unremarkable. What was remarkable was its surroundings. It stood on the fringe of a vast forest of prehistoric standing stones. There were hundreds of them, stretching to the horizon. Most of them were single rocks placed upright in the earth, but there were also a number of dolmens – groups of two or three vertical stones with a slab placed horizontally on top.

'I've heard of this place, but I've never seen it before,' said Tara. 'It reminds me of the dolmens in the Burren, near my home in Clare. But I've never seen so many stones together in one place.'

'It must have been a place of great spiritual importance to the ancients,' Andres mused.

'As it is to me,' said de Blaca. 'I find it a vast reserve of power, a huge battery of creative energy.'

He turned the page to reveal a photo of a very old wooden farm-gate with a carved sign that read: LA MAISON DES PIERRES FOLLES.

'House of the Mad Stones,' said Tara, translating it literally. 'The dolmens, I suppose.'

'Yes. It was the name of a farm that existed nearby, in the last century. It has long gone, but I find the name apt in view of my profession – and my reputation among the local community.'

The next page revealed an interior views of the barn. It was a spacious workshop with wooden benches and stone sculptures in varying degrees of completion.

But the fourth page came as a surprise. It showed two attractive young women flanking de Blaca as they all posed in his workshop.

In the next picture, one of the girls was shown hard at work polishing a sculpture. She was blonde, possibly Scandinavian, and she was wearing a pair of scuffed dungarees with no top underneath, the loose bib revealing a lot of her formidable frontage as she bent forward and concentrated on her labours.

The fifth photo showed the second girl, who must have been American. She was a small, plumpish brunette and she was flashing her perfect teeth at the camera as she sat up in a rumpled double-bed, clutching a duvet loosely around her naked body and raising a glass of red wine in a toast.

'My girls,' said de Blaca, proudly. 'Helga and Ronnie. Helga is from Scandinavia and Ronnie is from San Francisco. They share my house, they share my work, and they share my bed.'

He explained that they were art students who were learning the technique of sculpting. They were always there. This year it was Helga and Ronnie; last year it was Su Lin and Yvette; next year it would be someone else. Sometimes, he complained, it was impossible to get rid of them. There could be five or six girls in the house at a time.

'The beauty of austerity,' said Andres, straight-faced.

'Austerity?' repeated Michael de Blaca.

Tara wasn't listening to any of this. She was leafing her way through the album – more interiors, more works-in-progress, more shots of smiling girls in varying stages of undress.

It was all becoming very predictable...until she reached the final page.

This page, the one on the inside of the back cover, was entirely devoted to one photograph. It was a black-and-white studio portrait of a young Ann Kennedy, and, across it, a shaky hand had written: 'Ann. May you rest in peace.'

Tara felt de Blaca's eyes on her. She looked up and met his stare without flinching.

'I think,' he said at last, 'it's time I told the truth about myself and Ann.'

'I think,' said Tara evenly, 'that that would be a good idea.'

De Blaca was quiet now, still staring at Ann's portrait as though it were the key that would unlock the door to his past, that would change history and make everything all right again.

'My dear God,' he said at last. 'She was so beautiful.'

Tara thought she saw a shimmer, only a shimmer, of wet tears in his eye. But she couldn't be sure.

'She was certainly very pretty,' she agreed.

'What the hell do you know?' he exploded. 'Pretty? What sort of a word is that? Helga is pretty. Ronnie is pretty. This chap here' – he gestured rudely at Andres – 'might even find you pretty, God love his wit. But Ann was downright, twenty-four-carat, goddam *beautiful*.' He slammed his hand down hard on the table to emphasise the last two words. 'She had a face like a young nun's and a body like Salome's. Everything about her was understated sensuality – the way she moved, the way she talked, everything. Pretty? For God's sake! Have you any idea, any conception, of how it felt to be alone in that house with her? Have you the remotest notion?'

The unexpected outburst left his two visitors lost for words. Andres was the first to speak. 'When did you realise you had fallen in love with her?' he asked gently.

'You're missing the point. Yes, yes, I was obviously in love, but more than that. I wanted her more than I wanted my life, more than I wanted to breathe and – this was the intolerable part – more than I wanted to paint. I tried to work but I couldn't. Canvas after bloody canvas, all ruined, all useless. Nothing came to any good. Nothing worked out right. Something had to be done.'

He took a long draught of Badoit, almost as though the water would be enough to quench some inner flame.

'And was this feeling reciprocated?' asked Tara quietly.

'I believed it was.'

'Did she say so?'

'Damn it!' De Blaca's flat hand slapped the table again. 'She couldn't say so. She was a married woman, and it would have been a sin to admit her feelings towards another man. But I knew, all right. Or at least, I was sure I knew.'

A cloud drifted over the sun and its shadow, falling on the garden, seemed to darken the tone of the conversation.

'You were sure you knew.' Tara realised with surprise that she was playing the same word-game he'd earlier used against her.

'Yes.'

'But you were wrong.' She was following a hunch.

'Yes. I was mistaken.'

'Tell us what happened.' Tara, the prosecuting counsel, leading the witness.

De Blaca's tension seemed to ease immediately, as though he had resolved to tell everything and the mere intent of confession had lifted a great burden from his soul.

'It was a day I'll never forget as long as I'm allowed to live.' His eyes closed and his voice had dropped to a near-whisper. 'A bright, beautiful County Clare morning, everyone's ideal morning, sun glistening on the cobwebs in the hedgerows and the sea dancing with a million shimmering points of sunlight. I rose at dawn. I couldn't sleep. I walked on the beach at Claremoon Harbour, tossing bits of jetsam into the ocean, unable to think straight, unable to focus. I was angry with the world, and particularly angry with Ann for coming between me and the only thing that meant a damn to me, the only thing that made life worth living.'

He stared up at the top of the cedar tree, but his eyes were really looking upwards at the farmhouse at Barnabo, perched high on the crags above the beach.

'At last, maybe around seven in the morning, I knocked on the front door. It took her a while to answer. She was wearing a dressing-gown and her eyes were sleepy and full of innocent surprise. I'd never seen her like that before, her fair hair loose and tousled and golden, like the rough-stacked hay on the hillside behind her. I desired her more than I could bear.'

'And where was Martin during all this? Where was her husband?'

'Who knows? Over the hills and far away. Milking the cows, ploughing a field, or just behind a hedge with a naggin bottle of Jameson. Who knew, who cared?'

'So Ann let you in as usual,' pursued Tara. 'And you set up your easel as usual in front of the big window.'

'Yes. But my hand was shaking and my co-ordination was gone. I knew it was pointless.'

'And then?'

'I was consumed with anger. Not just anger, a volatile mixture of emotions – rage against her, and desire for her.

I went looking for her.'

'Why? What did you intend to say or do?'

He shook his head with impatience. 'I don't know. I couldn't help it. I found her in her bedroom. I pounded on the door. After a moment she opened it, just a crack. I could see her, still in her dressing-gown, but it had worked loose and I could see the pale Nordic skin of her neck and shoulders. She seemed afraid of me. She told me to go away, that she was trying to dress.'

'And did you?'

'Of course not. I could no more go away than...than give up my art. I told her everything, shouting through the door. How much I loved her and wanted her and needed her, and how I knew she felt the same. I begged her, pleaded with her to let me in to her bed.'

Tara glanced at Andres, but he was leaning forward, staring intensely at the artist's face.

'That's when it all went wrong,' said de Blaca at last. 'She told me to leave the house, to go away and never come back. She was furious, but also very, very frightened.'

He grabbed the empty Badoit bottle and tossed it angrily into the lower branches of the cedar tree. It rebounded and shattered against a stone.

'I think it was her fear that did it to me. I would like to say it was love, or lust, or desire, but it wasn't. It was her fear I found exciting. It was the sense that I had total power over her, that she was frightened and that I alone was the source of her terror. I kicked in the bedroom door as though it were made of cardboard. She stared at me, frozen like some small stricken creature. I grabbed her by the shoulders and pulled away the gown so hard that it ripped apart. Then I forced her on to the bed.'

He stopped and looked up, his eyes filled with naked anguish.

'My God,' said Andres slowly. 'You raped her.'

The artist nodded, his breathing laboured and

asthmatic. When he finally spoke, his voice was no more than a whisper. 'Yes. May God forgive me, but that is the truth.'

'So there never was a love affair,' said Tara. 'All those rumours throughout the years...they were all lies.'

'I never claimed there was an affair. Yes, I loved her with a passion I have never known before or since. As God is my judge, I still love her. But Ann Kennedy never, ever, not for one moment, forgave me.'

'I wonder why,' said Tara, not bothering to hide her contempt.

De Blaca wasn't listening. 'So I left the country after that episode. I abandoned my stuff at her house and ran all the way to my studio in the village. I packed a few things, grabbed a bus and fled to Dublin. I ended up in Liverpool, and then in Paris. For the next two years, I waited for the arrest warrant that never came.'

'It never came,' said Tara, 'because she didn't tell anyone. Not even her husband.'

'But why on earth not?' Andres exploded. 'She was the victim of an appalling attack. Surely rape was a crime in those days, even in rural Ireland?'

'It was a crime,' said Tara, 'but it was a different era, when women were held responsible for what their attackers did. She would have been asked why she was alone in the house, undressed, with another man while her husband was absent. The police would have come to what they felt was the obvious conclusion.'

Tara turned to de Blaca. 'Ann was an intelligent woman. She realised all this. So she quietly picked up the pieces of her life and carried on as best she could. She was strong. But she didn't reckon on one problem.'

De Blaca couldn't meet her eyes. He looked away.

'Ann became pregnant as a result of the rape, didn't she?'

De Blaca silently nodded.

'And you had the nerve to send the new baby a present

when it was born. A sculpture of a sheela-na-gig...a naked woman in an obscene pose.' Tara couldn't mask her incredulity at the tastelessness of the gift.

'You obviously don't realise the symbolism of the sheela-na-gig in history.' De Blaca was on more secure ground now, and regained some of his previous patronising tone. 'It was not an expression of carnality. It was the exact opposite – repentance for carnality, repentance on both our parts. That was the spirit in which I sent it. An act of atonement. I wrote an accompanying letter explaining all this. It was also,' his voice assumed a note of pride, 'my very first sculpture.'

Tara was about to reply in no uncertain terms, but Andres laid a restraining hand on her arm and gestured to her to drop the subject.

'I take it she didn't answer your letter,' he said.

'No.'

'So you simply put this shameful little episode behind you and forgot all about it.'

'Forgot it?' De Blaca's voice was a howl of distress. His fists clenched. 'I would give everything I possess, everything, if only I *could* forget it. Ever since that day, I have been living through hell.'

He was staring bleakly into the intertwined branches of the cedar tree, but looking at his eyes, Tara knew that he was really watching the twisting, writhing souls of the damned. She had never seen a human face so bereft of all hope.

'I ruined the life of a beautiful, kind woman,' he whispered hoarsely. 'The only woman I have ever loved. Ever since then I have ached for her. It is like an open wound that will never heal.'

'You're wrong,' said Tara, more sharply this time. 'You didn't ruin Ann Kennedy's life. She didn't give you that power. You had the physical strength to abuse her, but she did not allow her life to be ruined. She overcame the trauma. She pervaded.'

If de Blaca heard her words, he didn't show it. He lapsed into silence.

Andres cleared his throat. 'There is just one more question I'd like to ask,' he said. 'It's a very important question. In fact, it's the reason we have come here today.'

De Blaca drained his glass and glared at them both with undiluted hatred.

'Enough questions,' he said. 'You have learned the truth about me, something that no other person outside a confessional box has ever known. You have stripped me bare. Haven't you had enough? Go now.'

'But...'

'Please.' His voice had dropped to a whimper. 'Just go. No more questions. Now that Ann has gone, there are only two people I need answer to. One is my creator, and the other is the human being who I, in turn, helped to create that dreadful morning. My son.' His hand shook as it tried to pour out another glass of water. 'My only child. Manus.'

They rose wordlessly and left the house, leaving de Blaca alone with his immeasurable anguish, in the cedar-scented shade of the beautiful garden that had become his own personal Gethsemane.

'He mustn't be told,' Tara said firmly. 'He must never, ever be told.'

She fiddled aimlessly with the quiche on her plate. All around her, waiters and waitresses in colourful and elaborate folk-costumes from the Alsace area of France bustled back and forth, attending to the needs of the restaurant clientele with loud and good-humoured efficiency. But most of this carefully-arranged spectacle was lost on Tara.

'Who?' asked Andres.

'Well, I was thinking mainly of poor Fergal,' she said, setting down her empty fork. 'But it wouldn't be fair to either of them. Manus is already disturbed enough without being told he's the child of rape. Perhaps that's the reason he's disturbed in the first place, I don't know. Maybe it's responsible for his violent tendencies.'

Andres didn't respond. 'And Fergal?' he asked.

Tara gave an irritable shrug. 'It means a lot to him to believe that he's the son of Michael de Blaca. It's why he wanted to become an artist. It's the only thing that matters in his life. I'd be worried about the effect the truth might have on him. Especially at a time like this.'

Andres sipped thoughtfully at his glass of Alsace wine. 'I agree,' he said at last. 'It can do no good. It can only do incalculable harm.'

'He must never be told,' insisted Tara. She felt edgy and tense. Her wrist had started to hurt once again, sending regular spasms of pain up through her arm. 'Promise me.'

'Okay, okay, I promise.'

Tara looked at him for a moment, then picked up her knife and fork and cut another minuscule portion of the quiche. It was the genuine article, cooked to perfection, and in any other circumstances she would have found it irresistible.

'Why did you bring us to Paris, Andres?' she asked at last.

'To discover the truth. I knew Fergal could not be Michael de Blaca's son, despite all his protestations. The dates are all wrong. De Blaca created his first sculpture twenty-seven years ago, not twenty-nine. By the time the rape took place, Fergal was already more than a year old.'

'Not everyone is an expert on the life of Michael de Blaca.'

'Fergal certainly was not. And I find that surprising.' Andres studied the wallpaper pensively. 'Perhaps he did not want to look too hard. Perhaps he did not want to run the risk of reality destroying a myth that he had carefully nurtured since his adolescence.'

He glanced back at her, and his eyes widened with concern. 'Tara. You're crying.'

'I'm sorry, Andres. I'm just upset and...furious, to tell you the truth. That bloody hypocrite de Blaca, with his communion wafers and his fine talk about art and passion, and beneath all of it he's no better than Zip-Down Seanie.'

'Who?'

'Never mind. Just somebody who attacked me outside a pub the other day.'

'Someone else attacked you? Have you told the police?'

'Yes. It's not important.' She tried to relax, compose herself. 'How's your meal?'

Andres helped himself to another forkful of his own dish, another Alsatian speciality featuring tender pieces of lamb marinaded in milk. 'It's good. Really good. It's always good here. That's why I come here. That's why I brought you here. Listen' – now it was his turn to be irritated – 'you don't have to punish yourself, Tara. There is nothing you can do to alter the past. The only way we can honour Ann now – apart from respecting her obvious wish to keep this shameful matter secret – is to do whatever we can to bring her killer to justice.'

Tara set down her knife and fork together and pushed her plate aside. 'How can you understand? You're a man. Men understand nothing about what rape means to women. It's fear, pure and simple. Whether it happens physically or not, the threat is always there. It's the way men exercise power over women. It's always been that way.'

'Tara.' Andres was quiet but firm. 'You will have no argument from me about the evil of rape. But all men are not potential rapists. That is an extreme position and it is not helpful to anyone.'

'You heard him. His attack on Ann had nothing to do with desire. It was power. He was excited because he had power over her.'

Her voice had unintentionally risen. A couple at a nearby table had stopped talking to each other and were turning their heads curiously, drawn more by the tone of her voice than by her words.

'*L'addition, s'il vous plait, madame.*' Andres, his face expressionless, had caught the eye of a waitress and was calling for the bill.

'*D'accord, monsieur.*' The motherly-looking waitress smiled, then looked concerned when she spotted Tara's tense, pale face and her almost-untouched meal. '*Madame est malade?*'

'*Non, non, merci. Seulement un peu fatiguée.*'

The waitress had reached her own conclusion. She was tight-lipped with disapproval as she accepted payment from Andres, and she gave Tara a look which, in any language, means: Don't worry, love, he's not worth it.

It was still warm and sunny as they walked out into the busy Place de la Republique and hailed a taxi to take them back to the airport.

'Just what was the point of this trip anyway, Andres?' asked Tara after they had sat for ten minutes in silence while their taxi battled its way past the Boulevard Périphérique and out towards the northern suburbs of Paris. 'We've learned a sordid secret from the past. We've learned that Manus is the child of rape and that the only thing that keeps Fergal going from day to day is...just a stupid illusion. But essentially it changes nothing as far as our main objective is concerned. We're still at square one. We've achieved absolutely nothing.'

Andres shrugged and looked out the taxi window at the roadside cafés and Tabacs. 'Perhaps, perhaps not. This is just another piece of the jigsaw, Tara. We cannot judge anything until we find the gap in the puzzle that only this piece will fit. Then, and then only, can we decide how important it is.'

They didn't speak again until they reached Charles de Gaulle airport.

The Aer Lingus jet seemed to hang in the air over the damp green plains of Leinster, stationary and weightless as an airborne rock by Magritte. Just a slight downwards tip of the wing, and Tara could see the magnificent Wicklow Mountains, then the Hill of Howth, then the Liffey and Dublin Bay, all fading from colour to black-and-white in the encroaching dusk.

A little closer to earth and she could distinguish the individual lights of the fishing boats and ferries off the coast. Then – and she was always amazed at how rapidly this happened – suddenly the fields of north County Dublin were rushing up towards her, and then the fields turned into concrete, and they were swooping down on the runway at Dublin Airport.

Night was falling quickly as they made their way to the airport taxi rank, tired and ready for sleep after their five am start. It had been a long day. Tara wanted nothing more than a hot shower and a solid eight hours of total, wipe-out sleep.

By the time they reached the apartment, she was totally exhausted, and when she told Andres she didn't feel like coffee or a nightcap, he seemed to agree.

'Goodnight, then,' said Tara as she passed him on her way to the bathroom.

He stopped her. 'Tara...'

'Yes, Andres?' She was so tired that she could hardly keep him in focus.

He seemed to be gazing into her eyes. So much so that she wondered whether they were obviously bloodshot or something.

'There's something I'd really like to say to you. Something important. Can we sit down...?'

But she'd reached her threshold of exhaustion, and she was in no mood to listen to any of his new theories on the Kennedy case – especially theories about the loathsome

Michael de Blaca. 'Can it wait until tomorrow, Andres?' she pleaded. 'I'm sorry, but I just can't keep my eyes open any longer.'

'I suppose so.' He seemed disappointed.

'And thank you for the trip to Paris,' she yawned. 'See you in the morning.'

'Perhaps,' he nodded.

It was later, as she was drifting off to sleep, that his last word echoed in her head like some discordant note. Perhaps? Perhaps? What the hell did he mean, perhaps?

She tried to figure it out, but within seconds her thoughts were swamped in a dark and blessed tidal wave of oblivion.

CHAPTER SEVENTEEN

SOMEWHERE IN the apartment, a radio came on. It was tuned to the RTÉ news. The words forced themselves through Tara's warm, comfortable cocoon of sleep and into her consciousness. First item, another political corruption scandal. Second item, an old couple beaten up in their lonely home in some rural boreen for the five hundred pounds they'd saved up for their retirement and had kept hidden in a teapot. Third item, a priest given a suspended sentence for a sexual assault on a young girl entrusted to his care.

Welcome back to holy Ireland, she thought.

She listened for the morning-movement sounds of the man who had switched on the radio. The hiss of a shower, perhaps, or the muted roar of an electric kettle, or the welcoming pop of a toaster. But there was only silence.

After a while – she was in no hurry – she slipped into the luxurious dressing-gown and emerged, yawning, into the bright golden sunshine of the living-room. The curtains had been pulled open to reveal the panoramic view of the bay, Dalkey Island, Killiney Hill and, mistily in the southern distance, the cross-topped crag of Bray Head.

The radio was sitting on the table by the window. It had been set on auto-alarm.

Switching it off, Tara glanced down the corridor towards the bedrooms. The door of Andres's room had been left wide open to reveal a freshly-made bed and an empty room bright with sun. The bathroom, too, was obviously deserted.

Perhaps Andres has popped out to buy a paper or get more milk for coffee, thought Tara dozily as she wandered towards the kitchen.

Coffee. Now that sounds like a very interesting word.

She located the electric kettle, filled it with water, and switched it on.

And that's when she saw the note.

So much for pooling resources. So much for working together. So much for bloody co-operation.

Tara's unsteady hand hacked the toast into fragments as she tried to spread ice-cold butter from the fridge. She felt letdown, cheated, as though someone had offered her a comfortable chair and then snatched it away from under her at the last minute.

Why had Andres offered to help her if he was just going to disappear?

Why give support and then withdraw it just when she needed it most? Just when she was at her lowest ebb?

She topped the toast unevenly with dollops of lime marmalade, grabbed her cup of lukewarm coffee and flopped down miserably on the nearest armchair.

You idiot, she told herself. You bloody cretin. When will you ever learn?

It had been just another story to him. Just another headline, just another emotive colour article in some international magazine, just another bid to win a Pulitzer. He'd got the information he wanted from her, and now he'd gone on to the next story. He was no more concerned about justice than Gerry Gellick was concerned about ethics. The two men were exactly the same, she realised. They just used different tactics to the same end.

She uncrumpled the screwed-up note and reread it for the tenth time.

'Tara – I trust you slept well. Please help yourself to breakfast. I have to go abroad on a matter of great urgency. I am uncertain as to the date of my return.

'I *strongly* advice you not to return to Claremoon Harbour, at least for a week or so. You are most welcome to remain in my apartment for that period.'

There followed two paragraphs of terse, practical instructions on how to set the alarm system and operate the central heating. Then, finally: 'Be strong, Tara. Andres Talimann.'

And you go to hell, too, Andres, she thought.

Be strong. Looks like I'll have to be.

As her anger subsided, she began to feel the nagging pangs of self-doubt. Her behaviour yesterday, viewed in hindsight, had bordered on rudeness. She had been testy, moody, downright churlish, and the constant pain from her sprained wrist was no excuse. She'd been angry about Claremoon Harbour, angry about Bernietown and Ballymahon, angry about de Blaca, angry at the world. And she'd taken her anger out on him.

And yet. And yet he had appeared genuinely sympathetic, genuinely eager to help.

Part of the act, you moron, she told herself. Part of a smooth, polished, perfected stage routine which helped him win awards for his professional skills. What had Melanie's friend Carla said about Andres?

'As soon as he gets close to anyone, he jets off to the other side of the world and leaves her in the lurch.'

Grow up, Tara. Time to stop being so trusting.

You don't need him. You don't need anybody.

She finished her coffee and reread the note. Stay here? Stay in this luxurious flat while Fergal was still under suspicion? While a genuinely decent man was still being followed and hunted around County Clare by police who had yet to be convinced of his innocence?

She'd rather go for sculpting lessons with Michael de Blaca.

The phone rang when she was in the bathroom. Tara dashed out, practically at a sprint, but the answering machine cut in before she could lift the receiver.

She stood for a while, wondering whether she should

interrupt the process, and eventually decided she shouldn't. But as she was about to step into the shower, she had second thoughts. What if the caller had been Andres himself? Phoning her to explain his mysterious actions and leave a new contact number?

Wrapping a towel around herself, she returned to the sitting room and rewound the cassette on the answerphone. But when she played it, the tape began with an even earlier message. It had been logged the previous evening, as they'd been flying back from Paris.

'Andres? It's me.' A deep male voice, middle-aged, American but with a heavy foreign accent, possibly French. 'It's...uh...three-fifteen in the afternoon our time. Just to let you know I made the connection. I got the person you want. If you're still interested, book a flight and meet me at the airport tomorrow night, say eight, eight-thirty our time. Oh, and bring the cash, Andres. Otherwise, no deal.'

Tara hardly listened to the most recent message, a brief call from a garage to tell Andres that his BMW was ready for collection. The first call had left her stunned. Up until now, she'd been simply hurt and annoyed that Andres had let her down. But this message, which had obviously prompted his unexpected dash abroad, provoked thoughts that were much more disturbing.

What if Steve and O'Rourke had been justified in their concern about Andres's mysterious meetings with Villiers and the Limerick cannabis distributor?

'I made the connection...bring the cash, otherwise no deal.'

The mystery caller.

'I have to go abroad on a matter of great urgency.'

Andres.

Tara walked slowly back to the bathroom. She set the shower to maximum pressure, and focused the jet of water directly on her forehead, almost as though she could use it as a riot hose to chase the most frightening images out of her mind.

She finished her shower and dried herself off. Her heart had stopped beating so fast; she was beginning to calm down and think more logically. She had been making wild assumptions, she told herself. Jumping to crazy conclusions. There must be a rational explanation for all this.

Damn.

She'd dropped one of her earrings into the wastebin under the bathroom sink.

She knelt down beside it and began to rummage. Of course, the tiny earring had worked its way right through the rubbish to the very bottom. The bin hadn't been emptied for a while. She had to sift through the usual bathroom detritus to find it. There were empty shampoo bottles, tissues, disposable razors and...

She froze, transfixed by what she saw in the heart of the debris. There were five of them, altogether. She recognised them instantly. She'd done enough stories about them. Opaque plastic cylinders that had been used once and then discarded.

Hypodermic needles.

The little Fiat was waiting for her like an eager puppy. Well, no, it wasn't, it was waiting for her like a heap of rusted Italian metal, but Tara had always given personalities to cars and probably would go right on doing it for the rest of her life.

She put her overnight bag into the boot and mentally rehearsed the route home. Skirt the south city from east to west, then hit the motorway in the direction of Galway. Finally take that atrocious, winding, potholed road that led to the coast of northwest Clare, to Claremoon Harbour, and to what used to be home.

Tara paused for just a moment to take a deep breath of the sharp, cool air before flinging her handbag on to the passenger seat. It hit something hard and metallic: her mobile phone. She cursed her own stupidity. Had she really been daft enough to leave it there as an open invitation to any passing thief?

As she started the engine and drove slowly out of the car park, she lifted the phone and automatically punched the code that would replay her own taped messages.

The first one was an outdated message from a radio researcher who wanted to interview her about the Claremoon Harbour killing, for a programme that would have gone out yesterday.

The second one was a request for an interview from a famous magazine editor.

The third message was from a woman with a strong French accent who said she was from *Paris Match*.

The fourth said: 'Tara, it's Melanie here. Where are you, girl? We're all getting a bit concerned. Listen, please don't worry, pet, but your father's been taken ill. The doctors think it may be some sort of stroke. All the stress, I suppose. But they think he might be okay. He's out of hospital now and I've taken a couple of days off to stay with him and help out. I'm at his house in Claremoon Harbour. Give me a ring as soon as you can.'

Tara swung the car off the road and parked in a tiny lay-by overhung by a huge copper beech. Her fingers shook uncontrollably as she tried to punch the keys on the mobile phone. It was her father's phone number, as familiar as spelling her own name, but she still made three mistakes before getting it right. It rang and rang. It seemed to ring forever. Then, finally:

'Hello...?'

Melanie's voice, but not her usual voice. Uncertain, apprehensive, even fearful.

'Hello, Mel. I just got your message. This is terrible. How is he?'

'Tara! Thank God it's you.' Her relief was obvious.

'He's doing well. Don't worry. It's okay. He's out of danger and he's recovering. They kept him in hospital for only a couple of nights and then discharged him to the care of his GP and a visiting nurse. Lots of rest and he'll be fine, they say.'

'What's wrong with him? Was it really a stroke?' She was worried sick.

'They thought that at first, but now they're not so sure. They say it could have been anything. He can't even speak yet. But relax – it's not life-threatening.' She paused for a second as though wondering whether to go on. 'Which is more than I can say about the strange phone calls we've been getting.'

'Oh, dear God.'

'Some sicko has been phoning up late at night. When I answer the phone, he seems to think I'm you.'

'What does he say?' Tara waited for a reply. 'Go on, Mel. I'd rather know than not know.'

'That you should get out of Claremoon Harbour and stay out. Otherwise you could end up in the cemetery alongside Ann Kennedy.'

'Oh, no.'

'Words to that effect. Sorry, Tara.'

'Obviously someone who has lost touch with his inner child, Melanie.' Tara tried to put a brave face on it.

'Someone in good need of therapy, Tara. In fact, I have been giving him directive counselling. It comes in the form of two words, the second word being "off".'

'Have you notified the gardaí about the calls?'

'Of course. They asked if anyone had a grudge against you. I said: "You mean, apart from the entire population of Claremoon Harbour?" They didn't seem to think that was funny. They gave me the stock advice about handling nuisance callers, and told me to contact them if it happened again.'

'And did it?'

'Yes. Twice. More or less the same warning every

time. It's probably just some emotional cripple acting out his macho power-fantasies. According to the textbooks, they rarely translate these fantasies into action in real life.'

'So you don't think there's any cause for concern?'

'Are you joking? Textbooks, schmextbooks. I'm keeping your dad's shotgun loaded and ready by the front door.'

'Make sure all the doors and windows are properly locked, too.' Tara felt powerless, one hundred and fifty miles from home. 'Listen, why not call Fergal? He could stay with you until I get back.'

Silence. Melanie was obviously not impressed by the idea.

'Hello, Melanie? Are you still there?'

'Yes, I'm still here. You still haven't told me where you've been for the last couple of days.'

Tara hesitated. 'I've been with Andres Talimann.'

'The same Andres you can't stand?' asked Melanie. 'The same Andres who's a right pain in the neck?'

'Yes,' said Tara shortly.

'So he's not a pain in the neck any more?' Melanie was keeping her voice deliberately neutral.

'No. He's not a pain in the neck any more,' she said. 'He's graduated to being a pain in the ass.'

'Oh, my God.'

'He promised he would join forces with me to help find Manus Kennedy, then he just...he just pissed off without even saying goodbye. He's left the country.'

'Oh, Tara, That's awful. I'm really sorry.'

'Don't be. He's got too many shady connections for my liking. I couldn't care less if I never saw him again. I genuinely, honestly, absolutely, couldn't give a stuff.'

Melanie said nothing. She could hear the hurt in Tara's voice.

'When will you be home?' she asked at last.

'Very soon. As fast as I can drive from Dublin.'

Melanie sighed. 'Which in your old jalopy means next week sometime. I'll throw an extra spud in the pot.'

'Thanks, Mel. You've been an absolute tower of strength.'

'Hey, enough of the male-orientated phallic images. I'm a Freudian Feminist.'

'Goodbye, Mel.'

'Bye, pet. And remember – don't worry about a thing.'

Tara had driven another fifty miles before she'd noticed a fifth message, alerted by the mobile's insistent bleeping on the passenger seat. It was an unfamiliar voice – male, with a strong west of Ireland accent.

Judging from the noise he seemed to be calling from a public phone box near a busy highway. His message was curt and to the point.

He said: 'This is me. The guy you've been looking for, asking questions about all over Inismaul and Bernietown and Ballymahon flats.'

A pause on the tape as a coin rattled noisily into a kiosk slot. Cars were roaring past in the background. Someone sounded a horn.

'Well, don't worry about trying to find me any more,' said Manus Kennedy. 'Next time, *I* will find *you*.'

The weather turned as she crossed the Shannon. Leaving Athlone behind, she found herself driving towards great massed banks of tank-grey clouds, hovering like immense castles from a Grimm fairy tale just above the wet green flatlands of Roscommon and east Galway. Miles away, in the far distance, she could actually see the rain falling, connecting earth and heaven like some Victorian engraving of Jacob's Ladder.

By the time she drove past the gloomy pastures of Aughrim, scene of the bloodiest battle of the Williamite wars, the rain was pounding on her roof and windscreen like kettledrums.

And that was when her engine chose to give up.

It just ran out of steam, like a superannuated

locomotive, and drifted to the roadside, coughing and jud-
dering in hopeless resignation.

Rain in the electrics. Again.

It was already early evening before she managed to
thumb a lift to the nearest garage and find a friendly
mechanic. By the time she drove off with a brand-new distributor, a new set of spark plugs and a credit card slip
showing a bill for nearly ninety pounds, dusk was falling as
fast as the torrential rain. And by the time she reached the
west coast of Clare, Claremoon Harbour was enveloped in
a dense shroud of darkness and sea-mist.

Tara didn't even glance to left or right as she drove
down the deserted main street, past the bright lights and
music of Breadon's Bar, past the church and the cemetery.
She realised, with a sudden spasm of shame, that she was
hoping no one would notice her.

Was this what it had come to? Was this how she was
condemned to live her life? Like some furtive rodent scuttling from one cover to another under the protection of
darkness?

When she pulled in to the driveway of her father's cottage, she was shaking with exhaustion, anxiety and sup-
pressed anger. She killed the engine and sat for a
moment to let the caustic, poisonous emotions drain out
of her. Inside that cottage were new burdens, fresh
responsibilities, and she would need all her strength to
take them on.

But wasn't it strange, she thought, that no friendly
light went on in response to the noise of her car?

Strange that no familiar face peeked out through the
curtains with a smile and a welcoming wave?

She collected her bag from the boot, swung it across
her shoulder, and searched for her keys. Nowhere. They
must be in the pockets of her other coat.

She rang the doorbell and waited in the rain for Melanie to answer.

Nothing.

No answering footsteps. No shout of greeting. Just nothing.

She was about to go back to her car to fetch her keys when she realised it wouldn't be necessary.

The front door wasn't even shut.

It was almost closed, but not quite. There was the merest sliver of light between door and frame.

All her other emotions were swept aside in an all-engulfing wave of sheer dread.

Something was very, very wrong.

Dumping her bag in a puddle, she pushed open the door. It opened only a foot or so before jamming on a soft, yielding obstacle.

The obstacle on the floor was Melanie. Her body was twisted into an unnatural shape as it lay motionless on the cold tiles. The eyes were closed. And the glorious red hair was matted and covered with congealed blood.

CHAPTER EIGHTEEN

AT AROUND the same time Tara was leaving Dublin for Clare, Andres Talimann was sitting down to lunch with Wendy Killegar in an expensive restaurant in Dublin's St Stephen's Green.

Wendy was a statuesque strawberry blond, six feet tall and striking in an immaculately styled jade jacket by Rocha and a black Versace dress. Around her neck was a double string of freshwater pearls.

She ordered gravlax followed by lobster salad. Andres had salmon mousse and Dover sole. Over a shared and correctly-chilled bottle of Muscadet de Sèvre-et-Maine sur Lie, they began to talk. Their conversation was at first shallow and desultory, their voices quieter than usual in the reverent hush.

'Okay, out with it, Andres,' said Wendy suddenly.

Amused, Andres made a small show of looking at his lap. 'Out with what, precisely, Wendy?'

'You only ask me out to lunch when you want some information about the art world. Here we are at lunch. Ergo, you want to pump me for free info for which I would normally charge a breathtakingly exorbitant consultancy fee. If I ran my gallery the way I indulge you, I would be in *Stubb's* within a week.'

Andres sipped the bone-dry Muscadet. 'Instead of being on your way to your second million,' he teased.

'Don't be ridiculous. I've barely reached my first yet.'

'I was talking dollars.'

She conceded his point with a good-humoured nod. 'The only reason I indulge you at all, Andres, is that you are such good company. So' – she raised a fork with an impaled portion of salmon, as though in a mock-warning – 'don't blow it by talking of such vulgar topics as money.

What do you want to know about?'

Andres finished his last bite of salmon mousse, washed it down with a gulp of Muscadet, and plunged straight in at the deep end. 'Michael de Blaca,' he said simply.

'Well, well.' She pushed her chair backwards so suddenly that the wooden legs honked noisily against the terracotta tiles. She was genuinely surprised and not a little amused. 'Well, *well*, well. You *are* on the ball, aren't you? How in heaven's name did you find out?'

Andres hadn't a clue what she was talking about. He decided to bluff his way anyway.

'Oh, one has one's contacts,' he said vaguely. 'You would be surprised how many people indulge me. I'm such good company, you know.'

She dabbed her exquisite mouth with a linen napkin. 'It's all very hush-hush, darling. If you write anything at all before the auction next month, I'll personally turn your testes into gravlax.'

Wendy pushed her fork firmly into another roll of marinaded salmon as though to illustrate her point.

'That depends on the date. When exactly is it?' Andres was flying blind. He'd never heard of any auction next month.

'The twenty-first. The date was finalised only this morning. We don't have a lot of time, Andres, and secrecy is of the very essence. *Please.*'

She looked pleadingly at him with eyes that would have made Woodward and Bernstein tear up their notes on Watergate.

Andres was grateful for the arrival of the waiter, an angular young man in white shirt and faded blue jeans, who cleared their starter plates and delivered their main course. It gave him time to think.

'Is there a lot of money involved?' he asked at last.

'Oh, thousands, darling. Hundreds of thousands. And before you ask, I'm talking dollars. After all, the goods may be in Ireland but the auction is in New York.' She adjusted

the angle of her plate to a more aesthetically-pleasing position. 'Now come on, darling, spill the beans. How did you
manage to find out? Who else knows? That worries me a
teensy bit, I must say, Andres.'

She frowned and then pouted like a petulant child.
Wendy must be in her late thirties, thought Andres, but
the gesture still looked curiously endearing.

'If I tell you that, will you tell me everything you know?
I promise not to write anything before the auction.'

She looked relieved. 'On that basis, darling, I'll tell you
the colour of my knickers. Now, spill it. How did you
know?'

Andres took a swallow of Muscadet and gambled on
telling the truth. 'I said I'd tell you everything and I will. I
don't know anything at all. I was just bluffing.'

The Greek-goddess face broke wide open into a spontaneous grin. Conversations stopped all over the restaurant as Wendy Killegar tossed back her strawberry blonde
hair and laughed – not the sort of delicate, tinkling laugh
you might have expected, but a loud, alto-pitched belly
laugh of genuine, honest amusement.

She recovered her composure and dabbed her brown
eyes with a tissue. 'That's quite all right, darling,' she said
at last, 'because I was bluffing, too. I'm really not wearing
any.'

The coffee was accompanied by fine brandy – cognac for
Wendy, Armagnac for Andres. As other diners departed
one by one and the restaurant became quieter, Andres told
Wendy the truth. Or at least an edited version of the truth.

'So Ann Kennedy, the murdered woman, had a painting
of de Blaca's on the wall at Barnabo,' he concluded. 'I think
it was one of his Atlantis series. And I had the feeling that a
local dealer called Godfrey Villiers was terribly keen to get
his hands on it. That's why I wondered whether something
was moving in the art world as regards Michael de Blaca,

for up until now he has not exactly been in strong demand.'

Wendy smiled, broke a petit-four and popped it into her mouth. 'You were absolutely right, darling. Here's the full SP from Auntie Wendy. One of the most prestigious art houses in New York has begun secretly buying up early de Blacas. That wouldn't be remarkable except for two factors – firstly, they're going to extreme lengths to avoid making it look like a mass buy-up. Every purchase is separate, anonymous and, most importantly, dirt cheap.'

'And the second factor?'

'This is no ordinary art house. This is Cedric Maxwell we're talking about here.'

Andres looked blank.

She sighed. 'Cedric Maxwell Associates. They supply all the major-league fat cats who are looking for solid, and I mean rock-solid, art investments. You know the sort of people, darling – the merchant bankers and the insurance corporations who don't appreciate art, but like what appreciates. They want something that looks good in the boardroom, gives the MD something to brag about to the visiting Taiwanese, and still triples in value every five years. No risky stuff. No risky stuff at all.'

Andres ordered more coffee. 'But up until now, nobody has wanted to know about de Blaca,' he objected. 'He was regarded as old-fashioned, slightly embarrassing. All that passion and expressionism. It was thought very passé.'

'That's the way it goes, darling. He's been what the City might describe as a solid but unimpressive performer. If you bought one of his early works twenty years ago, for instance, its value might just have kept pace with inflation.'

'And now?'

She leaned over and delicately popped the other half of her petit-four in Andres's mouth. 'And now...he's becoming an icon. The usual process. Yesterday's rebel artist is today's sound investment and tomorrow's museum exhibit. Whatever the reason, darling, and I'm not entirely sure what it is, the art world has decided de Blaca has been seriously undervalued. His hour has come. The sky's the limit.' She leaned closer and dropped her voice to a husky whisper. 'The rumour is that, during the last US Presidential visit to Ireland, the First Lady bought one. And that's what sparked it all off.'

Andres thought for a moment. 'So tell me. How much would one of his early paintings be worth now?'

She brushed the question aside with a wave of her long, elegant fingers. 'Oh, not a lot. Five thou', perhaps. It may rise to eight, ten, on the back of this surge, but nothing to get excited about.'

Andres was confused. He ordered more brandy and tried to make sense of what he was hearing. 'But you said we were talking hundreds of thousands,' he said.

'Thanks.' She accepted the cognac from the blue-jeaned waiter. 'My word, he *is* rather dishy, isn't he? I wonder if he would like a hand in the winecellar?' Her loud, sibilant whisper carried across the entire restaurant as clearly as a shout. Over at the till, the waiter flushed and tried to concentrate on marking up their bill. Then, returning to the subject: 'You did ask me about paintings, darling. I told you about paintings. But we're not interested in silly old paintings, are we?'

'We're not?'

'No. Sculptures. That's what the fuss is all about. My God.' She stared at him in sudden realisation. 'You really didn't know anything, did you?'

'I told you I didn't,' Andres said. 'Sculpture.'

'Yes, sculpture. That's what the New Yorkers are buying up. Early de Blaca sculptures. They're paying big money.'

'Does de Blaca know about this?'

She snorted. 'He'd be the last to know.'

'The twenty-first. What's happening at this auction on the twenty-first?'

Wendy hesitated. 'A few of us here in Ireland have

been tipped off about the big buy-up, and we don't see why the New Yorkers should have it all their own way with one of our own artists. We're buying up as many de Blaca sculptures as we can, from collectors and galleries and private owners. Then we're holding our own joint auction in Manhattan on the twenty-first. If all goes well, we should make megabucks, darling. Unless all the sellers get tipped off first. Which is why you could ruin everything by rushing in with your big, ignorant, clodhopping journalistic feet.'

Andres accepted the bill from the waiter. 'This man, Godfrey Villiers, the art dealer in Claremoon Harbour. Have you heard of him?'

'Minor league player. Small time conman. He runs an outfit called the Michael de Blaca Museum and Gallery, or some such nonsense. That's probably why he'd been contacted by the New Yorkers, who took the name at face value. They didn't realise that it's all a grand-sounding cover for a glorified pound shop that specialises in selling badly painted, mass-produced watercolours of Loop Head and the Cliffs of Moher to gullible tourists. Anyway, my theory would be that he has been instructed to prowl around Claremoon Harbour and hoover up as many of de Blaca's early chippings as he can. Which won't be very productive, since he didn't start sculpting until he left there and moved to Paris. *Everybody* knows that.'

She discreetly studied the far wall as Andres signed the credit card slip for an amount which would have more than covered the car repairs that Tara Ross, soaking wet and stranded by the side of the road in Galway, needed at that precise moment. When Wendy turned back, Andres had completed the transaction and was looking very thoughtful.

'Suppose I had an early de Blaca sculpture,' he said at last.

'How early?'

'Let's say the very first one he did.'

Wendy laughed. 'You're talking about one of the Dirty Dozen – that's what we call his sheela-na-gig series. You know, all those ugly naked Celtic goddesses, in poses that would embarrass a Bangkok bargirl. Those were his first works. He did twelve of them, but several have gone missing over the years.'

'Yes, those are the ones.'

Wendy was suddenly serious. 'Darling, if you had one of the sheela-na-gig series I'd marry you here and now. If you had the first one, guaranteed to be the first one, authenticated by the artist, I would not only marry you but let you sleep with me as well. We're talking a quarter-million or so. In pounds.'

'Two hundred and fifty thousand.' Andres hid his surprise with a smile. He changed the subject, trying to give himself time to think. 'I must say, your price for that particular service has gone up considerably over the years, Wendy.'

'Well, darling, one moves onwards and upwards, doesn't one?' She flashed him a good-natured smile. 'Those were strange days, weren't they, Andres? I still keep a cutting of the article you did about me and the girls when we founded a trade union all those years ago.'

'Professional association,' Andres reminded her.

'Whatever.' She drank her cognac. 'I was in Bonn only the other day and I passed by the old place. It's become dreadfully seedy, darling. The latest management are even calling it a "sexy kino den". How tacky. How unimaginative. It's a far cry from the days when we used to operate under the name of the Holistic Healing and Therapy Centre and some of the most powerful politicians in the land came to get healed every night. Sometimes twice a night. We'd heard of well-heeled politicians, but that was ridiculous.'

Andres smiled at the memory. 'I suppose a lot of their political clients have shifted to Berlin. Anyway, you were always meant for more than that, Wendy.'

'Of course I was, darling. Top graduate of my year from art college, and I couldn't even get a job anywhere in Ireland. And when I ended up broke on the streets of Bonn, it seemed like the only way out.' She became suddenly serious. 'I admit I was a bit low in the old self-esteem department when you happened along.'

Andres dismissed the subject. 'All I did was take you to hospital.'

'At a time when nobody else gave a damn whether I lived or died. If you hadn't found me, it would have been curtains for Auntie Wendy. One more hour, the doctors said, and all those paracetamol tablets would have caused irreversible liver damage.'

'But we got over it, didn't we, Wendy?'

She smiled and nodded. 'We did. My only regret was that you didn't take up my invitation to join me as a partner when I set up that first gallery. We would have made such a wonderful team, darling.' She took another delicate sip of cognac. 'And who are you teaming up with these days, Andres? Is there any special lady in your life? Any prospect of your marrying and settling down?'

He shook his head. 'You know the reason. We've talked about it often enough.'

Wendy sighed. 'Andres, you've got to stop punishing yourself over Manuela. Repeat after me this simple phrase: It Wasn't My Fault.'

'But it was my fault, Wendy. I should have been there.'

'Even if you had been there, you couldn't have prevented it.'

'But I wasn't there.' He shook his head defensively. 'It was not intentional, I was involved with another woman, but...'

'Andres, Andres.' Wendy was smiling. 'You'll have to do a lot more work on your idioms. In English, when a man says he was involved with a woman, it means he was having an affair with her.'

He looked horrified. 'It does?'

'Yes. What you're trying to say is that you were *kept occupied* by her, *detained* by her, at a business meeting that lasted longer than you'd intended. I hope you didn't put it that way to anyone else!'

Andres looked away, remembering that he'd put it exactly that way to Tara in Paris, just twenty-four hours beforehand.

Wendy caught his eye and held it. 'Whatever way you phrase it, Andres, it doesn't matter. You weren't to blame, and you can't go on for ever using this as a pretext to avoid relationships.'

The Estonian began to move the table condiments around like advancing chess pieces, a sure sign that he was ill at ease with the topic of conversation. 'I know it's irrational,' he said at last. 'But I can't risk going through all that again. Besides, it would be unfair to her.'

'Ah, so there is a *her*,' said Wendy triumphantly. 'Who is she? She must be a stunner. Tell me everything about her. You can confide in Auntie Wendy. I'm the soul of discretion. All my gentlemen in the Bundesbank used to say so.'

Andres shrugged uncomfortably. 'A young woman I met on an assignment in the west of Ireland. She's a journalist. She has her own Internet newspaper. And you're right, she *is* the most beautiful woman I've ever seen, apart from Manuela obviously.'

Wendy was highly amused. 'I trust you didn't say that to her.'

'I haven't said anything to her. Not about that, anyway.'

'So she doesn't even know how you feel about her?' Wendy was exasperated. 'Andres, this is perfectly ludicrous, even by your standards.'

Andres said nothing.

'Can't you see what's happening?' Wendy said. 'You're playing safe again. Deep down, you feel responsible for Manuela's death and you feel you'd be betraying her if you had another relationship. So every time you feel yourself attracted to another woman, you disappear off to the Congo or Croatia, or somewhere equally ridiculous, and stand up in front of a machine-gun.'

'That's playing safe?' he mocked.

'As far as you're concerned, it's a damn sight safer than risking possible heartbreak in another relationship,' she challenged. 'You know as well as I do, that's what's at the centre of it all. You're afraid to open yourself up and experience normal emotions again.'

Andres took a larger-than-usual mouthful of cognac. 'I did try to tell her,' he said defensively. 'Only last night. We'd just flown back from Paris...'

'Paris?' Wendy's sculptured eyebrows arched suggestively.

'Business. Purely business. She fell asleep on the flight home, and her head ended up resting on my shoulder. I could feel her hair on my cheek and I could smell her perfume. Flying normally bores me, Wendy,' he confessed, 'but on this occasion I wished the flight would never end.'

Wendy's lips pursed in a soundless whistle. 'My, my, we have got it bad, haven't we? What's so special about this one? What makes her different to all the others?'

'You mean, apart from the fact that she's intelligent, talented and exceptionally beautiful?' He was only half-joking. 'I don't know. How does one measure these things?'

'Body shape?' suggested Wendy. 'That's how we used to grade the girls at our place. Ectomorph, endomorph, mesomorph? Tall, slim and leggy? Or Mediterranean type, all tits and bum? Draw me a picture of her, darling.'

Andres ignored her. 'She simply intrigues me,' he said, half to himself. 'She's so volatile and moody she irritates the hell out of me, and yet when she tosses her hair back and gives one of those throaty giggles I just feel I want to...'

His voice trailed off helplessly.

Wendy gave a tiny, pleasurable shudder. 'You shouldn't be telling *me* these things, Andres. You should be sitting down to dinner with this special lady and telling them to her. Just make sure there's a candle on the table and gaze into her eyes, darling, and I promise you she'll melt like butter.'

'I can't.'

'You *won't*.'

'I can't, because she's already involved in a relationship. At least, I think she is.'

'You think, or you know?'

'I know. At least, I think I know.'

She shook her head despairingly. 'So you're just going to give up, and hop on the next plane to Colombia or somewhere?'

Andres glanced at his watch.

'My God, Andres, you're insufferable!' cried Wendy. 'You *are*. You're running away again. You're catching a flight this very afternoon!'

He nodded. 'Five-thirty.'

Wendy lifted her handbag on to the table. 'Well, I can't force you to stay, darling. It's just that I feel a certain responsibility to save you from yourself. Still, if you're absolutely determined to play the wounded Fisher King for the rest of your life, there's absolutely nothing I can do.'

Andres checkmated the salt with the pepper and avoided her eyes.

She leant across the table mischievously.

'Nothing, that is, except offer you a quick cup of coffee in my apartment before you leave.' Her voice dropped to a whisper and she smiled wickedly. 'No complications. No untidy biscuits, no messy dark chocolate, just pure *concentrated* coffee. What do you think, darling?'

Andres took a deep breath. When Wendy sang her siren song, she was almost impossible to resist.

He smiled and touched her arm affectionately.

'Thanks, Wendy, but I must refuse. I have to get to the airport two hours before the flight to collect my ticket.'

Wendy seemed disappointed, but grateful that he'd let her down gently with a plausible lie. 'Perhaps another time, then.'

'Perhaps.' Andres patted his pockets. 'Where did I put my syringe? I forgot to take my insulin before lunch. I'd better do it now, before I leave for the airport.'

'Right. Oops, must dash. I have a consultation at the Dáil this afternoon. Can't keep my politicians waiting.'

'Really?' Andres stood up. 'I didn't think you were giving those sort of consultations any more.'

She smiled and drained her glass. 'Not that sort of consultation, silly. An artistic consultation. A genuine one. Some addled nitwit is offering to sell a Jack B Yeats to the nation for an absolute song and my politicians want to know, God bless their cotton socks, whether it would be a waste of public money to buy it. I shall be assuring them that it's not. I shall then present them with an outrageous bill which will certainly qualify as a waste of public money.'

She stood up and gave the waiter a dazzling smile. He turned bright scarlet and fetched her coat and her Louis Vuitton briefcase.

'So you see, darling,' said Wendy as she kissed Andres lightly on the cheek, 'I'm still screwing politicians. Only nowadays I do it at their place.'

CHAPTER NINETEEN

TARA SQUEEZED through the door. She stepped over her friend's body and checked the hall for signs of immediate danger. It was deserted, but the air was thick with the acrid smell of gunpowder.

A shotgun lay on the floor near Melanie's grotesquely-twisted leg. She touched the barrel. It was still warm.

Tara dashed to the nearby phone and dialled 112, choosing it rather than the more familiar 999 because the number-pulses were shorter and it saved a few vital seconds.

She gave the address and asked for police and ambulance, stressing that an intruder might still be on the premises. Then she got another line and phoned the local GP as well. She was taking no chances. God knows how long it might take to get an ambulance out here.

All of this took precious minutes, during which she had to restrain herself from the one thing she wanted most to do – run upstairs and check her father.

Fearing the worst, hardly daring to hope, she replaced the receiver, mounted the stairs three at a time and threw open his bedroom door.

There he was – pale and gaunt, but sleeping as peacefully as a baby. She noted the bottle of medication on the table. He had probably slept through the entire episode, shotgun blast and all.

Next, a quick check around. Nothing. All the rooms were empty and undisturbed. The intruder, whoever he was, had gone. He had failed to get past Melanie, who had guarded her charge well.

Tears welling in her eyes, Tara ran back downstairs, practically clearing the entire flight in one long jump. She searched for a blanket and spread it carefully over the prostrate figure in the hall. The blood on Mel's hair had come from an ugly head-gash and was already congealing. Tara winced as she looked at the unnatural angle of the leg.

Hurry, she willed the emergency services. Please hurry.

Steve McNamara, the garda sergeant, got there first. Cool and professional, he first examined Melanie, then checked the entire house, garden and surroundings. Finally he returned and questioned Tara.

'Are you OK?'

'Yes. Just a bit shaken.'

'Sure? Nothing physical?'

'No.'

'Tell me what happened.'

She told him as succinctly as she could, pausing only to admit the GP in response to his anxious knocking. Dr Eoin Maguire threw back the blanket and examined Melanie thoroughly.

'Simple concussion,' he finally said to the garda sergeant. 'She's sustained a very bad blow to the head, but there are no other wounds. The leg seems to be dislocated, not broken. She'll need to get to hospital as soon as possible. Concussion is always a dicey business, of course, but the chances are good.' He delved into his bag. 'Who the hell could have done this, Steve?'

'Who do you think?' said Tara in frustration. 'The same man who killed Ann Kennedy, that's who.'

On the floor, Melanie groaned and opened her eyes.

She looked directly at Tara and winced as she tried to fight off a spasm of pain. Then...

'Manus,' she said in an almost-inaudible whisper. 'It was Manus Kennedy.'

Steve McNamara turned to Tara, and his eyes were aghast as he realised the enormity of his mistake. 'God, I'm sorry, Tara,' he said. 'I'm so sorry.'

It was now three-thirty am, and Tara's eyes were almost crossing with fatigue as she sat in an upstairs anteroom at Clare County Hospital and told her story for what seemed like the thousandth time.

'It was meant to be me,' she told Inspector Phil O'Rourke. 'If my car hadn't broken down on the road to Galway, that would have been me in there.'

She gestured to the door of the private ward where Melanie lay, conscious but sedated into a semitrance, with several disfiguring stitches across the left side of her head. The matted, blood-covered hair had been partially shorn. The dislocated leg had been repositioned. X-rays had revealed no skull fractures or other broken bones, but the doctors were still monitoring her for complications.

O'Rourke's bloodshot eyes followed her pointing finger. He had the look of a man who had gone to bed after a few pints and fallen straight into a deep sleep, only to be hauled out of bed an hour later.

'It certainly looks that way, Tara,' he agreed. 'You were the intended target. First there were the threatening phone calls. Then the actual attack – he seems to have mistaken Melanie for you in all the confusion. It looks like she put up quite a fight. She's some girl.'

'Woman,' corrected Tara icily. 'She's an adult woman. And the fact that she's still alive is no thanks to you. You didn't even take the warnings seriously enough to put a guard on the house.'

O'Rourke sighed. 'We were taking them seriously. We were monitoring the calls, using the latest technology at our disposal to identify the caller.'

'Right. But you didn't think he meant what he said. You thought they must have been hoax threats. Because you thought you had Ann Kennedy's real killer either locked up or under close surveillance at all times since the murder.'

'In our business, we never jump to conclusions about other people's thoughts or motives,' said O'Rourke calmly. He looked at the notes he'd made of her statement. 'So you really hunted Manus Kennedy all the way across Ireland? I'm impressed by your tenacity, but, let's face it, it wasn't the safest thing to do. Squats in Bernietown, smack-dealers' shooting galleries in Ballymahon Flats. And all alone, unprotected.'

Tara picked up the unspoken reproach and realised he had a point. She'd disappeared for days, exposing herself to the gravest danger, and now she was complaining that the gardaí had not done enough to protect her.

But at that moment a dark surge of pain flared from her injured wrist and travelled up her arm with agonising slowness to join the anvil-pounding of a headache. She was in no mood to listen to a lecture.

'Someone had to do your job for you,' she said shortly. 'You had your minds firmly made up. You had your culprit. As far as you were concerned, the case was a cinch and you could all relax.'

O'Rourke said nothing but shook his head in silent denial.

'Don't shake your head. You know it's true. You already had Fergal Kennedy tried and convicted for murder. Even my evidence as to his whereabouts that night didn't convince you. It took this' – she pointed angrily at the hospital ward – 'to prove his innocence.'

O'Rourke still remained silent.

Tara sighed with exasperation at his lack of response. 'Unless you think Fergal has developed bloody bilocation and is responsible for this crime too?'

The detective took out a packet of cigarettes and absent-mindedly placed one in his mouth before remembering that he was in a hospital. He removed it again and carefully replaced it in the pack.

'No, we're not claiming that Fergal was responsible for the attack on Melanie,' he said wearily. 'As you point out, we've had him under surveillance at all times. And besides, you also know, Melanie has clearly identified her attacker as Fergal's brother, Manus.'

He flipped back the pages of a black notebook to his earlier notes of Melanie's statement. 'She's quite clear about it,' he repeated. 'She heard someone outside, assumed it was you, and opened the door to let you in. Instead she saw a wild-looking, unkempt figure crouching at the window trying to peer through the curtains. She tried to slam the door but he made a run for her, shouting some garbled threat that she was going to die. With admirable presence of mind, Melanie backed up, grabbed your dad's shotgun, cocked it and pointed it at him. He kept coming, shouting at her. She can still remember his eyes, she says. They were crazy eyes, as though he was out of his mind on something. Anyway, the gun went off with a godalmighty roar and that's the last thing she remembers.'

'He must have hit her over the head with something,' said Tara. 'A very vicious blow. He could easily have killed her.'

'Melanie has certainly sustained a serious head injury, yes. But it's not life-threatening, and the doctors are confident that she'll make a full recovery.' She could hear the genuine relief in his voice. 'Thank God for that, anyway. For a while there, I thought we'd another murder on our hands.'

Tara was still not placated. 'I wouldn't speak too soon. You've got a man on the run out there who's shown his willingness to kill, twice.'

'We're fully aware of the dangers, Tara. We've got road blocks all around the area. We've notified all garda stations and we'll have a full description on the radio news in the morning. In the meantime, you'll be placed under twenty-four-hour police protection.'

'One question.' Tara couldn't keep the note of hopefulness out of her voice. 'Was Manus wounded when the gun went off?'

'As far as we can establish, no, he wasn't.' O'Rourke shook his head. 'There's no sign of his blood anywhere in the house or grounds, and there's a huge hunk of plaster-work missing from the ceiling of your hall. Don't look so disappointed. It's probably for the best. It would only complicate our case when it's time to take a prosecution.'

'When? You mean if. If you catch him.'

'We'll catch him.'

'And then you're going to charge him with Ann Kennedy's murder.' She tried to make it a statement rather than a question.

'That's a matter for the Director of Public Prosecutions. You know that, Tara. You're familiar with the law.'

'But you'll be sending a file to the DPP recommending his prosecution for the killing.'

'We can't send any file until we complete the investigation, and we can't complete the investigation until we get all the evidence.'

Tara felt like exploding with frustration. 'But what more evidence do you need? The man is crazy as a lamp, he has a history of violence and he's in the area. He even had a motive for Ann's killing. I've already told you the drug bosses were after him over a disputed three thousand pounds. He probably needed cash desperately and he went home to get it from his mother. She would have refused – and that's all it took to push him over the edge.'

O'Rourke kept his cool. 'There's still the forensic stuff to complete. That takes time. The DNA tests, for instance, might not be completed for another few days.'

'DNA?' It was the first Tara had heard of DNA tests.

'It's routine these days. We look for skin, hair, minute traces of blood, and check their DNA configuration. The most important samples in this case were taken from under the victim's fingernails. When there are defence wounds – that is, when the victim gets injured trying to protect herself with her hands and arms – it's not unusual to find tiny portions of the attacker's skin under her nails.

We took nail scrapings and found workable samples. They're being tested at the lab now.'

'That's great news,' said Tara. All of a sudden, she felt like hugging him instead. 'So it's only a matter of time before we get official confirmation.'

'Before we hope to get a result, yes.'

Tara looked out of the window of the little room and saw the night sky begin to lighten with the dawn. It wasn't much of a change, you could hardly call it sunrise, but it was a start.

'Yes, what is it?'

Tara turned around as O'Rourke snapped at the uniformed garda who had entered the room.

'Sorry, sir, but there's a fella in the downstairs waiting room wants to see Ms Ross urgently,' he said. 'I checked his ID and he seems kosher.'

Tara looked surprised. 'I'm not expecting anybody. What does he want?'

The garda frowned. 'He claims you know him. And he says it's a matter of life or death.'

'A matter of life or death?' challenged Tara.

'Okay, so I exaggerated a bit,' said Gerry Gellick. 'Journalistic licence. Would you have talked to me otherwise?'

Her jaw dropped at the sheer gall of the man. There he was, lounging casually in his sharp Armani suit, arms extended along the entire length of the waiting-room settee, smiling cockily at her as though they were old friends. The only thing that prevented her from exploding in a torrent of outrage and invective was that she knew it would be a total waste of energy. Phrases about ducks' backs leaped to mind.

'Smart tactic,' she said, turning on her heel. 'I'm sure Inspector O'Rourke will agree when he interviews you for wasting police time. In fact, I'll get him right now. You'd better leave the rest of your day free for making statements.'

'If you go out that door,' said Gellick clearly, 'you'll never know why Ann Kennedy died.'

She froze in the doorway. Her brain told her to keep moving, but her feet refused to obey.

'I thought you'd already made up your mind on that,' she said without turning around.

'Flexibility of thinking is the hallmark of genius.'

'Which is a fancy way of saying you got it all wrong.' She turned around to face him. 'At least you admit it.'

He shrugged it off as a minor objection. 'That story in the *Evening Report!* was yesterday's truth. I'm only interested in today's. I want to find out why Manus murdered Ann Kennedy.'

She tried to laugh sardonically, but it emerged as an incredulous gasp. 'And you're here to ask for help? From me?'

'I'm here to offer you information you need. In exchange for information I need.'

Something in his voice made her take him seriously.

'Keep talking,' she said. 'You have thirty seconds to start making sense.'

He propped his ankle across his knee and lounged back. A man who had plenty of time at his disposal.

'It's becoming obvious that Manus was the murderer, but as far as I can see, there's no real evidence against him,' he said. 'No witnesses, no decent forensic.'

Tara said nothing. He obviously didn't know about the DNA tests.

'So they'll get him for the assault on your friend Melanie. But they won't get a murder charge to stick. Unless he talks, he walks. That means the file will stay open for ever, and your boyfriend will never be totally cleared. Is that what you want?'

'Go on.'

'So we're both looking for more information about

Manus. You need it to clear your boyfriend. I need it because I want to write the definitive story.' He extended his arms in a gesture of good faith. 'As far as I can ascertain, you know some things about him I don't, and I know some things about him that you don't. Together they may make up the full picture. What I'm proposing is a pragmatic alliance to enable us both to get what we want. Are my thirty seconds up yet?'

Tara hadn't even bothered checking her watch. 'I'm still listening,' she said.

'Think of it this way, Tara. It's as though an item we both need is locked in one of those bank deposit boxes, the ones that need two keys to open them. I have one key, you have the other. I know you hate me, and personally I don't give a shit. The question is: do you hate me enough to give up the chance of opening that box?'

There was a knock at the door. The garda she'd seen earlier poked his head in.

'Just checking everything's okay, Ms Ross?'

She hesitated.

'Yes. I'm just having a chat with Mr Gellick.'

'Fine. I'll be right outside.'

The door closed, and Tara sat down slowly on the armchair facing Gellick. She couldn't believe she was even entertaining this bizarre suggestion of a practical alliance. But in a world gone mad, his proposal had a sort of absurd logic to it.

'You show me yours,' she said, 'and I'll show you mine.'

Gellick set down his empty coffee cup on the formica table. 'What you don't realise,' he told Tara, 'is that you stumbled into a hornet's nest in Ballymahon. You were there to witness the death-throes of Philo Romero's heroin gang.'

'I already knew that those two scumbags were tied in with the Romero gang. They said so.'

'But you didn't know how big they were. The tall skinny guy, the one with the hatchet face and the hate tattoo, was Romero's top lieutenant. Christy Geaney. Career criminal, totally ruthless. He's sold more drugs in Dublin than Boots the Chemist.'

'And the other man?'

'The Star Trek fan? Carl Ryan. Chemistry graduate, helped the Romero crowd mass-produce their own Ecstasy at a factory in the suburbs. Until the police busted it. And that's the problem.' Gellick sat back. 'Ever since Philo went down for fourteen years, the Romero gang has been having a run of bad luck. The word from my mates in the underworld is that Christy is in big trouble. Most of his main men have defected to other gangs, and his top heavy, Paul Lawless, has been locked in a loony-bin for assessment over his recreational hobby of roughing up old ladies.'

'And Geaney's up in court soon himself,' Tara pointed out. 'He said so in Ballymahon.'

'Yeah. Caught last April with thirty grand's worth of coke in his soccer holdall at Dublin Airport. Carl Ryan was on a separate flight. He had ten grand's worth of smack in a rucksack. But the cops were waiting for them both. "Excuse me, sir, may I have a look in that bag, please?" Ba-boom. We're talking a total street value of over one hundred and fifty thousand pounds. They're both going down for a long time – if anyone can find them, that is.'

'But what has any of this to do with Manus Kennedy?'

'I was coming to that. The cops couldn't believe Geaney could be so stupid as to carry his own gear. But my man says he was forced to take the risk. It all started a couple of months earlier, when Christy took out a ten percent share in a shipment of cheap H from Amsterdam. Then suddenly Christy wasn't able to find the money, and the sweetest deal of the decade fell through. The Irish importer, the guy who was organising the shipment, was not a happy man. And the only way Christy could keep his kneecaps was to agree to act as courier for him on his next drugs run.'

Tara nodded. It had all the hallmarks of a classic set-up. 'And the importer tipped off the police?'

'Maybe. It might have been worth his while to lose the drugs in order to kill off the Romero gang. We don't know. What we do know is that, for some unknown reason, Christy blames Manus Kennedy. The way he sees it, Manus started off the whole chain reaction that left Geaney flat broke and headed for jail.'

'He told me that Manus owed him three thousand pounds.'

Gellick nodded. 'That's about right. Three grand would have been his ten percent stake in the Amsterdam shipment. But there's more to it than that. And this is where I need to see *your* key. So to speak.'

Tara raised her eyebrows inquiringly.

'You see, Christy Geaney was spotted in Claremoon Harbour about a week before the murder,' Gellick explained. 'According to my dodgy sources, he met a guy called – let's see – Godfrey Villiers outside the Kennedy home at Barnabo. Who is this guy Villiers? Do you know him?'

Tara took a giant leap of faith and told Gellick all she knew about Villiers and his money laundering. She told him about his reckless skimming of funds to feed his gambling habit. And how, as a result, he was now in big trouble with the vicious Viney drug-dealing clan in Limerick. 'For some reason,' she concluded, 'the art dealer seems to think that Manus can get him off the hook. He's managed to persuade the Vineys to launch a full-scale hunt for him.'

'Meanwhile, Christy seems to be searching for him, too,' said Gellick. 'And it can't just be for the money. Three grand's a lot of dosh, but it's not worth that amount of trouble.'

Tara looked puzzled. 'So we've got two major criminal organisations searching for Manus Kennedy.'

'Yes. The Vineys in Limerick, none of whom will get out of bed for less than twenty grand, and the bigtime Romero gang in Dublin. Both expending a lot of time and effort to find one flat-broke, jobless no-hoper who's so crazy he can hardly tell what day of the week it is.'

He turned to Tara in bewilderment. 'Just what the hell has this guy got that everyone wants so much?'

Fergal didn't hear her come in.

He was sitting with his back to the door in the empty waiting-room, surrounded by posters promoting needle-free injections and well-woman services, idly leafing through a six-year-old edition of *What Car?* magazine. He seemed somehow smaller, his sturdy frame weighted down by trouble. He was hunched and deflated, and the sight tore at her heart.

She stood behind him silently for a few seconds. Then she softly said his name.

Fergal sprang to his feet. 'Tara! Thank God you're all right.'

He grabbed her in a bear hug, leaving her almost smothered. She tried to respond, as best she could with her arms pinioned to her sides. At last he released her and she was able to return his embrace.

'I'm okay, I'm okay,' she smiled. 'At least, I was until you cracked my ribcage.'

She examined his face. It was anaemic and ghostlike. The horrific experiences of the past two weeks had aged him by years. 'You're looking very pale,' she said with concern. 'You're not ill, are you?'

'No, I'm fine. I'm terrific. The worst part was worrying about you.' His relief at her safety was rapidly being replaced by indignation. 'You had us all worried sick, disappearing for days like that without letting anyone know where you were. Why didn't you phone?'

Tara was fed up being told how inconsiderate she was.

'It doesn't matter now,' she said. 'All that matters is that I'm back and I'm okay. More importantly, it looks like Melanie's going to be okay, too. All that matters is that you're okay and you're innocent and the police know you're innocent, and it's only a matter of time before they catch Manus and jail him for life for his mother's murder. That's all that matters.'

She took a deep breath and immediately felt her head swim with dizziness. The flow of words had come out without a pause, delivered with such passion and intensity because, she realised, she was willing it all to come true.

Fergal stroked her hair. 'You've been through a lot, I know,' he said kindly. 'Sit down for a moment. I'll fix us both some coffee.'

She sat down on the worn tweed sofa and put her head in her hands to block out the merciless fluorescent light for just a moment. Down the corridor, she heard two coins rattle into a vending machine and the sound of liquid pouring into a plastic cup.

'Here. Drink this.'

The beige plastic cup was filled with a stomach-churning watery brown liquid topped by loose granules of brown powder and a foam that looked like dishwashing solution. It tasted like dishwashing solution as well. She drank it anyway.

'Thanks.' She motioned at him to sit down beside her. Then, choking back tears, she told him everything about her strange odyssey around Ireland -- from the mental hospital at Inismaul, through the flats at Bernietown and to the drug den in the tower-block at Ballymahon. She said nothing about Paris or Michael de Blaca. Finally, she told how she had arrived back late to find her best friend lying bloody and unconscious on the floor in an attack which had been clearly aimed at her.

For a long while Fergal sat silently, staring at the false tiling on the vinyl floor. He sat quietly for so long that she began to wonder whether he had fallen ill. At last he spoke.

'That little bastard,' he finally said, with an ice-cold calmness that surprised her. 'That bastard. I'll kill him.'

'Fergal. Stop. I know you don't mean that literally, but it's not the smartest thing to say in the circumstances.' She glanced around, even though she knew the room was empty.

'The hell I don't mean it literally. I'm going to tear him limb from bloody limb.' He looked at her, eyes burning with a righteous fury. 'What do you expect me to say? He murdered my mother and now he's come back to kill you. The two women I love most in the world.'

She laid a hand on his shoulder. 'Don't do this to yourself, Fergal.'

He moved away irritably. 'Can't you see what this is all about? He's getting back at me for all the years he's been put away in a nuthouse. He thinks I'm responsible for it all. He knows that if he attacked me face-to-face I'd make dog-meat out of him. So he's taking the coward's way out. He's trying to kill me indirectly – by killing the people I love.'

Tara stared at him in bewilderment. Then she shivered involuntarily. His words, finally making sense in her tired head, chilled her to the bone. Up until now, she'd assumed that Manus was targeting her in a temporary fit of anger over the Ballymahon drugs episode, or simply because he wanted to stop her asking questions about him. She could somehow cope with that. It was understandable. It had its own warped logic. But the idea that Manus had calmly and deliberately set out to kill her, as an insane act of revenge on his elder brother, filled her with dread.

'But why?' she managed to blurt out.

'You know about the bad blood between us. We have different fathers and nothing in common. Don't tell me you haven't heard about the time he tried to take revenge on Martin by setting the cowshed ablaze and killing all the cattle. I was the one who ruined his plan by catching him in the act and forcing him to go on the run. He's never forgiven me.'

Fergal looked at her accusingly. 'Don't look so surprised. You're bound to have heard the story. Your father was one of the men who brought the blaze under control.'

Tara averted her eyes and nodded. She remember that peaceful evening down at the harbour, a few weeks and several centuries ago, when her father told her the story for the first time.

'Yes, I heard,' she admitted. 'But there's no point opening up the old wounds of the past, Fergal. It's out of our hands now.'

He looked at her tiredly. She wondered whether her own eyes were as dark-ringed as his own.

'What do you mean, it's out of our hands?' His anger was passing and his voice sounded dejected.

'The police are combing the countryside for him. They've got roadblocks everywhere. They'll have Manus in custody within forty-eight hours.'

He walked slowly away and stood at the window, looking out at the early dawn.

'You don't understand,' he said at last. 'Roadblocks are pointless. Manus doesn't travel by road. He takes laneways and boreens and forest trails and even mud-filled roadside ditches when he has to. He's tough and he's fit. He can cover twenty, thirty miles across rough countryside in a single night. He can spend weeks on end living off the land. It doesn't bother him if he has to forage crops from a farmer's field, or raid a henhouse, or sleep under a hedge. He's used to it. They'll never catch him.'

Tara followed him to the window and put her arms around him. 'Leave it to the police,' she said. 'They're putting everything they have into this hunt. They must know by now that they were wrong to suspect you, and they're directing all their energies into hunting for Manus. It's a full-scale murder hunt now, Fergal, not just a search for a missing person. Once the news goes out on the radio tomorrow morning, we'll have every farmer and every landowner looking for signs of him in their fields. It won't take long to narrow him down to a small area. But whatever happens, however long it takes, you shouldn't forget that there's been a major development tonight – the cloud of suspicion isn't hanging over you any more. You're free, Fergal. You're free to start all over again.'

Still looking away, he took her hand and squeezed it gently. 'Thanks to you, Tara. It's all thanks to you. If you hadn't smoked Manus out of hiding, forced his hand, and made him carry out a blind attack that he hadn't planned out properly, they'd still be convinced that I was the killer.'

Tara hadn't thought of it that way. An innocent woman lay bruised and beaten in hospital, but at least something good had come out of this dreadful business. What had she said to Andres in the taxi in Paris? 'We've achieved nothing. We're back to square one.' How wrong she'd been. Fate moved in strange ways.

'Perhaps all my crazy travels weren't wasted after all,' she mused. She hugged him warmly. 'I've a feeling it's all over, Fergal,' she said with a confidence she didn't feel. 'It's all over.'

Fergal's eyes were fixed on the horizon, beyond the civilised, ordered rooftops of Ennis town, beyond the disciplined ranks of the suburban housing estates, toward the fields and forests and rock-strewn wildernesses of the vast County Clare countryside. 'It's not over, Tara,' he said quietly. 'Until he's dead, or I'm dead, it won't be over.'

CHAPTER TWENTY

'NETWORK RADIO news at nine o'clock. Gardaí in County Clare have named a man they wish to question in connection with last month's murder of Mrs Ann Kennedy in Claremoon Harbour. He is twenty-seven-year-old Manus Kennedy, of no fixed abode, who is believed to be have been living rough in the County Clare countryside following another attack on a young woman in Claremoon Harbour three days ago.

'He is described as being five feet seven inches tall, of stocky, powerful build, with brown curly hair and a heavily pockmarked face. He may have grown a beard.

'Detectives at Ennis say that anyone spotting the man should inform them as soon as possible, but warn that he should not be approached by the public as he may be dangerous and could possibly be armed.

'Another man who was previously arrested in connection with the murder, and subsequently released without charge, is no longer at the centre of their inquiries.

'Now some political news, and it seems certain that the Government will survive today's vote on...'

Tara leaned over and switched off the radio. She whipped up a mixture of scrambled eggs and smoked salmon and, as they cooked, put several rashers of bacon, some fat sausages, and half a dozen tomatoes under the grill. The sun poured in through the window of her cottage, making the old pine dressers and the waxed wooden table glow like home-made honey. Even the simple routine of cooking a full Irish breakfast lent its own comfort. It was a long time since she'd felt so much at peace, so relaxed.

'They say they'll have him caught soon,' she told Fergal and Melanie as she passed round a large jug of freshly-squeezed orange juice and a plate stacked high with warm toast. 'They've got him pinned down in a forest near the Galway border, and the place is practically surrounded.'

'It can't happen soon enough,' said Melanie. She wore a black Atlanta Braves baseball cap to hide the stitches on her partially-shaven head. With her red hair spilling out of the back of the cap in a cascading ponytail, she looked more like a perky teenager than a woman recovering from a serious assault. 'Speaking as a caring social worker,' she continued, 'I hope they shoot the little *putz*.'

Tara glanced at her, relieved to see that her friend had made a total recovery. Melanie was regaining colour, and the headaches had gone. Plenty of rest, recuperation and gentle exercise, her doctor had instructed her, and you'll be as right as rain.

('Mind you, he did warn me there was a slight chance I might suffer from disorientation, euphoria, lack of concentration and poor co-ordination,' she'd told Tara on the way home from hospital. 'And I told him: More than a slight chance, doc. It's a cert. I'm going out partying tonight.')

Tara served the first portions of scrambled eggs. 'Easy on. We *are* talking about Fergal's brother,' she said.

Fergal poured himself some orange juice. 'I agree with Melanie,' he said. 'I just hope they get a good clear shot at him and get it over with quickly.'

Tara placed a third plate in front of Garda Sergeant Sean Gurrane, who had just joined them at the table.

'*Go raibh míle maith agat*,' the policeman said gratefully, his round, friendly face splitting wide in a smile of appreciation. 'I wish all the people I was assigned to protect were as good a cook as you are, girl.'

'You're welcome, boy.' She mimicked his Cork city accent good-naturedly. It had become something of a running joke between them since he'd begun guarding her and Melanie as part of a twenty-four-hour protection roster. 'And we've even got some Barry's Tea as well. Get it down you, boy, you never know where your next meal of spuds is coming from.'

'You never said a truer word, girl.'

Tara made a meal of invalid-food for her dad and left it to cool while she ate her own breakfast. John Ross had still not recovered from the sudden and devastating illness that had robbed him of speech, but Tara was convinced there had been some improvement. Hospital tests had shown that both brain and bodily functions were undamaged, and Tara believed, without any real evidence, that he was aware of his surroundings. Although he didn't seem able to communicate in any way, Tara would still sit with him for hours, stroking his hands and talking quietly to him as though he understood everything she was saying.

'Oh – there was a phone call for you while you were in the shower,' Melanie said through a mouthful of toast. 'Andres. Again.'

'Really.' Tara's voice was flat.

'He wants you to ring him. I wrote the number down. It's a mobile. He says he's out of the country but you should be able to reach him on the digital system.'

'He can wait.'

'That's the fourth call he's made,' Melanie reminded her. 'He says it's important.'

'If it's so urgent he can leave a message.'

'I've suggested that. He won't. Why won't you talk to him? Fergal, tell her to talk to him.'

Fergal said nothing.

Melanie shrugged. 'So *don't* call him. It's none of my business. It's not as though you owe the man anything. After all, what's he ever done for you? Apart from saving your life.'

'And I saved his, so we're even.'

'But Tara...'

'Don't want to talk about it, okay?' She was smiling, but her tone was firm. She looked down and concentrated on buttering her toast. She had no time for fair-weather friends like Andres who deserted her when the going got tough, and then had the nerve to phone her from some beachside bar on the other side of the world to boast about his suntan while he ordered another Pina Colada.

I have to go abroad on a matter of great urgency. A couple of days later, she'd heard the truth about Andres Talimann's movements. She'd been chatting generally on the phone to Jean Murphy, her former colleague at the *Evening Mercury*, when Tara happened to mention that she'd met the famous war correspondent.

'Oh, yes, I saw him the other day,' Jean said. 'Was it yesterday or the day before? Anyway, he was sitting in the most pricey restaurant in St Stephen's Green drinking wine at thirty-five quid a bottle with the most classy strawberry blonde I've ever seen. Face like Claudia Schiffer and legs so long they seemed to start somewhere around her neck glands. They obviously knew each other very well. She was all over him – popping petits-fours into his mouth and hanging on his every word. They seemed to be having a great laugh about something or other.'

I have to go abroad on a matter of great urgency.

No wonder they were laughing, Tara thought sourly. They had plenty to laugh about. She was lucky to have her real friends here – friends who had stood by her through thick and thin, friends she could depend upon.

But why had everyone gone so quiet?

She looked up. Melanie was sticking out her tongue at her, the way she always did when Tara got stroppy.

Tara burst into laughter and twisted her own face into a schoolyard grimace.

'Now, girls,' warned Sergeant Gurrane, 'this may constitute conduct likely to lead to a breach of the peace. I must caution you to desist.' He cleared his plate first, the way he always did. 'God, that was grand altogether. It was as good a meal as you'd get in the Arbutus Lodge, and that, as you know, boy, is the best restaurant not only in Cork city or county, but in the entire universe.'

Tara returned his smile and studied his pleasant, man-in-the-moon face. She liked him immensely but she had serious doubts about his ability to protect her. He looked as though he would have trouble dealing with a pushy encyclopaedia salesman, never mind a psychotic murderer. He was highly experienced and well-trained, without a doubt, but he was definitely overweight and out of condition and unable to walk very far without panting and running out of breath. She just hoped that Sean was handy with the .38 that he kept tucked in his belt-holster on his ample rear, just under his tweed sports jacket. If he didn't, they were all in big trouble.

Tara jumped and clutched involuntarily at his sleeve as the phone and the doorbell both rang at the same time.

There was no question about who should answer the door. The sergeant was already on his feet and heading for the hallway.

'I'll get the phone,' said Fergal. He was determined to protect Tara from the sickos, freaks and hopeful journalists who were still jamming the line every day.

'It's okay. I've got it.' Tara lifted the cordless phone and pressed the talk button before anyone could stop her.

'Allo?' A woman's voice, far away and crackling.

'Hello. Who is this?'

'Ees thees Mees Tara Ross?' The line was getting worse. Oh, no, thought Tara. Not another continental journalist.

'Speaking.'

The French woman hadn't heard her reply. 'I would like to speak, please, to Mees Tara Ross. Eet is very important.'

'This is Tara Ross.'

'Allo?'

Tara sighed. 'Okay, which publication are you from? *Le Monde*? *Figaro*? *Paris Match*?'

'Allo? Ees Mees Ross there, please?'

Tara lost patience. This was, after all, about the

dozenth call from foreign-language news outlets, French, German, Belgian and Dutch, all seeking to do the same 'murder in paradise' feature which would serve to shock their thousands of continental readers who flocked to the west of Ireland every summer in search of peace and serenity. What was the matter with these European newspapers? Didn't they have any crime on their own doorsteps?

'Listen,' Tara said, loudly but not unkindly, 'I don't know who you are, but please don't phone again. My father is ill and I just want to be left in peace.'

The line crackled and hissed like a winter bonfire. 'Allo?' said the voice again. 'I need to speak with Mees Tara Ross. Eet is important.'

Tara raised her eyes to the ceiling and hung up.

Now it was mid-afternoon and the sun, beaming through the window of Tara's bedroom, was beginning to bounce annoyingly off the glass of her computer monitor. She made a mental note to buy a non-reflecting screen shield.

She checked her event guide and the local tourism links, then double-checked that the vital adverts and sponsorship notices were in place. After all, they paid the bills.

Finally she pressed a combination of keys, and her cheap modem trilled like an electronic budgie as it connected her PC to the big server-computer in Ennis and propelled her publication into the vast realm of cyberspace.

She yawned and stretched, and switched off the machine. Throwing open the bedroom window for more fresh air, she could see the narrow mud track that led invitingly up to the pine forest that covered the side of the hill behind her house. It had been planted in the sixties and seventies, over what had previously been scrubland not even fit for grazing sheep. Its rambling acres provided home for dozens of sika deer, and the state forestry agency provided a network of pathways for hikers and joggers.

Tara looked at the distant trees longingly, smelling the sharp tang of the sappy wood and imagining the crunch of the pine needles underfoot. Over the past few days, she had barely left the cottage and was beginning to suffer from cabin fever. More than anything else in the world, she longed to be running through the forest, free as a young deer, feeling the fresh mountain wind in her hair.

She looked back into her bedroom. By sheer coincidence, her Adidas running shoes had spilled out of her wardrobe and were lying on the floor, tongues hanging out like twin puppies demanding walkies.

Tara made up her mind in an instant. Her father was being cared for by a visiting nurse; Fergal and Melanie were busy elsewhere; she could risk a quick run up to the edge of the wood and back. She could hardly ask for police protection – judging from the way Sean Gurrane puffed and wheezed after the mildest of exertion, he wouldn't make it even a tenth of the way up the steep slope before collapsing of a heart attack.

Quickly, she threw off her clothes and put on black cycle shorts and a Puma sweatshirt. Her well-worn running shoes fitted her like a familiar pair of jeans, soft, supple and yet supportive.

After taking a few minutes to limber up, she tied her long black hair into a ponytail, put on a pair of light in-ear headphones, and firmly clipped a Walkman to her sweatshirt. Now she was ready.

Feeling a bit like a teenager sneaking off to an illicit disco, she crept downstairs and glanced in to the kitchen. Sean Gurrane was busy doing the *Star* crossword. He didn't notice her as she softly opened the door and slipped outside. Things were simpler that way.

The air was warm and heavy as she began the steep ascent up the mud pathway that climbed through the bracken and gorse to the main entrance of the forest. Within a couple of minutes her muscles were protesting and her lungs were bursting. Her body was demanding that she give up and go home, but she was familiar with the feeling – it was a physical barrier she had to pass. Enjoying the tension on her thigh and calf muscles as she mounted each fresh metre of hillside, she persevered and before long was rewarded with her second-wind. Soon she was in her stride, her breath deep and regular and under control, feeling that she would be able to run for miles and miles.

At the car park at the entrance to the forest, Tara paused to stretch her muscles and enjoy the view of the Clare coastline. In one direction lay Ballyvaughan and Kinvara; in the other, Liscannor, Quilty, Kilkee and Kilrush. But through today's heat haze, she could only just distinguish the towering Cliffs of Moher – each black headland plunging into the churning waters of the Atlantic in a dizzy ninety-degree drop.

The sun was almost unbearably hot on her perspiring forehead. Behind her, the forest road looked cool and inviting as it vanished into the dark shade of the woods.

Straight up to the edge of the forest and then home, she had promised herself. But a few hundred yards into the woods, say maybe a half-mile, wouldn't do any harm. Who did she think she was, Little Red Riding Hood?

She snapped a cassette of *Revenge*, the classic Eurythmics album, into her Walkman. Then she took another deep breath and got back into her stride, clearing the low bar-gate with a clean jump and plunging into the forest shade like a diver slicing into cold water. After the searing heat of the sun, the combination of cool breeze and shade was pure bliss. Her muscles responded like those of a racehorse on the final straight. She increased her stride and her speed, loving the invigorating smell of pine in her nostrils as she drew the clean forest air deep into her lungs.

In her best foxy, throaty, rock'n'roll voice, Annie Lennox was wailing about her love for a missionary man. The guitars, bass and drums pounded precisely to the beat of Tara's stride. Within fifteen minutes, she was more than a mile into the forest and feeling as though she was never going to stop.

At this rate, she could easily do a 10K by the time she doubled back and reached home. Maybe this would be the year she would do some serious training for a full-scale marathon. They did say that the first thirteen miles were the worst. After that, it was just a question of endurance, pacing yourself, thinking of nothing but putting one foot in front of the other, in front of the other, in front of the other...

Rounding a blind bend, she almost careered into a figure standing in the centre of the path, blocking her route. His clothes were torn and dirty. His face was covered in crude camouflage daubings of brown and green. And he was carrying a high-powered rifle.

Tara skidded and almost fell. She wanted to turn and run away. But she knew she'd be wasting her time. She knew a long-range hunting rifle when she saw one. Nobody could outrun a bullet from a .270 Winchester.

She just stood rooted to the spot and stared at the gunman in front of her.

He was not tall, but he was powerfully built and his features looked intimidating behind the warpaint mask of camouflage.

As if on cue, the tape ended and the Walkman clicked itself off. For a few seconds – it seemed like hours – there was silence. Even the birds seemed to have stopped singing. The only sound was the harsh rasping of Tara's breath and the pounding of her heart.

Then the man spoke.

'Good Lord,' he said. 'You frightened the life out of me.'

A West Brit accent. Diffident and polite.

'I frightened *you*?' she said incredulously. She studied him for a moment. He was wearing a filthy, torn, Army surplus jacket and baggy pants with several zip pockets. On his head was a peaked military-style cap in olive green. His coat pockets bulged with cardboard boxes which presumably contained rounds of ammunition.

He nodded and smiled, his perfect white teeth flashing from behind the camouflage paint on his face. 'I mean, coming that fast. I was prepared for someone coming along the path, but I wasn't expecting bloody Sonia O'Sullivan.' He thrust out a hand that looked surprisingly clean and well-groomed. 'I'm Dr Charles Lifford. Please call me Charlie.'

He shook her hand and pointed to a clipped-on ID card that identified him as the chairman of a local rifle club.

'Doctor?' Tara suddenly burst into a fit of giggles. 'I feel like Stanley in the jungle. Doctor Lifford, I presume.'

After the sheer terror of the initial encounter, the sur-realism of the situation seemed hilarious. Tara sank back on a nearby tree trunk and tried to recapture her breath.

'I say,' said Dr Lifford, 'are you okay?'

'I'm fine, Charlie. Just fine.' She introduced herself. 'Now tell me. What the hell are you doing standing in the middle of a public road with a .270 Win, scaring the living bejasus out of innocent joggers?' Even asking the ques-tion, she couldn't keep from laughing.

'Well, you see, that's my job. To stop people coming along the path.'

'But we're allowed to come along the path. It's a public forest.'

'Yes, but not today. If you'll just let me explain.'

'Fire ahead. Oh, don't take that literally.' She stood up and bent forwards, hands on her knees, regaining her breath. Her heart was only just starting to regain its natu-ral rhythm.

'You see, our gun club is authorised to co-operate with the Office of Public Works, which is responsible for the deer herd.' He took off his military cap to reveal a pale bald head. Contrasting with his heavily-painted face and neck, his white, shiny pate looked like an egg sitting in a pat-terned eggcup. 'We help out with culling, to stop the popu-lation getting out of control. But today we've been called in specially because there's been a report of a deer that has injured itself pretty badly. It's bleeding heavily and it's in a lot of pain. It could pose a danger to the public.'

'So you're going to shoot it?'

'Put it out of its misery, yes. It's too badly injured to be helped, so it's the only decent thing to do. We've tracked it down to a certain area of the forest, and our best marksman is going to wait until he gets a clean shot at its head. It'll be all over in a second. The deer won't know a thing.'

'Just like Bambi's mum.'

'I beg your pardon?'

'Don't tell me you never saw *Bambi*. I got very upset when Bambi's mother was shot dead.' Tara walked around to stretch her muscles. 'It's a funny thing. For years I was convinced that her shooting was shown on screen. I could actually remember seeing it as a child. Then, many years later, I went to see the movie again. And you know what? They don't actually show Bambi's mother being killed at all. You hear the shot, but everything else is left to your imagination.'

She glanced at Dr Lifford, expecting a stare of bewilderment or condescension. Instead, he was smiling and nodding.

'I know *exactly* what you mean,' he said, emphasising the adverb in a very English manner. 'It's like the shower scene in *Psycho*. People imagine they see the knife plunging into the woman's body over and over again, but in fact you don't see any contact between killer and victim at all. It's all done by shadows and clever editing. Quite a tribute to Hitchcock's skill as a director, I always think, when you compare it to the gory rubbish you see nowadays...oh, dear. Have I said something to upset you?'

Tara shook her head. 'No, it's not your fault. Everyone in this village is a bit sensitive about the subject of stabbings these days.'

He looked at her blankly, then the penny dropped. 'Oh,

yes, of course. How insensitive of me. I'm sorry. Cigarette?'

'No, thanks. I'd better be getting back home. Good luck
with the hunt.'

'Thanks. It's more or less over, anyway. If you hear a
shot, you'll know we've got it.' He pointed to a fork in the
track leading into a side-path. 'If you go down that path,
you'll be well away from the action. It circles around and
brings you right back to the main forest entrance just
above Claremoon Harbour.'

She nodded and began running on-the-spot in a bid to
get back into form. 'Yes, I know the route. See you
around.'

'Cheerio for now. Oh, and Miss Ross,' he called after
her, 'if you ever need a colonic irrigation, be sure and give
me a call.'

One pace at a time. One foot in front of the other.

Tara was starting to regret she'd come so far. The road
through the forest was still climbing inexorably upwards,
and she was finding the effort increasingly exhausting.

She knew the forest well, and realised that the pathway
she had taken looped upwards for a good two miles before
reaching its peak and beginning the slow, winding descent
back down towards Claremoon Harbour. But the descending part of the road was actually very close to the point she
was at now. If her memory was true and her sense of direction accurate, she had only to leave the path, cut in through
the trees and run in a straight line for a quarter-mile or so
to join up with the downward portion of the same road.

Keeping up her steady pace, she wheeled off the path,
jumped the narrow ditch and plunged into the semi-
darkness underneath the closely-knit canopy of the pine
trees. It was a different world in here. There was virtually
no sunlight. Underfoot was a dense carpet of pine needles
which had withered to a light brown colour. They tinted

the weak light and turned everything into a strange tea-coloured monochrome, like a Victorian photograph. Adding to the sense of isolation and unreality was the intense silence – the pine needle carpet absorbed all sound and deadened it. Her running feet made no noise. Tara felt as though she had been transported into one of those old-fashioned sepia-coloured drawings that used to illustrate fairy tales by the Brothers Grimm – with hidden eyes everywhere, silently watching and waiting.

Hearing no sound but her own rasping breath, she plunged on through the densely-planted trees, changing direction and slowing down to negotiate drainage ditches and avoid fallen tree trunks.

At one point she found herself heading into a thicket of brambles and had to do a U-turn to get back on to her route. Or what she thought was her original route...she wasn't sure any more.

She paused, semi-stooped with hands on her knees, to regain her breath. A pigeon clattered noisily out of the undergrowth. The sudden clamour made her jump. She smiled at herself as the bird, scolding loudly, rose up towards the vaulted ceiling of the forest and escaped through a hole towards a patch of blue sky.

Which way was she going?

Come to that, which way had she just been?

She looked around and admitted to herself that she hadn't a clue. Every direction seemed exactly the same. There wasn't even a glimpse of sun to give an inkling to the compass points.

Tara began running again, but she was tired and not taking enough care. Her foot hit a hidden tree root and she plunged headlong on to the ground. It wasn't a bad fall and the pine needles were soft and yielding, but the impact knocked the wind out of her lungs.

It took a few moments to regain her breath. By now she was thoroughly exhausted and fed up. She had to fight to control the wave of irrational panic that was welling up from deep inside her as she looked all around and saw no clue to direction. For a few seconds, she felt she was incapable of breathing.

Get a grip. Calm down.

Breathe.

Now, walk, Tara. Don't run – walk.

You'll get there sooner or later, she reassured herself. This forest isn't that big. In fact, it's not even a forest at all. It's only a little wood. Fall over twice in any direction and you're practically on the other side.

She hardly noticed the second man from the gun club until she had almost stumbled over him. He was crouched in the brambles, just behind two large trees, obviously on the lookout for the wounded deer. His clothes, like Dr Lifford's, were dirty and torn and his face was smeared with earth-coloured camouflage.

But this one looked lupine, predatory, like some sort of wild creature of the forest. Just like the wolf in the fairy tale, she thought to herself. That's what you get for straying off the path, Little Red Riding Hood.

The man rose slowly as she approached. Behind the earthy camouflage his face seemed dark with displeasure, even anger. She suddenly realised that she must have strayed far from the original route and ended up in the middle of the shooting zone – the very area she'd been warned to avoid. No wonder he seemed so hostile.

'Hello, there!' called Tara, trying to sound cheerful. 'Dr Lifford's warned me about the hunt for the injured deer, and I'm trying to stay clear. If you can just point me in the right direction, I'll get out of your way.'

The man continued to stare at her, eyes burning through the muddy stains on his haggard face.

Muddy stains. Streaky stains of mud. Not facial camouflage, carefully painted like the doctor's. Just mud.

The hair, matted and filthy.

And no identity card on his ripped, mouldy, slept-in street clothes.

Tara felt the back of her neck prickle with a dreadful sense of impending danger.

Her smile slowly faded as she recognised his face...and realised the dreadful truth about the man who had stalked her all the way across Ireland to this godforsaken clearing deep in the forest.

She was looking into the eyes of a murder suspect who was being hunted by police in five counties – Manus Kennedy.

'I told you I would find you,' he said.

CHAPTER TWENTY-ONE

ANDRES THRUST a folded banknote at the taxicab driver. 'Can't you go any faster?' he pleaded. 'I really have to get to the airport as soon as possible. It is vitally important.'

The driver shook his head. He was obviously making some sort of facial gesture, but all Andres and his woman companion could see were his dreadlocks shaking from side to side and a fragment of his cheerful brown face in the driving mirror. 'Can't be done, man, can NOT be done. This a car, not a helicop-TER. Who you think I am, James Bond?'

He broke into a brief burst of Desmond Decker's reggae classic, 'Shanty Town'. 'Oh-oh-seven...oh-oh-seven...', banging his hands on the steering wheel in ska rhythm. It didn't seem to bother him that the radio was simultaneously blasting out an REM song in three-four time.

The driver gestured at the traffic which was locking him in on all sides. 'Rush hour, man. You must have heard of the rushhour where you come from in the United States of Ameri-CA.'

'I'm not American.'

'However. You get too much traffic, they build better roads, the cars fill up da roads and they become big car parks. It makes no sense, brother. No sense at all.'

'And there's no other route you can take to the airport?'

'Not unless you want the pleasure of my sweet company even longer.'

The six-lane highway had become gridlocked. Angry drivers blasted their horns for no good reason other than to relieve their tension. Lights turned from red to green and back to red again with nobody moving. Dense clouds of exhaust fumes pumped into the air from trucks whose drivers were revving up their engines in frustration. Anything more than fifty feet away was lost in a shimmering haze of smog and heat.

Andres looked at his watch and sighed. 'We're going to miss the flight.'

The woman looked out the window and said nothing. She was a pretty, dark-skinned brunette who wore her hair in a short bob. Her eyes were brown and enormous. Her mouth was wide and voluptuous. Her attractive snub-nose usually gave her a pert, cheeky-urchin expression, but right now she seemed apprehensive and jittery. She wore a black woollen miniskirt and sheer black tights on long, slender legs which she kept crossing and re-crossing nervously. She was a chain-smoker, and the no-smoking rule in the cab was driving her crazy.

'Damn. Damn. Damn.' Andres was looking at his watch again. 'We should have left more time.'

Silence. The lights turned green, and this time the traffic began to move sluggishly. Then, just after the car in front got through, the signals turned red again.

Andres gave a grunt of annoyance. Then: 'Why on earth won't she take my phone calls?' he asked the woman.

She shrugged and resumed her silent study of the traffic jam.

'She won't even phone back. God knows how many times I've left the number.'

'Hey, I been there too. You want my advice on dealing with women?' The driver was about to launch into a spiel.

'No.'

'The less you phone them, the more they want you, man. My rule is, never phone them. They come runnin' to your door.'

'Just concentrate on the road, friend.'

'Okay, but you missin' out on lessons from the best teacher in town. Wasn't it Desmond Decker who said,

"You Can Get it if You Really Want"?'

It took another hour of frustrating stop-start driving to get to the airport, but the taxicab driver was still smiling and seemed as calm and fresh as though he'd just come back from a relaxing spin in the countryside. The grin widened even further when Andres paid the extravagant bill and added on the banknote he'd proffered earlier. 'Thanks. Take it easy, man.'

They dashed to the terminal only to find that the flight had been exactly on time and had left seven minutes beforehand. Andres never ceased to marvel at the great cosmic rule which ensured that flights for which one was on time were always delayed, and flights for which one was late were always on time.

'No more flights and no connections. What do we do now?' he asked in near-despair.

'Find somewhere we can have a cigarette,' said the brunette pragmatically.

'What do you mean, she's gone?'

Fergal was almost speechless with outrage. He paced up and down the hallway of the cottage like a caged animal, banging his open palm with his fist. Sergeant Sean Gurrane was in no doubt about whose face was represented by the palm into which the fist repeatedly smacked.

'Mr Kennedy, I share your frustration, but please don't take it out on me,' the Corkman said with dangerous politeness. His attitude was coldly formal. 'Sit down. We've done all that can be done.'

'You've done damn-all except screw up the only job you had to do – keep guard on Tara.'

'You're not being helpful with that attitude, sir. Ms Ross was not under arrest. If she wants to secretly leave her house, for whatever reason, without notifying us, there's not much we can do to prevent her.'

'Leave the house? How do you know she wasn't abducted?'

Sean Gurrane sighed. 'It's a small village, as you know, Mr Kennedy. At least two witnesses saw her running up the hill towards the forest, wearing jogging gear. I think her intentions were perfectly clear.'

Fergal looked at his watch. 'How long ago?'

'Around three-thirty this afternoon.'

'But that's three hours ago. She should have been back ages ago.'

'I am aware of that, sir. I've notified headquarters and we're arranging a search with the help of local volunteers.'

'Well, I'm volunteering too.'

Sean Gurrane didn't respond. 'So you see, sir, we're doing everything in our power to find her.'

Fergal glared through the window at the top of the hillside, where the trees stood rank upon rank like an advancing army.

'I know you are,' he said at last. 'But it's not enough. He's going to find her first.'

'We're running out of time. For all we know, she could already be dead.' Andres pressed another series of numbers on the mobile-phone and talked urgently down the line to the downtown travel agent. At times he had to shout to make his voice heard over the airport tannoy announcements.

Outside, jets were being refuelled and loaded with baggage under the blasting heat of a sun that baked the asphalt and cooked the air into a simmering soup.

The brunette sighed and placed a fourth cigarette butt into a polystyrene cup half-full of cold coffee. They floated there like repulsive insects. She brought out a soft pack of Marlboro, shook a new cigarette directly into her mouth, and lit it with a small gold lighter. She looked around the airport nervously, as though expecting to be attacked from behind at any minute.

'Thanks. That is a confirmed booking, yes? Okay.' Andres pressed the off-button on the mobile and smiled for the first time that day.

'Good news?' asked the woman.

'Well, the best we can hope for. In thirty minutes, we can catch an internal flight to here' – he pointed to an airline map – 'where, if we wait for three hours, we can get the last two seats on a chartered flight to Belfast.'

The brunette looked at him blankly.

'Belfast, capital of Northern Ireland. Then we have a choice. We can either fly to Dublin and then travel to Clare on my BMW, or we can hang around Belfast Airport for several hours, take a direct flight to Shannon, then hire a car, and drive to Claremoon Harbour. Knowing the standard of the roads, I am not sure which would be faster. Either way, it's a long haul, but it is the only option we have. The only alternative is to wait until tomorrow.'

The woman took a deep drag of her cigarette. 'One question,' she said.

'Shoot.'

'Do they allow smoking on Irish planes?'

Inspector Phil O'Rourke arrived at Tara's cottage pale-faced with fury.

'I don't believe it,' he whispered angrily to Sean Gurrane as he hurled closed the door of his car with a resounding slam. 'What the hell can she be thinking of, running off like that? I tell you, if Manus Kennedy doesn't kill her, I bloody will.'

'Keep your voice down, Phil. Everyone's a bit highly-strung in there.' Gurrane nodded his head in the direction of the cottage.

'I'll bet they are. They'll be even more highly-strung when they hear the worse news.'

Gurrane looked at his feet. 'I have the feeling I'm not

going to like this.'

'Manus Kennedy gave them the slip along the Galway border. They had him pinned down along the shores of Lough Derg, with nowhere to run. Trouble is, he didn't run.' O'Rourke patted the pockets of his Donegal tweed jacket angrily, looking for cigarettes. 'He swam.'

Gurrane shook his head disbelievingly. 'He swam all the way across Lough Derg?'

'Across it, along the shoreline, out to one of the islands, whatever. The only thing we know is that he's escaped, and that he's had plenty of time to travel across country since.'

Gurrane watched his boss pat his pockets some more, then placed a hand on his arm and pointed to the packet of cigarettes lying on the passenger seat. 'Worst case scenario?' he asked.

'Worst case scenario is, he's in Claremoon Harbour again.' O'Rourke opened the car door again and grabbed the packet. 'He can travel across country like a bloody fox. I'm telling you, if he ever gets out of jail they should sign him up for the SAS.'

He lit a cigarette and looked around at the two uniformed gardaí who had travelled with him from Ennis and who were now standing outside the cottage awaiting orders. 'Okay,' he said to Gurrane. 'We'd better get things moving before nightfall. Give me an update.'

'We've had three gardaí searching the woods for the past hour. There are half a dozen members of the Civil Defence up there, too. All good men. The only problem is...'

O'Rourke clapped his hand to his head. 'Oh, Holy Divine. Not more problems.'

Gurrane pointed up at the hill. 'Part of the forest is sealed off. There are about a dozen armed members of a local gun club hunting for an injured deer.'

The inspector stared at him blankly. 'An injured deer,' he repeated flatly.

'Yes. A deer. They've got authorisation from us and from the OPW. Nobody's allowed into that part of the forest because they're likely to stop a bullet if they do.'

'Well, I sincerely hope they've told Manus Kennedy that,' said O'Rourke with heavy sarcasm. He flicked his cigarette on to the ground and stepped on it aggressively. 'Call them off.'

'We're doing that at the moment. But they're spread out all over the place. The good news is that we've talked to the club chairman, Dr Charles Lifford, who encountered Miss Ross and stopped her from wandering into the protected zone. He showed us the path she took, but we've checked every inch of it and she's not there.'

O'Rourke was silent for a few moments. 'What a pig's breakfast,' he said at last. 'Why can't anything be simple and straightforward with this woman?'

'Because she's not a simple and straightforward type of woman,' said Gurrane in irritation.

They both looked up beyond the treeline, studying the terrain and working out tactics. But as they watched, a frantic cloud of birds suddenly emerged from the forest and scattered in all directions.

A split second later they heard the shot. It cracked sharply, almost like a snapped twig, and then rolled and echoed around the hillside.

O'Rourke signalled to the waiting policemen to follow him up the hill. 'For all our sakes,' he said to Gurrane, 'let's hope that was aimed at your deer.'

CHAPTER TWENTY-TWO

FOR A long time they just stared at each other, Tara Ross and Manus Kennedy.

He was smaller than she remembered him, but brawny and sturdily-built. His hair had grown longer and hung down over his eyes in greasy, matted hanks. His heavily pockmarked face was disguised by mud and several days' growth of beard, but his blue eyes still burned and glowed like those of some Old Testament prophet as he glared at her, measuring her, assessing her.

'What exactly do you want from me, Manus?'

Tara was surprised at how steady her voice sounded. Inside, she felt petrified, sick with terror. Every cell in her body screamed at her to panic, cut loose, run. But she knew she wouldn't get far. Instead, she willed herself to remain calm. Her only chance was to stall, bluff, engage, wait for an opportunity that might never come.

She leaned casually up against a tree, trying to look as though she had all the time in the world to stay and chat. But the main purpose was to stop herself shaking.

To her relief, Manus did not move any closer. He stood stock-still, watching her with slow, wary eyes.

There was a long, long silence.

Tara bit her cheek inside her mouth until it hurt. She must not break the silence. If she did so, she would sound panicky and afraid. She had asked a question. It was his turn to speak.

Finally, he replied. If you could call it a reply.

'You're to be next to die,' he said.

His voice chilled her. It was the quiet, soft, unhurried voice of a rational man. But its pitch was unnervingly high and the tone was shattered and unnatural.

It was the same sort of voice she had heard dozens of times, from the people who would drift in to the front office of her newspaper in Dublin on cold winter nights, claiming they had an important story to reveal. The sort of people who looked like your kind uncle or your friendly neighbour and sounded fine until they suddenly started shouting about the Stone of Destiny or Satan's Children and began overturning chairs and grabbing you by the throat. She had learned to spot such people in advance by looking into their eyes. And listening carefully to their voices.

Voices just like this.

The sweat from the run was cooling rapidly on her skin, and suddenly Tara felt very cold. She tried to stop the crawling of her flesh turning into a shiver which would be obvious to the man in front of her. What she had to do now was put on an act. She had to deliver the performance of her life. But which act would keep her alive longer? Fear and submission? Anger? Indifference?

As his relentless eyes continued to bore into hers, she forced herself to wait for a few long seconds before she spoke. And when she did, it was with a careless shrug.

'What do you mean, I'm going to die, Manus.' She kept her voice light and matter-of-fact, the voice of a nurse tucking in the bed sheets and reassuring a patient on the morning after a nightmare. 'Sure didn't I go to school with you? We're both only young pups. Neither of us is going to die for a long time, I hope.'

That's right. Keep it light. Keep it easy. Two friends having a bit of a chat.

'It makes sense when you think about it,' he said, and he could have been discussing the weather or the economy instead of her imminent death. 'First the beasts of the field, then the mother, then the lover. That's how the devil thinks. That's how he works.'

'The devil?'

'That's how he thinks, that's how he does things.'

'What did you mean about the beasts? What beasts?' She was desperately stalling.

'The beasts of the field. The cattle. The ones who died.'

Suddenly she knew what he meant. 'Manus, are you talking about the time those cattle died on your farm? The time the cowshed burned down?'

He looked at her slyly. 'You know about that? Yes, the devil did it. Everyone thought it was my fault, but the devil was the one who really did it.'

He fell silent, as if everything had been made clear. The afternoon air hung heavy with thunder. Nearby, a huge bluebottle buzzed angrily around the decomposing carcass of some tiny forest creature.

Far away, from down below in the village, voices drifted up in the hot summer air. A child's excited cry of pleasure. A man's spontaneous laughter. Here, time had frozen into one endless, terrifying moment. But elsewhere, life just went on as usual. In the middle of this long, lingering dance of death, this slow-motion horror, life still went on as usual.

'That must have been terrible for you,' said Tara, realising too late that her sympathy sounded forced and false.

All the time her mind was in freefall. What way would it happen when it happened? When he finally attacked, would it be with a razor-sharp knife clutched in his dirty, pudgy hand? Or with a crude stone snatched from the forest floor and raised and lowered, raised and lowered, again and again? Or would his fingers lock around her throat and keep squeezing until her thrashing body became limp and still?

She forced herself to stop the pointless speculation and concentrate. Keep him talking. The longer he talks, the longer you stay alive. Simple as that.

But he had picked up on the tone of her voice. 'What would you know about it? You have no idea what it was like!' For the first time, his voice registered emotion.

Bad move, Tara. Talk him down.

'You're right, of course,' she agreed, taking time to think about it. 'Yes, how could I know? Nobody could possibly know unless they were there.'

Get ready, Tara. Ready for whatever it takes. But not ready to die. Not yet. Please God, not yet.

'You don't understand, you don't understand at all. First the beasts, then the mother, then the lover. That's how it's going to be. First the animals, then the mother, then the lover,' he repeated as though reciting a verse from scripture.

Tara tried to keep up her rational-nurse act. But inside, she was a frightened child longing to scream with terror and run away.

'It doesn't have to be that way, Manus,' she said. 'Nothing ever has to be. We can change anything we want.'

'No, no, no.' He shook his head in vehement denial. 'The devil doesn't change. He killed those animals in the cowshed. He killed my mother. And he will kill you, too.'

'It doesn't have to happen, Manus.'

'You didn't see those cattle die,' he said. 'You didn't look into their eyes as they clambered over each other to try to get away from the flames. I'll never forget it, not ever, not as long as I live. It gives me...scary nightmares, awful dreams. I couldn't stand it and they put me away and gave me medicine and it stopped for a while and the devil went away. But then they let me out again and the nightmares started. Every time I went to sleep, I could see them...their eyes...staring at me. And the devil came back to me again, and my mother died too.'

He stared at her as though everything had been made clear and a logical point had been proven.

Tara shrugged with exaggerated carelessness. She said: 'You've been through a rough patch, I know, Manus, and so have I. But to tell you the truth, I'm starting to get cold. You know my cottage? It's just down below. Why don't we go down there and we'll talk it all out over a nice hot bowl of soup and home-made bread. Maybe some rashers and eggs?'

It was worth a try. For a brief moment she saw his eyes flicker with indecision as the hunger gnawing at his stomach almost overcame his willpower. But it lasted only for a split second. He looked at her with a sly cunning, as though she had almost succeeded in putting one over on him.

'Oh, no,' he said. 'That wouldn't do. That wouldn't do at all.'

'Please yourself.' Tara affected superficial annoyance. 'But I'm off.'

'Don't go YET!'

The last word was a strangled scream. With surprising speed, he was on his feet, by her side, holding her arm in a grip like an iron clamp.

'Manus! Let go!' Tara could hardly control her panic. She had mentally rehearsed half a dozen moves to stop him doing exactly this. But she hadn't had time to do any of them.

He shook his head, growing more and more excited. 'I can't. You have to understand why I can't. The devil wants you. The devil.'

Far, far away, more faint voices. Nearer at hand, much nearer, the sound of something rustling through the undergrowth.

'No, *you* don't understand,' she said, trying hard to keep authority in her voice. 'There are men with guns all round here. They're looking for me.'

He paused, as though unsure whether to believe her. 'It's not true. You're lying. Just like all the others. Everybody lies to Manus Kennedy.'

'Listen!' Her voice was a command. The rustling and crunching of undergrowth sounded again, this time nearer at hand.

His eyes flickered to the right and he appeared almost to sniff the air like some creature of the forest. 'You're lying,' he repeated. 'That's not a man. That's an animal. Squirrel or a rat – no, not a squirrel. Bigger. A dog, maybe.'

The ferocity of his grip brought tears to her eyes. She couldn't play any more roles. 'Please let me go, Manus. I've done you no harm.'

'No, you've done me no harm, and you've done the devil no harm, but the devil wants you dead anyway.'

'But why? Why does the devil want me dead?'

'I don't know. He doesn't tell me, does he? Maybe he doesn't know himself. But it's going to happen, and it's going to happen very soon. You have to come with me.'

The rustling had ceased and the forest had become eerily quiet once again.

Then Tara's eyes open wide with astonishment and disbelief. Behind Manus's shoulder, at the edge of the little clearing, she caught sight of movement. Painful movement, dragging movement, movement with excruciating slowness.

'The animals that died in the fire,' she said, a desperate plan forming out of despair. 'Those animals, Manus. You can still see their eyes in your dreams?'

He stopped suddenly in the act of dragging her away. 'How do you know about my dreams?' he demanded. He began breathing fast, heavily, regularly, as though building up a head of steam of uncontrollable emotion. 'The eyes are the worst part. I can always see their eyes.'

She leaned towards him so that her voice became a whisper in his ear. 'Look behind you, Manus. The eyes are still watching.'

Still holding her firmly, he spun around.

The first thing he saw was a pair of large, brown eyes, staring into his with suffering and a dumb incomprehension that could almost have passed for pleading.

There, half dead with pain and exhaustion, lay the wounded deer, collapsed in an untidy heap after its last few desperate steps. Bluebottles buzzed furiously around the dried blood on its injured, torn haunch. Its broken leg, trailing uselessly behind, seemed to have collected half the debris of the forest in its wake. Now the deer was lying down to die, and its eyes mirrored its anguish and despair.

The eyes of Manus Kennedy met the eyes of the beast, and his dark nightmares came to life.

He screamed, a long drawn-out, animal scream of unendurable dread.

And he released Tara's arm.

She pushed him as violently as she could, trying to knock him off-balance before leaping away and plunging into the forest undergrowth. Briars ripped at her skin, pine branches tore her clothes, but she didn't care as her heart pounded against her aching ribcage and her breath roared through her opened lungs, running, running, running for her life.

The last thing she saw, from the corner of her eye, as she sprinted out of the clearing, was Manus Kennedy falling slowly to his knees. He wasn't running after her. In fact, he wasn't even moving. He was a statue of stone, a kneeling, praying penitent confronting the demons of his innermost soul.

And that's how they found him, ten minutes later, after Tara had plunged out of the forest into the protective arms of Sergeant Steve McNamara.

He was still kneeling there motionless, his blue eyes fixed on the brown eyes of the stricken beast, his face transformed with something halfway between terror and ecstasy.

As the clearing slowly filled with uniformed men, and the air became loud with the crackling stutter of radios, Manus Kennedy's expression didn't flicker and his eyes didn't move.

But when the man from the gun club stepped forward and dispatched the panting, suffering deer with one

expert, close-range shot, it was Manus Kennedy who collapsed on the forest floor, groaning and whimpering as
though a silver bullet had entered his own confused brain
and put an end to the turmoil of his own anguished life.

CHAPTER TWENTY-THREE

THEY TOLD Tara that the shock of the ordeal would strike her later, with all the force of a runaway juggernaut, and that it would come when she least expected it. But it never did. Declining Dr Maguire's offer of a sedative, Tara settled instead for a single stiff brandy, and rode it all out with the help of Dr Remy and Dr Martin.

She watched the television news bulletin in which Manus Kennedy was shown, looking even more werewolfish in the harsh glare of the TV lights, as he was escorted from Ennis Garda station to a special sitting of the district court, where he was remanded in custody on a holding charge of assaulting Melanie. He had refused to answer the charge and a solicitor had been appointed by the State to conduct his defence. The judge was told that a more serious charge was pending against the defendant and bail was opposed on the grounds that witnesses could be intimidated.

'The arrest and charge follows one of the most intensive manhunts ever mounted in County Clare,' said RTÉ's crime correspondent. 'Involving more than a hundred gardaí and scores of civil defence workers, it was instigated following the brutal murder of a local mother-of-two, Ann Kennedy, and a subsequent assault on a young woman at another house in Claremoon Harbour.'

The report ended with an interview with the Garda Commissioner, who paid tribute to the outstanding work of the gardaí in the operation and promised that vigilance would be maintained to protect the people of outlying country areas.

Tara turned off the television. 'Funny sort of world,' she said.

'What?' asked Melanie, absent-mindedly swishing the

remains of a measure of brandy in her glass. She had taken the same medical treatment, in a selfless gesture of solidarity with her friend.

'All the times I sabotaged stag hunts during my student days,' said Tara. 'I never thought I'd see the day when a deer saved *my* life in return.'

Melanie laughed. 'It must have been a one in a zillion chance,' she said. 'You must be the luckiest person in the entire universe, if not beyond. Can you give me six numbers? I'm filling out a Lotto ticket and I want to be sure of winning.'

'Perhaps it wasn't just luck,' argued Tara. 'The OPW man told me that some of the deer in the forest are quite tame, so perhaps it heard the voices and came towards us for help. Besides, I think I deserve just a few awards of merit in the quick-thinking and presence-of-mind categories.'

'Which nearly – but not quite – cancels out your incredible stupidity in getting yourself into that situation in the first place,' Melanie reminded her. 'Anyway' – she raised her glass in a toast – 'the creep is safely behind bars by now, and if there's any justice he'll be there for a long time.'

'And so say all of us.' There was a belated tap on the living-room door. The two women looked around to see a tall, heavily-built figure in garda uniform.

'Oh, hello, Sergeant McNamara.' Tara's voice was stiffly formal. She still hadn't forgotten the hostility Steve had shown towards her after she'd given Fergal his alibi. 'Have a seat. Melanie, I'd like you to meet Sergeant Steve McNamara, who used to be a good friend of mine.'

The sergeant's rough-hewn face turned bright red with embarrassment. 'Tara, I...'

'Oh-oh,' said Melanie, sensing the atmosphere, 'I can see you two have things to say. Excuse me, I'll just nip out to the kitchen to...check the oven.'

'But there isn't anything in the oven, Mel.' Tara was poker-faced.

'Well, I'll just check that the oven's still there. There've been several cases of unexplained oven abductions.' Melanie flashed the bewildered sergeant her brightest smile. 'Cup of tea, inspector?'

'Thanks, love. White, three sugars.'

There was a long, awkward silence after Melanie left the room.

'Well, Steve, to what do I owe the pleasure?' Tara asked at last.

The big policeman shuffled uncomfortably in his seat. 'I just thought I'd congratulate you on the way you handled that situation in the pine woods today. If you hadn't kept a cool head, you'd have been another murder victim. I've no doubt about that.'

'Comforting to know you had faith in me, Steve.'

He accepted the reproach with good grace. 'We took him to Ennis Station,' he said, changing the subject slightly. 'He just stared at the wall and said nothing. Nothing at all. Admitted nothing, denied nothing.'

Tara sipped her brandy. 'It doesn't really matter,' she said. 'Confessions are pretty useless these days without hard evidence. When you get the right evidence – the DNA results, for instance – it won't matter what he says or doesn't say.'

McNamara nodded. 'Our main aims right now are to locate the murder weapon and to establish a motive. It's clear from what you've told us that he was in dispute with some pretty heavy Dublin drug dealers over a sum of around three grand. If we can prove that he came to Claremoon Harbour at the time of the murder, we can work on the theory that he came to borrow the money from his mother. He was pretty desperate and not in any mental state to handle a rejection.'

'That's one theory,' agreed Tara. 'But there's another possibility. Fergal is convinced that Manus was out to get him through the women in his life. First Ann, then me. And that makes some sort of sense in view of what Manus said in the wood – "first the beasts, then the mother, then the lover". He seemed to believe that Satan made him kill the farm animals first, then Fergal's mother second, and finally me.' She looked directly into Steve's eyes. 'Mind you, he wasn't the only one who made my life miserable because of my relationship with Fergal.'

She fell silent. Cue Steve.

'Tara...' McNamara was shamefaced. 'I have to admit I didn't just come here to congratulate you on your escape and to inform you of developments. I came to apologise.'

'Really?'

'I've behaved like a gobshite, and I've regretted it ever since. I made a lot of unfounded assumptions about our relationship and where it was going, but you had done nothing to justify that. You said nothing that led me to believe we were any more than friends. It was all inside here.' He tapped his angular forehead.

'What I'm trying to say is that, if we could only' – he fought to find a word, then his eyes rested on the video recorder – 'if we could only *rewind* things to the way they were before, I would consider it a great honour to be counted as your good friend once more.'

Tara said nothing for a moment. Then: 'I'm afraid that's not possible, Steve,' she said.

'It's not?' His craggy face collapsed like a landslide on Mount Rushmore.

Tara rose to her feet, walked over to him, and put her arm around his shoulder in a warm hug. 'We'll be friends as before,' she smiled, 'but Steve, the honour will be all mine.'

'Where's O'Rourke, anyway?' she asked as she walked Steve outside to the police car. 'I thought he'd be here tonight.'

The sergeant banged his forehead with his fist. 'Jaze, Tara, I nearly forgot to tell you. The Inspector sends his apologies. He had to dash off to Dublin to interview some druggie. And while he's there, he's going to visit his daughter.'

'I didn't know O'Rourke had a daughter. How old is she?'

'Twenty-six. Same age as you.' Steve peered at Tara, as though comparing her face to another woman's. 'In fact, she looks a lot like you, too. Same black hair, same big brown eyes. Sad case.'

'Thanks a lot, Steve.'

'Oh!' He looked horrified, as though he'd put his foot right in it again. 'I didn't mean you. I meant his daughter.'

'And why do you say she's a sad case?'

'Well.' Steve fidgeted with his cap. 'It's just that she had everything going for her. Loving family, great university career, whole world of opportunity ahead. But she threw it all away.'

'How?' Tara was intrigued.

'Oh, she fell for some smooth-talking conman from England. She was really besotted with him. But he was one of these cold-hearted bastards who was only out for himself. One of those fellas, he could carry a shaggin' bottle of Heineken around in his inside left pocket, and at the end of the day it would be cooler than when it went in.'

He planted his cap on his head and opened the door of the patrol car.

'Anyway,' he said, 'the way I heard it, he gave her this hard-luck story about owing money to the banks. Said he was about to lose his house. Wanted to marry her and said everything would be OK if he could just get wipe the slate clean and start again. He talked her into leaving college, getting a job and going guarantor on a big loan for them both. Turned out, all he really wanted was ready cash to skip the country with another woman. He had it all planned out from the start. Last thing she heard from him was a postcard from Malaga with one word on it: "Thanks".'

'My God. How did O'Rourke react to all this?'

'How do you think? We practically had to scrape him off the ceiling. But there was nothing he could do.'

'So his daughter's been left penniless?'

'Worse than that, Tara. She owes a fortune, and the banks are determined to screw every last cent out of her. She'll be spending the rest of her days working to pay off the debt.'

'Her life's been ruined,' she said slowly.

'Yep,' he agreed. 'All because of one lousy bastard with a heart of stone.'

The car's suspension groaned in weary protest as Steve eased himself into the driver's seat.

'O'Rourke says he has only one regret in his life,' the sergeant said thoughtfully. 'And that's that he was too busy with his police work to spend more time with his daughter. He never had a chance to warn her against people like that.'

The huge jumbo soared eastwards, away from the midnight of the west and into the rising sun. The last movie had finished long ago, and the first rays of dawn revealed sardine-packed passengers with sleeping bodies splayed at ungainly angles – feet over each other's ankles, heads rested on the shoulders of strangers as they tried to snatch a few hours' sleep before a morning that their internal body clocks were not expecting.

Andres awoke to find a pretty, red-haired stewardess tapping his shoulder and asking him if he wanted a drink of mineral water or orange juice. Beside him, the brunette was still fast asleep, her head cradled against her hand.

The freckle-faced stewardess repeated her question, and Andres accepted a Ballygowan mineral water. 'What time is it?'

'Five o'clock Irish time. We're due to land in Belfast around seven-thirty.' She smiled professionally and moved on.

The brunette awoke in her turn, stretched stiffly and ordered a Buck's Fizz. She leaned forward. 'What time is it in Irish currency?' she asked.

'Five in the morning,' he said. 'That delay before take-off cost us two hours. Even if we clear Belfast Airport by eight, we shall not reach my home in Dublin much before noon, and that means late afternoon before we get to County Clare. It's much the same story if we have to wait around for a direct flight to Shannon. I wish there were some faster way.'

'I wish I could smoke,' replied the brunette.

The breakfasts came around, hermetically sealed plastic containers of bacon, sausage and black pudding. 'Damn. Damn. Damn. We may be too late,' Andres muttered to himself.

'I beg your pardon?' said the navy-suited businessman by his side. He spoke in a broad Belfast accent.

'I apologise. I was just – what is the phrase? – thinking aloud.' Noticing the man's puzzled expression, he elaborated. 'I'm trying to reach Claremoon Harbour in County Clare before noon. It is very, very urgent. Very important. But I have to travel from Belfast and that could take all day.'

'Well, you may have hit it lucky,' said the businessman, producing a business card. 'I own a commercial helicopter company. You could always hire one of my pilots. It won't come cheap, but it'll get you there in time.'

He whipped out a Sheaffer pen and did a few calculations on the back of a napkin.

'Including VAT and insurance, we could do Belfast-Clare for you at this price,' he said. 'And believe me, there's a quare wee bit knocked off that figure for luck.'

Andres picked up the napkin and blanched as he read the figure.

'Well?' asked the man. 'Is it important or not?'

Andres was silent.

'If it's important, then it's worth the money,' said the

man, holding his open palm out in a gesture of impatient invitation. 'Take it or leave it. You snooze, you lose.'

He began clicking his pen restlessly, miming the sound of a ticking clock.

Andres took a deep breath. 'It's important,' he said.

'It's a deal, then,' said the man. 'I'll call ahead and have the chopper waiting on the tarmac.'

Andres shook his outstretched hand.

'It'll save time if I do the paperwork here and now,' said the man, searching under the seat and producing a briefcase. 'How many passengers?'

'Two.'

'Names and addresses?'

'Andres Talimann, from Killiney in Dublin.' He turned and smiled encouragingly at the beautiful black woman beside him. 'And a Ms Mathilde Bresson, from Montreal in Canada.'

The Belfastman shook the brunette's hand. 'Visiting family in Ireland?' he asked.

Mathilde Bresson nodded.

'I'll bet you're looking forward to it.'

Mathilde nodded again. It was easier to agree than to tell the truth. That she was flying to Ireland to confront the man who had been responsible for her worst nightmares.

Her husband. Fergal Kennedy.

It had taken Andres Talimann ten full days to track her down, and another two days to persuade her to return to Ireland with him. To start with, the only lead he'd had was the short news item he'd found on the Internet: a mere two paragraphs stating that a warrant had been issued for the arrest of a Mr Fergal Kennedy on a charge of assaulting one Mathilde Bresson.

Dozens of phone calls from Ireland had yielded nothing. In the end, he'd had to hire a private investigator, a French Canadian ex-cop with impeccable police contacts.

The investigator had left a message on the answerphone while Andrés was in Paris, confirming that he'd made a tricky flight connection and had managed to contact the woman. But he wanted money upfront.

Flying to Canada was no big deal for Andrés. His magazine had a discount arrangement with a major airline, so travel was cheap. But he'd been reluctant to leave Tara. She had been showing all the symptoms of delayed shock after her experiences at the hands of the Ballymahon drug dealers.

The morning after their return, he'd twice tried to waken her with tea and toast, but she'd been flat out. Rather than force her awake from the healing sleep she so obviously needed, he'd left her a note. He couldn't tell her exactly where he was going, but he had every intention of returning in a couple of days and, anyway, she should be safe so long as she remained in his apartment. God knows, he'd thought, she could do with the rest.

Andrés flew to Canada not knowing whether he was wasting his time. But when he finally sat down opposite Mathilde Bresson in her tiny low-rent apartment, he didn't just get confirmation of Fergal's identity. He heard a story of bullying and brutality that made his blood boil with anger.

Fergal Kennedy and Mathilde Bresson had married on a freezing day in late October. The sky over Montreal Harbour was the colour of festering wounds, and a dirty sleet blew off the St Lawrence River and through the streets to the grim civic offices where they signed the papers. There were two witnesses, both strippers in the seedy clip-joint where Mathilde was working as a topless waitress and Fergal worked as a part-time barman.

When he made his vows, Fergal was satisfied that Mathilde had told him the truth about her life – how she had travelled just a few months before from her birthplace in Metz, in the north-east of France, to live with her relations, first-generation French immigrants in Quebec.

In contrast, he had told her nothing but lies about himself. He was a famous Irish artist who was about to make an important breakthrough in Canada. His first major exhibition was due to open soon, but there had been a delay and, in the meantime, he had to take menial jobs where he could find them.

It was all fantasy, just like all the bogus stories he was later to tell Tara about art galleries in Vancouver and healthy lumberjack work in the great Canadian outback. The less romantic truth was that Fergal had never set foot in Vancouver and the closest he had come to the great outback was stacking beer-crates out back of the grimy bars where he scraped a living.

Lies came easy to him. They always had. In Fergal's world, there was no substantive difference between truth and falsehood. Truth was relative. What you said depended on who you were talking to, and what they wanted to hear. It was easy. All it took was practice. Years of practice to mimic all the emotions he saw in the faces of other people, but would never experience himself – emotions like sincerity, love and trust. To him, they were just words, meaning nothing more than the word 'icebergs' might mean to a desert Bedouin. He knew they existed, he knew they were out there somewhere, but they just didn't have any relevance to him or his life.

When he said 'I do' on that cold October afternoon, it meant nothing, either. It just gave him the exclusive right to possess the body of this sensuous black woman who had somehow resisted everyone's advances for the past five months.

At first, their marriage went like a dream because they were both great in bed. For a full month, they hardly left their attic bedroom as she tested her limitless inventiveness against his inexhaustible energy.

But when the first fires faded and they rejoined the

humdrum, everyday world of alarm clocks and greasy dishes and dirty underwear and ironing, the mask started to slip.

Mathilde began to be spooked by his unpredictability and frightened by his white-hot flashes of anger. But most of all, she was bewildered and lost in the endless fog of lies and deceit that had engulfed their relationship and left her life without any sense of direction.

'I never know when he is lying and when he is telling the truth – even in the little, unimportant things,' she sobbed to her Tante Jeanne one dismal afternoon. 'It seems that lies are simply part of everyday life to him, as basic as washing one's face or combing one's hair.'

'Men, they are all like that,' Tante Jeanne assured her.

But all men were not like Fergal Kennedy. All men would not ask for a cup of coffee and slap her hard across the face if she forgot the sugar. All men would not strike her in the stomach with their fists if she asked where they'd been to four am. All men would not fly into terrifying rages for reasons that could never be anticipated or controlled.

She had her first warning that something was seriously amiss when they were working in the nightclub together. Their income depended on her tips. One night she became flustered and spilled a Bloody Mary over the suit of a regular client who was famous for leaving large gratuities. The customer stormed out, swearing never to return. Fergal witnessed the encounter. His face became darkened and twisted with rage. He ran the full length of the club, hurled Mathilde on to the floor, and began to beat her with his fists. It took two bouncers to haul him off. If they had not, he would have killed her, there and then, in front of a dozen witnesses.

She swore to herself that this was the end. But after only a week's token separation, she accepted his apologies and tearful pledges and returned to him. He had drunk too much cheap wine, he assured her. It would never happen again.

Their marriage lasted eighteen months, and finally died on a misty April night as the foghorns boomed their mournful note across the St Lawrence River. He had come home at five am, red-eyed and irritable and smelling of another woman.

Mathilde knew better than to ask him where he'd been. She just sipped her coffee and looked at him.

It must have been the look, or how he interpreted the look. Or maybe it hadn't anything to do with the look. Perhaps there was no trigger at all. Perhaps there was no need for one.

She spent the next six days in hospital and the next three months attending orthodontic clinics as therapists worked to realign her broken jaw. Her dental work took even longer. Even the most hardened cops were stunned by the savagery of the beating, and the courts issued a warrant for Fergal's arrest on serious assault charges.

But Fergal was no longer in Canada. He had scooped together his few belongings and had taken an internal flight to Toronto, then onwards to London. It was the first leg of a long journey that would take him home to Ireland, where he reinvented himself, made up a new set of lies, and met the new girl of his strange, twisted dreams. A young journalist named Tara Ross.

CHAPTER TWENTY-FOUR

FERGAL KENNEDY was a rock, a bulwark of support in the hours that followed Tara's ordeal in the forest. While others ran around shouting, panicking and generally adding to the air of mayhem, he was the calm centre of the storm, tending to the practical problems such as ensuring that everyone who mattered had a seat and a cup of tea, and everyone who didn't was kept at a distance. He was the one who organised a caterer to supply sandwiches and soup to the volunteer searchers, and the one who compiled a statement to satisfy the waiting reporters. While Tara was swept up in a storm of activity, being examined by doctors and questioned by police, he was the solid, dependable anchor who kept her firmly secured to ground.

Eventually, late at night, it was all over and peace returned to the cottage. Leaving the residue of the chaos until later, Fergal and Tara retreated to the garden to reclaim some peace of mind under the stars of the clear summer night.

From a garden bench sheltered by a huge bank of red and purple fuchsias, they could sit and look over the bay. A full moon, high in the black sky, cast a wide pathway of glittering, shimmering gold across the still water. The giant rocks and headlands that flanked the bay had become silhouetted against the sea like two-dimensional stage sets in a Japanese play. But awe-inspiring as it was, the seascape could not compare with the drama of the night sky above them. There, low on the horizon, was Jupiter, largest and most enigmatic of the planets. There was the Plough, and there was the North Star. And occasionally, a communications satellite would traverse the sky on its ceaseless journey around and around the globe.

'What a beautiful night,' murmured Tara as she sipped a chilled lager. 'We may have made headline news again, but when you look up there, it somehow seems all so...insignificant.'

Fergal grunted and opened a bottle of Rolling Rock.

'Some of those stars we see have been dead for millions of years. Yet we still see them shining.' Tara was sleepy and just slightly tipsy from her self-prescribed medication of a brandy and two beers. 'Will we shine on, Fergal, do you think?'

Fergal said nothing.

'After we die, I mean? Will we shine on?'

'I have no idea,' said Fergal.

'I can't believe that the people we love just disappear for ever,' said Tara. 'They're still there, somewhere, shining just as brightly. We just don't know how or in what form.'

Tara stared at the night sky and the dusty drifts of stars dissolved into the features on a face she remembered and loved. The years disappeared and suddenly she was sitting beside a hospital bed listening to her mother's faint whisper. The once-healthy face was growing paler and paler, the voice weaker and weaker.

The hepatitis had wreaked havoc on her liver, sapping her energy, turning her skin a sickly, jaundiced yellow. There was talk of compensation from the Government, but no amount of money could ever repay her for the irreversible damage caused by the tainted blood product she had received all those years ago.

'Promise me,' she had told Tara. 'Promise me you'll look after your father.'

Tara had held her limp hand and fought back the tears. 'I promise,' she said.

Christine Ross had always said she would not give in easily. She told Tara she would follow Dylan Thomas's advice to his own dying father, and rage against the passing of the light. But in the end she was too weak to resist.

She simply faded away, gently, into the goodness of the night.

Now, under the stars of this spectacular Van Gogh sky, Tara felt closer to her than ever.

'I think what's important,' Fergal said, after a long silence, 'is that we do what we can to realise our dreams while we're still alive.'

'Mmm,' said Tara in general agreement. It was one of those vague statements everybody agreed with in theory.

'No, I mean, right here, right now,' Fergal insisted. He paused, as though summoning up all his nerve to deliver his next words. 'What would you say if said I could make *your* dream come true, Tara?'

She giggled. 'I don't know, Fergal. Is it something you're likely to say?'

'Be serious, Tara. I mean it.'

'Okay, you mean it. You can make my dreams come true. But do I have to be back by midnight, or will the coach turn into a pumpkin?'

He ignored her. 'Listen to me. Remember what you told me? How you've always longed to buy the old Victorian spa house on the hill overlooking the village?'

She nodded, still smiling.

'What if I could make it come true for you? Not just right away, but soon? In the near future? What if we could get possession early next year, get the structural engineers in, get the plans drawn up and hire the builders and carpenters, and have it all restored by the end of next year, in time to get a big Christmas tree up in the front room?'

'I'd say you've had too many Rolling Rocks.'

He grunted impatiently. 'This is my first drink all day and I'm absolutely serious. What do you think?'

Tara yawned and stretched. 'I think I'm very, very tired and I think I need some sleep. Can we talk about it, if there is an "it" to talk about, in the morning?'

He held out an arm to stop her rising from the bench. 'Tara, I'd like you to come to a celebration dinner with me tomorrow evening. Out to La Belle Époque in Ennis – no expense spared – where we'll have oysters and lobster by candlelight, and toast your future in champagne. At the end of the evening I'm going to ask you a very important question. If you say yes, you'll make me very happy and we can grasp that dream of yours and never let it get away from us. If you say no, I'll get out of your life, and out of this village, forever.'

Her eyes widened as she looked at him. 'What on earth...?'

'There's no in-between, Tara. After the way things have gone, there's nothing left for me here but you. Think about it. Goodnight.'

He rose abruptly and stalked towards the gate.

'Fergal, wait.' Tara sat bolt upright, shaken out of her reveries. 'Come back. Let's talk about this.'

He shook his head and left without another word.

Sleep eluded Tara that night, no matter how hard she tried to relax her restless body and tame the hurtling, runaway thoughts that raced through her head.

Her mind kept returning to the last conversation she'd had with her father...perhaps the last conversation she would ever have with him.

It had been over a week ago. He'd travelled all the way from Claremoon Harbour to Galway, where she'd been staying with Melanie, and they'd met down by the salmon weir near the cathedral.

The River Corrib had been low and sluggish. At other times of the year, when it was in full flood, it could be spectacular. You could sit and watch the salmon flashing up through the waterfall, struggling against the cascading stream to return to their spawning grounds in the lakes and rivers of Connemara.

'Thanks for coming, Dad,' Tara had said softly. 'It's a long way.'

John Ross shrugged and lit a cigarette as they sat down together on a wooden bench. 'It's only a ninety-minute drive, Tupps. Christine used to say that, if you love someone enough, you'll go to the ends of the earth for them.'

She took his roughened hand and squeezed it fondly. She knew how much John Ross had adored his wife. For twenty-nine years, she had been the centre of his life, the very core of his heart and the reason for his existence; and when she'd been stolen away from him, he had been almost literally disabled. It was not as though one individual had died and another individual had been left behind. It was more as though a single entity had been severed in half, like a worm under a garden spade, leaving one part struggling to find a new life without the other.

Tara thought of her own relationship with Fergal.

'What was it like when you met Mum?' she couldn't resist asking. 'How did you know you'd found the right person?'

He lit a cigarette. 'Now, that's a hard one,' he said. 'That's a really hard one.'

He lapsed into silence, and she resisted the temptation to break it with a prompt or a clarification. John Ross had his own rhythm of speech and would not be rushed.

'It happened while I was in the merchant navy,' he said at last. 'I was on leave in Dublin, and I met her at a dance in the old Ierne Ballroom in Parnell Square. She was wearing a red dress. And my goodness, how she could dance. She danced with a sort of easy, unconscious grace. She moved across the floor like a swallow moves across the sky in summer, gliding, dipping, as light as the air.'

Tara nodded encouragement. She'd heard the story many times before, but she'd never grown tired of it.

'I couldn't believe that anything that walked on God's earth could move so beautifully,' he said, as he stared at the wall of the cathedral and the scene replayed itself on his mind's eye. 'I knew I had to ask her to dance.'

He took a long, reflective draw on his cigarette. 'But

you've heard what the ballrooms were like in those days,' he said. 'You had the boys lined up along one side and the girls lined up on the other, with this vast empty space of floor in between. It was a long, lonely walk across to ask a girl to dance, but it was nothing compared to the loneliness of the long-distance walk back again if she refused you.'

John Ross had made that long walk across...and she'd turned him down right away.

'I wasn't going to make that long walk back again,' he said, and Tara could see the glint of determination in his eye. 'I told her outright that there was only one way I was going to go back across that dance floor, and that was with her in my arms.

'Christine was absolutely outraged. She said: "Well, I hope you've brought your tent and sleeping bag, because you'll have a long, long wait."

'I said: "That's fine by me."'

Tara smiled. She could just imagine them facing each other, two hot-headed personalities, equally determined, her father looking like the young Connery, and her mother looking like some haughty Spanish contessa, the way she did when her Latin blood was up.

'She looked me straight in the eye, and I looked at her, and suddenly we both burst out laughing. Next thing, the band struck up a waltz and we were away.' He tapped the ash from his cigarette. 'Well, I'm no dancer, Tupps. Normally I'd move as gracefully as a cow coming off the trailer at a mart, but somebody was looking after us that night, because my feet flew as smoothly as a skater's on ice. By the time the night was over, we knew we were meant for each other.'

Tara sighed. 'That's really romantic. And you were married before the year was out?'

He nodded. Then, reading her mind: 'But we were lucky, Tupps. It's not always as straightforward and clear-cut as that. With most people, it needs time to develop slowly.'

Her eyes followed a tourist couple – probably Dutch or German – who were strolling arm in arm along the riverside.

'But how can you possibly tell for sure?' she persisted. 'I mean, I know I'm very fond of Fergal, but I'm just not sure whether...' Her voice trailed off.

He took her hand. 'You've always been the thoughtful type, Tupps. You question everything, analyse everything. No harm in that,' he added hastily as she began to object, 'except that it doesn't always apply in matters of the heart. When your heart tells you it's right to do something, then nothing your head says will make any difference at all.'

'But how will I *know* when it's right?'

John Ross shrugged. 'When it happens, you'll know.'

She felt like shaking him in frustration. He was behaving like a guru from a bad Kung Fu film.

Instead, she burst into laughter. 'But how?' she persisted.

Her father joined in her laughter. 'When you meet someone you'll go to the ends of the earth for,' he said.

She stood up and helped him to his feet. 'That doesn't help, Dad,' she admonished him, taking his arm and leading him back along the riverside. 'That doesn't help at all.'

Now, as she tossed and turned sleeplessly, Tara replayed this conversation over and over in her mind. Finally, she gave up on sleep. By five-thirty am, she was searching through the fridge when she felt a presence looming behind her.

She started and looked around sharply.

'Only me,' said Melanie quickly. 'Sorry to frighten you. I couldn't sleep either.'

She filled the kettle and put it on the range.

'When I can't sleep,' Mel continued, 'I find it's a waste of time to toss and turn and count sheep. I usually get up and make myself a cup of tea. If that doesn't work, I raid the fridge. I see you're at the fridge-raiding stage.'

Tara smiled. She never stopped marvelling at her friend's ability to interpret her moods.

'It's okay,' she said. 'Nothing that a good chocolate ice-cream wouldn't cure. Or an extra-creamy tiramisu.'

'That bad, eh?'

'Well, nearly. I'll settle for a low-fat fruit yoghurt.'

'Make it two and we'll form Insomniacs Anonymous.'

The kettle boiled quickly on the hot range, and soon Melanie had produced two steaming mugs of tea.

'What is it, Tara? Is it Manus? If that's what's keeping you awake, you know the answer is to talk it all out, and get him out of your head.'

Tara sipped the strong tea gratefully. 'No, strangely enough, that's not what's bothering me at all,' she said. 'I'm more worried about dad.' She nodded towards the upstairs room where her father lay motionless, still locked in some kind of coma that had left the specialists bewildered. 'I feel he's slipping away from us.'

Melanie laid a comforting hand on the arm of Tara's dressing-gown. 'No one lives forever, Tara. You may be right, you may be wrong, but there's no point putting yourself through the mangle over something you can't control. Take heart from the fact that you're doing your best and that your father is getting a standard of care that's second to none.' She smiled. 'When trouble comes all at once like this, one giant wave after another, all you can do is body-surf the waves. Go with them. It's pointless trying to battle against them.'

'But I still lie awake thinking that there must be something else I could do,' said Tara in despair. 'You see, the doctors say there's nothing physically wrong with him – at least, nothing more than there was a few weeks ago. The brain scan, the hospital tests...they're all fine. He just seems to have retreated into himself. Up to now I've been kidding myself that I've been getting through to him, making some sort of contact, but if I'm honest with myself I have to admit it's just not true. He's not responding to me at all.'

'And you feel it's up to you to shake him out of this...this coma, or whatever it is.'

'It sounds silly, but yes. I feel I should be at his side twenty-four hours a day, playing his favourite music, reading his favourite books, until I find something that releases the trigger and brings him back to consciousness.'

Melanie finished her mug of tea. 'That's an awfully heavy burden to impose upon yourself, love. It's too much for one set of shoulders to bear. You're assuming you have a control you don't have – power over sickness and health, control over life and death. But that's not within your gift. Change the things you can change, accept the things you can't. First principle of Insomniacs Anonymous.'

She handed Tara a box of tissues and watched as she dabbed a dampened eye. 'You're probably right, as usual, Mel,' said Tara. 'But I feel so helpless. If dad is aware of his surroundings at all, it must torture him that he can't even see the ocean from his bedroom. He lived for the sea. I sometimes think that if he could only get at the helm of the *Róisín Dubh* for just one hour, and taste the salt wind in his face and feel the swell of the ocean, and hear the breakers pounding on the rocks at Chicken Point, it would do more for him than any medicine the doctors could prescribe.'

She rose from her wooden chair and pulled the curtains on the kitchen window. It was already dawn, and the morning sea was dead calm, its surface moulded around the points and headlands and inlets of the coast as still and flat as though it were made of solid ice. An early-rising fisherman was already checking his lobster pots. His little rowboat left a wake as precise as plot lines on a navigational chart.

She felt Melanie at her shoulder. 'Well – why not?' Mel said suddenly. 'That sea is as calm as a boating lake. Your dad might not be able to take the helm, but there's no reason why you shouldn't take him out in the *Róisín Dubh* – as a passenger.'

Tara thought about it. 'Why not, indeed?' she said slowly. 'We could put him into his wheelchair and fix it solidly to the deck. It's not as though there's any danger, and it just might work.'

'Don't build up your hopes,' cautioned Melanie. 'But I suppose you've nothing to lose.'

Tara checked the big schoolhouse clock on the kitchen wall. 'Right! As soon as it gets to a decent hour, I'll phone Dr Maguire and ask his opinion. If he says it's okay, I'll ring Fergal. I'm sure he won't mind helping out.'

'Yes, I suppose so. But take Steve along too, if he's off duty.' Melanie paused as she saw a frown appear on her friend's face. 'Okay, own up, Tara. There's something else bothering you. What is it?'

Tara shrugged. 'Oh, nothing. I've just remembered that Fergal is taking me out to dinner at La Belle Époque in Ennis tomorrow night.' She glanced at the clock again. 'I mean, tonight.'

'Oh, that's a real problem,' mocked Melanie. 'What are you worried about – whether you should choose the Latour at six hundred pounds a bottle or the Lafite at seven hundred and fifty pounds?'

'It *is* a very generous gesture,' admitted Tara. 'And it will be a wonderful way of celebrating the end of a long ordeal for both of us. It's just...'

'Come on, out with it. There should be no secrets at IA meetings.'

'I'm almost certain he's planning to propose marriage to me.'

'And?' Melanie's face was blank.

'And I don't think I'm in any state to make decisions right now.'

Melanie's entire body had been tense as a tautened bowstring. It relaxed visibly. 'I'm glad you said that, because I couldn't agree more,' she said. 'Listen, Tara, if I were in the state you're in, I wouldn't trust myself to choose a TV channel, never mind choose a partner for life.'

'That's the way I feel. Spaced out. Confused.'

'Fine. You've every right to be.' Melanie rose to her feet and paced around the table in agitation. 'I don't want to be a pain and go on and on about it, Tara, but at a time like this, there's a danger that he could push you into commitments you don't want to make. Don't let it happen.'

'I'm not taking any decisions either way. I'm just tired, Melanie.' Tara poured herself more tea. 'I just need some time to get my head clear, that's all.'

Melanie was still pacing. She swung around to face Tara. 'Fergal can be very forceful. I'm just concerned that he might be able to wear you down. And I'm worried that, the way you're feeling right now, you won't have the will-power to resist.'

Tara blew her nose. 'And would that be such a bad thing?'

'Yes, it would!' Melanie rarely raised her voice, but this time she made an exception. 'I've skirted around this subject before, Tara, but this time I have to be direct. Fergal is a volatile man. He may be able to pull the wool over your eyes, but he can't fool me. The man is bad news. If you married him you'd spend the rest of your life regretting it.'

'Jesus, Melanie.' Tara stared at her, taken aback by the outburst.

Melanie sat down again, drained. Her face seemed pale and drawn.

'You need time,' she repeated. 'You have a right to ask for time. Just tell Fergal that. He'll understand.'

Tara looked out to sea again and remembered Fergal's words of just a few hours ago – his warning that he would leave Claremoon Harbour for ever if Tara gave him the wrong answer to his very important question.

'That's where you're wrong,' she said slowly. 'I don't think he will.'

CHAPTER TWENTY-FIVE

A FEW hours after Manus Kennedy's arrest and appearance in court, Inspector Phil O'Rourke stepped off the late train at Heuston Station and took a taxi to Store Street Garda Station in Dublin's north inner city. It had been a long, exhausting day and he had a lot of work still to do before his head could hit a pillow.

From the outside, Store Street Station looked like an advertising agency or a computer software firm. But it was often nicknamed Hill Street because it policed one of the capital's toughest districts. Every day, as a matter of routine, it dealt with vicious muggings, bag snatchings, syringe raids, knifings, and assaults on holidaymakers who'd innocently wandered a few hundred yards off the main tourist beat and ended up in Apache territory. The criminals who passed through its doors ranged from affluent drug barons and career shoplifters, through pathetic alcoholic prostitutes and half-dead junkies, to hard-chaw youngsters whose favourite trick was to lob a live rat into a car at a traffic light, and grab a handbag or mobile phone from the passenger seat as the driver screamed in panic.

Every serious thug, hood, con artist and pimp came through its gates at one time or another – but Phil O'Rourke was interested in only one of them.

The detective introduced himself to the sergeant on duty and was escorted into a tiny upstairs cubbyhole where a tired and overworked plainclothes garda sat among a mountain of paperwork. The Dublin detective shook his hand and led O'Rourke downstairs again, this time to an interrogation room where Christy Geaney waited with his solicitor.

'He's all yours,' whispered the Dublin detective just outside the door. 'Just be careful. We've got him dead and buried on the cocaine dealing charge. But he's a sharp bastard, and so's his lawyer. Don't do anything that might blow our case.'

'Don't worry. I'll steer clear of it.' O'Rourke thanked him and walked into the tiny room. Like all interrogation rooms, it was bare of any pictures or decorations that could distract the subject. A plain wooden table, a few chairs, an ashtray and a couple of polystyrene cups half filled with cold tea and fag-ends...it may have been on the other end of the country, but it was an environment in which O'Rourke felt instantly at home.

Christy Geaney didn't even look up as O'Rourke walked in. He was a thin, wiry six-footer with close-cropped black hair. His jacket, denim with leather trim, was labelled 'Smashing Pumpkins On Tour'. His collarless red shirt revealed the purple letters HATE on his neck, and his wrist bore an angry bite-scar that was taking a long time to heal.

Clement Zeicker, his lawyer, sprang to his feet. 'I sincerely hope this isn't going to take long, inspector. My client has co-operated fully with the Store Street gardaí in relation to the cocaine charge ever since this afternoon's arrest – an arrest, incidentally, which we shall be claiming was unconstitutional, which may itself carry implications for this interview.'

O'Rourke said nothing. He was used to this.

'Well?' said the lawyer belligerently. 'I have other cases to attend, you know.'

'How long it takes depends entirely on your client,' O'Rourke grunted. 'Want a fag, Christy?'

Christy Geaney yawned and gave a long, simian stretch. Finally, as though it hardly mattered to him one way or another, he put out a hand and grabbed the proffered cigarette. He didn't say thanks.

'Okay,' said the solicitor. 'Can we at least be told what this is all about?'

O'Rourke had his strategy carefully worked out. He

intended to keep the nature of his business secret for as long as possible, wandering around the crucial issue in ever-decreasing circles until he had learned everything he needed to know.

But Christy Geaney got there first. 'It's about the Kennedy murder in County Clare,' he said, glaring directly at O'Rourke as though challenging him to deny it.

The solicitor stared at the detective incredulously. 'What? Well, if that's the case, you're certainly wasting your time, inspector, and mine too. We have absolutely no involvement in the Kennedy murder and we wish to say nothing about it. Now, that didn't take long, did it?' He began gathering his papers together with calculated insolence.

Christy Geaney ignored him. He was still eyeballing the detective. 'See, I saw Mano Kennedy arrested on telly,' he explained. 'I saw you behind him outside the courthouse. Therefore, you're involved in the case. You think he did it but you don't have enough evidence. You need motive and opportunity. You need somebody who knew Mano and knew his movements just before the killing. You need to know what was on his mind at the time. Someone's told you that I hung around with Mano for a bit. Therefore, you want my help. That's why you've come all the way from the bog, from muck-savage culchie land, to talk to me. Well, better bog-off back to the bog, bogman, because unless you can quash a coke trafficking charge for me I'm not even going to tell you the colour of my pee.'

O'Rourke struggled to hide his amazement and frustration. The verbal stream of connections, delivered fast and furious like the stutter of a one-armed bandit dispensing the jackpot, was not only logical but undeniably true. O'Rourke felt like an accomplished chess player who has set up an elaborate strategy of attack only to be checked after the first couple of moves.

It was the solicitor who first broke the silence. 'You've said more than enough,' he warned his client. 'As your appointed legal representative, I advise you to shut the feck up.'

Phil O'Rourke's poker face didn't flicker. 'You think you're a hard case, don't you, Christy?' he said.

'They don't come any harder, bogman. Where I come from, you learn how to snatch handbags before you learn how to walk. It's the only way you can put food on the table when you ma is lyin' under it, legless drunk, and your da is doin' a stretch in the Joy. You get to your teens, and it's either go out robbin', or sell your body to the pervs up in the Phoenix Park. But you wouldn't know anything about that, would you, bogman?' he sneered. 'Where you come from it's all clash of the ash and comely maidens dancing at the crossroads, isn't it? You don't know nothin' about real life in the Mun or the Mansions or Bernietown. Don't talk to me about hard cases, bogtrotter. You wouldn't know one if you stuck your turf spade into one.'

He spat the last words out with an intense, deeply-felt contempt. The solicitor looked at O'Rourke with interested amusement. Both lawyer and cop realised that Geaney had turned the established pattern of interrogation – hard cop on the attack – back to front and inside out. What are you going to do now? the solicitor's eyes challenged O'Rourke.

The detective wasn't fazed. He had served his apprenticeship in one of the roughest districts of the capital's south inner city, and had spent five years policing an estate in Limerick where fatal stabbings were just another form of Saturday night entertainment. But he didn't mention any of this.

'So the fact that you're going to prison won't bother you at all?' he countered in the same even tone, as though Geaney's outburst had never happened.

'Been there, done that, tried to hang myself with the T-shirt.'

'It won't bother you, even if you know you're going down for a long time?'

Geaney grinned with genuine pleasure at the cop's naïveté. 'Long time, me arse,' he said disdainfully. 'You know the justice system as well as I do, bogman. The jails are too full. By this time next year, I'll be turning up at the Joy every Monday morning and they'll write down me name and send me straight home again. You know how it is.'

O'Rourke didn't smile back. Geaney was exaggerating – drug importers didn't get temporary release – but what he was saying had a core of truth, and it was a source of immense frustration to every working cop in the land. He let the silence build up and hang heavily before speaking again.

'But when you *are* in jail, there's a sort of hierarchy, isn't there, Christy?' he said, lighting another cigarette and tossing another one over to the drug dealer. 'You've got this sort of pyramid of respect. At the top, you've got the organised criminals – the serious drug barons, the cash depot gangs, the big-time blaggers and so on. Then you have the murderers and the sadists, particularly if they're unpredictable bastards. Nobody likes to mess with them, just in case. A bit lower down you've got the drug smugglers, like yourself, and at the bottom of the pyramid there's the poor pathetic junkies who are in and out of jail all the time because they're too stoned or strung-out to plan their crimes properly.'

Geaney stretched again and yawned rudely. 'I've got a sick note,' he said to his lawyer. 'Can I be excused the criminology lecture?'

The solicitor opened his mouth to speak, but O'Rourke raised a hand for patience. 'Mind you, there are some jail-birds who don't even figure on the scale of respect at all, aren't there, Christy?' he asked. 'They're so low that they don't get to be on the pyramid – they live beneath the foundations, scuttling around underneath like rats. They're hated so much by the other prisoners that they have to be kept segregated for their own protection. Otherwise they'd be used as human punchbags every night of their lives.'

Geaney was no longer bored. His eyes followed O'Rourke warily.

'Oh, come on, Christy, you know this as well as I do, and you know who I'm talking about, too. The sex offenders. The rapists, the child abusers, the sickos who get their kicks from torturing prostitutes. Everyone detests them. They're the lowest of the low. The nearest they're going to get to respect is listening to a song by Aretha Franklin.'

'This is utterly irrelevant,' sighed the solicitor weakly, but Geaney silenced him with a glare.

'Just what the hell are you driving at, bogman?' he asked.

'And it doesn't stop,' O'Rourke pressed on. 'It doesn't stop when they leave prison, does it, Christy? We all know what happens to convicted rapists. They can't drink in their local pubs, they get filth shoved through their letter-boxes. And they'd better lock their doors and windows soundly on a Saturday night, because there are lots of people out there who'd call round after closing time to rough them up, just for fun.'

'Jesus. What is this?'

'Funny, you don't look so bored any more, Christy.'

O'Rourke reached into his briefcase and made great show of opening a thick file of typescript. He asked the garda on duty to organise tea for three people and began to flick through it.

The file actually contained a series of statements from a west-of-Ireland farmer convicted of using illegal animal growth hormones, but nobody else in the room knew that. He frowned and pursed his lips as he scanned page after page.

Then, with the brass neck of a seasoned poker-bluffer, he began reading extracts from a non-existent statement.

'Just looking over this, Christy, I'd say we have you for

attempted rape and indecent assault, not to mention the ordinary-decent-crimes of GBH and false imprisonment,' he mused.

'I demand to examine that file,' snapped the solicitor.

'All in good time. Milk? Sugar?' O'Rourke closed the file as he took the three cups and proceeded to pour with infinite slowness. 'Christy knows what I'm talking about, don't you, Christy? Small matter of an attack on a young woman who visited your flat while you and Carl were cutting heroin and sorting it into deals?'

Geaney said nothing. For the first time his face had turned pale and the ugly indigo tattoo on his neck throbbed like a neon sign. The insolent grin had faded from his lips.

'Oh, come on, Christy,' cried O'Rourke, like a teacher encouraging a talented child. 'You're not concentrating. She was a good-looking girl from the west of Ireland, long black hair, name of Tara Ross. She came to your flat asking about Mano Kennedy. You grabbed her, hauled her inside, locked the door and attempted to rape her in front of witnesses. Bad case.'

'You're bluffing, bogman.'

O'Rourke was bluffing higher and wilder than the Maverick Brothers on speed, but he wasn't going to let on. The truth was that Tara had flatly refused to press charges over the Ballymahon flats incident. Since the attacker was going to jail for a long time anyway, she just wanted to put the whole episode behind her and forget about it. That had essentially closed the police file on an already-shaky case.

'Bluffing?' O'Rourke shook his head and smiled mirthlessly. 'You wish.'

He flicked over a few more pages which in fact contained a list of cattle hormones. 'Ah, here we are. Your friend Carl, the Star Trek fanatic, the one who was with you in the flat, has been very helpful to us ever since we told him that he's likely to spend the next five years in the company of serial sodomites. He's been begging Scotty to beam him up. He's been singing like a Romulin soprano.

Ever since I explained the consequences to him, he has accepted the wisdom of co-operating with the State in this case.'

The solicitor tut-tutted loudly and raised his eyes to the ceiling. 'Oldest trick in the book, Mr Geaney. Don't fall for it.'

'Oh, that's not all, Christy. We're not so stupid as to rely on tainted testimony from a fellow-accused. We've got the evidence of Ms Ross, an upstanding pillar of the community in her native County Clare – that's part of Bogland, by the way – and the corroborating evidence of Mr Andres Talimann, a respected international war correspondent, the one who found you grappling Ms Ross on the floor. We've also got your young lady friend, the girl who answered the door when Ms Ross called round.'

Geaney grinned cruelly. 'Now I know you're talking through your arse. The Madra wouldn't say nothin'. Bitch knows better. She knows I'd make her face even uglier than it is already.'

O'Rourke shrugged. 'I hope you keep on spouting like that during the trial, Christy. Your smooth-talking charm will help our case no end, particularly if you indulge in that attractive habit of describing women as dogs. But it doesn't matter whether your pathetic junkie friend gives evidence or not. We've more than enough to make an attempted-rape charge stick. I'd say the judge would take a very serious view of it. What do you think?' He turned to face the solicitor. 'Four years? Five years? It would probably run concurrently with your cocaine sentence, but the good news is that you'd serve it in a segregated jail for sex offenders, where they *don't* operate a revolving door policy.'

There was a long silence. Elsewhere in the draughty old building, phones were ringing and doors were slamming. Outside in the street, in the shelter of the main bus station, a drunk began singing incoherently.

'Unless,' said Geaney, heavily.

O'Rourke looked innocent. 'Unless what, Christy?'

'Unless I give you the information you need about Manus Kennedy.'

The detective was shocked. 'As a mere country bogman, I would never be so devious as to suggest that, Christy. Did I suggest that?' He turned to the solicitor for corroboration. The lawyer looked down at his legal pad and didn't reply.

'However,' said O'Rourke, 'since you have raised the subject, I would certainly welcome any information you might volunteer that might help us in a major murder investigation. It is, after all, your duty as a good citizen. As your solicitor will no doubt agree.'

The lawyer sighed. 'I need to be alone with my client,' he said. 'I shall require some time.'

O'Rourke sprang to his feet with surprising agility. 'You've got it,' he said. 'In fact, you've got all night. This bogman is going to see if he can find a haystack to sleep in.' He gathered up his files and turned to Geaney.

'Sleep on it, Christy,' he urged. 'And make sure you have a good night's sleep. When you're in among those nice friendly fellas in the segregation unit for sex offenders, you won't get too many of them.'

CHAPTER TWENTY-SIX

'YOU'RE BACK at sea, Dad,' she whispered into his ear. 'Back at the wheel of the *Róisín Dubh.*'

Tara was overcome by a deep, indefinable sadness as she watched her father return to the battered old fishing boat he had skippered, suffered, controlled and cajoled for the past twenty years. First they'd pushed his wheelchair to the pier, and then Fergal had lifted the old man out of it as delicately and as gently as a first-time parent might lift a new-born child. He'd stepped carefully on deck and waited patiently while Tara had folded the wheelchair, brought it on board, and reassembled it near the controls in the open wheelhouse. They'd positioned him in the chair and made sure he was comfortable before strapping him firmly in and securing the chair to the structure of the boat. At last they were satisfied that it would not move, even in the heaviest of seas.

Dr Maguire had already given his blessing to the strange expedition. 'I'll be honest with you, Tara,' the GP had told her, 'we've no way of treating what's wrong with your father. It's not a coma in the strict sense of the word – our tests have eliminated that possibility. Hospitalisation won't help. It could be some form of dementia, possibly Alzheimer's, or it could be related to depression. Whatever the reason, he's retreated into his own world, and he could stay there for days or weeks or even months. We'll carry on with the tests, but, in the meantime, your idea of leading him back out by means of external stimulus is as valid as any other approach. If a sea trip seems the most likely to succeed, then by all means go ahead. If it doesn't work, at least you've tried. Good luck.'

Now, Tara watched her father's face carefully, hoping for some flicker of response to the sight of his beloved

Róisín Dubh, to the smell of the salt air and diesel, to the slight rocking of the boat in the harbour swell. But there was no sign of life in the sightless eyes that stared, unfocused, into the middle distance and recognised nothing.

Fergal joined her. He double-checked that the old man was seated comfortably, looking directly into his eyes and patting his arm encouragingly. When he talked to him in a calm, reassuring voice, as though John Ross could hear and understand every word, Tara felt another emotion swell up inside her. It could have been gratitude or it could have been pride, or it could have been something more. She didn't know. All she knew was that Fergal was giving her the strength and support she so badly needed at this time. What would it be like to be able to rely on that sort of strength for the rest of her life? She knew she was confused and unable to think straight. But she couldn't help wondering if she would have the willpower, or even the inclination, to refuse if he were to offer her something like that.

She was tired, in more ways than one. Tired of being the strong one, the coper, the carer. Why not marry Fergal, a dependable partner who would help share her burdens and make life more tolerable? Well, why not? She could do a hell of a lot worse.

'Penny for them.'

'Oh...nothing.' She smiled and kissed him lightly on the cheek.

Fergal spent a long time sorting everything out and making sure the craft was seaworthy. He prepared the ropes, made sure the anchor was functional, checked the fuel and safety equipment and ran the old diesel engine for fifteen minutes to ensure there was no problem that could blight their trip.

'Okay,' he said at last, 'let's go.'

He pointed to the nets that lay at the stern of the boat, ready for 'shooting' or letting out into the sea. 'Do you want to do some serious fishing? We could just about manage those tangle-nets by ourselves.'

She shook her head. 'No. We'll just make this a pleasure trip.'

'Fine by me.' Fergal walked over to the helm. 'We'll head out to the fishing mark on the other side of Chicken Point and use a couple of boat-rods. With a bit of luck we'll get enough pollack, cod and mackerel to stock up your freezer for a few weeks.'

'Hello there!'

Tara looked up at the pier.

'Morning, Steve,' she called back. 'We're just going out for a spot of fishing. Want to join us?'

'I heard what you're doing. And I'll keep my fingers crossed that it works. No, I can't come along' – he gestured at his uniform – 'because I'm due on duty in half an hour. I just came to see if I could help.'

'You could cast off if you like.'

The sergeant cast off the mooring ropes that secured the boat to the pier and, with easy skill, Fergal manoeuvred the *Róisín Dubh* from her berth and into the centre of the tiny port. The slow, deep bass note of the diesel engine changed to a faster rhythm as he pushed open the throttle and headed through the harbour entrance, past some tricky rocks and out to the open sea.

Tara had always loved the experience of leaving behind the safe womb of the port and entering the vast and unpredictable Atlantic Ocean. It was a feeling that was timeless and universal – the same emotion that the mediaeval Irish sailors had experienced when they set out to sea in their frail, flexing currachs in search of fresh fishing grounds and ultimately to uncover new worlds that lay beyond the setting sun.

Today the ocean was as still as a mountain lake. But Tara knew that this could be deceptive. In these conditions, huge swells born out of Atlantic storms could build up a momentum that they could never achieve in rougher, choppier weather. These inshore groundswells, as they were called, could hit you suddenly and unexpectedly, even though the ocean surface retained its flat, imperturbable calm.

But that didn't concern her at all. Tara knew that the *Róisín Dubh* was well able to handle anything the Atlantic could throw at her. The boat would simply roll on her round belly, absorbing the energy of the surge before returning to her centre of gravity as surely and inevitably as a child's roly-poly toy.

Seagulls, sensing the potential of an easy breakfast, wheeled and soared above the boat's wake as she chugged steadily out to sea. The houses along the coast became smaller and even the hills became dwarfed with distance. Scudding clouds turned the hills from solid geological objects into moving displays of light and shade. The bright sunlight, beaming through the gaps in the sky like a precise spotlight, highlighted first this purple peak, then that green slope, like a natural *son-et-lumière* show.

The spray flew over the bow, but the *Róisín Dubh* protected its crew well. Fergal sat on the skipper's perch, sheltered by a wheelhouse constructed of wood and glass. Just below it lay the enclosed cabin, which held four berths, the tiny galley, and several storage lockers. By Fergal's side, John Ross sat comatose in his wheelchair, facing astern towards the open deck, where Tara was working to prepare two sturdy boat-rods with feather-traces and weights.

They rounded the scraggy headland of Chicken Point, keeping a respectful distance from the jagged rocks that lurked unseen just a few inches below the treacherously calm surface. The colonies of seabirds that nested there, safe from predators, shrieked and scolded at the unwelcome intruders who'd invaded their stormy and chaotic home.

The entire village of Claremoon Harbour had now disappeared behind a solid wall of stone. They were alone in this strange world of rock and water, where the sky itself had almost vanished in a maelstrom of feathers.

Finally Fergal pulled the throttle and verified that the markers on the shore were lined up. This was 'the mark' – the best sea-angling spot anywhere along this coastline. As the engine died, the *Róisín Dubh* slowed. Robbed of her forward momentum, she began rolling with the swell of the water, rising and falling with an uncontrolled motion that would have sent weaker stomachs into spasms of nausea. Under her sturdy hull, the water slapped and dragged and slopped with an almost metronomic regularity.

Then, suddenly, there was a different kind of noise.

Tara halted on her way to the cabin. 'What was that?'

'What was what?' Fergal was checking his feather trace. He didn't even look up.

'I thought I heard a strange sound. From inside the cabin. It sounded like somebody moving around.'

'My God, Tara, you're easily spooked these days.' He shook his head. 'Can't say I blame you after yesterday. It's probably just something rolling around in the bilges.'

'Probably.' She rubbed her eyes with her hands. She really would have to curb her imagination.

It was hot – too hot for comfort. Tara went down into the cabin and stowed her jumper in the rickety locker that hung on the wall. It was even more wobbly – 'bockety', her father would have called it – than usual. The whole structure moved as she opened the door, and she made a mental note to have it repaired as soon as possible.

Back on deck, Fergal had already put his fishing line over the side. Tara followed suit. The big wooden reel rattled noisily as the weight sank rapidly towards the seabed. But not all the way down. Below, on the jagged rocks, the wreck of a ship had lain for as long as anyone could remember. Local legend said that it was the remains of a vessel from the mighty Armada. Gold lay down there, said the old men, and cases of silver coins. Whatever the truth, the carcass of the wreck held silver treasure of a different kind. It was a feeding ground for thousands of fish.

Careful not to snag the weight or the feathered hooks, Tara found the right depth and began moving the line in a regular up-and-down motion. Within seconds she felt a succession of rapid, violent tugs which she instantly recognised as mackerel. She drew up her line. Three fish had taken the hooks at once. As she hauled them in, she took a glance at her father. Had he noticed her catch? Was he aware of anything at all? The unfocused stare and the sightless eyes gave her the answer she didn't want.

The line went down again and returned with a fine-sized pollack.

At the stern of the boat, Fergal had already landed half a dozen mackerel, a pollack and a cod. Tara caught a few more mackerel and then left him to it. She sat beside her father and began stroking his hand, urging him gently to open his senses to the sights and sounds and smells around him.

Meanwhile, Fergal's rod kept pulling in cod and mackerel. In less than half an hour, the big fish-box in the centre of the deck was filled.

'Okay, I suppose that's enough,' called Tara. 'No point catching more than the freezer will hold. We're drifting off the mark, anyway.'

Fergal stowed away the rods. He wandered over to the wheelhouse where Tara was sitting, her father's hand clasped gently in her own.

'Anything?' Fergal asked quietly.

She shook her head. She had spent the past twenty minutes talking to her father and checking his eyes for signs of awareness or consciousness. There were none. His pulse was strong, his breathing was relaxed and regular, but he still inhabited another world.

Eventually, she had to admit to herself that the experiment had been a total failure. Well, at least they'd tried. Grateful that the salt spray disguised the tears that sprang up in her eyes, Tara took the wheel and fired the engine. 'I'll take her back in while you gut the fish,' she called to Fergal.

He made a grimace. 'I'll do it when we get home.'

She looked at him with surprise. 'Come on, Fergal, it's always best to gut them at sea. It saves time and mess, because you can throw the waste to the gulls.'

'I don't feel like it.'

'Okay. You take her into port and I'll gut them.' She was annoyed at his intransigence. She dived into the cabin and emerged with her father's toolbox.

Fergal's male pride was wounded. 'All right, all right,' he said testily. 'I'll do it. You stay at the wheel.'

Tara smiled. 'Thanks. It's just that you do it so well. You can gut a dozen fish while I'm still struggling over the first one.'

Fergal grunted. 'You just watch where we're going,' he said.

He took the first fish, the large pollack, out of the box and set to work.

The helicopter was waiting on the tarmac at Aldergrove, just as the Belfast businessman had promised.

Andres had to admit the man had done a good job. As part of the same package deal, he'd arranged with the cabin crew for Andres and his companion to get priority exit from the jumbo; he'd arranged for their swift passage through immigration at Belfast's international airport; and he'd arranged to have their luggage collected and forwarded to them at Shannon Airport.

Within ten minutes of touchdown, the couple were being ferried across the airport in a baggage truck and dropped off at the helicopter pad.

Andres recognised the chopper, a dependable Bell 206B Jetranger III, capable of a top speed of 132 mph. It had a range of over 360 miles, more than enough to cover the distance to Clare without stopping.

The pilot had already powered the engine, and the rotors were slowly spinning ready for takeoff. Buffeted by noise and downdraught, they ran crouching to the doors, hoisted themselves into the passenger seats and fastened their seatbelts.

Clearance came through almost immediately from Air Traffic Control. The rotors chewed hungrily into the heavy, fuel-stinking air. With contemptuous ease, the big machine battered gravity into submission. It rose high above the sparse hillside terrain of County Antrim, and began shadowing the M1 motorway southwards and west-wards on the first stage of its long journey to Claremoon Harbour.

As the neat, pretty villages of Antrim, Down and Armagh passed underneath, Andres Talimann did a rapid calculation of speed and distance and crossed his fingers, hoping against hope that they would not be too late.

Back in Store Street Garda Station, Geaney's lawyer no longer feigned an air of busy impatience, and his client no longer looked bored.

'My client has agreed to co-operate,' the solicitor announced as soon as Phil O'Rourke ambled through the door, refreshed and relaxed after a sound night's sleep in a nearby hotel.

'I thought he might,' said the detective.

The solicitor looked anything but relaxed and refreshed. The top button of his shirt was undone and his tie was slightly askew. He looked as though he'd come to regret taking on Christy Geaney as a client.

'The quid-pro-quo, of course, strictly off the record and without prejudice, is as follows. My client will give you all the information at his disposal about Mr' – he had to con-sult his notes – 'Manus Kennedy, and in return you will guarantee that he will face no charges of any nature in relation to the incident involving Ms Tara Ross in Bally-mahon Flats.'

O'Rourke peeled open a new pack of cigarettes, opened the flaptop, and passed the entire packet over to Geaney. It was a gesture of good faith. 'Agreed,' he said. 'Let's go.'

Christy spoke for the first time. He was more relieved than resentful. 'Okay, bogman. What do you want to know?'

'When did you first meet Manus Kennedy?'

'Couple of years ago. He was in and out of the loony bin at Inismaul. The guy was sick in the head.'

O'Rourke leaned over with a lighter and put a flame to Geaney's first cigarette. 'We know that. Go on.'

'They kept giving him medication and letting him back into the community. But Manus didn't have a bleedin' community. He kept getting into trouble and had to be taken back inside. He would come to Dublin and began wandering around places like Bernietown with a head full of prescribed uppers and downers, looking for somewhere cheap to stay. He was like a bleedin' lamb to the slaughter.'

'What do you mean by that?'

'Well, he got a private flat and the health board paid for it. We got to know him, chatted him up, gave him the all-mates-together crap, and screwed the bastard.'

'You mean, you took his money?'

Geaney shook his head in frustration at O'Rourke's lack of cop-on. 'More than that, bogman. We moved in with him, Paul Lawless, myself and a few other heads. We told him we were poolin' money for food and rent. But what we did was, we took his disability money and used it to buy dope. We brought the junkies in and let them shoot up in his flat. We stored the gear there, too – at one stage there was enough bleedin' heroin stashed there to supply half a' Dublin, and Mano didn't even cop on. His head was so screwed up on medication that he'd totally lost the plot. He thought we were just all mates together, just watching videos all day and hanging out and having a bit of a laugh.'

He sniggered unpleasantly. O'Rourke's poker face concealed the deep disgust he felt. 'And then?' he prompted.

'Lost touch. I went to jail for a bit, Mano went back into hospital. Paul Lawless was in there for a while, too. We all met up again earlier this year and organised a great stroke.'

'This was the scam that ended up with Manus owing you three grand?'

'Yeah, yeah, I'm coming go that. Don't be so impatient, bogman. What's the matter, your cows need milking or something?'

O'Rourke sighed. 'You don't know much about farming if you think cows can wait to be milked until this hour of the morning, Christy. Keep talking.'

'Lawlo had noticed that the pharmacy in Inismaul Mental Hospital was wide-open. They didn't close it until late at night, with only one woman in charge, an oul' wan of nearly sixty. Mano was friendly with her. He used to keep her company, playing chess with her in the evenings when things were quiet. Lawlo's scam was deadly. Real simple. When they got back into Inismaul, Mano would get together with the oul' wan, play chess with her as usual, and then keel over as if he wasn't well. The oul' dear would lean over him to see what was wrong, Lawlo would sneak up from behind and whang her over the head with a metal golf club from the recreation cabinet. Then Mano and Lawless would take her key, get into the pharmacy, and fill a couple of kitbags.'

O'Rourke looked over at the lawyer, who couldn't hide his expression of nausea. He glanced back at Christy, who looked as cool as though he'd just outlined the tactics for a five-a-side soccer match.

'What with?' asked O'Rourke.

'What with, what?'

'What were you going to fill the sports bags with? Which drugs?'

Christy stubbed out his cigarette. 'Morphine. Phy. Napps. Gee-gees. Roches. Uppers. Anything you can sell easily on the streets.'

'So what went wrong?' asked O'Rourke. 'Did Manus do the job himself and cut you fellas out?'

Geaney laughed rudely. 'Nah. Jesus, you have got it all arsewise, haven't you?' He helped himself to another cigarette and waited silently for O'Rourke to produce the lighter.

'Mano didn't know anything about the plan until the last minute,' he said through puffs of smoke. 'Then when we told him, he didn't want to play ball. We did everything to persuade him – even roughed him up a bit – but he just kept comin' off with this oul' hippie shite that he couldn't bring himself to harm anybody, couldn't hurt another living creature.' Geaney frowned as though trying to remember something. 'Kept ramblin' on about cows' eyes burning, some crap like that. I already told you, he was sick in the head.'

The solicitor's head turned sharply, but Geaney didn't appear to notice the irony. 'So,' continued Geaney, 'what our good mate Mano did – what he did, was shit all over our great scam. He warned the oul' wan in the pharmacy. She was moved to safer duties. The hospital put up a grille and extra locks and a security man. So we never got a chance to pull it off.'

'When did all this happen?'

'Early April this year.'

'And Mano?'

'He'd planned to go back into the hospital, but he didn't. He disappeared, which was a bleedin' wise thing to do since both Lawlo and myself wanted his testicles on toast.'

'Come on, Christy!' O'Rourke was incredulous. 'You're overreacting by a mile. It was just a plan that went wrong. Nobody was hurt. Nobody was busted. You didn't lose any money because there wasn't any money in the first place.'

Geaney hissed in frustration and leaned forward until his face was only inches from O'Rourke's.

'What went wrong, bogman, was that this wasn't just one scam. It was part of a series of operations that would set me and Lawlo up for life. And it all hinged on the Inismaul pharmacy job. As far as we were concerned, that was money in the bank. It was our cash-cow.'

He smiled with temporary pleasure at having landed another bogman insult. 'Once we got the stuff, we would have had no trouble shifting it on the streets. It sells fast 'cos everyone knows it's the real thing, straight-up, uncut. We reckoned it would get us three-K each, so we promised that amount of money to take a share in a big shipment of heroin from Amsterdam. Somebody in Holland was in trouble and needed to shift it cheap. It was the sort of chance you get once in a lifetime. When the time came to collect and we'd no money to pay for our share, the whole deal fell through and we were in deep shit with a lot of heavy people.'

'It's a tough world out there, Christy.'

'As I said earlier, you've no idea how tough, bogman.' He smiled wryly. 'For me there was only one way out of the problem, unless I planned walking on crutches for the rest of my life. That was to volunteer as a mule for the big fellas who'd organised the shipment. And that's why, one nice April morning, I ended up being busted at Dublin Airport with a shit-load of cocaine.' He pulled viciously at his cigarette. 'And that's why I'm facing ten years in the Joy instead of lyin' on the beach in Tenerife.'

O'Rourke nodded. 'And what about all the gear you were cutting and packaging at the flat at Ballymahon a few days ago? The time Tara Ross came round?'

'A different deal. Other people's stuff. More favours, more bleedin' risk. It all went down the tubes thanks to your bogwoman friend. And that's only because she was looking for Mano.' He grimaced. 'One way or the other, that little bastard has set me back the guts of ten grand.'

O'Rourke sat in silence for a moment, taking notes. Then: 'You know a fella called Godfrey Villiers?' he asked at last. 'Runs the Michael de Blaca Gallery in Claremoon Harbour?'

'Yeah. Only I knew him before he was Godfrey Villiers. I knew him when he was plain Paddy McGurk. We did a bit of time in Spike Island Prison together, before he went into the art business.'

'The laundry business, you mean.'

Christy shook his head. 'Dunno what you're talkin' about, bogman.'

'Course you do, Christy. He launders drug money for your old mates the Vineys in Limerick. Only problem was, the art shop turned out to be more successful than anyone bargained for. And before long, Godfrey was skimming off the cash to fund his seven-card stud.' O'Rourke began counting out imaginary piles of money. '"Ninety-five quid for the Vineys, five for me. Ninety for the Vineys, ten for me." Then it was eighty, then seventy-five.'

'You know all this already, bogman, why you asking me?' Christy began picking his teeth. 'I never get involved with the Vineys' business. As long as they stay in mucker-land and we stay in the city, everything's cool. They learned that the hard way. A few years ago, they tried to move in on us and we pissed all over them.'

'Nice way of putting it, Christy. You left three people dead.'

'Get to the point, bogman.'

'That is the point, Christy. The current deal is, you stay in Dublin and the Vineys stay in Limerick and Clare. So what were you doing in Claremoon Harbour last month? And why were you spotted with Godfrey Villiers?'

Christy looked at his lawyer. Clement Zeicker gave a shrug. He was past caring.

'I was on the run on the coke smuggling charge when I got a message from Villiers. He'd heard that I'd put a contract out on Manus Kennedy. He wanted me to drop the contract and spread the word that it was safe for Mano to come out into the open again. In return, he would personally give me my three-K back, plus another three for my trouble.'

'Maybe he was just in a generous mood,' said O'Rourke.

'Yeah, and my arse is parsley. I wanted to know what was behind all this shit, so I arranged a secret meeting. We got together in Claremoon, he got pissed drunk and told me everything.'

'Go on.'

Christy hesitated. 'The Vineys weren't as stupid as he'd reckoned. They'd figured out that he was skimming off their hard-earned cash. So they took him for a walk along the mudflats on the Shannon estuary and asked him very nicely if they could have their money back again.'

'Only he didn't have the money any more. He'd gambled it all away.'

'That's right. Now Villiers likes lazin' around on the beach as much as the rest of us, but it kind of spoils your day out if you're buried up to your neck waiting for the tide to come in. Which is what's going to happen to him if he doesn't get the readies.'

'Nothing surer,' said O'Rourke.

Clement Zeicker, who was out of his league in this sedate discussion of savagery, glanced from one face to the other in horror. His mouth opened, and then closed again. He said nothing.

'The poor fecker can feel the water lapping up round his chin already,' continued Christy. 'Then, out of the blue, he gets a call from some big art house in New York.'

'Cedric Maxwell Associates.'

'Yeah. Something like that. Seems the Yanks are going daft for Michael de Blaca – he's some Irish artist who used to live in Claremoon Harbour – and they want Villiers to buy up whatever he can get. Big money, big commission for a small-time loser like him. So he promises them the sun, moon and stars and starts asking around.'

Christy flicked his cigarette ash on the floor. 'Trouble is,' he continued, 'he can't find nothin'. Not a bleedin' thing. Until somebody tells him that de Blaca used to work up at Barnabo, the Kennedy family house. So up goes our Godfrey to Barnabo, and he talks to Ann Kennedy. And she gives him good news and bad news. The good news is, she's got the very first sculpture de Blaca ever done, some naked woman or something. The bad news is, it's not hers to sell.'

'Whose was it?' O'Rourke leaned forward.

'She didn't say. But Villiers looks up his books, does his sums and works out that it has to be Manus. So he phones up New York and asks the guy what he'll pay for the first sculpture de Blaca ever done, and the guy practically creams his pants and says, get it to us by yesterday and we'll send you a bank draft for three hundred thousand dollars. At least' – Christy's brows lowered in suspicion – 'that's the figure he told me, so I reckon the true offer was nearer four.'

O'Rourke did a few rapid calculations. 'Godfrey must have thought he'd died and gone to heaven,' he said. 'With that kind of money, he could get the Vineys off his back and also set himself up for a nice peaceful retirement.'

'Yeah. Remember, Mano was broke and living rough. Even if he was offered a tenner for the statue, he'd take it. It was a shit-hot deal. It was perfect. It couldn't go wrong.'

'Except that it could,' said O'Rourke. 'Because nobody could find Manus anywhere.'

Christy nodded. 'The Vineys pulled out all the stops to find him, because the way they saw it, it was the only chance they had of getting their missing money back. They knew Mano was living rough around Claremoon, but they couldn't pin him down. Because Mano wasn't like their usual target. He didn't have a house. He didn't drive a car. He didn't drink in pubs or play in pool halls. He was their worst nightmare.'

'Tell me about it,' said O'Rourke, with feeling. 'So in desperation, Villiers called you in. He thought that Manus might resurface if you made it clear you weren't looking to disembowel him any more.'

'Got it, bogman.'

'And did you lift the contract?'

Geaney glowered. 'Temporarily. But it's back on again. Bigtime.'

'What happened?' O'Rourke leaned forward. This was getting interesting.

'Well, I had my own interests to protect. I figured, since I'm playing such a bigtime role in this, I should get a bigger share of this payout. That way I could pay off the importer in Dublin, make a fresh start, maybe move to Amsterdam and set up in biz there.' Christy nodded, agreeing with himself that it all made sense. 'So I made a deal with Godfrey that we'd bypass the Vineys, split the profits from the statue, and get out of the country.'

'You never learn, do you, Christy? There you go, counting your chickens again.'

Geaney ignored him. 'We put a lot of messages out, hopin' one would reach Manus. And eventually, after a long time, the little bastard came out of the woods.'

'And you put the deal to him?'

'We tried. He wasn't even listening, half time. He was in a world of his own. Animals' eyes. Flames. Cows burning up. That's all we could get out of him.' Geaney stubbed out his cigarette savagely. 'So we had to give him a little bit of grief, a little bit of pain, just to concentrate his mind. Then we took him up to the farmhouse and told him that if he didn't go in there and bring the bleedin' statue out, we'd burn *him* up. With a blowtorch. Slowly. Bit by bit.'

He was breathing heavily.

O'Rourke felt the hair on his neck rise. 'When was this, Christy?'

'What?' Geaney seemed distracted.

'Which date? When did he go into the farmhouse looking for the statue?'

'I knew you'd jump to that conclusion, bogman.' Christy sneered with perverse triumph. 'Sorry to disappoint you. But it was a week before the murder.' He lit another cigarette. 'Nothing at all happened that night. Because Mano just disappeared.'

'He what?' O'Rourke was incredulous. 'After taking all that trouble to find him, you just let him go?'

'We didn't let him go, bogman. He just vanished. We had seven guys there, all around the building. He went into the house to get the statue, and he didn't come out again. At least, we think he didn't come out again.' He sucked his cigarette and sent a cloud of smoke jetting aggressively towards the detective. 'Coupla minutes later, I thought I saw somebody disappear into the hills. None of us have any idea how he got away. He just seemed to fade away into the night.'

'Just like his father at the funeral,' said O'Rourke.

'What?'

'Nothing. Did you check the house?'

'Yeah, it was empty. No Manus. No statue, either, at least nowhere that we could see. We moved a few things around a bit, but not too much. We didn't want anyone to know we'd been inside.'

O'Rourke checked his file and stroked out a question mark beside one of his notes. 'Where did you go from there?' he asked.

'I went back to Dublin. What's the point of hangin' around? But Villiers was hitting the jar, bigtime, and was getting even more desperate. He told me he was going to work on Manus's brother. Try to persuade *him* to get the statue. Mad stuff. I didn't want to know. Jesus, man, I'd enough on my plate without getting tied up in a murder

I'd nothing to do with.'

He spread his palms outwards towards the detective. 'And that's all I know, bogman. God's honest truth.'

O'Rourke believed him. But he felt more puzzled than ever. Christy's story hadn't helped him to build up his case against Manus. On the contrary, he thought, as he silently scanned through his notes of the conversation, it had just muddied the waters further.

The detective was already confused enough. All his attempts to dig up information about Manus Kennedy's alleged history of violence had come to nothing. All the promising leads had vanished like froth on a bad pint.

'Let me get it straight, Christy,' he said at last. 'You're telling me that Manus was never involved in this plan to sell the statue?'

'No.' Christy Geaney shook his head emphatically. 'Too spaced out. Didn't know what was goin' on.'

'And he's never been involved in drugs or drug dealing?'

'Nope. Too stupid.'

'Never committed *any* crimes in your presence or to your knowledge?'

'I never even seen him drop litter.'

'What about arson, fire-raising? Any obsession with fire, hanging around fire stations, getting friendly with firemen, anything like that?'

Geaney shook his head again. 'Unless you count putting a few peat briquettes into the grate when his arse was freezing.'

'Acts of violence? Assaults? Intimidation? Threats?'

Geaney's face twisted into a look of pitying contempt. 'Watch my lips, you poor muck-savage. Mano was so un-violent he made Mahatma-bleedin'-Gandhi look like Mike Tyson.'

O'Rourke stared deep into the cruel eyes. There was no doubt about it – Geaney was telling the truth.

'So in your opinion,' he said at last, 'Manus Kennedy

would not be capable of murder?'

Geaney laughed again, a hard metallic sound like a Stanley-knife falling on the tiles of a prison shower. 'In my opinion, bogman,' he said, 'Manus Kennedy would not be capable of swatting a wasp if it got under his vest.'

O'Rourke spent quite some time sorting through his notes.

He reminded himself that many killers had no previous history of violence. And that around five per cent of murderers were psychotics who killed because killing made sense within the context of their fantasy; most of them didn't have records of violence, either.

'Did Mano ever talk about demonic possession?' he asked Geaney.

'What?'

'Did he ever claim to be possessed by Satan? Did he do things and blame them on Lucifer? Anything like that?'

Geaney grinned and shook his head. 'You mean like in *The Exorcist*? I never saw his head spinning around, if that's what you're asking.'

O'Rourke sifted through pages of notes until he reached Tara's statement. The part about Manus's bizarre remarks in the forest.

'Let me read these sentences to you and then you can tell me if Manus ever talked in these terms.' O'Rourke directly quoted Manus's words to Tara. 'The devil did it. Everyone thought it was my fault, but the devil was the one who really did it.' He put aside his notes. 'It seems he has a habit of committing acts and attributing them to the devil. Does that sound familiar in any way?'

Geaney's hard face lit up with sudden recognition. 'Oh, the devil!' he said, as though recognising the name of an old friend. 'Why didn't you say so? That was nothing to do with possession, bogman. Manus used to tell me all about the devil after he'd had a few ciders late at night.' He snickered.

'Go on, Christy. I'm waiting.'

'He told me his brother Fergal was a really sick bastard who used to do all sorts of twisted, off-the-wall things and blame them on Mano. At school he used to rip the legs off frogs and things and tell the teachers it was Mano that done it. He even set the bleedin' cowshed on the farm on fire, and blamed that on Mano too. He sounded like a real crazy bollix.'

He grabbed another cigarette and snapped his fingers insolently, demanding a light. O'Rourke ignored him. The detective sat as though welded to his chair, unable to move.

'Wake up, bogman,' Geaney shouted into his ear. 'You hear what I'm sayin'? The devil wasn't anything that Mano dreamed up out of his head. It was a sort of nickname. That's what Mano called his brother.'

Ten minutes before he was due to go on duty, Sergeant Steve McNamara was watering the crimson geraniums in the window-box outside the part-time garda station in Claremoon Harbour. The slugs had been busy, leaving silver trails across the peaty soil and shredding the soft green leaves. McNamara was on his way inside to get some slug pellets when something made him look up in surprise and annoyance.

A blue Mazda sports car was racing down the hill towards Claremoon, its exhaust roaring as the driver expertly switched gears to negotiate the treacherous bends at high speed. Instead of slowing down at the 30 mph sign at the entrance to the village, the car accelerated. It rocketed along the main street and came to a screeching halt outside the garda station.

Steve wiped the peat from his hands, stuffed his sergeant's hat firmly on his head and stalked across to the driver.

'May I see your licence, sir?' he said with ominous politeness.

He thought he recognised the driver, a young red-haired man in a sharp-looking suit, but he wasn't sure.

Ignoring the request, the man jumped out of the sports car and slammed the door. 'Where's Tara Ross?' he demanded.

Steve loomed over him threateningly. 'I said, may I see your licence, sir?'

'Never mind all that. I was speeding, big deal, the office will pay the fine. I need to find Tara Ross. Quickly.'

There was something in the man's tone that Steve found immensely irritating. 'Okay, what's your name?' he asked, producing a notebook.

'My name's Gerry Gellick. I'm a reporter.'

Steve sighed. Now he remembered. This was the man he'd seen grabbing Tara's arm outside the Kennedy house at Barnabo.

'You'll get no information from me, Mr Gellick,' he said firmly. 'But I'm going to ask you one more time to...'

'*Where is she?*' The words were almost a snarl.

There was a desperate urgency in his voice that Steve couldn't ignore. 'She's gone out in her father's fishing boat. With Fergal Kennedy.'

'Oh, Jesus. Jesus.' The man rubbed his eyes in frustration. 'This is worse than I thought.' He made an effort to calm himself down. 'Sergeant. I promise you that I'll show you my licence and pay any fine you want. Later. But right now, you have to listen to me.'

Steve just stared at him.

Gellick walked ahead of him into the garda station and slapped a sheet of paper on the counter. 'We haven't much time. Just read that.'

The sergeant lifted the paper. It was a flimsy fax containing several closely-typed paragraphs. Some of the words were smudged and illegible.

'What is it?' he asked suspiciously.

'It's a fax message.' Gellick took a deep breath. 'Listen, I have a contact in the Garda Technical Bureau who tips me off about forensic evidence as soon as he gets it. This is the latest finding in the Ann Kennedy case. Your detectives in Ennis won't even see it until the morning.'

'And what are *you* doing with it?' Steve was outraged.

'What do you think? I'd planned to stick an exclusive in the *Evening Report!* tonight. But there are some things that are more important than breaking a story. Even for me.'

Steve began reading the report. 'It's an analysis of the bloodstains on the dead woman's nightdress,' he said slowly.

'That's right.' Gellick couldn't hide his impatience. 'Skip the next couple of pars. Nearly all of it is her own blood, as you might expect, but in a couple of cases, the fabric bears faint traces of another type of blood.' He pointed to the relevant section. 'Since it's confined to areas where the fabric was cut by the knife, it probably came off the murder weapon. In other words, we're talking about a residue of dried blood that had been on the knife *before* the attack.'

Steve's eyes widened with surprise. 'You mean, the same knife had been used in other killings?'

Gellick wasn't listening. 'The traces were only microscopic – but the forensic people still managed to identify the species,' he continued, grabbing the sheet of paper and running his finger down the smudgy lines of type.

The sergeant leaned over his shoulder. 'Species? You mean it wasn't human blood?'

'No, sergeant, it wasn't human. Look, they've got the exact name written down here – *Scomber Scombrus*.'

'And what the hell is *Scomber Scombrus* when it's at home?'

'I'd never heard of it, either,' said Gellick. 'But apparently it's the common North Atlantic mackerel. The weapon was obviously a knife used for gutting fish.'

Gellick looked up from the sheet of paper, his eyes pleading with the sergeant to understand.

But Steve McNamara had already gone. He was sprinting towards the harbour, faster than he'd ever run when he represented his county at the football championships in Croke Park. His worried eyes were fixed on the massive outcrop of Chicken Point, behind which the *Róisín Dubh* lay drifting, unprotected and completely hidden from view.

Fergal's hands were like the hands of a skilled surgeon. Rapidly yet with pinpoint precision, he inserted the razor-sharp gutting knife under the pollack's neck, slid it smoothly downwards, removed the innards, and moved swiftly on to the next fish. Tara, who was used to filleting and cooking fish, envied his speed and dexterity. She knew how to do the job, but she'd never been that good.

'You must give me lessons some day,' she called to him from the helm.

He glanced up. 'You just keep your eyes on the sea ahead,' he warned.

She adjusted the throttle to compensate for slight changes in the sea-swell and rechecked the course. Everything was fine and the route ahead was totally clear.

She turned back to Fergal. His hands were thick with blood, but they still moved speedily and precisely, the guts flying into one bucket and the prepared fish into a container of salt water.

Tara watched closely, hoping to learn something as Fergal picked up a large mackerel and pierced its skin. She was surprised at the awkwardness of the initial cut, when the point of the knife first penetrated the skin. For all his smooth skill on the downward cuts, Fergal was slow and ungainly at this first stage.

Then she saw the knife and realised why. It had broken at some stage. There was a big break, a chunk of steel missing, just near the point. It snagged on the fish's tough skin and slowed things up.

'It must have been broken near the tip. So we're looking

*for a knife with a distinctive notch or cut at the end. Inciden-
tally, Tara, we're keeping that bit quiet...'*

The instant she made the connection, Fergal glanced
up, surprised and annoyed that she was still looking at him.

But Tara's eyes were locked on the knife.

His eyes followed hers, down to the ugly, jagged notch
of broken steel.

Then their eyes met.

She tried to smile, tried to act naturally, although her
blood had become as chilled as the steel-grey depths of the
ocean that surrounded them. But as his eyes locked in on
hers, it became clear that deception was futile. She knew.
And he realised she knew. In that fleeting microsecond,
friendship died and innocence was lost, and it was pointless trying to reclaim them.

He set down the knife. 'I told you to watch where we're
going,' he said, and there was a cold, hard edge to his voice
that she'd never heard before.

'Okay, okay. I'm watching.' She turned back to the
wheel, instinctively looking to her father for assistance.
But he still sat like a dead man in his wheelchair beside the
controls, his unseeing eyes forever focused on some
meaningless point in mid-air.

Trying not to make it seem obvious, she nudged the
throttle forward bit by bit and prayed that the boat would
soon emerge from the shadow of Chicken Point into the
benign openness of Claremoon Bay. But there was still a
long way to go, and both tide and current were against
them.

Meanwhile, smelling blood in the bottom of a dirty
black plastic bucket, the thousands of robber gulls and
guillemots circled and wheeled and swooped around her.
Their harsh keening wails seemed to cry out like the ban-
shee of Irish folklore, venomously screaming, echoing
Manus Kennedy's warning that she was to be the next to
die.

CHAPTER TWENTY-SEVEN

FOR A long time, neither of them spoke.

All you could hear was the steady throbbing of the *Róisín Dubh's* diesel engine striving against the tide and overcoming the swell. The hypnotic surging and splashing of the ocean on its hull. And all around, the frenetic howling and grieving of the gulls.

The bright, cheerful sun of the early morning had vanished. The sky had turned grey and the surface of the sea had become the colour of old lead.

Tara's hands were fixed so tightly on the wheel that her knuckles had turned white as dry bones. Her heart was palpitating in time to the motor. She silently pleaded with the boat and the engine to make faster time. The headland seemed as remote as ever.

She tried desperately to play down her terror, to rationalise it. There was a knife with a notch in it. A broken knife. So what? How many fishing boats had broken knives? It didn't mean their crews were murderers. And even – she gritted her teeth – even if it were true, even if that blade had been the same blade that had plunged dozens of times into Ann Kennedy's thrashing, dying body, it didn't mean that the same thing was going to happen to Tara. She could easily have misinterpreted that look he gave her, that cold look that said: You know, and I realise you know, and that means things can never be the same again.

Tara shuddered at the memory and again eased the throttle forward as far as she dared. Once she got beyond the headland and into public view, she was safe. Ten minutes, perhaps. Just ten minutes.

Looking at the pale reflection in the glass of the wheelhouse window, she saw that Fergal had finished his job and was chucking the fish guts, handful by handful, to the greedy, clamouring gulls. His hands were bloody and sticky. In a minute he would come forward to the wheelhouse and they would have to talk. She couldn't risk that. She wasn't a good liar. She could never trust herself to maintain a deception for ten seconds, never mind ten minutes. She must avoid conversation at all costs.

He kicked aside the empty bucket and lumbered forward towards her. Perhaps it was just as well that the reflection in the dark glass showed only his silhouette – she couldn't see the expression on his face and she didn't want to.

As he came closer, she faked a shiver – it wasn't hard to do – and abandoned the wheel. 'Take her for a bit, would you, Fergal?' she called out casually. 'I'm going to get my jumper from the cabin.'

She didn't meet his eyes. She turned her back on him and went down into the tiny cabin. Once inside, she closed the door behind her and slowly, silently, eased the inside-bolt into place. She glanced out the window. Fergal hadn't noticed. His eyes were still fixed on the sea, checking that he was on the correct course.

If she could just stay in here until the boat rounded the point and entered the safe haven of Claremoon Bay...

The inside-bolt on the cabin door had been Tara's own idea. The *Róisín Dubh* had no proper sea-toilet, just a 'bucket and chuck-it' in a tiny alcove. The privacy bolt had been John Ross's only grudging concession to civilisation.

Sensing Fergal's eye upon her, she opened the rickety plywood storage locker and mimed the action of searching for her pullover. It didn't take much searching – it had been the last item she'd put in – but she searched anyway. The shaky locker creaked and flexed and shifted on the wall as she moved her hand. After a few minutes she couldn't prolong the process any more. She hauled out her jumper and pulled it over her head, hoping it would quell her shivering.

Before moving in to the hidden alcove, she mentally rehearsed how she would react if Fergal were to try the cabin door and find it bolted. What would she say? I'm feeling sick. I'm spending a penny, darling, can you hold on a moment? Could she fend him off long enough for the *Róisín Dubh* to round the headland and get within sight of the village?

Then, with terrifying suddenness, something happened that made it all irrelevant.

The deck beneath her feet seemed to rise up and corkscrew at the same time, hovering for a stomach-heaving instant before plunging downwards again. It was a groundswell – a powerful surge of energy erupting from the ocean depths and sending the craft into a dizzy roll. Unprepared, Tara stumbled, lost her balance and reached out for the nearest thing to hand. For a fleeting instant she thought it was too late, that she would be sent sprawling across the cabin, but she managed to grab hold of the wooden strut of the storage locker and hold on tight, practically swinging on it like a primate on a tree branch, trusting it with her entire weight.

And then it gave way, as she somehow knew it would, screws tearing out of the wood like tin tacks as the whole structure ripped off its flimsy foundation. Tara fell backwards on to the opposite wall, the locker crashing down on top of her, and then she was flung forwards again as the groundswell surged past them and shattered itself into icy shards of spray on the granite cliff-face.

Tara was unhurt – but she couldn't see. Something had fallen off the wall and on to her head. Something made of cloth but unnaturally heavy. It had wrapped itself around her eyes and face. Parts of it were dry and hard and parts of it were sticky-wet. It felt unpleasant and smelled nauseating. She fought to get it off her face and saw to her horror that her hands were dark-red. She held the material at arms' length and screamed and screamed and screamed as she recognised it as a lumberjack shirt that had once been tartan and a pair of denim jeans that had once been faded blue. Now they looked as though they had been worn on the killing floor of a slaughterhouse. They were stained, matted and stuck together with blood. A huge amount of blood.

And suddenly there was Fergal, alerted by her screams, looking through the window, witnessing the horror in her face, realising the import of her stomach-churning discovery.

And then he was at the cabin door, trying to turn the handle as her hysterical screams became louder and louder, drowning out the shrieks of the bloodthirsty sea-birds that were still circling greedily overhead.

Fergal, face distorted with anger, stepped backwards and landed his size-twelve boot square on the door, smashing the steel bolt aside like a piece of tin. He pushed through the broken door, past the devastation of the cabin, and grabbed Tara brutally by the hair. He pulled her upwards and out on to the open deck, and savagely spun her around so that her long hair twisted tighter around his fist and almost tore itself from her scalp. He held her face up close to his until they were only a couple of inches apart.

'Why?' he roared, his voice rising above her own hysterical screaming. 'Why could you not just leave...things...alone.' The last three words were emphasised by painful tugs at her hair. 'All you had to do was do nothing. But you had to go around pushing...your nose...in...'

His saliva spattered her face. His face was twisted and black with rage.

'Stirring up things. Turning up stones that should have been left alone. Why? Why?'

He paused, seeming to expect an answer. But the screaming from the deep pit of her soul had assumed its own identity, taken a life of its own. It was like a frightened animal running amok inside her. She couldn't have stopped even if she'd wanted to. Her breath came inwards in harsh, rattling moans and immediately expelled itself in cries of sheer anguish. She was out of control.

'They had *nothing* on us! Nothing! All we had to do was sit it out and call their bluff. They would all have gone away and we would have ended up in that big house, the one you always wanted, set-up for life! People could talk all they wanted, but there was no proof. We would have been up there, you and me, laughing down at them all!'

It was the excruciating pain from the repeated tugs on her scalp that forced Tara back from the brink of hysteria. Somewhere deep down within her, she discovered some burning instinct for survival. It cooled, found its shape, and became hard as steel. She forced herself to stop screaming, take deep steady breaths and concentrate on staying alive.

'But you had to destroy everything. Everything. It's all gone, now. Everything's in ruins.'

The survival instinct within her began assessing, compiling, analysing. The first thing it computed was that this was no meaningless rant. Fergal was working himself up to a fever of self-justification, stoking up a righteous anger that would give meaning and purpose to whatever terrible action he planned to take.

'When I think of what I did for you. I did everything for you! I even killed my own mother for you. For us! And what do you do, you stupid ungrateful bitch? You throw it all back in my face!'

The admission had been made, but it had lost all its power to shock. Tara had stopped listening. She felt the crazy lurching of the boat and realised that there was yet another threat to her survival. The *Róisín Dubh* was still under power, but out of control. Rudderless, she had abandoned her striving against the swell and had taken the course of least resistance, wallowing with the waves instead of pushing through them, heading straight towards the cliffs and towards the treacherous rocks that lurked just beneath the surface.

But Fergal was lost in his own world of righteous, white-hot fury. 'What do you do? What do you do? You lie to me. You cheat on me. You betray me. I know all about your trips to Paris with that Russian guy. I know all about your nights in his apartment. Don't try to deny it, you two-faced whore!'

'It wasn't like that. It's not what you think,' Tara tried to blurt out. But in Fergal's world of stark black and white, there was no room for grey.

He hauled her across the deck towards the side of the boat. '*You* did this,' he said with cold fury. 'You brought this on yourself.'

And suddenly she was knocked backwards across the gunwale until her lower back hurt like hell against the hard wooden edge, and his fingers were closing around her throat, strangling her, choking the life out of her.

She grabbed at his wrists and tried to pull them away, but it was hopeless. His grip was locked as solidly as bolted metal.

As the blood pounded in her temples and she felt herself beginning to black out, a voice came into her head, as cool and clear as it was unexpected. She recognised the voice of Ciarán, the security man and martial arts expert who'd taught her so many street-survival techniques:

'If someone's got his hands around your throat, Tara, you're in big trouble. You've got to break the hold, but it's no good going for his wrists. You go for the vulnerable parts. And what's the most vulnerable part of the hand?'

Obeying the inner voice, her frantic, clutching hands left his wrists and moved swiftly forwards along the bone to locate Fergal's little fingers. Working blind, she grabbed each of them in a firm grip. Then, with one strong co-ordinated wrench, she hauled them outwards and backwards.

'Son of a *bitch!*'

He hadn't been expecting resistance. He didn't like

pain. The hold was broken and the shock sent him reeling backwards, his arms crossed and his maimed hands stuffed under his armpits as he tried to block out the all-engulfing wave of agony.

Tara struggled to her feet, dizzy, disorientated. Standing upright on the deck, the first thing she saw was the black cliff-face, immense and implacable, bearing down on them.

There were less than a hundred yards of water between boat and cliff. She had no choice, no time to think. She dashed forwards and spun the wheel to port, pushing the throttle to full speed to avert the catastrophe. The *Róisín Dubh*'s bow swung around and ploughed back into the waves, heading out to the open sea. Tara saw the water churning and swirling on the evil rocks on either side as the craft struggled to reach safe water.

And then, without a single moment to pause and catch her breath, Fergal was upon her again, grabbing at her, spinning her around. She skidded and landed on the hard wooden deck with a crash.

Through a miasma of white fog from her air-starved brain, Tara could just make out the glimmer of steel a few feet away from her. The gutting knife. It had been knocked out of the bucket and it was lying on the deck. No time to lose. Go for it...

She rolled over twice. Her hand reached out towards the knife, but it was just beyond her grasp. Her fingertips could touch it, feel the warm wooden handle beneath them. She scrambled frantically to pull it within reach. She'd almost made it when Fergal's boot came from nowhere and kicked the blade away.

As it clattered to the far side of the boat, Tara slumped to the deck in exhausted defeat. She saw Fergal's boot rise again. But this time the toe was aimed directly at her head.

The garda sergeant's eyes were fixed on the horizon,

desperately willing the outline of the *Róisín Dubh* to emerge from behind the jagged rocks of Chicken Point. But, as Steve McNamara knew only too well, willing something with all your heart was not enough to make it happen.

He barely noticed the helicopter as it appeared on the horizon, flying low over the Burren from the northeast, its dark shadow pursuing it across the white limestone hills. Dogs barked and sheep scattered in terror as it circled the cliffs near the harbour, looking for a landing point. And then the streets of the sleepy village were filled with the scything, buffeting roar of its rotors as it descended slowly, warily, to settle on a grassy outcrop near the harbour.

At any other time, the sergeant would have gone straight across to investigate. And at any other time Steve – like any other red-blooded male – would certainly have been transfixed by the mini-skirted brunette who climbed out of the back seat of the Jetranger. But he ignored her, just as he ignored the tall dark-haired man who shepherded her, crouching, away from the helicopter and raised a thumb to the pilot.

The sergeant briefly considered commandeering the aircraft, but he didn't have time. Within seconds of the thumbs-up signal, the machine had soared into the sky, heading southwards to Shannon for refuelling.

Steve's eyes scanned the harbour. He rejected the rowboats and the tiny sailing dinghies and the slow, round-bottomed fishing skiffs. Instead, he settled on a nineteen-foot Orkney Fastliner with a semi-displacement hull and a punchy forty HP Yamaha motor capable of powering her along at twenty knots or more.

'Excuse me. Sergeant!'

McNamara looked around. It was the tall, sun-tanned man who'd alighted from the helicopter.

'Can't talk to you right now, sir. Urgent business. Later.' Steve was jumping down the harbour steps two at a time and leaping into the Fastliner.

'This is urgent, too, actually.'

Steve stared at him. He recalled that accent from somewhere. Yes, now he remembered. That strange Eastern European who'd been hanging around with Villiers.

'Yes? Can it wait?' Steve was already starting the engine.

'It's about Tara. Tara Ross.'

Steve hesitated. He couldn't afford to ignore this man, and yet he couldn't risk standing around.

'Jump in,' he ordered curtly.

The two passengers leaped into the Fastliner just in time. With Steve's next attempt, the motor kicked into life and the boat surged through the water, its bow rising sharply into planing position long before it left the crowded little port. Shouting above the nasal roar of the engine and the rhythmic sluicing of the water, Andres began telling the sergeant everything he knew.

A convulsive shiver brought Tara back to consciousness. Unexpectedly, her first sensation was of physical comfort. She was no longer lying on the hard wooden deck. Her battered, pain-racked body was stretched out on something soft, yielding and yet supportive.

For a fleeting instant, as she lay with her eyes closed, she thought her nightmare was over – that she was lying on a hospital bed or an ambulance stretcher. But she could still hear the shrieking of the gulls and feel the cold sea air. Cautiously, she put out an exploratory hand and encountered the familiar texture of mesh netting.

Keeping her eyes closed, she feigned unconsciousness while she took stock of her situation. She realised she was stretched out on the netting at the stern of the boat. The *Róisín Dubh* seemed to have returned to the open sea and the engine was idling, out of gear – she could tell by the tone of the motor and the wallowing motion of the boat on the ocean swell.

'Come on, Tara. I know you're awake.'

She opened her eyes. He was squatting beside her on the deck, staring down at her. His anger seemed to have subsided. But his face and voice registered no emotion at all.

'I'm sorry,' he said softly.

Tara felt an irrational surge of relief. She knew the circumstances hadn't changed, but at least she was no longer dealing with a man consumed by a violent and unreasoning fury. Fergal was himself again.

'Let's go back, Fergal,' she pleaded, her voice weak and hoarse. 'Give yourself up. The courts will give you credit for that. If you plead guilty to manslaughter, you'll be out in six or seven years.'

But Fergal didn't appear to hear her.

'I'm sorry,' he repeated, in exactly the same tone. 'I'm sorry that you have to die like this.'

The relief that had surged inside her soul subsided like a retreating wave on the shoreline, leaving her empty and drained. She felt her eyes swell and fill with tears.

'But why?' she whispered weakly. 'Why?'

He misunderstood her. 'Because you're too good a swimmer,' he explained patiently, 'and I'm too good at handling boats. You wouldn't just fall overboard and drown in a calm sea. Nobody would believe that.'

She stared at him, speechless and nauseated. This man she had grown to know so intimately, this man whose lips she had caressed with her lips, and whose body she had loved with her body, was dispassionately explaining how he intended to murder her.

He pointed to the net that lay folded beneath her. 'She fell in as we were shooting the nets,' he said distantly, assuming a frank, honest gaze that seemed fixed on an imaginary face on the other side of a desk. 'Just slipped and fell over. She's a strong swimmer, but she got tangled up under the nets. And you know how it is – once those nets fly out across the stern under the weight of a four-stone concrete block, nothing can stop them.'

Tara's tear-filled eyes opened wide with dawning comprehension and terror. She knew Fergal was absolutely right. If he managed to get her entangled in the strong meshes, the impetus of the shooting nets would carry her deep beneath the waves where no amount of swimming or struggling could free her.

Her body shuddered involuntarily. Like most people in fishing communities, she'd always had a primal, atavistic terror of drowning. She often had nightmares about it. The swelling pain in your lungs as you tried to keep the air trapped inside you for as long as possible. The knowledge that you couldn't hold on for much longer. The inevitable gasp, the explosion of bubbles, then the relentless surge of cold salt water into the mouth, nose and airways, the horrific final seconds as your lungs pounded hopelessly like broken bellows and your body thrashed and convulsed and died.

Fergal's eyes focused on her again, but if they noticed her tears at all, they showed no emotional response. His expression didn't even flicker. His impassive tone didn't waver in the least.

'Accidents like that do happen,' he said distantly. 'Nobody can prove any different. They'll suspect. They'll question. But I'll be there, leading the mourning at your funeral. Just the way I was at mom's.'

She stared disbelievingly as his expression changed for the second time, this time crumpling into a totally credible one of tortured grief. 'I wish I could talk about it,' he said emotionally, 'but there...just...aren't...any...words...'

Then, just as suddenly, the expression changed, as though a mask had been removed, and he was smiling coldly down at her.

Tara felt her weakened body become taut with anger. He was repeating the same words he'd said to her when she'd comforted him on the day of his mother's funeral.

The bastard was mocking her.

'Anyway,' he said as he stood up and began the routine of shooting the net, 'they can gossip all they want. I'll be out of this shit-kicking little dump by the end of the month. Australia, perhaps. Or maybe Paris. But then, you know all about Paris, don't you, Tara?'

He was getting angry again. He hurled the net's marker system – the buoy and the twenty-fathom sling rope – over the stern.

'Maybe it's just as well I found out about Paris,' he said. 'I really was thinking of settling down here with you. For the rest of my life.'

She could hear the same dangerous tone of aggrieved self-pity in his voice. He grunted with effort as he stooped and lifted the huge anchor-stone that would send the net plummeting into the depths of the ocean.

'Don't get me wrong, Tara,' he said, turning to look at her directly as he left the big concrete block balanced precariously on the six-inch wide wooden gunwale. They both knew the slightest push would send it plunging into the sea, and all three hundred metres of net would go shooting inexorably after it. 'Don't get me wrong. You're a good-looking girl. And you're a *great* lay. But much as I like screwing you, there's no way I'm going to waste the best years of my life caring for some crippled, dribbling imbecile.'

As he turned his head pointedly towards her father's chair in the wheelhouse, Tara felt herself electrified by anger. Within a single transforming instant, all her pain and weariness were swept aside in a power-jolt of sheer fury. She knew she'd only a split second in which to act.

Now!

Her foot drew back and lashed outwards and upwards towards his unprotected groin. Her aim was perfect. And the vicious kick contained every ounce of her remaining strength.

But at the last moment Fergal glanced back, saw the

advancing blow, and turned sharply to avoid it. Her foot landed harmlessly on his thigh, but it caught him off balance and sent him flying backwards to land sprawling against the stern of the boat.

'Do you never give up?' he snarled.

And then he's lunging at her, and they are struggling again, rolling together on the deck.

Tara clawing, hitting, kicking, biting, trying desperately to break free from his grizzly-bear grip. Fergal, hampered by his injured fingers, lashing out at her and trying to push her backwards on to the ground so that he can get a clean blow at her face with his fist.

Tara scrambling free, pushing him back. Fergal, sliding and skidding on a deck made slippery by seawater and fish-gut. His feet suddenly giving way under him, sending him sprawling face-down on the heap of netting.

Tara, in desperation, throwing heaps of the tangled net on top of him, twisting it around him, trying to bury him in it. Fergal thrashing like a captured eel, turning, his head emerging through a hole in the chaotic heap of net. Tara close to exhaustion, fighting through a daze of white fog, managing to struggle clear but unable to move fast enough to escape as he forces her back towards the stern.

Fergal, crawling towards her on his hands and knees, taking his time, knowing she can't get away. Then pausing, finding himself unexpectedly constrained by the hank of twisted netting that has become looped around his neck.

Fergal, reacting with mere irritation as his hands move upwards to tear off the noose of netting. It's hanging loose around his neck, it's no big deal. It'll only take him a few seconds to get free.

Then, suddenly, both of them becoming aware of a noise that shouldn't be there at all – the harsh metallic sound of the *Róisín Dubh's* engine crunching into forward gear.

Tara sussing it out first, looking forward with disbelieving eyes towards the wheelhouse. Fergal's eyes following hers, first with incredulity and then, when he finally understands, with naked terror. He hears the dull bass throb of the engine rise to a powerful roar. He feels the sudden forward surge of the boat. The bow of the craft rising sharply, the stern descending behind him. His frightened eyes go back to the stern just in time to see the heavy concrete block dislodge itself from its narrow shelf of wood and fall backwards over the edge. As the anchor-stone plunges into the ocean, drenching them both with its splash, the netting follows, flying outwards at incredible speed. The ropes at either side buzz like angry hornets. Fergal pulls desperately at the mesh wrapped around his neck, but it's too late.

For a second his eyes meet Tara's, begging for life, pleading.

And then it happens, faster than anyone could have believed possible. The shooting net tightens around his neck, and his entire body flies backwards like a puppet's, slamming up against the woodwork of the stern. His head jerks to the side, his neck gives a sound like a cracking branch, and then his entire body is catapulted over and across the stern, like a cork over a waterfall.

Tara scrambling to her feet, sprinting forward towards the wheelhouse, towards the throttle control that's located just beside the wheel. But she takes only a few steps before the white fog smothers her brain in a dizzy, overwhelming rush, engulfing her, blanking everything out. She finds herself fainting, swaying, falling, hurtling downwards towards the wooden deck just before the inside of her head explodes in pain and the world turns black and silent.

They located the *Róisín Dubh* about three miles off the coast, moving at nearly full speed and locked on a course that would ultimately have taken her to Newfoundland.

Steve McNamara hailed her several times as he

manoeuvred the Orkney Fastliner closer and closer amid the treacherous swell of the open Atlantic. There was no response. At last he managed to steer the smaller boat alongside, and Andres Talimann put the Orkney's rubber fenders over the side to prevent one craft smashing the other as they rose and fell at their different angles.

Then Andres took over the wheel of the Fastliner while Steve judged the moment and leaped across the heaving gap between the two boats.

He scrambled to the wheelhouse and cut the engine, bringing the fishing boat's relentless transatlantic journey to an end. Had her course had been landwards instead of seawards, he thought to himself, the *Róisín Dubh* would have been a wreck by now.

Grabbing a rope, he strapped the two boats to prevent them drifting apart. Then he took a deep breath, steeled himself, and looked around him.

The big garda sergeant was used to confronting death in all its forms. But nothing could have prepared him for the horrific scenes he was to witness on board the *Róisín Dubh* that day.

The area around the deck and wheelhouse was a bloody, chaotic mess of overturned fish-boxes and buckets.

The aft section of the boat was a scene of breathtaking devastation. It looked as though a maniac had run amok with a chainsaw. The stern had been half-demolished where the second anchor-stone, attached to a rope at the end of the shooting net, had torn huge chunks out of the woodwork as it catapulted free of the boat.

In the wheelhouse, his invalid chair still fixed solidly to the woodwork, was John Ross. The old man sat stock-still, in exactly the same position as Steve had last seen him at the harbour, and with exactly the same vacant expression on his face. He heard nothing and saw nothing. His open eyes remained focused on nowhere.

And only a few feet away from him, Tara lay motionless

on the deck, an irregular red-brown stain surrounding her head like a halo.

It took them more than four hours to find Fergal's body.

They knew he was out there somewhere, trapped in the tangle-nets, but they didn't know exactly where.

It wasn't until late afternoon that the *Róisín Dubh*, crewed by volunteers from the Claremoon Marine Rescue Service and helped by local fishermen, located the floating buoy that marked the spot where the nets had been shot.

From that point on, it had been a routine exercise to haul them in.

Within a few minutes, Steve was on the radio to base.

'We've found Kennedy,' he said.

'Is he dead?' asked O'Rourke. The static on the radio failed to disguise the anxiety in his voice.

Steve looked over towards the net-hauler, the large mechanical drum they'd used to haul in the first thirty metres of netting. The body was suspended from it like some macabre puppet. The meshes around the throat had been twisted and pulled and warped to the hardness of steel-cable. The darkened face still retained its expression of ghastly, hopeless pleading, but one glance at Fergal Kennedy had confirmed that he was beyond all help.

'He's dead. How's Tara?'

'She's in pretty bad shape. But she'll be okay.'

Steve McNamara heaved a sigh of relief. He'd done what he could to stop the bleeding, but he knew that Tara would require emergency treatment for the ugly gash on her head. And her pulse had been frighteningly weak.

'What the hell happened?' asked O'Rourke.

'I know exactly what happened,' Steve replied slowly. 'But you're not going to believe it.'

Steve McNamara had always been quick on the uptake when it came to mechanical matters. Within seconds of hauling in the net he had worked out what had happened to

Fergal. He'd understood how the shooting net had tightened around his throat and snapped his neck like a twig. He'd understood, too, that this had happened after someone had thrust the *Róisín Dubh* into forward gear and had pushed its throttle lever to its utter limit, deliberately dislodging the anchor-stone that had been balanced on the stern.

He'd also realised, as he'd carried out a cursory medical examination shortly after boarding the boat, that the old man seated in the invalid chair would never see the sky, hear the crash of the waves, or breathe the salt air of the ocean again.

But what he couldn't understand, what he would never be able to explain until his dying day, was how John Ross's paralysed right hand had somehow left its position in the wheelchair and had moved a full eighteen inches to the right, across the controls to the throttle-lever...and how the cold hand had become locked there in such a solid death-grip that it had taken all of Steve's strength to prise it free.

CHAPTER TWENTY-EIGHT

'FERGAL KENNEDY was obsessed with the belief that his real father was the artist Michael de Blaca,' said Inspector Phil O'Rourke. 'It wasn't just a fantasy – it was his very reason for living. It made him feel special, superior. And it gave him an excuse for not trying very hard at school, for failing to hold down a job for any length of time, and for his chronic inability to sustain any meaningful relationship.'

He held out a nicotine-stained hand and began listing points on his fingers. 'According to all the romantic clichés, artists are rebellious, quick-tempered, unfaithful, and easily capable of betraying personal friendships and trust. Those also happen to be the personality traits of Antisocial Personality Disorder. Any artists who behave like that can get away with it because they're talented. Unfortunately for him, Fergal was far from talented.'

'And he wasn't Michael de Blaca's son, either.' Tara shifted uncomfortably in her hospital bed, trying to ignore the pain of her injured head and battered body.

Outside the glass door of the private ward, a nurse looked daggers at O'Rourke and mouthed the words: 'No excitement.'

The detective gave her a reassuring nod. 'I've always known that, Tara,' he said. 'It's obvious when you check the dates. Which makes you wonder how he was able to sustain this delusion for so long.'

'Perhaps he didn't want to risk finding out the truth. And perhaps everyone else in the village just preferred to forget it.'

'Yes. Small communities have a habit of developing collective amnesia when it comes to shameful episodes from their past. Particularly when it might involve recalling their shoddy treatment of a woman who went on to become a national heroine.' O'Rourke shrugged. 'In any event, all Fergal did was put together a lot of local gossip, some of it misheard and some of it just misinformed, add a few facts that his mother reluctantly gave him, and use these few shaky bricks to create an entire fantasy castle. Here, let me help you with that.'

Tara was shifting her pillows in a bid to find a position that didn't make her back hurt like hell. It was difficult. Her body seemed to be one massive bruise. Her forehead, where she had fallen and hit the gunwale of the boat and knocked herself out, had turned a rich purple. But at least, she consoled herself, there had been no permanent damage. The doctors sympathised, but they had seen a lot worse injuries in victims of minor car shunts. Within a week or so, they assured her, she would be well on the way to recovery.

'So he lived in fantasy land,' she said at last. 'A lot of people do. But it still doesn't explain why he was driven to kill his own mother.'

'I'll come to that in a minute. Let's order tea.' O'Rourke was becoming irritated at the nurse's fixed stare. He opened the door and politely asked for a pot of Earl Grey. The nurse didn't move from her desk. She simply lifted a cream-coloured phone, notified the catering staff, and continued her task of ensuring that this intrusive policeman did nothing to damage her patient's stress level.

O'Rourke returned to the ward. There could be a lot worse places to recuperate, he thought as he glanced around the cheerful, sun-filled room with its TV, stereo and minibar – all facilities on a par with those of a first-class hotel. The air was heavy with the scent of more than a dozen bouquets of flowers sent by well-wishers. Some of the most elaborate were from neighbours and friends in Claremoon Harbour.

Tara, lying on top of the blankets in her silk dressing-gown, thought it was all a bit over the top. But it had all been provided courtesy of Andres Talimann's gold Amex credit card, and she deeply appreciated it. She'd never felt so pampered and cosseted in her life. From its gentle piped music to its gourmet menu, the Whiterock Clinic definitely deserved the Egon Ronay Award for Best Place To Recover from a Murder Attempt.

'I'm going to need a bit of help to answer your question,' O'Rourke said at last. 'Do you mind if I bring in a couple of other visitors?'

Tara shook her head. 'If you think it's necessary.'

'I'll just be a moment.'

O'Rourke left the room again. When he returned, he had two people with him.

The first was Andres Talimann, carrying a bunch of long-stemmed red roses. The second was an equally long-stemmed black woman in a red leather miniskirt and a figure-hugging black polo-neck. She had what the advertising industry describes as a 'bob and gob job' – that is, hair in a trim sexy bob, bright-red lipstick emphasising sensual lips.

Tara sighed inwardly. Thanks a million, O'Rourke, she thought. My face looks like an apple that's been kicking around the floor of a greengrocer's for three days and my body's so bandaged-up I could get a starring role in *The Curse of the Mummy's Tomb*. And just to make me feel better, you introduce me to Andres's supermodel girlfriend.

But O'Rourke was busy rearranging chairs. His usual old-world courtesy had deserted him and he had forgotten all about introductions.

'Hello, Andres,' said Tara, after an awkward moment during which all three of them waited for the detective to do the necessary. 'It's good to see you again.'

'It's good to see you again, too. How are you feeling?'

'Oh, not so bad. According to the hospital bulletins, I'm "comfortable", but I must say that isn't the word I'd choose.'

'I am sorry about your father. Please accept my condolences.'

She nodded. 'Thanks. He had a good life, all in all. And I suppose, in a way, it was fitting that he should die at the helm of the *Róisín Dubh*, back in control of things, rather than wasting away in a hospice. It's how he would have wanted it.'

And at least, she told herself for the hundredth time, the massive coronary attack that had stopped the lifeblood flowing through John Ross's courageous heart had also made his death quick and painless.

Tara felt her eyes sting with tears and she tried to blink them away before they began to flow again. 'Well,' she said, smiling at the supermodel. 'Aren't you going to introduce me to your friend?'

'I'm sorry. Tara Ross, I'd like you to meet Madame Mathilde Bresson.'

Madame. So she was married.

'Mathilde. How do you do.' Tara's voice was polite but unenthusiastic.

They shook hands. The brunette, sensing that some misunderstanding was in the air, began talking rapidly in French. It was much too fast for Tara to understand, but she'd spoken only a few words when she was sure of one thing – this was the voice of the French woman who'd left a message on her phone. The woman she'd taken for a French journalist.

Andres translated. 'She says she feels for you at this time, and especially so because she herself has suffered the same ordeal at the hands of Fergal Kennedy,' he said.

Tara was totally, absolutely, profoundly lost. 'I don't understand,' she whispered weakly.

Andres looked quizzically at O'Rourke. He'd obviously assumed the policeman had already explained everything. But O'Rourke smiled apologetically and shook his head.

Andres placed his hand gently on Tara's.

'I'm so sorry, Tara,' he said. 'I thought you already knew.'

He nodded towards the beautiful black woman. 'Mathilde is from Canada,' he explained. 'She's Fergal Kennedy's wife. Or should I say...his widow.'

Tara turned ashen-faced as she heard the full, horrific story of Mathilde's nightmare marriage to Fergal. Her hand trembled as she reached for a glass of water.

'Are you sure you're able for all this, Tara?' O'Rourke's gravelly voice interrupted the silence that followed. 'Just tell me if you find it too upsetting. There's no hurry. We can come back tomorrow, if you like.'

Tara shook her head. 'No, I'm fine. I want to know the truth. All of it.'

Glancing across the bed, Tara noticed that Mathilde's brown eyes were dissolved in tears and her mascara had started to run. The effort of reliving her ordeal had obviously left her emotionally drained.

It was obvious, now, that Mathilde was much older than she'd seemed. Stripped of their protective make-up, the eyes were surrounded by tiny wrinkles.

Tara leaned forward and squeezed her hand reassuringly. Andres placed his arm around her shoulder.

'Yes, I think it's best that we get it over with.' O'Rourke nodded agreement. He wanted Tara to know all about Fergal Kennedy – all about his background and his lies and why he had become a killer. He wanted her to know it all as soon as possible, so that the healing truth could become firmly established in her mind before the inevitable flood of pointless, corrosive guilt engulfed her.

'Okay,' he said. 'You asked me what could have driven Fergal to kill his own mother. It's taken a long time, but at last I think I know the answer.'

The detective had done a lot of work on the case – a lot more work than he'd needed to. He'd talked to Godfrey

Villiers, he'd talked to the owners of the gallery in New York, he'd talked again to the fisherman who'd spotted Fergal down by the harbour on the morning of the murder.

Connecting these witness statements and filling in the gaps though his policeman's intuition, O'Rourke was able to piece together almost everything about the horrific twenty-four hours that culminated in Ann Kennedy's death.

And his story went something like this.

Fergal Kennedy had a problem. He wanted Tara from the first time he saw her in the courtroom. He wanted her more than he'd wanted anything in his life before. He knew there was a key somewhere. He knew there was a button to push. It was just a question of being patient until he found it.

But patience wasn't Fergal's strong point. For instance, he knew that, one day, he would be recognised as a great artist. He had to be. It was in his genes. The way he saw it, you couldn't be Michael de Blaca's son without inheriting some of his talent. But that day was a long time in coming, and in the meantime he was reduced to earning pin-money by digging drainage ditches and hauling nets.

All that changed when Godfrey Villiers approached him out of the blue with an offer to buy his paintings. All of his paintings.

They met in a snug in Breadon's Bar. Fergal had a pint of Guinness, and Villiers, to Fergal's mortification, ordered a 'vodka-tini'. Then they got down to business.

'My dear chap,' Villiers began, trying to sound calm, although Fergal noticed he was tense and agitated. 'I am extraordinarily impressed with the quality of your work. Last week I took the liberty of consulting some prestigious colleagues in a gallery in New York, and I am happy to say they share my faith in your future. The only problem is that, at this juncture in time, you are an unknown quantity. One hates to raise the base subject of finance, but in commercial terms you are a gamble. What I suggest is that we offset the risk by including, in our deal, any works of Michael de Blaca which you happen to possess. That seascape in your dining-room, for instance, and of course the sculpture, too. May I suggest a generous sum of thirty thousand pounds, all-inclusive?'

Fergal hadn't come down the St Lawrence River in a bubble. In Canada – at least in the circles he moved in – you learned all about hustlers fast, or you went under, fast. He knew this guy was trying to hustle him. He just couldn't figure out how or why.

So he just sat back and let Villiers buy him pints all afternoon while he hummed and hawed and hedged his bets, until finally, around the sixth vodka-tini, Villiers let it slip out. The name Fergal had been waiting for. The name of the New York art gallery that had been so keen to buy his paintings.

Only by that time, Fergal knew they didn't really give a damn about his paintings. He knew that all they wanted was the sheela-na-gig.

Twelve hours later, as he lay in bed with Tara, their limbs entangled, the sweat cooling on their skin, Fergal suddenly made up his mind. He was going to marry this girl.

The fact that he was married already didn't pose a problem in his mind. He just had to have this woman. He had to own her, like he owned his Corvette. If that meant marrying her, then he'd marry her. If it meant saying a few empty promises, like he'd had to do in Canada, then he'd say a few empty promises.

But he had yet to find the right key to turn, the right button to push...

As they lay there together, Tara began talking sleepily about her dreams for the future. She told him all about the ruined Victorian spa on the hilltop, and her crazy plan to restore it.

'But it'll never happen,' she yawned. 'I haven't two pennies to rub together, never mind the money it would take to do a proper restoration job.'

'Why?' Fergal demanded. 'How much would it cost?'

She snuggled in to him. 'Oh, let's forget it. I tend to waffle on sometimes. But talking about rubbing things together...'

'No, really.' He extracted himself from her embrace. 'I want you to tell me.'

She popped him a kiss, threw on a long white cotton shirt and headed for the bathroom. 'Forget it,' she said, over her shoulder. 'I talked to a builder friend and he said that the work would cost at least two hundred grand.'

A sudden idea came to Fergal, blinding him, like a flash of burning magnesium. When she left the bedroom, he dashed downstairs, picked up the phone and asked Directory Enquiries for the number of the Cedric Maxwell Gallery in New York City.

It was five in the morning, around midnight in Manhattan, but one of the gallery's principal partners was still on duty, cataloguing items for an exhibition. Yes, he knew Godfrey Villiers. In fact, he was awaiting important news from him. Had Mr Villiers dispatched the de Blaca sculpture, as he'd promised?

Fergal wasted no time in putting him straight. He said Villiers was out of the picture. His name was Fergal Kennedy, he was de Blaca's son, and he was the legal owner of the sheela-na-gig. Other galleries were interested, too. Could he talk turkey? Could he make a deal there and then?

Within sixty seconds, they had settled on four hundred thousand dollars, subject to verification, bank draft to be made out to Fergal personally.

He slammed down the phone and bounded up the stairs, nearly colliding with Tara as she emerged smiling from the bathroom. Her sexy, just-made-love smile took his breath away. He swept her up in his arms and threw her on to the bed. This time, their lovemaking was even better. It was more than good sex. It was the triumphant performance of a rutting stag.

Afterwards, he pulled on his blue jeans and plaid shirt, kissed her goodbye, and almost ran out the door.

Fergal was convinced he had found it at last. The secret key to turn, the right button to push, that would allow him to possess Tara Ross and have her all to himself.

He glanced at his watch. Just before six am. Perfect, he thought with satisfaction. His mother would soon be up, making herself a cup of tea in the kitchen. He would tell her all about his plans to sell his sheela-na-gig sculpture and use the cash to buy the spa house for the woman he planned to marry.

He had made up his mind in an instant, with all the impulsive generosity that characterises people with ASPD, and he wasn't going to change it. Let anyone dare to stand in his way.

'I can't stand the sight of blood,' said Ann Kennedy.

'Sorry,' muttered Fergal.

'It's okay, love. But I've told you before, when you come home after helping John Ross on the boat, and you have some fish to clean, could you tidy up after yourself? I had a late night, and it doesn't help my stomach when I come into the kitchen in the morning and see a plate swimming with fish-innards and a dirty old gutting knife.'

'I said I was sorry, Mom. It won't happen again, honest.' He kissed her on the cheek and shook his head to decline the proffered cup of tea. 'Listen, I can't wait to tell you. I've had great news. It's going to change my whole life.'

Ann Kennedy listened, and her face grew paler. She sat down and poured herself a second cup of tea without emptying the dregs of the first cup. That was something she never did.

Fergal didn't even notice. He bounded into the living-room and returned with the sheela-na-gig clasped in his hand. 'You don't think my da will mind?' he asked. 'I mean, it was my birthday gift. He'll love the spa house, once we've done it up. He can come and visit us there, me and Tara, and we'll all sit on the front deck together and paint the ocean, the way da used to...'

His voice trailed off. He knew something was dread-fully wrong.

'Mom, you're not saying anything,' he said quietly. 'What's the matter?'

Ann's voice was barely a whisper. 'It's not yours,' she said.

'What? What are you talking about?' Fergal knew she was going to make petty objections and he could feel his temper rising like lava in a volcano.

'Sit down, Fergal. Please.'

'No, I won't sit down,' he said, his face darkening. 'Tell me.'

Ann was renowned for her tact and diplomacy, but there was no tender or humane way to tell this man that the very core and centre of his existence was a sham.

Gently but firmly, she told him the truth. The sculpture was not his to sell. It belonged to his younger brother Manus, because it was Manus who was the real son of the artist Michael de Blaca.

Fergal stood rooted to the ground in shock. In the course of a dozen softly-spoken sentences, his mother had destroyed his life. In those few minutes, he saw his great self-myth, his reason for living, exposed as a lie. He saw himself revealed, not as the tempestuous rebel artist, but as the good-for-nothing son of a drunken abusive farmer. And worst of all, he saw Tara slipping inexorably from his grasp.

'You're lying,' he whispered at last.

Ann shook her head. She left the room and returned with battered, dog-eared envelope. Her hands were shaking, because she recognised the darkness in her son's features and she was frightened by it. She pulled out a letter and read it aloud. It was signed by Michael de Blaca, and dated only a few days after the birth of Ann's second child. It stated clearly that the enclosed sculpture, de Blaca's first work in stone and marked *sng1*, was to be given to his son Manus.

Fergal stood up, knocking over the heavy pine chair. He had taken the path of denial, but it had turned to quicksand. He was floundering. He was gasping for air. He couldn't contain his anger. It boiled up, spilling out, venting itself in rage and fury against his mother. The world turned red, blood red, the way it had with Manus at the cowshed, the way it had with Mathilde in Canada. He saw the razor-sharp gutting knife. It was in his hand. He plunged it into Ann Kennedy's body...again, and again, and again, long after there was any need to go on.

When he came to his senses, he was standing in the shower, hosing his body down. He had no idea how he got there. But the blood-soaked shirt and jeans that lay beside his feet, leaching red stains into the draining water, immediately dispelled his hopes that it had all been a terrible nightmare.

He moved fast, hardly bothering to dry himself before he pulled on a clean pair of jeans and another plaid shirt. He had only minutes to spare. His brain was focused now, cool and sharp and focused. His mind was a crystal-clear pool. He could see right down to the seabed. He knew what had to be done.

He walked quickly back into the kitchen, and when he stepped over the body of his mother, it meant no more to him than stepping over a sleeping drunk lying in the gutter outside the nightclub in Montreal. He lifted the knife from the floor. He lifted the letter and stuffed it into the breast pocket of his blood-stained shirt. He walked to the door, scrupulously careful to avoid stepping in the splatters of blood on the tiles.

The harbour was deserted as he jumped aboard the *Róisín Dubh*. Quickly, furtively, he stuffed his blood-stained pants and shirt behind the rickety locker in the cabin. It was a temporary measure. Next time they were out at sea, miles into the open Atlantic, he'd put them in a weighted bag and dump them overboard.

He tested the strength of the locker. It would be okay for a while. It would hold. Finally, he washed John Ross's gutting knife in the seawater and replaced it in the toolbox under the seat. The whole process had taken only a few minutes.

As Fergal waited for the police to arrive he felt satisfied, in a strange sort of way. All he had to do was sit tight, put the New York dealer on hold, and wait for all the fuss to die down before selling the sculpture.

He would have to shed a lot of tears over the next few days, because that was expected, but he had learned a long time ago how to fabricate emotions like that. He didn't understand words like sorrow or remorse. The way he saw it, deep down inside himself, it had all been inevitable. He had wanted something. And so he had removed the only obstacle that had stood in his way. It was as simple, as terrifyingly simple, as that.

The Earl Grey tea finally arrived. As the door opened, Tara could hear a faraway speaker piping Elgar's *Enigma Variations* through the corridors of the clinic. The smell of bergamot suffused the room as the white-aproned maid poured the beige liquid into four china cups.

Tara reached for her bottle of painkillers. The ordeal of listening to the full story had left her feeling as though her head were about to explode. And it wasn't the full story, anyway. No living person knew exactly what had happened in the kitchen at Barnabo on that dreadful Sunday morning, and no one ever would.

'Well, it's over,' she whispered at last. 'Thank God it's all over.'

O'Rourke took a mouthful of tea and stood up. 'Yes,' he said. 'It's over. We can close our files on Ann Kennedy's murder, instead of leaving them open for ever.'

'I don't understand,' Tara objected. 'You told me you would have had a conviction anyway. You said it was only a matter of time before you got DNA results, and they would have established Fergal as the killer.'

O'Rourke shook his head. 'It didn't work out that way, I'm afraid. Word just came through this morning that the DNA tests were inconclusive.'

'So you'd never have caught him?'

O'Rourke drained his tea. 'We had nothing on Fergal,' he agreed. 'Nothing at all. We had no idea that he occasionally worked with your father on the *Róisín Dubh*, and we had no reason to search it. He would have ditched those clothes without anyone knowing. The truth is, Tara, that if it hadn't been for you and your crazy idea of taking your father out on a boat trip, we might never have found any evidence worth a damn. It's all too likely that Fergal Kennedy would have lived a long and happy life in a big house overlooking Claremoon Bay, without ever being brought to justice. And if he'd had his way, Tara – you would have been right there beside him.'

He reached into his pocket, produced a little buff envelope of the type used by jewellers, and handed it to her. 'We found this in Fergal's pocket,' he said. 'I believe he intended to give it to you that night.'

The envelope showed the crest of a local goldsmith. Inside was a small black jewellery box. She opened the lid and took out the ring that nestled on a cushion of red velvet.

It was an engagement ring, wrought from fine gold

with a cluster of miniature diamonds. But in the centre of the cluster, where the main diamond would usually be set, was her birthstone. It was a minuscule pearl...spherical, creamy-white, and absolutely perfect, the type you might find concealed within the shell of a mussel during lunch at a seafood restaurant on a mild Saturday afternoon in spring.

CHAPTER TWENTY-NINE

MATHILDE BRESSON'S plane was on time. They saw it land as they sipped cappuccino in the airport bar. At a quarter to eleven, according to the terminal screens, passengers would be permitted to board, and half an hour later the plane would leave Dublin Airport on its journey to Paris.

'You're positive you don't want to go back to Montreal?' Andres asked in French.

'Quite sure.' Mathilde smiled. 'The memories are all bad memories. Besides, one cannot be a topless waitress all one's life. When a woman reaches a certain age, she fights a losing battle against gravity.'

Her eyes were rueful, but her thousand-watt smile – perfect white teeth highlighting flawless dark skin – lit up the dim lounge. She may indeed have been entering that phase of life which the French tactfully call 'a certain age', but the shapely figure, poured into skin-tight leather trousers, still threatened to cause whiplash injuries to every head-turning male in the airport.

'That's one problem you don't have to worry about,' said Tara, struggling with her own inadequate French. 'But you *do* deserve a better career.'

Mathilde sipped her coffee and kept a careful check on the digital clock on the terminal screen. 'Me, I began my career as a hairstylist,' she said. 'I enjoyed the work and I was good at it. The only problem was my employer.' She grimaced. 'Today, he would be sued for sexual harassment. But in those days, it didn't work like that.'

She shrugged as only the French can, and her troublesome employer simply disappeared. 'I have decided. I will return to Metz, my hometown, and try to open my own salon. It will be hard work, but I will be answerable to no one except myself.'

'That's the spirit,' Tara encouraged her. 'You'll be a huge success, I just know it. And I'll be one of your first customers.'

She meant every word. She'd enjoyed Mathilde's company over the past weekend, a fun-filled but hectic two days in which she'd shown her the sights of Dublin and given her a taste of Irish pub life in bars like the legendary Johnny Fox's. Andres had joined them on most of these outings. They'd shared an embarrassed laugh about Tara finding the insulin syringes and jumping to conclusions. And, yes, Tara had to admit that she'd enjoyed his company even more.

'My heart goes with you, Tara,' Mathilde was saying. 'I wish you happiness in whatever you choose to do, and wherever you choose to go.'

The tannoy announced that the boarding gate was open. Spontaneously, Tara and Mathilde embraced – two survivors out of an ill-matched trio of women whose lives had been blighted by one man. Mathilde dabbed her eyes with a handkerchief. She nodded urgently towards Andres, who'd wandered off to fetch her luggage trolley.

'That one, he is crazy in love with you,' she whispered rapidly to Tara. 'But you are in danger of losing him.'

'What?' Tara was taken completely by surprise.

'He loves you. But yet he will leave. He will leave, not in spite of his love for you, but because of it. Be careful.'

Andres rejoined them. Tara could only stare open-mouthed as Mathilde gave her an encouraging smile, patted her arm and headed for the departure gate.

They watched her walk away towards the security scanners, her svelte hips sashaying with an unconscious and confident sexuality that caused luggage trolleys to collide all over the departure lounge. She didn't look back.

'I've a feeling she'll do OK,' said Andres.

Tara nodded. 'I've a feeling you're right.'

'Now,' smiled Andres, taking her arm, 'how about lunch?'

Damn. She couldn't.

'I'm sorry, Andres, I'd love to,' she apologised, 'but I've got something else on. What about tomorrow instead?'

He shook his head. 'I have to go to London on business.'

'Next day, then?'

'Perhaps.'

Damn Andres and his 'perhaps'. With him, you could never tell whether 'perhaps' meant yes, maybe or never.

'Goodbye, then, Tara,' he said, giving her a hug which seemed to go on much longer than necessary for two friends parting company for a couple of days.

'Okay, Andres, see you later,' she said cheerfully. 'And sorry I can't make lunch. It's just that can't break this appointment. I promised to visit someone in hospital.'

'Oh?' He looked surprised. 'Relative or friend?'

'Neither,' she said thoughtfully. 'It's someone I don't even know.'

All the other doors in the beautiful Georgian terrace had several brass panels and half a dozen doorbells apiece. Each lofty house, with its fanlight-crested door and multi-paned windows, was shared by solicitors' offices, insurance companies, accountants and architects, all paying a fortune in rent for a few square metres of office space.

But the door Tara was interested in had only one brass panel, a modest rectangle that bore the two words: RUS-SETT CLINIC. There was no further explanation of its purpose, no elaboration as to why it should occupy an entire multi-storey building in one of the most expensive terraces in central Dublin.

Tara pressed the bell and gave her name into the intercom. The yellow-painted door buzzed like an angry wasp and an electronic bolt snapped back.

'Good afternoon, Ms Ross.' The receptionist smiled warmly. A pleasant woman in her early fifties, she had the jolly, roly-poly face of a farmer's wife from an Enid Blyton book. 'We were expecting you. Please take a seat. Mr Fitzpatrick will be with you in a moment.'

Tara sat on the plush white leather sofa and leafed through the current issue of *Country Life*. A hidden sound system was softly playing an Andrew Lloyd-Webber tune on panpipes.

'Ms Ross?'

Tara looked up. Mr Frederick Fitzpatrick, consultant psychiatrist to the Russett Clinic, was not the stuffy middle-aged man she had expected. He was in his early thirties, he wore his hair long, and he had a well-trimmed black beard that framed his ready smile. He had on blue Levis and a light denim shirt, and his multicoloured, multi-patterned waistcoat seemed to be the result of days of painstaking labour by some Third World craft worker.

He must have noticed her expression. 'I know, you were expecting a suit,' he said in a disarming Liverpudlian accent. 'Everybody does. But I don't believe in pinstripes. They're symbolic barriers – prison bars you wear.'

Tara was glad she hadn't worn her chalk-striped charcoal suit. Her own outfit – light blue jeans and white cotton shirt – would no doubt meet with the good doctor's approval.

'You must be Dr Fitzpatrick,' she said, shaking his hand.

'Well...*Mister* Fitzpatrick, actually. It's a funny old profession. You go in as a Mister, you work for years to get called a Doctor, then they make you work like a Trojan for another few years for the privilege of getting called a Mister again. But it's all pretty irrelevant, really, because everyone around here calls me Fred.'

'And may I?'

'Of course, and I'll call you Tara. Please.' He opened the door of the reception area and led her up a flight of varnished stairs with plush red carpeting and brightly-polished brass stair rods. The old-wood banisters were immaculately polished. High above, on the ceiling, she could discern white, perfectly-preserved plasterwork moulded into intricate shapes of fruit and leaves.

'I'm delighted that you decided to come,' he said, taking the stairs two steps at a time and obviously expecting Tara to do likewise. 'Not everyone would have the courage, after what you've been through.'

'I wanted to come.'

'I know.' He paused on the stairway and dropped his voice to a whisper. 'Our patient is just up here.'

'How is he, anyway?'

'Making steady progress. Meeting you in a friendly, non-threatening environment could do wonders for him. But...' He paused again. 'It might be a very short meeting. You don't mind that?'

'Not at all.'

'I know I can rely on you to be calm and non-judgmental,' he whispered as they reached a landing. He knocked on a polished pine door marked 'Private'. Without waiting for a reply, he turned the handle and threw the door open with the confident air of someone who has ready access to all areas. 'This is Ms Ross. Sorry, I mean *Tara*.' He smiled at her. 'She's travelled a long way to see how you're getting along, our kid.'

Tara hesitated in the doorway. The room was warm and sunny, and simply but expensively furnished with half a dozen armchairs. On the wall, pinned to cork notice boards, were watercolour paintings that had obviously been created by the clinic's patients. They looked like depictions of dreams.

At first, she wondered who the figure in the armchair was. Then, as logic prompted her towards recognition, she stepped forward and held out her hand.

'Hello, Manus,' she said.

The man in the smart Ralph Lauren sweatshirt smiled shyly and returned her handshake with surprising warmth. 'Hello, Tara. I'm glad you were able to make it.'

'I couldn't wait to come, Manus. May I sit down?'

'Yes, of course. Sorry.' He motioned to the five empty armchairs. 'Do you think you can find a seat?'

They shared a smile. As she sat down beside him, she glanced at him again. His brown hair was shiny, clean and neatly-cut. He was clean-shaven, and his eyes were quiet and content. With his plain, pockmarked face, he would never be considered a movie star, but he looked good in a boy-next-door, butcher-delivery-lad sort of way. She could hardly recognise him as the filthy, wild-eyed fugitive who had confronted her in the forest.

'And how are you doing?' she asked at last.

'Fine. I like it here.' His voice drawled slightly – he was probably on some sort of sedative, she guessed – but otherwise he sounded normal. 'They treat me really well.'

'I'm glad. It's a good place. They're good people.' God, she sounded like a presenter on *Sesame Street*.

'I'm sorry I scared you.' He was staring at her a bit apprehensively, like a nervous puppy. 'I didn't mean to.'

'I know you didn't. You were just trying to warn me.'

'Yes.' He looked relieved. 'Is your friend all right? The red-headed girl?'

'Melanie? Yes, don't worry. She's made a full recovery. She realises now that you weren't trying to hurt her. She knows that you'd come to the cottage looking for me. To warn me about Fergal.'

Manus nodded. 'What happened was, I looked through the window to make sure *he* wasn't there. Then I went to the door. But when your friend made a go for me with the shotgun, what happened was, I panicked and pushed the barrel upwards away from me. The gun went off and knocked her backwards. She banged her head on the floor. I just got scared and ran.'

'It's okay,' Tara reassured him. 'It could have been an awful lot worse. I suppose Melanie did overreact a bit. She was terrified because your warnings sounded so much like threats.'

Manus looked remorseful. 'I know. The doctors have explained to me that I have a real problem...' he frowned, trying to remember the phrase...'communicating with people.'

He yawned, stood up, and lifted a brown parcel from the table beside him.

'I want you to have this, Tara,' he said. 'My mother's solicitor says it belongs to me and I can do what I like with it. So I said I wanted to give it to you, and he told me that would be all right.'

The parcel was small and heavy.

'What is it, Manus?'

'Just something.' Manus's face began to redden. 'The solicitor tells me it's worth an awful lot of money, but I don't care. It never brought us nothing but bad luck. Please just take it and do whatever you want with it.'

Tara put it into her bag.

'There's a letter inside,' said Manus. 'Promise you'll read it before you decide what to do?'

'I promise. Get well soon, Manus.'

She stood to leave, shaking his hand again and wishing him well. She was able to meet his eyes and she knew, with a deep inner satisfaction, that she had confronted her worst fears, and that the figure in the wood was exorcised for ever. Manus Kennedy would never again visit her in her nightmares.

'Thank you for coming here, Tara,' he yawned as she walked away. 'Thank you for doing that for me.'

'You're very welcome, Manus,' she said. 'But I didn't do it for you. I did it for me.'

CHAPTER THIRTY

NEXT DAY Tara Ross rose early and took a lengthy walk along the shoreline near Claremoon Harbour. For a long time, perhaps half an hour, she did nothing more than lift gnarled hunks of driftwood and toss them aimlessly into the ocean.

Back at her cottage, Manus Kennedy's package still lay unopened on the kitchen table, exactly where it had lain since her return from Dublin. She knew what was in the heavy little parcel, but she couldn't bring herself to open it. The memories were too vivid and the wounds were still too raw.

Besides, another matter was weighing even more heavily on her mind. It had begun with Mathilde's enigmatic warning at the airport. Andres was in love with her, she'd said, but he would soon be gone. He would not leave in spite of his love for her; he would leave because of it. What on earth was that supposed to mean?

And yet, Mathilde's cryptic remark explained a lot of things Tara hadn't understood before. It explained Andres's oddly protective attitude towards her – an attitude she'd wrongly interpreted as arrogant interference in her affairs. It explained why he'd gone to such enormous lengths to help her. It explained all the mystifying occasions when it had seemed he was trying to say something to her, but had drawn back at the last minute...

She tossed a jagged, bone-white stick of driftwood far out to sea. Yes, it explained all those things, and, if she were honest with herself, it also explained something about her own tangled and confused emotions towards him. The feelings she'd refused to acknowledge because of her misplaced loyalty to Fergal. Now that Fergal was gone, she could suddenly see things clearly, as though a dense and impenetrable sea-fog had abruptly lifted and she could glimpse the true, wide horizon for the first time.

She looked out at the real ocean horizon, shimmering gently as the rising sun burned off the early morning mists. With a sudden jolt, she realised that she would miss him more than she could bear. She would miss his strange accent and his quaint, old-fashioned, Indian Raj way of talking. She'd miss his tales of foreign places, his Far Eastern paddy-field cooking, his Swiss wines, and his droll, understated sense of humour.

No, it was more than that. It was much, much more than that.

Tara quickened her pace as she walked back towards the cottage, filled with a renewed sense of determination. She would phone him at his apartment in Dublin and arrange to meet. She would treat them both to a long, luxurious dinner, and for once, they would stop shadowboxing and be honest about their feelings for each other. If Mathilde had been right, if he did feel the same way about her, then anything was possible.

Tara saw the grey Mercedes car outside her cottage long before she saw the statuesque strawberry blonde at the wheel. She felt her heart give a sudden leap of trepidation. She'd never seen the woman before, but she immediately recognised Jean Murphy's description of the stunning beauty she'd spotted having lunch with Andres in the restaurant off St Stephen's Green.

As Tara walked up, feeling scruffy and disreputable in her blue-ringed Breton fishing-smock and ancient Levis, the woman got out of the Merc and smoothed a non-existent wrinkle out of her immaculate Paul Costelloe suit.

'So *you're* Tara Ross,' she smiled, as she stretched out an elegantly-manicured hand. 'I'm Wendy Killegar. And you've got something I want.'

They shared a pot of Java among the fuchsias in the back garden, enjoying the warmth of the morning sunshine. Bumblebees mumbled drowsy complaints as they struggled in and out of the purple flowers. In the background, the ocean whispered gently across the stony beach.

'The sheela-na-gig, darling,' explained the gallery owner, her shrewd eyes watching Tara closely from behind her darkened Ray-Bans. 'I've been talking to Manus, and he tells me you're now the legal owner. Has anyone else made you an offer for it?'

Tara shook her head. So she'd been right about the contents of the mysterious parcel.

'No,' she replied. 'And to tell you the truth, I haven't even looked at the thing yet, let alone made any decisions on what to do with it.'

Wendy took a sip of her Java. 'I'm so glad, darling. Because Auntie Wendy will be only too pleased to look after you. With an offer I'm sure you will regard as *extremely* generous.'

Opening her briefcase, she extracted a printed sheet of A4 paper and passed it across to Tara, whose eyes immediately widened in disbelief at the sum of money shown on the bottom line.

'We *are* talking about the same thing?' she gasped incredulously. 'A disgusting little sculpture of a naked woman looking like the centrefold in *Hustler* magazine, except she's ugly as sin?'

'Personally, I share your philistine views, darling,' said Wendy, 'but it seems that Sluts in Stone are this year's thing in the best circles of Manhattan society. Don't question it. Just sign here.'

Tara ignored the outstretched pen. She continued to stare at the series of noughts on Wendy's contract. The figure had become considerably inflated, grossly inflated, even since Fergal's abortive attempt to sell the sheela-na-gig to the New York gallery in June. Over-whelmed by the idea of having so much money, she couldn't help glancing up at the ruined shell of the old spa house on the hillside.

'You could buy yourself a nice house,' purred Wendy, reading her mind. 'Or a decent car.' She winced as she looked at Tara's rust-bucket. 'Or,' she suggested casually, 'you could use it to set yourself up in South Africa.'

The astute eyes studied Tara's face keenly, awaiting a reaction to the final suggestion.

Tara shot her a puzzled look. 'South Africa?'

'Don't be silly,' chided Wendy. 'It must have crossed your mind, even if you don't actually *do* it.'

Tara set aside the contract. 'I haven't a clue what you're talking about, Wendy. I've never been to South Africa, I don't know anyone in South Africa, I've absolutely no inclination...'

She stopped short. Wendy was staring at her in genu-ine astonishment.

'I don't believe it,' breathed the art dealer. 'That idiot. That absolute...moron. He hasn't even told you?'

'Who hasn't told me what?' Tara's head was starting to swim.

'Andres. He hasn't told you he's off to South Africa.'

'What? When?'

Wendy shook her head slowly in despair. 'I don't know when. Sometime today. He may even have left already, for all I know. You know what he's like.'

Tara took a desperate gulp of coffee, hoping that the rush of caffeine would sharpen her senses to the point where she understood what was going on. All right, she thought. So Andres was taking a business trip to South Africa. It wasn't the end of the world. She'd postpone that dinner until he returned.

'Do you know when he'll be back?' she asked.

'He won't *be* back, silly. That's what I'm trying to tell you. He'll be gone for good. He's taking up a job there. In

Cape Town.' She poured herself more coffee. 'The South African government's been after him for years to come and work for them as a sort of...well, as a sort of ambassador to the world's press. After that Robben Island interview, Mandela used to say that Andres was the only journalist who truly understood his vision of the new South Africa.'

'He's staying there? He's not coming back?' Tara could hear her own voice in the distance, and was aghast at how desperate it sounded. She felt as though she were on the verge of tears. 'He didn't even tell me.'

Wendy laid a gentle hand on her arm. 'It's obvious that you feel the same way towards him as he does about you,' she said quietly. 'Yet neither of you will admit it. You, Tara...you don't seem to be able to see the wood for the trees. And as for Andres, he's absolutely terrified that you'll be taken away from him, the way Manuela was. That's why he's leaving before he gets in too deep.' She sighed. 'What a pair of prize idiots. You deserve each other.'

For a long moment she sat there, shaking her head in silent wonder. When she spoke again, her voice was hushed and carried undertones of some ancient sadness. 'When will people like you realise that opportunities for happiness don't come along in fleets, like buses?' she asked in quiet frustration. 'Like, it's okay to miss one, because there'll be another one along in a minute? It doesn't work that way, Tara. When it comes your way, you take it. You grab it. You leap on board.'

For a second her eyes, behind the dark Ray-Bans, flickered with reawakened pain. Then, suddenly, she stood up.

'I can't let you do this to yourselves,' she said. 'I *won't* let you do it. Here.'

She thrust a hand into her briefcase, lifted out a small notepad, and scribbled out a number. 'This is the phone number of the house he's been staying in, in London. If you're lucky, you'll get him before he catches his flight for Johannesburg.'

She put the unsigned contract back into her briefcase, and shut it with a loud snap. 'You're in no condition to sign anything,' she said decisively. 'We'll talk about it another day. No, don't bother to see me out. You'd just be wasting valuable time. Go and phone.'

Ignoring the imperious command, Tara escorted Wendy through the arch of fragrant honeysuckle towards the front of the house. The gleaming Merc flashed four orange lights and beeped dutifully as its mistress approached.

'Look after him,' pleaded Wendy with deeply-felt concern. 'He can come across as a bit arrogant, but it's all just a front. He's one of the few genuinely kind, compassionate and unselfish men I've ever met – and, Lord knows, I've met a lot.'

Tara stared at her. 'My God,' she said as the penny dropped. 'You're crazy about him, too.'

'As a loon, darling. As a coot.' Wendy smiled brightly as she got into the car, closed the door, and pressed a button that made the driver's window sigh downwards. She turned the ignition key and the engine murmured an obedient response.

'When I said you had something I wanted,' she said, with forced breeziness, 'I wasn't just talking about a sculpture, you know.'

Tara watched the grey Merc disappear down the dusty road. She returned to the house, poured a glass of ice-cold Perrier and forced herself to take long, slow, deliberate breaths to steady her nerves.

Then she phoned the London number.

'Hello?'

A woman's voice.

'Hello. Could I speak to Andres Talimann, please?' Tara tried to keep her voice calm and businesslike.

'He not here. He gone.'

The woman's voice was high-pitched, Oriental. And with that poor command of English, she obviously wasn't a receptionist or secretary. Tara had a ludicrous vision of a Filipino beauty stretched naked on Andres's bed filing her nails.

'I'm the housekeeper. I take a message?'

Tara felt like kicking herself. 'Did he say when he'd be back?' she asked, biting her cheek apprehensively as she waited for the reply.

'He not coming back. Mr Talimann gone for good.'

'Oh, my God. Are you sure?'

'Yes. He pack bags, leave for airport, catch plane at three-fifteen.'

'Which flight? Which airline?'

'I dunno. Sorry.'

'Thank you.'

Tara hung up. She rapidly flicked through a phone book, and dialled the number of the Springbok Airways desk at London Heathrow.

'Hello. Do you have a flight leaving Heathrow for Johannesburg this afternoon?'

'Yes, we have, ma'am,' said a voice with a heavy South African accent. 'There's one at three-fifteen.'

'Is there a ticket reserved for a Mr Andres Talimann?'

'I'm sorry, ma'am. We can't divulge information about our passengers.'

Tara tutted impatiently. 'This is Mr Talimann's secretary,' she said, summoning up the appropriate tone of indignation. 'We need to confirm our reservation. Is that a problem?'

'Hold on, please.' She was treated to two minutes of a song by Ladysmith Black Mombazo before the woman returned. 'Yes, we can confirm that Mr Talimann is booked first-class for the three-fifteen flight,' she said.

'Thank you.'

Slowly, Tara hung up the phone. Damn, damn, damn. What could he be thinking of? Why was he running out on her like this, just when she'd realised how important he was to her? She felt anger and self-pity flare up inside her, but it was rapidly doused by cold reason. How could she blame him? She'd never given him the least encouragement. She'd practically sleepwalked through their time together, her eyes blind to his kindness towards her, his courage, the extreme lengths to which he'd gone in a bid to save her from herself. If anyone was to blame, it was...

Her thoughts were interrupted by the clatter of the letterbox. Zombie-like, she walked into the hallway to collect the mail. Her stomach performed a sickening somersault as she saw the white envelope lying on her mat, with her name and address scrawled across it in a hurried, masculine script.

She'd seen the same handwriting before. In the note Andres had left for her in his apartment, just after their trip to Paris.

Tara's hands shook as she ripped open the envelope. It had been posted the previous day, she noted – just one hour after they'd said their casual goodbyes at Dublin Airport.

She leaned her back against the wall for support and forced herself to read the letter. As she worked her way through Andres's hasty scrawl, her whole body slumped downwards until she was seated, knees raised, foetus-like, on the wooden floorboards of the hall.

Dear Tara,

I am sorry to say goodbye to you in a letter. I wish I had the strength to talk to you face-on-face, but I know that if I see you one more time I will never be able to leave you.

I cannot get you out of my head, Tara. You are on my mind night and day. Your face is the last thing I see when I fall asleep and the first thing I see in the morning. Whether we are in Ireland or Estonia, there is only one diagnosis for this strange disorder, is there not? I have fallen deeply on love to you, Tara, and for me there can only be one cure.

I have decided to leave Europe, to take up a job in faraway South Africa.

I do not know how you feel about me, Tara. Perhaps it is better that I never know, for it is best that we forget one another.

This is the cure for my complaint. Like many drastic remedies, it will hurt for a little while, but, in the end, it is better than running the risk of long-term unhappiness.

Be strong,

Andres

For a long time Tara sat motionless, watching the words swim before her eyes. Andres was doing it again: exactly as Melanie's friend Carla had predicted, exactly as Wendy had warned. He was running away before he became too involved. He'd done it so many times before...

Well, perhaps no one had ever tried to stop him before.

Tara shook herself out of her despondency and rose resolutely to her feet. There must be something she could do, she told herself. If only she had more time, she could even fly to Heathrow and try to talk to him before he left...

But there wasn't time. That was the point. And anyway, the very notion – flying all the way from County Clare to London just to head off a flight to South Africa – was patently ridiculous.

She phoned Aer Lingus.

'Let me see,' said the woman who answered the phone. 'Yes, there's a direct flight from Shannon to London Heathrow at five past one.'

'Hold on, please,' Tara told her. She glanced up at the big schoolhouse clock on the kitchen wall. Eleven-twenty. My God, it would be close. Scarily close. But if she left right now, without delaying to change clothes or pack a bag, she could make it to Shannon Airport by twelve-thirty. Catch the flight. Arrive at Heathrow at two twenty-five. Say twenty minutes to change terminals. She could be at the Springbok Airways desk a good half-hour before the flight. With a bit of luck, she might even catch him before he checked in.

If she could get just five minutes with him, face to face, she just might be able to persuade him to change his mind.

'Book me a seat,' she said.

CHAPTER THIRTY-ONE

THE JOURNEY to Shannon Airport was a nightmare. Juggernauts, tractors, hydraulic diggers...they seemed to be working on a rota basis for the sole purpose of holding her up. It seemed that, as soon as one crawling, smoke-belching truck left the road, another would appear in the distance to take its place. She'd never seen so many steamrollers, white-line sprayers, and hedge-cutters on one single road in her entire life. And why did every learner driver in the county have to pick this particular morning to practise driving at fifteen mph?

At one stage, immobilised behind a beer-keg delivery truck in Ennis, she took out her cellphone and dialled Melanie's number.

'Hi,' said Melanie. 'Still okay to meet for drinks tonight?'

'No, that's why I'm phoning,' she explained. 'I have to go to London. Would Saturday night do instead?'

'Fine by me,' said Melanie. 'But why London?'

'I've just been told that Andres is leaving for South Africa. I'm going to try to catch him before he gets on the three-fifteen flight to Jo'burg.'

'You're *what?*'

Tara swallowed. 'I know this sounds ridiculous, Mel, but I've only just realised how important he is to me. I've realised I'm crazy about him.'

Melanie laughed. 'Sure I know that already,' she said, as though it were patently obvious.

'You do?' Tara was slightly miffed by Melanie's casual dismissal of her earth-shattering news.

'Of course I do,' said Melanie, highly amused. 'You're the only one who didn't realise it.'

Before Tara could respond, the line fizzed, crackled

and went dead. She'd hit another twilight zone of reception.

She continued her nightmare journey, and made it to the last traffic lights before the airport with a mere twenty-five minutes to go before take-off. The lights were green as she approached. She was nearly there.

Then...

Damn it! Damn it to hell, she thought. This can *not* be happening...

A garda motorcyclist had just pulled up, siren blaring, and had raised a hand to stop all the traffic. He sat there motionless, as the lights turned from green to red, then back to green, then red again. Nothing happened. Tara banged the steering wheel with the heel of her hand in sheer frustration.

Then, at last, a black limousine with motorcycle outriders flew past on its way to the airport. Oh, well, thought Tara cynically. Everyone else may have missed the flight, but at least the Minister's girlfriend won't have any problems.

The garda roared off, leaving the honking, swearing drivers to sort themselves out. The light was green. Please let it hold at green until she got through. Please...

It held.

She put her foot down firmly on the accelerator, ignoring the airport speed limit, and abandoned her Fiat in a semi-legal space between two larger vehicles.

At the check-in desk, the Aer Lingus official had just one word to say to her: 'Run.'

She made the London flight with only seconds to spare before it closed.

Flopping into her seat, she tried to relax, but couldn't. Even though it was a perfect flight, her stomach swirled and churned as though affected by serious turbulence. And despite the textbook landing, her pulse still raced and her head pounded with tension.

Her hurried footsteps, clattering on the airport floor,

echoed her heartbeat as she changed terminals. She passed through seemingly endless corridors, through a maze of escalators and people-movers, checking her watch every few minutes. Two-forty. Two forty-five. Two-fifty. This was impossible. She'd never make it.

Two fifty-five. At last, there it was in the distance. Springbok Airways flight desk. There was only a handful of flustered passengers in the queue. And Andres wasn't among them.

'Boarding. Boarding,' flashed the monitor overhead.

Tara ran up to the desk. 'Excuse me. I have to get an urgent message to a passenger...'

'Hey,' snarled a hatchet-faced American woman. 'Get in line.'

'But it's urgent.'

'So's catching my flight, honey.'

The airline official took the safe way out. He kept tearing tickets and tapping his keyboard, eyes downcast.

'Boarding,' echoed the tannoy system.

Helplessly, Tara took her place in the queue and waited for five agonisingly-long minutes until it was her turn.

'I need to talk to one of your passengers,' she said to the man behind the desk. 'A Mr Andres Talimann. Can you tell me if he's gone on board yet?'

'I'm sorry, ma'am. We cannot disclose the identities of any of our passengers without due authorisation. If you contact our public-liaison officer at this number, she'll be only too pleased to help you with your query.'

It was almost like listening to a robot.

'I haven't time to do that,' Tara pleaded. She glanced at the monitor. Five past three. 'It's really important. Couldn't you just...get a message to him?'

'Is it an emergency, ma'am?'

Tara hesitated. It was...to her. But there were probably all sorts of dire penalties for delaying an international flight without due cause, and she doubted if the regulatory authorities would agree with her definition of an emergency in this case.

'It's really important,' she repeated.

The official studied her face and seemed to relent slightly. Then he frowned as a message appeared on his computer monitor.

'I'm terribly sorry,' he said, the sympathy in his voice failing to disguise his obvious relief. 'But that flight has just closed. It's already received clearance for take-off.'

Tara nodded dully. She felt the tears of frustration well up in her eyes until the official's face became blurred and indistinct. She tried to blink them away and found she couldn't.

Ignoring his formulaic apologies and suggestions, she slowly made her way upstairs to a café where she could watch the planes land and take off.

Yes, there it was, the Springbok Airways jet, taxiing slowly towards the runway. For a moment, she thought she could see Andres's face at one of the windows, but she knew it was just her imagination. The plane negotiated itself into position, roared its engines, and shot down the smooth black runway. Its nose lifted, and then its entire body gracefully shed weight until its tyres were merely kissing the tarmac. As it finally broke contact with the earth, Tara felt as though she, too, had lost contact with some part of her soul.

She watched the plane rise until it was just a tiny glint of silver light in a perfectly blue sky. Then she turned her back on it and walked miserably away.

What would she do now?

Phone him in South Africa, she supposed. E-mail him. But she was under no illusions about the difficulty of building up a relationship half a world away, with a man who was determined to forget her.

In the meantime, she had to get back home.

She'd have to go back to the domestic terminal and book a flight to Shannon. And while she was waiting for the plane, she would have a bite to eat, maybe drink a glass or three of wine, or even four, while she worked out how to clear up this godawful mess she'd made of her life.

The Aer Lingus desk at Terminal One was crowded. An entire brass band was checking in, all at the same time, loading drum kits and euphoniums on to the luggage scales and passing tickets over their heads to a check-in official who was doing her best to achieve some sort of order out of the chaos.

Tara didn't really care. She was at the next check-in desk, and she was in no hurry any more. And after the events of the past month, she was well used to chaos. In fact, chaos seemed to be the natural order of things in her world.

Handing over her ticket for Shannon, she waited as the official filled out her boarding pass. She felt suddenly tired and hungry. It would be nice to retreat to the restaurant for a long-awaited meal and a much-needed drink...

'Excuse me.' A tall man, hidden from her view by a forest of bandsmen's caps, was talking to an official at the far check-in desk. The voice wasn't particularly loud, but it was strangely familiar.

'Yes, sir?'

'Flight EI 377 to Shannon. What time is take-out, please?'

'I'm sorry, sir?'

'What time is take-out?'

'Oh. You mean take-off, sir.' The Aer Lingus woman smiled.

'I apologise. It flies *out*, but it takes *off*. I shall remember in future.'

Tara stood rooted to the spot, hardly daring to breathe.

'Excuse me, ma'am? *Ma'am?*' The woman at her own check-in desk was impatiently holding out her boarding pass. 'Boarding is in forty-five minutes, Gate...'

'Thanks, I know.' Tara grabbed the pass and dashed towards the sound of the man's voice. She had to fight her way through the throng of bandsmen who had all, naturally, decided to walk away from the desk at that precise moment.

'Excuse me, excuse me.' Tara pushed her way through the crowd and burst out in front of the next check-in point.

But by that time, of course, Andres had gone.

She was perched on the first-floor balcony, her eyes desperately scanning the crowded terminal building, when she finally caught sight of him.

There he stood, directly beneath her, at the bottom of the upward escalator. And for some reason, he, too, seemed to be scanning every face in the crowd.

'Andres!' she yelled, waving her hand. 'Andres!'

But her words were swept away in some interminable tannoy announcement. He turned and began to walk away.

'Andres!'

Tara felt a surge of anxiety. She glanced over her shoulder at the downward escalator, which faced the opposite side of the building. If she took that, she would lose sight of him – and she couldn't bear to do that. By the time she'd reached the ground floor, he could easily have disappeared.

Throwing caution aside, she ran downwards on the ascending staircase, dodging irate passengers as she fought her way down against the flow of rising metal.

'Andres!'

This time he heard her and turned around. His tanned face split into a wide grin that could have signified either relief or amusement, or possibly both. Laughing at her antics on the moving stairway, he quickly returned and hopped on to the bottom step. They met halfway, in a chaotic tangle of outstretched arms. The escalator continued to carry them upwards.

'Careful,' he laughed, his lips finally pulling free from hers, 'we're nearly back at the top again.'

'I don't care.' She kissed him once more, and he was forced to hoist her in his arms as the metal teeth at the top of the escalator closed in upon her heels.

As he deposited her on solid ground, she confronted him with an indignation that had been boiling up inside her all day.

'Just what the hell do you think you're up to, Andres?' she demanded. 'Heading off to the ass-end of the globe without even saying goodbye? You might at least have talked to me about it. You might have told me face to face.'

The words spilled out, unplanned and uncontrolled, but the emotion that drove them was unmistakable.

He must have understood that, because he responded simply by holding her more tightly to him. His mouth kissed her hair and his hand stroked her cheek soothingly.

'I couldn't do it, Tara,' he whispered at last. 'I couldn't bring myself to board that plane. I couldn't run away any more. I was able to take flight from other women, other relationships. But not from this one. Not from you.'

She hugged him, lost for words.

'When I heard that you were travelling all the way from Claremoon Harbour to try to stop me, I was...simply overwhelmed,' he said. 'I could not believe anyone would care about me so much.'

'Hang on a minute.' Tara felt her head reeling again. This didn't make any sense. 'How did you know I was coming to Heathrow? I wasn't able to make contact with you. I tried to phone, but you'd already left your London base.'

He smiled. 'We have your friend Melanie to thank for that. She has always had our best interests at heart.'

'Melanie?'

It was the last name she expected to hear. Any minute now, the Mad Hatter and the March Hare would come bounding across the terminal building.

'Yes. You called Melanie from County Clare on your way to London. She knew you'd never make it across in time. So she phoned me on my mobile to let me know.'

'You have a mobile,' repeated Tara flatly. All of a sudden, she felt very idiotic indeed. 'I could have contacted you on a mobile phone?'

'Yes,' he said, deliberately keeping his tone light. 'Remember the number she kept trying to give you when I was in Canada? The number you refused to take because you had jumped over the wrong conclusions about me?'

He looked at her. She looked at him. They both burst into laughter at the same time.

'Jump *to* conclusions,' she corrected him, in an effort to save some shred of dignity. 'The phrase is, jump *to* conclusions.'

'I sit corrected.' He put his arm around her shoulder and steered her towards the stairway.

'I was queuing at the boarding gate when Melanie's call came through,' he explained. 'In fact, I was next in line to board the plane. One more minute, and I would have had to switch off my phone. But when I heard how hard you were trying, how much effort you were making, to stop me running away from you, I could not bring myself to go on board. I simply handed in my ticket and walked away.'

She held him tightly. 'So you're not going to South Africa after all?' she asked.

For the first time, his voice sounded uncertain. 'South Africa can wait,' he said. 'Right now, we have more pressing matters to consider.'

'Such as?'

'Where we shall eat tonight. Have you checked your own cellphone for messages recently?' he asked suddenly. 'If you had, you would have found a message from me, recorded one hour ago, inviting you to join me for dinner tonight. Not in Cape Town. Not in London. But in County Clare.'

'I see.'

He took her hand and led her towards departure. 'Let's hurry,' he said, checking his watch. 'If we can catch that plane to Shannon, we'll still be back in Clare in time for that dinner.'

'I accept your invitation, Mr Talimann,' she said with mock formality. 'But on two conditions. Number one: I cook the meal for us at my house. Estonians aren't the only people who are good at entertaining at home.'

He nodded. 'Agreed. And the other?'

She snuggled close to him as they walked. 'Condition number two: you don't make any promises to behave like a gentleman.'

Andres's face lit up with pleasure when Tara opened the door of her cottage. And it wasn't just the warm flow of pleasant cooking smells wafting from her kitchen, although he could recognise thyme, marjoram and lemon grass among the herbs in this symphony of scent and he knew dinner was going to be special.

'You look...*wonderful*,' he said, his voice revealing something close to awe as he handed her a bunch of red roses and a curiously lumpy package wrapped in crimson paper.

It was Tara's turn to feel a surge of pleasure. She had swapped her shirt and jeans for a black evening dress of a classic early 1960s style. Her only jewellery was a necklace of jet-black hematite that echoed the colour of her swept-up hair and completed an ensemble that made her look like the young Jackie Kennedy.

Andres had never seen her dressed to kill, and she was enjoying his reaction.

'Well, thank you. You look pretty good yourself, Andres.'

He glanced down at his stone-coloured linen suit and open-necked cotton shirt. He accepted the compliment with a shrug. His eyes returned to Tara and seemed to light up again, with something akin to wonder and delight.

She laughed. 'Don't you want to come in?'

'Forgive me.' He seemed to snap out of his temporary trance and followed her through the cottage door. A stereo was playing slow, mellow torch-songs by Ella Fitzgerald.

'Dinner smells delicious,' he said.

'It should be ready soon. Would you like an aperitif? I've got most of the usual things. Except your exotic Swiss wine. Sluther's off-licence has run out of it, unfortunately.'

She gave that throaty giggle that always sent sensual shivers down his spine.

'Any sort of wine would be fine,' he said.

He sat down on the sofa, feeling the warmth of the late evening sun as it filtered through the honeysuckle around the window. There was a pop and a splash of pouring liquid, and a moment later she handed him a tall crystal glass half-filled with pale white wine.

'To us, Tara.'

'To us, Andres.'

She sat down beside him and took his hand.

'Come with me to Cape Town,' he said suddenly.

'What?'

'I want to be with you. Always. Come with me to Cape Town. It is very beautiful. You'll like it there.'

'But I thought...I thought you weren't going to South Africa.'

'You have been jumping on conclusions again, Tara. I should really like to take that job. But I want you by my side. I want you to share this new life with me.'

She looked out through her window towards Claremoon Harbour. The pretty little port, bathed in the saffron glow of sunset. The beach, stretching to vanishing point. The beautiful old spa house on the hill...

'Let's not talk about South Africa right now, Andres,' she said. 'Not tonight.'

'No,' he agreed. 'Tonight is special.' He leaned forward. 'Tonight I want to tell you, face-on-face, how I feel. For years after Manuela died, I was sure I would never be able to love again. But all that has changed. My whole life has changed since I met you, Tara. No more running away. No more self-blame. This is my one chance at happiness, and I'm not going to let it pass.' There was not the slightest trace of doubt in his voice. 'I want to tell you that I am badly in love for you, Tara.' He suddenly frowned. 'Have I got that right?'

'Oh, yes,' she confirmed. 'Yes, you've got that absolutely right.'

He glanced down at their joined hands. His eyes slowly rose again and looked into hers. For a few moments neither of them stirred a muscle. Then, as inexorably as drifting objects in space, their faces began to move slowly closer together. Their lips were about to meet when the romantic atmosphere was suddenly shattered by the piercing shriek of a smoke alarm.

Tara sprang to her feet and dashed into the kitchen. Andres followed. A pan had boiled dry and was emitting a dense cloud of acrid smoke.

'Damn!' shouted Tara when she'd got everything under control. She pointed to a blackened, charred nuclear-meltdown of meat and vegetables at the bottom of the pan. '*That* was our dinner.'

He fanned the smoke alarm with a newspaper until the shrieking stopped, then opened a window to allow the smoke and smells to escape.

'I'm sure it would have been delicious,' he consoled her.

She shook her head ruefully. 'Yes. It would have been.'

'You know, Tara, I am not really *that* hungry,' he said. 'We could always have that most impressive salad' – he gestured to a large pottery bowl filled with a Greek salad of lettuce, olives, sun-dried tomato and feta cheese – 'and skip straight to dessert.'

Her face fell. 'I didn't plan any dessert,' she said.

He pointed to the unopened crimson package he'd given her earlier.

'I did,' he smiled.

For new lovers, eating fresh lychees is a deliciously sensual experience.

Tara and Andres sat facing each other across the narrow table, with the Indian lychee fruits placed between them in a simple white bowl. Near them on the table was an empty salad dish, two plates with discarded olive-pips and chunks of bread, and two bottles of New Zealand Sauvignon Blanc – one empty, the other chilled and glistening and ready to pour.

Two candles lit up the scene, flickering over Andres's tanned features as he looked deep into Tara's eyes. He was entranced by the way the soft candle-glow lit up her face with a magical, almost mystical light, transforming her into an angel from a Leonardo painting.

However, Tara was feeling anything but angelic. Keeping her eyes fixed on his, she lifted a single lychee fruit and rolled it between her fingers and thumb until the hard, brittle exterior shell cracked and a small drop of deliciously sweet juice came through to the surface. She removed it with the tip of her tongue. Then slowly she began to peel off the tough, reddish-pink skin, revealing the delicate pale, fleshy fruit concealed just beneath the surface. She teased the flesh gently with her tongue to savour the luscious juices trapped in the folds, before removing the rest of the husk and biting softly into the firm, yielding fruit. The top part of the lychee disappeared into her mouth. She ate it luxuriously and slowly, nibbling it away from its hard smooth core, savouring its spongy, resistant texture and the beguiling honey flavours. Then, with a single abrupt motion, she popped the remainder of the tiny fruit between her lips. She took her time, enjoying the sudden rush of flavour, the sudden and intense release of the fruit's hidden secrets.

Andres watched, and relished her enjoyment. He wanted to share it, be part of it.

His hand went forward to the bowl of lychees. But her hand intercepted it, her fingers softly touching his, silently asking him to hold back. Instead, she herself lifted another lychee. Holding it up between their two faces, and keeping her eyes on his eyes, she peeled it with infinite care and passed it over to him. Three of her fingers gently stroked his cheek as her thumb and forefinger moved towards his mouth, ready to pop the peeled fruit between his half-opened lips.

But he wasn't going to let her control the situation completely.

Rather than take the tiny prize from her immediately, he raised his hand towards her outstretched wrist, took hold of it and drew her palm towards his mouth instead. Gently, not at all hard, he bit into the soft fleshy mound under her thumb – the erogenous region known as the mount of Venus. He felt her entire hand ripple with pleasure. It was only then that he allowed his lips to start their nuzzling journey across her palm towards the proffered lychee. But even then he refused to take it all at once. The tip of his tongue rolled across its moist, membranous surface, exploring all its raised surfaces and hidden folds, before he finally allowed her to put the lychee between his lips.

Tara felt her entire body give a secret squirm of pleasure as she watched and shared in his enjoyment. For the first time since she had known him, his face seemed entirely free of pain. The last lingering traces of anguish were being slowly erased. The bad memories were being steadily peeled away like the hard skin of the lychees, leaving only the pure, innocent heart of peace, contentment and pleasure which every soul possesses at its inner core, which every soul deserves to rediscover.

She caught sight of her own face in a distant mirror and realised, with a jolt of pleasant surprise, that exactly the same thing was happening to her.

They said nothing at all during these magical few minutes, or those several hours, whatever it happened to be – words, as well as time, had become irrelevant.

Somewhere far away, the smoky, dark-chocolate voice of Ella Fitzgerald was singing her heartstopping, bittersweet version of Jerome Kern's ballad 'The Way You Look Tonight'.

Around midnight, Andres poured the last of the wine.

'We've finished the lychees,' said Tara at last.

It was the first time either of them had spoken for a long time.

'Yes,' he said. 'We've finished the lychees.'

'What was the tradition about lychees?' she asked, almost dreamily.

'That they should be shared only by lovers.'

'Yes.' She smiled contentedly. 'Yes, that was it.'

She looked into his eyes and blew out the candle on the table.

Without another word he rose, lifted her in his arms, and carried her towards the bedroom.

CHAPTER THIRTY-TWO

TARA LAY on the bed, watching him sleep, as the first traces of light stole through their curtains and lent sepia-tinted colour to the patchwork bedspread. The past few hours of lovemaking had left her exhausted, but deeply at peace. She knew now, as she watched his body stir gently in sleep, that she had never really loved anyone until this moment; she knew why the feelings she'd had for other men had been illusory, self-deceiving, and plagued with uncertainty. For the first time in her life, the insistent questioner inside her head was silent. For the first time in her life, there was no doubt. She was sure. She was sure about everything.

Softly she left their bed, threw on a silk dressing-gown, and crept quietly downstairs to the kitchen.

She made herself a large pot of Japanese green tea and sat down at the table. Now it was time, she told herself. At last she had the strength to do it.

She took a deep breath and opened the parcel Manus Kennedy had given her.

Inside, as she had always suspected, was Michael de Blaca's first sculpture, the sheela-na-gig, looking more repulsive than ever in the innocence of the dawn sunshine. She stared into the monkey-eyes of the gruesome old hag for a few moments, trying to understand the mind of the man who had created her. Then she opened the accompanying envelope to discover the fatal letter that Michael de Blaca had sent to Ann Kennedy after the birth of their son Manus twenty-seven years ago.

Tara had expected a lengthy document filled with apologies and excuses, but in fact it was cruelly curt and to the point.

'Ann,' it began coldly, 'this is my first sculpture and I would like you to give it to your new-born son Manus on my behalf. After all, he is my son, too. I am confident that, at some stage, this sculpture will be of some value, and he may sell it or keep it as he chooses. You might also explain to him what it signifies. The sheela-na-gig is an ancient symbol of the essential ugliness of carnal lust and was designed to protect good men from the evil temptations presented by licentious women. May it remind him of this and give him the strength that his father did not have in his weakest moment. I hope you, too, will somehow find peace and forgiveness, Ann. As you will not be hearing from me again, you may regard this as a full and final discharge of my responsibilities as the boy's father. Yours sincerely, Ml. de Blaca.'

Tara read it and reread it, stung and left breathless by its brutal insolence. Forgiveness? For *her?* Unbelievable as it might seem, de Blaca was effectively blaming Ann for her own rape. In his eyes, the victim had become the perpetrator.

Furious, Tara had to fight to remind herself that the letter had been written nearly three decades ago and that the same arrogant de Blaca was now a broken man, existing in a living hell, his soul daily gored and prodded and torn and bleeding by the demons of his own guilty memories.

But of course, that would have been no help at all to the young Ann Kennedy as she cradled her new-born child and read this appalling litany of self-justification from the man who had blighted her life.

Tara gave a sudden shiver, almost as though she were sharing in Ann's anguish and humiliation. Across the yawning chasm of years, she felt for Ann Kennedy, longed to offer her words of support and consolation, yearned to hold her hand and comfort her.

She rose and poured herself a glass of water. Then, for a long time, she simply stood at her kitchen window and gazed down towards the harbour where the *Róisín Dubh* lay beached on the sand, her hull repaired and newly painted, ready for sale to another fisherman who would take her out to sea once more and hunt the wild salmon of the Atlantic.

CHAPTER THIRTY-THREE

'SOUTH AFRICA?' squawked Melanie. *'You're* going to South Africa?'

'I don't know,' Tara replied honestly. 'I just can't make up my mind.'

Melanie frowned. 'But what would you do there?' she asked. 'You can't speak South Africa-ish. Or whatever it is they speak.'

'English is one of the official languages. I'd get by.'

'What would you work at?'

Tara shrugged. 'I don't think that's a problem, either. Ever since the *Clare Electronic News* won that award for Best Online Newspaper in Ireland, I've been inundated with job offers. Including one from Hibernian Newspapers. They own lots of papers in South Africa.'

'But you haven't accepted anything yet?'

Tara shook her head. 'I'm stuck in a bit of a dilemma,' she confessed. 'You know how much I love Claremoon Harbour, Mel. If I had my way, I'd stay here for ever. But I love Andres too, and I don't want to lose him.'

'Can't you have both? Couldn't he stay here with you?'

Tara grimaced. 'I wouldn't ask him to do that. The South African job means a lot to him.'

'And I presume *you* mean a lot to him, too.'

'I suppose so. But how could he refuse an offer from Nelson Mandela?'

'Easy. He just says: "Not on your nelly, Nellie".'

Tara ignored that. 'It's an impossible decision,' she mused, half to herself. 'I could stay here and continue to build up a successful business in Claremoon Harbour. Or I could take a chance and start a new life in a scary country in another hemisphere, with no guarantees of anything.

Either way, I lose something very important to me.'

She searched in her bag, produced a five pence coin, and pushed it across the table without explanation.

Melanie's face became serious. 'I can't give you an answer,' she admitted frankly. 'You've always talked about finding your dream in Claremoon Harbour, Tara, but when it comes to achieving happiness, the location isn't really important at all – no matter what the estate agents might say. It's not a matter of where you are, but who you are – and who you're with. All over the world, the shrinks' waiting-rooms are full of people who thought they'd suddenly find paradise if they bought a vineyard in Tuscany or converted a barn in Provence. But you can't run away from yourself. If you can't find peace of mind in the centre of Dublin, you're not going to find it by moving to west Cork or Connemara. If you can't find it in Cape Town, you're not going to find it in Clare. And vice-versa.'

'That's a great help!'

'Tara, you're the sort of person who will find happiness anywhere in the world,' said Melanie encouragingly. 'As for guarantees? One thing I've learned in my job is that there are no guarantees this side of the great divide.'

Tara still didn't think she'd got good value for her five pence. 'What would *you* do, Mel?' she persisted.

Melanie smiled. 'This is a bit of a Jean-Paul Sartre set-up job, I'm afraid.'

'A *what*?'

'Old J-P believed,' explained Mel, raising her voice above the session music, 'that we're often deluding ourselves when we seek advice from other people on major life decisions. Because first we have to select the person we ask for advice. And that's a choice in itself.'

'What are you on about, Melanie?'

'That if you asked Steve McNamara, or Phil O'Rourke, or old Mrs McLaughlin who cleans the church, you know what their answers would be. They'd tell you to stay here. It would be the most sensible thing to do. But you're not asking them. You're asking me. And you already know what I'd do. You know me well enough, Tara, to realise that if I were in your situation, I'd be over there in South Africa before you could blink an eyelid. It doesn't mean it's the right thing to do. It doesn't mean it's sensible. But if I were in your shoes, you wouldn't see me for Kalahari dust.'

'Well, my father once told me,' Tara said thoughtfully, 'that if you loved someone enough, you'd go to the ends of the earth for them.'

Melanie shook her head in mock despair.

'You want my advice?' she asked directly. 'Stop looking to other people for advice. Nobody can make this choice for you. Find somewhere quiet, somewhere very quiet, and just listen to your soul. It's a still, small voice, and it gets overwhelmed so often that we sometimes forget it's there. But when you do listen, when you just remain silent and really listen, you'll find it will rarely let you down.'

Tara stared out through the window at the darkened skyline of Claremoon Harbour. She knew her friend was right. It was her decision, and her decision alone.

She looked back in time to see Melanie gently pushing the five pence coin back across the table to her.

CHAPTER THIRTY-FOUR

TARA HAD a secret place, a spot nobody else knew about. She had discovered it as a child. If she ever needed time to herself, away from her friends or from her family, she would steal down a narrow, steep path towards the rugged coastline, clamber down the rocks, through a tiny hole between two huge boulders, and on to a perfectly flat ledge that could be seen only from the open sea. There, with the solid rock slabs of County Clare at her back and on either side, and the seemingly limitless Atlantic Ocean ahead of her, she would feel suspended between the old world and the new, between the past and the future.

So when she rose early one morning, and her feet began walking in a direction of their own choosing, she knew exactly where they were headed. Following the overgrown sheep-track through the brambles, she stole down a gully between the rocks, hardly looking downwards because her feet knew each slope, each sharp angle, each tiny slippery precipice.

She paused for a moment to look across at her father's cottage. The windows of her childhood home stared sightlessly back at her, stripped of their protective curtains, the rooms behind them empty and bare. A large FOR SALE sign had been planted in the front garden, in the middle of John Ross's treasured petunias.

As she thought about her father, trying to stem an overwhelming flood of memories and associations, she saw Andres emerge from her own cottage and load her few suitcases into the boot of a hired car. Spotting her, he smiled, waved their airline ticket, and pointed at his watch.

Tara swallowed hard. She waved back, and then raised her hand with all five digits extended. He nodded and gave her an OK sign.

Round the corner, through the hidden niche between the boulders, and she was back in her own simple childhood world in which the only elements were stone, sea and sky.

She sat down, with her back propped against an inward curve in the warm rock, just as she had done so many times as a little girl. Above her, the blue sky was streaked with mackerel clouds. In front of her, the sea stretched vast and empty.

What had Melanie said when she'd asked her for advice?

'*Find somewhere quiet,*' her friend had counselled, '*somewhere very quiet, and just listen to your soul.*'

So Tara sat for a little bit longer – just listening.

Once again, she found herself suspended between her two worlds. Behind her, the familiar rocks of her Clare home town, sun-warmed, comforting, nurturing, their banks of heather and fuchsia loud with the summer hum of bees. But those same rocks could be savage and pitiless. They could crush and pound, and tear and rip. In either guise, they were still comforting because they were known. Much more challenging was the unknown – the empty horizon, the vast, wide pathway of silver-cold water that led to who knows where.

Then she rose, her mind made up. Scrambling on to the top of the rock, she could just glimpse the old spa house she'd yearned for so long to own. God, it was so beautiful, nestling there in the shade of a copper beech tree, like some sort of slumbering fairy tale castle just waiting to be brought back to life.

She glanced down at the ugly little sheela-na-gig that rested heavily in her hand. Wendy had been right. Incredible as it seemed, that little stone was worth so much, it could have paid for the house and the renovation work, with money to spare. A few weeks ago, sitting amid the drone of the bees in her back garden, she could have grasped that statue, signed a simple contract, and known that the realisation of her lifelong dream lay literally in the palm of her hand.

But she hadn't. She'd resolved to take a different course of action, and now she was determined to see it through. There could be no going back on her word.

Her five minutes were nearly up. She thought of Andres, waiting by the car. She thought of the plane that was even now refuelling at the airport, ready to take them thousands of miles away to the southern sunshine. She had to force herself into action. She had to dispel the final doubts, and go for it.

But Tara did not move. She stood rooted to the spot, overwhelmed by the enormity of what she was about to do. No matter how hard she tried, no matter how much she willed herself to do it, her limbs refused to obey.

Andres was by her side. 'It's time, Tara,' he said softly, understandingly. 'It's time to go.'

She took a deep breath. 'I can't do it. I'm sorry, Andres. I just can't do it.'

'Yes, you can, Tara. *We* can.'

'Is it really time to go? Already?'

'Yes. Our plane will leave in ninety minutes.' He took her hand in his. 'Don't worry. It's only for four weeks, and then you'll be back in your beloved Claremoon Harbour again. You'll enjoy Bali. It's the most romantic place in the world for a holiday.'

'I know.' Her face lit up. 'I can't wait. Hopefully the builders will have the place ready when we return.'

He nodded. 'Let's hope so. Whoever designed that old spa house really knew how to build. It's as solid as a rock. It'll last at least another hundred years.'

She smiled. 'Long enough for us to raise our family, anyway.'

He kissed her neck. 'Long enough for us to raise our grandchildren. And great-grandchildren.'

'No second thoughts about turning down the job in South Africa?'

'None at all.' He glanced fondly down towards Claremoon Harbour. 'I never thought I would grow to love this village so much. It's so peaceful, so silent, so inspiring...I find I can work better here than anywhere else in the world.'

'Like having Bach in the background all the time.'

'Yes. The same peace of mind.' He looked down at the sheela-na-gig in her hand. 'You really can't bring yourself to do it?' he asked sympathetically.

She closed her eyes and shook her head. 'Don't get me wrong,' she said. 'I want to do it. I really want to do it.'

He squeezed her hand silently.

'I want to take this ugly little statue and chuck it into the deepest depths of the sea, where nobody will ever find it again,' she said angrily. 'I don't care how valuable it is. I don't care if it's the latest fashion in Manhattan. As far as I'm concerned, it's a symbol of everything that went wrong in Ann's life. The violence she had to endure from that brute of a husband. Her humiliation at the hands of Michael de Blaca. But it's more than that, Andres.' She turned to him, her eyes bright with tears. 'It's also the symbol of everything she rose above. Everything rotten she fought against for the past five years. Everything she challenged and overcame.'

'Then the best tribute you can pay to Ann is to destroy it forever.'

'I know that. It's just...'

Her voice trailed off helplessly.

'Just what?'

'I know it sounds ridiculous.' Tara grimaced. 'But whether I like the damn thing or not, I'm depriving future generations of an important work of art.'

'If you can't do it alone,' Andres suggested, 'then let's do it together.'

'All right. Let's do it.'

They didn't hesitate for another moment. Together, they took hold of the statue, summoned up all their strength, and hurled it in a graceful arc towards the horizon, far out into the ocean, where no tide could ever salvage it.

Tara saw the splash, and felt herself become suffused with a sense of release and liberation as all her troubles sank alongside the ugly little stone, Michael de Blaca's mad stone, all the way down to the bottom of the deep Atlantic, leaving not a single ripple of regret.